Born in Birmingham, Michael F_____ _____ _____ ___ _____ ____
as head of art in secondary schools in the city. He left teaching in 1988 to devote his time to painting and has exhibited
regularly in local galleries and further afield. His short stories, poems and articles have been published in the *Sunday
Times*, *Mayfair*, *Private Eye* and *London Magazine*. This is his
first novel. He has a grown-up son and daughter and lives
with his wife in Rubery, Birmingham.

# The Pig Bin

Michael Richardson

TINDAL STREET PRESS

First published in 2000 by
Tindal Street Press, 16 Reddings Road,
Moseley, Birmingham B13 8LN
www.tindalstreet.org.uk

Copy-editing: Penny Rendall
Typesetting: Tindal Street Press

All the characters in this book are fictitious and any resemblance to
actual persons, living or dead, is purely coincidental.

A CIP catalogue reference for this book is
available from the British Library.

ISBN 0 9535895 2 8

Printed and bound in Great Britain by
Biddles Ltd, Woodbridge Park, Guildford.

For Anny
and in fond memory of the Bos

# Acknowledgements

I am deeply indebted to the following for, variously, their encouragement, advice, reminiscences, anecdotes, patient reading of text and invaluable specialist assistance on matters historical, military, medical, linguistic and religious: Sister Joan Brian, Shirley and Graham Cartwright, Jim and Pat Charles, Craig Clarke, Valerie Croix, Louise Cusack, Lucia del Vecchio, Roma de Roeper, Dr Dorothy Gibbs, Mariette Gretton, Fenella Harcourt, Major Alan and Janet Hoe, Ken Kennedy, Professor Margaret Lingard, David Lodge, Michael Ludlow, Ina Murphy, John Narbett, Ann Over-the-Road, Sylvia and Jeff Perry, John Prangley, Arthur and Betty Pritty, Patrick Pritty, Alice Richardson, Emma and Tim Richardson, Gym Sherlock, Roger Smith, Mary Traves, John Traves, Victoria Trenberth, Norma and Barrie Wedgbury, and innumerable people met briefly in pubs and Rackham's Café whose names I never learned.

Special thanks to Kate Packwood, who pointed me in the right direction at the beginning, and to Jane Harris, Martin Flynn, Alan Mahar and Penny Rendall, who helped substantially in giving the story its final shape.

Above all, thanks to Anny Richardson, whose idea it was and who unfalteringly supported me throughout.

**WASTE FOOD**
**FOR THE FEEDING OF PIGS**

**Put IN Bin.**
Potato and Apple Peelings.
Pea Shells.
Scraps of Meat.
White Bread.
Cabbage and Lettuce Leaves etc. etc.

**Do NOT put in Bin.**
Rhubarb and Potato Tops.
Tea Leaves.
Coffee Grounds.
Skins of Oranges, Lemons, Grape Fruit
and Bananas.
Salt, Soap and Soda.

**KEEP DRY AND FREE FROM GLASS,
BONES, METAL, PAPER ETC.**

**YOUR COUNCIL WILL COLLECT.**

# Author's Note

For reasons determined by the plot, I have taken liberties with the geography of some Birmingham and Worcestershire locations in the narrative. Use of their real place names therefore seemed inappropriate as my descriptions would conflict with local readers' experience of those places. The book's fictitious suburban villages of Redhill, Redwell and Upfield and the Ickley Hills remain, respectively, close relatives of the Rubery, Rednal, Northfield and Lickey Hills of 1940s Birmingham.

# Chapter 1

Freshly dosed with malt and cod liver oil and wearing his best trousers and new lumber jacket, Morley Charles paused uncertainly at the end of his road, wondering how he could safely occupy himself for the next hour or two. With over two shillings in his pocket, the shops at Redhill beckoned and there would be schoolmates around to whom he could show off his new jacket. But Redhill village was dangerous territory. It would just be his luck to bump into one of his mother's friends or even, perhaps, his mother herself on her way to the Co-op. He sighed, turned his back on the roofs and chimneys of Redhill and the huge green-domed tower of Redhill Asylum to his right, swung left into Eachley Lane and walked briskly towards the narrow gully which would take him to the Ickley Hills.

This was the second time he had missed confession. A month ago on his last visit Canon Reilly asked at the end, 'Are you *sure* that there is nothing else, my son?' Morley replied, quite truthfully, that there wasn't, but in the middle of his penance with the canon's curiously insistent question still reverberating in his head, it suddenly dawned on him that there *was*; and he had been doing it enthusiastically and regularly since the beginning of January.

The gully ended at the foot of Redwell Hill, the smallest of the Ickley Hills. Morley decided against his usual route, which zigzagged up to the Scots pine-crowned summit. Although this would deny him the mild satisfaction of seeing the upper half of his distant house, it would avoid the risk of his mother recognizing his distinctive red lumber jacket, should she be looking out of a bedroom window. Instead, he took a rising, meandering path round the lower slopes that eventually joined the broad track leading to a point safely behind the summit.

Carefully avoiding the wet bilberry bushes and bracken in case they soaked his trousers, he tried to organize his thoughts. He was sure that what he got up to most nights of the week was sinful, but how really serious was it?

It might, of course, be only a venial sin, but if it *was* a mortal sin and he did not confess it, he ran the risk, should he die, of eternal damnation. 'This does not *literally* mean roasting in perpetual fire whilst being relentlessly pierced by Satan's fork,' Canon Reilly had often explained. 'This is a primitive image that was created for the benefit of our forefathers. No, what hell *really* means is experiencing all the most terrible, horrible and vile things that you can think of, but multiplied a billion times.'

Searching for a crumb of comfort, he turned his thoughts to his new jacket. It was a genuine Yankee jacket. 'Made in USA', it said on the label. He looked approvingly at its intricately woven colours and glanced at his new long trousers. He was glad of both: it was chilly up here on the top of Redwell Hill, in spite of the recently emerged April sun.

He hoisted the trousers to his knees to remind himself what it felt like to wear short trousers. Instantly, his legs became unbearably cold. Yet, he reflected, he had been happily bare-legged for most of his life, until last September, when Uncle Walter had handed down a pair of long trousers. His mother had shortened them but reducing the size of the waist was beyond her skill. This meant that he had to wear a belt as well as braces and, every time he put them on, painstakingly arrange numerous equal-sized tucks to make the enormous reduction as inconspicuous as possible. He also had to wear a well-pulled-down jersey or pullover to

10

cover up his handiwork. 'They don't look *too* bad,' his mother said. 'Anyway, what do you expect? There's a war on.' But so voluminous were they, falling in such generous, luxuriant folds from beneath his jacket, that Maureen from next door said, 'I thought you was wearing a long skirt for a minute, Morley, when I seen you with your legs together.' And he didn't wear them again until Big Gwen Pinder performed major surgery on them with her Singer, for twenty Player's Weights.

Today, however, he was wearing his best pair, bought new from the Co-op in Upfield. As he let them fall, his legs were immediately surrounded by deliciously warm air. He savoured the luxury. He did it again, this time hitching them up with some difficulty with his hands inside his pockets: a blast of cold air. He dropped them again: bliss. He continued doing this until he reached the bridle path at the bottom of the hill.

Morley slowed down, wondering where to go: the duck ponds or the amusement arcades and shops at Redwell, where he might be able to get an ice-cream.

Indecision. His mother was always on to him about it.

'Well, don't leave it, go now if your books are nearly overdue. I don't want you paying any more fines.'

'Yes, but knowing you, you might forget.'

'If you're just at a loose end, why don't you go for a walk?'

'All right, don't go for a walk then. Mind, it wouldn't hurt you to just pop up to Hiller's for me and see if they've got any Minors, that'll hardly tire you out.'

'Micky Plant's? How is it you've suddenly remembered you've got to go to Micky Plant's? Anyway, Micky Plant's is further than Hiller's.'

'All right. Then you can try the pub for some Minors on the way back from Micky's, it'll be open then. Get a Family Ale as well – and I'll let you have a drop.'

'Well, it's the first time I've ever heard you say you didn't like Family Ale. In any case, why don't you think of what *I* might like for a change?'

'It doesn't matter how late it is, so long as you're back before ten.'

'All right, all right, don't bother. I'll go myself. Though why you can't do a simple job like anybody else, I shall never know.'

'No, no, it's all right, you just go off to Micky's.'

'*Now* what are you doing?'

'But you just said that your books weren't overdue yet.'

'You're never right, son, never right in all this world.'

'No, you're not. Or you'd be able to make your mind up like a normal person.'

'No, you can't, not with *your* mind. Your mind's too full up of rubbish . . . just like that pig bin.'

He decided he would treat himself to an ice-cream if, before reaching the end of the bridle path, he had worked out what to do about his – and the probability was growing – Mortal Sin. Of course, whether venial or mortal, it still had to be confessed. But what on earth was it called? Reggie Kelp, Reggie Nolan and Perky Beswick were always on about it, and even seven-year-old Bernard Inch, who said it felt like a neat pain. But he could hardly tell Canon Reilly that he had neat pains, still less tossed off, racked off or wanked. He cringed at the very thought of such words in the confessional. But they were the only words he knew, and the only ones the Reggies and Perky ever used.

David Meyer, the boy he sat next to in class, might know, but so far Morley hadn't thought of a way to bring the subject up casually. And his friend Micky Plant, whether he knew the answer or not, would just give him a funny look and say, 'What d'you want to know that for? Hey, Morle, is that what you get up to? You *dirty* little bugger, no wonder your teeth stick out.' Then go round telling everyone.

One way or another, he would find out the proper, respectable word before next Saturday, when he would *definitely* go to confession.

Supposing Canon Reilly didn't know what the proper word meant, though, and asked him to explain exactly what he did? Or if he did know, what would he say? Either way, he could imagine his roar of, 'You did WHAT?' with everyone outside the confessional hearing; he would stammer badly and the priest would know who he was. He could, of

12

course, go to Father Smythe, the curate, who always had the longer queue because he was more easy-going. But that might be worse, as Father Smythe knew Morley better than the canon did. He used to draw Morley and two other lads aside after confirmation class and talk to them about the priesthood as a vocation. He also asked them to serve at Mass, but Morley refused because of his stammer. Father Smythe said that serving at Mass was a great privilege and, if Morley had enough faith, Our Blessed Lord would, if it was His will, stop Morley stammering during Mass and might even cure it completely. No, he would prefer the canon's rage to Father Smythe's hurt silence. What about another church? One in town: St Catherine's or St Chad's? But these were big intimidating places where perhaps things might be done differently and which might confuse him more than ever.

No, it had to be Canon Reilly and he *must* not stammer. The canon must not identify him as the son of Mrs Charles, whom he knew well. He would practise the long-abandoned drill taught to him by the expensive specialist May, his aunt, had taken him to – and paid for – a couple of years ago. 'Relax, breathe deeply; pause before you speak; imagine that you are reading the words you want to use on an imaginary white screen.' The trouble was, when his stammer threatened, he was already too agitated to remember to get out the non-existent screen and do all the other stuff. Still, he would really try on Saturday, *and* deepen his voice – another of the doctor's tips. Even *disguise* his voice. Or – dare he? Was it possible? Pretend to be French. That was the answer!

If he couldn't find the respectable word before next Saturday, it wouldn't matter, he could just boldly explain that he did a rude thing seven or eight times a week but did not know what it was called in English. Perhaps Canon Reilly would supply the missing word . . . which would certainly lessen the ordeal for future confessions. There was no need to rehearse: on the few occasions when he had been French, what needed to be said just popped into his head like magic,

13

and he didn't stammer. He had made this discovery the term before last, when rehearsing for the Christmas play.

Mr Davies, who was responsible for drama at school, chose Morley to play the escaped convict in *The Bishop's Candlesticks* – a dramatized portion of *Les Misérables* – to be performed as the second-year seniors' contribution to the Christmas Drama Evening. This wasn't such a surprising choice as it may have appeared, since Morley had already demonstrated that he was much less inclined to stammer when acting or singing.

It was a major role and Morley was delighted at the honour and anticipated fame but then became terrified at the prospect of learning his forty-two lines. Discouraged and miserable after his third floundering rehearsal, he asked Micky Plant, a mere sergeant of gendarmes, if he would swap roles. Micky was only too pleased but Mr Davies, when he was told, was not. He punished Morley by admitting that he had only chosen him for the part because of his haunted and hungry look. So then, regretting his decision and stuck with a minor role which gave him only three minutes on stage, Morley set about finding a way to enhance it. He decided to do it in a French accent and throw in the odd French word. He already had a model: Armand Bechoux, a refugee boy from Liège who served at Mass and whom Morley had known and occasionally mimicked in secret for a couple of years. He could get the French words from 'Jacques Wins Through', a story in *Stirring Tales for Boys*, a present from May. Morley worked very hard at it and Mr Davies was amused by his interpretation at the next rehearsal. But afterwards he explained that the French, when speaking French, did not have foreign accents or throw in foreign exclamations; that Morley and the other members of the cast were supposed to be speaking the language of their birth – which they spoke fluently. The cast were native English speakers *representing* native French speakers. Morley wasn't sure that he followed all this but he nodded, trying to hide his bitter disappointment.

Morley's new-found talent wasn't wasted, though. Whenever difficulties loomed and his stammer impended among people he didn't know, he became French and strangely confident.

He had first put this to the test on the trolley bus coming back from Grandma Morley's. He had lost the halfpenny for his fare and all he had was a half-crown. He panicked at the fierce old conductor's approach, then calmed down when he realized that there was a simple solution. The conductor's fury when he saw the half-crown turned to bewilderment when Morley said, 'Eur, one shild, please, *pour* ze city, *s'il vous plaît, monsieur,*' and confidently proffered his half-crown.

'I dunno what you're agoing on about, son, but for a start off, I can't change that! I'd be using half me change up.' He shrugged and looked helplessly at the other passengers, who were whispering, 'Foreigner', and 'Refugee', until a cheerful, gap-toothed sailor paid Morley's fare.

# Chapter 2

The day was warming up as Morley reached the end of the bridle path and entered the Old Birmingham Road. From the direction of the tram terminus at Redwell came the Saturday trippers in their summer frocks, sports coats, service uniforms and suits made informal with open-necked shirts. Many were carrying overcoats or macs. The agile were climbing Bilberry Hill, which rose steeply on the other side of the road; others were making for the ornamental pools and waterfalls which lay at the foot of Rose Hill. Satisfied that he was now close to the solution of his problem, Morley turned towards Redwell and the amusements and shops.

Two American soldiers went by, their arms around the waists of their girlfriends. One of the soldiers was saying something which had the others doubled up with laughter. He felt an affinity with the soldiers because of his American jacket. He was impressed with the way they walked: carefree, relaxed, confident. He did his best to emulate it. Two scruffy, cheerful lads of about ten were approaching, one swinging a golf club with an improvised bamboo cane shaft, the other pushing a near-wrecked pram containing a snot-streaked child, its many scabs daubed with gentian violet. As Morley passed them, the child leaned out of the pram and shouted 'Boo!' almost in his face. Morley inwardly jumped, but walked on, apparently unconcerned, continuing his new-found American walk.

The boy wielding the golf club turned round. 'What's amarrer with you, mate?' he asked.

Morley took no notice.

'Why you walking like that for, then?'

Morley ignored him.

'Ay, you know what?' he heard the other boy say. 'I bet he's shit hisself.' They hooted with derisive laughter and the small child joined in.

But then lots of people were laughing and smiling (though not necessarily at Morley) or whistling or humming, or talking good-humouredly. The fine Easter weather combined with the prospect of Peace were generating an almost palpable excitement, but Morley felt excluded from it. If only confession was out of the way and he was free to feel a part of all this gaiety. If only he wasn't a Catholic . . . He sighed: this was a sinful thought.

He had seen nobody eating an ice-cream and sure enough the first shop in Redwell bore the sign 'NO ICE-CREAM' on the door. He walked on to a general stores and joined the promising-looking queue, which stretched two or three yards along the pavement. Then an irate voice inside shouted, 'Don't they learn you to read at school no more? No, we haven't and won't have till next week.' Morley hesitated, then decided to stay put as if buying an ice-cream had never occurred to him. A few people detached themselves from the queue, a red-faced boy stumbled out of the shop and Morley saw the notice – until then hidden by somebody in the queue: 'ICE-CREAM SOLD OUT'.

From the back of the shop came the smell of boiling fish and a voice from the wireless saying, ' . . . *Deutschlandsender* long-wave station at Koenigswursthousen, which resumed transmission on Thursday, continues to broadcast but reception is extremely weak. All other medium- and short-wave stations are reported to be off the air . . .'

In spite of his preoccupations, the German words thrilled Morley. Not for the first time he wondered whether he wanted the war to end – just yet. The war coloured and directed everything in his life, giving it an exciting, purposeful edge

17

and a perverse sense of security; Peace was strange and unknown territory. He recognized the thought as an indulgence, however: he wanted an unscathed Dad back and a film for his cherished but unused camera and some decent watercolour paints.

When he got to the counter, he bought the 'Reporters' Notebook' he had seen in the window. It was a small pad of thin, speckled, lined paper. He had hoped for plain so that he could draw in it, but it would do, and he hadn't stammered. This minor triumph emboldened him enough to risk asking the time. It was important that he didn't return home too early.

'Excuse me, please,' he said to a well-dressed old man standing near the amusements, 'but can you p-please tell me the time?'

'I most certainly *can*,' said the man, 'if by that you mean, have I the ability to tell the time and the ability to convey this intelligence to you. But the question is, am I willing to do so?' He paused, teasingly.

Morley wondered what to say next, but the old man continued, 'Yes, of course I'm willing to tell you the time. It would be churlish of me to refuse such a polite, if somewhat imperfectly phrased request.' He drew out a watch from his waistcoat pocket. 'It is precisely seven minutes and twenty-three seconds past noon. You must pay no attention to me, young man, I'm afraid I'm growing into a boring old pedant.'

Morley thanked him, wondering what it was about himself that seemed to invite such queer responses and whether the man would have said the same things to Perky Beswick or the Reggies.

Seven minutes past twelve. He had been out nearly as long as it would have taken him to go to confession and back, so he could either begin to walk slowly back home now or hang around for another half-hour. It made little difference. His mother knew he often went to Woolworth's or the library in Upfield after confession.

The pavements were thronged with people now and a newly arrived tram was disgorging still more. Four more trams, two in wartime battleship grey, were waiting on the loop before returning to town.

It occurred to him that it might be an idea to pick up a couple of discarded tram tickets as evidence that he had been to Upfield. He could pull out his hankie in front of his mother and let them fall to the floor. Although, did he usually hang on to his tickets and make sure his mother saw them? No, of course not. It was stupid, the act of somebody with a guilty conscience. It was the sort of barmy thing that George Formby might do. 'Ee, look, Mother. I'm getting proper daft. I've just dropped me tram tickets to Upfield and back where I went to confession. I'll just pick 'em up and throw 'em on t'fire.'

He laughed aloud but stopped abruptly as he felt the eye of a tall young man on him. He was standing in front of the amusements, chewing gum, a cigarette dangling from his lips, rocking back and forth on his heels, hands in pockets rattling loose change, with an air of one who owned the place. His face was a mass of deep red, erupting pimples. But he had made the best of a bad job with sunglasses, a pencil moustache and several elaborate corrugations pushed into his long, oily, black hair. Morley wondered, given the choice, whether he would swap his protruding teeth for the youth's bad skin. No, he decided after little reflection, he wouldn't. What about the bad skin for his stammer *and* his protruding teeth? No again. For all his faults, he was better off than the festering youth. He felt almost relieved to be who he was. Grandma Morley was always saying that there were plenty of folk worse off than yourself.

When Morley was ten, on a Saturday morning visit to Nechells, Grandma Morley asked him to go on an errand.

'Be a lamb, duck, and do your gran a favour. Go up Newton's and get us two gas mantles and you shall have sixpence. Just say, "Two gas mantles for Mrs Morley." He knows the sort I have so you needn't say nothing else. Just speak up nice and clear and remember your manners and don't get frightened. He's ever such a nice gentleman, always asmiling and alaughing and ready with a joke or two.'

Morley walked up the entry, into the street and along to Newton's Ironmongery and Paints reciting, 'Two gas mantles for Mrs Morley, please, two gas mantles for Mrs Morley, please,' quietly and fluently until confronted by the smiling Mr Newton, when all he could manage was 'Two g-ga, two g-ga, two g-ga . . .' He was still persevering when a boiler-suited customer came in.

Mr Newton said, 'God strewth, Mr Allcock, it's wicked innit, but I reckon they forgot to give this one his birdseed this morning – or perhaps he's gone and got his needle stuck!' He laughed loudly at both jokes.

'I reckon he needs more than birdseed,' said Mr Allcock, taking an apple from his pocket. He polished it on his paint-covered sleeve and handed it to Morley. 'How about this, son?'

The gas mantles were sorted out and Mr Newton gave Morley a broken piece of whitening, to use as chalk, to make up for his laughing and joking. But it was clear to Grandma that something was amiss when Morley returned. She persuaded him to confide in her.

'You haven't got much to mither yourself about, duck,' she said. 'Just tek no notice – I never do. It's just that you get a bit nervy sometimes, just like your mom used to. You'll grow out on it, and remember there's always plenty of them that's worse off than what you are.'

She told him about the man who used to live in the next yard: he'd had his ears cut off in the Boer War and ran a pub and drove a motor and got on with everybody a treat. In the end he made a lot of money. Then there was the lad whose head was bigger than his body and had to be pushed round in a baby carriage and fed with a titty bottle even when he was fourteen. He used to live up Bloomsbury Street but he was dead now.

Morley was still looking down in the mouth, so she continued in a lighter vein. 'There was this lad that was helping his mom to wring out the washing, see, and he went and got his threepenny bit caught in the mangle. We-e-ll, they couldn't get it out; they tried and tried but they still couldn't shift it. So in the finish they took him up th'ospital – with the mangle an' all – in th'ambulance. But th'ospital couldn't get it out neither. So the fire brigade had to come to chop the mangle up to get his bit out. But when they got it out, it was all squashed out flat like a great big pancake. We-e-ll, he couldn't get it down his breeches; and when he went out it was always adragging along the horse road; and everybody laughed at him and chucked bricks at him. So, anyroad, in the finish th'ospital had to chop it off for him. And all his life after that, he had to piddle out his mouth. But he never mithered about it, he just carried on and never took no notice.'

Although he wasn't sure if he believed this one, Morley laughed heartily – but when you are only ten (unless you are Bernard Inch), threepenny bits are only fit for the one, rather ridiculous function.

'So remember, my duck' – Grandma never called him Morley, after all, it was her own surname – 'you astuttering a bit now and again in't nothing much really. You just think of all them that's far worse off. *Everybody*'s got somebody worse off.' But Morley was left thinking about the somebody at the bottom of the pile who had no somebody worse off to console *himself* with because he was the worst off of the lot.

The spotty youth might well have been worse off than Morley but he was bigger and stronger, and was giving Morley a challenging look. Morley shifted his gaze to a punchball, as if this had been the object of his interest all the time, and, to leave no room for doubt, he walked purposefully over to it. He would love to have a go, but this was strictly the province of the athletic, such as his father and Mr Grant, his PT teacher, and the reckless, such as Reggies Nolan and Kelp – and he was neither. Anyway, it was broken: a piece of gummed brown tape over the penny slot said, 'Out of Order'. He should have guessed – it was one of the few attractions with no jostling crowd round it.

The amusements were noisy, shabby and hugely enticing.

On a quiet rainy evening a couple of months earlier, Morley, heart pounding, had guiltily watched the three peep shows inside: *Sir Archibald's Dream*, *What the Butler Saw* and *Percival's Seaside **Miss**adventures*.

With the eagerness to spend still with him, he was tempted to go inside but the big notice which hung like an inn sign from the ceiling made him pause. It began piously in old English lettering, 'God helps those who help themselves,' and finished threateningly in sloping capitals, '*BUT GOD HELP THOSE WHO HELP THEMSELVES IN HERE!!!*'

The sign decided it: a place which took the name of the Lord in vain was no place for a boy who was supposed to be in Upfield confessing his sins, let alone that it was full of paraphernalia associated with sex, violence and gambling. On other occasions it had seemed harmless; and he had never been forbidden to go there. His father had even taken him, before the war, when he was only six. Not now, though. The amusements would keep.

Another packed tram creaked up the hill, its rear platform crowded with lads poised to leap off the step as soon as they dared. Not far from the amusements, the Hare and Hounds was doing a roaring trade. All the tables and benches in its forecourt and paved garden were occupied; the remaining patrons leaned against walls or squatted on the kerbside. The queues at the bars and outside hatch were huge and the glasses must have run out: an old man and three boys were making frantic searches.

As Morley drew alongside the pub, a large group of people were rearranging their tables and making room on their benches for a couple of just arrived soldiers. Both wore the blue uniform of the wounded – though such an indication seemed superfluous in their case. One was in a wheelchair, an empty sleeve safety-pinned to the chest of his blouse and a section of empty trouser leg folded and pinned over what remained of his leg. His companion, who had probably pushed him from the military wing of Redhill Asylum, had a large area of furrowed and discoloured flesh surrounding a narrow, irregular slit where once his eye had been.

Morley stopped, leaned against the pub's garden wall and took off his boot to remove an imaginary stone while he looked and listened.

Eager hands were helping to slide the wheelchair into the narrow space they'd made. Its occupant said in a public-school accent, 'Sorry to be a pain and all that . . .'

They fell over themselves to protest.

'No, no trouble at all.'

'Don't be daft, it's the least –'

'Shift that bag of yourn out the road, Marge.'

'You're okay, son.'

'Don't crowd him, Gordon.'

And when the one-eyed soldier was seated:

'Now, gents, what'll you –'

'No, it's my shout, Gordon.'

'Shurrup, both of you, I've had a bit of a win.'

'Have one of these –'

'Put that Yankee horse muck away, Don.'

'I bet Arthur's got some cigars hid away, come on, Arthur.'

The soldiers' wounds horrified Morley. These men were worse-offs with a vengeance. He watched fascinated as, about to raise cigarettes to lips, they both laughed, not knowing which to choose from the half-dozen instantly proffered lights. How *could* they laugh after what had happened to them?

He held his breath to stop the tears. A vision of his father in a tattered, bloodstained battledress, writhing in agony with a shattered leg, jumped into his head; then another, blundering around, arms outstretched, a bloody bandage covering his sightless eyes. He held his breath again, gritted his teeth and made loud discordant sounds in his head to prevent further images. He crossed the road to the grass reservation on which the trams ran, leaned against a tree and fished from his trouser pocket the last letter from his father.

It wasn't really a proper letter but a fragment cut from the bottom of his father's letter to his mother. His mother seldom allowed him to see entire letters. She just read aloud

23

selected bits from them, unless as with this one, there was a part at the bottom specially intended for Morley. He read:

Dear Son (he never called him Morley),
How are you? I hope you are well. I am quite well and fit and the food is quite good, much better than it was a few months ago. I have not yet got any decent Jerry souvenirs but am always on the look out and will let you know as soon as I have got a decent collection together for you. Look after your mother for me, and remember what I've always told you, *keep that eye of yours on the ball!!!*
Love Dad.

The letter had been written just over two weeks ago by an uninjured father. It was hardly likely that anything had happened to him since; and the war was practically over. No, he was going to be all right. Somewhat calmed, Morley crossed the road again, his eyes carefully averted from the soldiers, and looked at the huge retaining wall which kept a portion of Redwell Hill from sliding into the pub garden. On it, someone had painted a vast, white V for victory with the Morse code dot dot dot dash underneath.

A hundred yards beyond the wall lay the body of Cardinal Newman, in the cemetery of the Oratory Fathers' Retreat House, a secluded spot to which Father Smythe had once taken Morley and fellow scholars on a Saturday instruction class outing. 'A very, very holy man,' Father Smythe had said, reverently. 'One day he will become a saint. What do you think of that, boys and girls?' Nobody had thought anything very much so they had remained silent.

Now, in a curiously changed mood, Morley soundlessly answered, Neat, Father, neat. And when Cardinal Newman was a kid, Father, did he ever rack off?

From inside the pub came the chorus of a song, popular a couple of years ago:

Heil (prrrzz), heil (prrrzz),
Right in der Führer's face.

24

A military band was playing somewhere in the distance; a near-empty tram started back to Birmingham whilst a full one lurched up the hill; the wounded soldiers and their new-found friends were knocking back pints; over the road, a man in shirt sleeves and a grey trilby was selling things from a suitcase to the women queuing outside the giant public lavatories, oblivious to a policeman who was chatting to a group of sailors near by; and the well-dressed man who had told Morley the time was peering curiously into the street-seller's suitcase.

Redwell village, which Morley despised – as a village – because its main street was almost entirely composed of jerry-built souvenir and refreshment booths and amusement arcades, and bore no resemblance to any proper village that he had heard about, read about or seen at the pictures, was suddenly the pulsating centre of the universe, and Morley felt almost at one with it. He felt unusually patriotic, God and his Mortal Sin had almost disappeared and the glamorous aspect of the war depicted in his books and boys' papers had, for the moment, lost some of its enchantment.

Morley wished that life could always be like it was at this moment. To make things perfect, he wanted to do something exceptionally brave – provided he wasn't maimed – or good, or just something . . . magnificent. But he knew that the feeling wouldn't last long. He was hungry. Reluctantly, he turned into Eachley Lane and home.

# Chapter 3

A familiar Sunday afternoon ennui had settled upon the Charles household. Morley's mother was half-listening to the wireless, half-reading *Reynold's News* whilst half-lying on the settee. The now unappealing smell of roast beef and the still less appealing smell of Brussels sprouts lingered from dinner time in spite of the open windows and kitchen door.

Morley had been to eight o'clock Mass, his mother to high Mass at eleven o'clock and Frank, the lodger, who made the curious claim that his job at the Aero Works absolved him from his weekly obligation, had lain stinking in bed, as Morley's mother put it, until twelve o'clock and was now at the Hen and Chickens.

Morley had taken a few listless turns around the garden to pass the time. He would have finished off his balsa model of a Messerschmitt, had the balsa cement not run out; read a story, had he a story to read; or started a painting, had he some paper. To this last end, but with little hope, he rummaged through the two big dresser drawers and the lidless old suitcase under the stairs which contained magazines, his pre-war copies of *Gem* and *Magnet*, brown paper and carefully preserved pieces of old Christmas wrapping paper. But in vain.

He stood on the kitchen chair and searched through the

household's thirty-odd books on top of the dresser, in case he could find a previously missed clean endpaper somewhere. *Monroe's Universal Reference Book*, *Modern Home Management* and others in this vein were sacrosanct, of course, as were the Rexine-covered Dickens and the prize-awarded books from his mother's childhood. As he had feared, all his own books had already been stripped of all paper that didn't bear text. What space remained, in margins and beneath chapter endings, was tightly packed with doodles and drawings representing years of changing subject interests and techniques.

There were cars, aeroplanes, ships, tanks, lots of soldiers – mainly German – in a variety of uniforms; Disney cartoons and caricatures of Hitler and Churchill; the picturesque: thatched cottages, watermills, idyllic villages, streams and woodlands; and, more recently, women. Nearly every blank area of *The Picts and the Martyrs* was filled with drawings of fur-coated women, sitting, standing or reclining. Once naked, they had acquired underwear, stockings and shoes, then a frock or a smart two-piece and finally a heavily shaded censoring fur coat.

He glumly examined the Enid Blyton books recently given to him by Maureen from next door. He had originally disregarded them as all three were small and printed on poor, war-economy paper which did not take well to watercolour, or even pencil. But even here the biggest undrawn-on area he could find was a meagre five-inch square soiled with a teacup ring – useless for a serious picture.

Morley's persistent searching and fiddling with books were getting on his mother's nerves. 'For goodness sake, duck, can't you settle down and do something useful? I can't stand all this pithering.'

Morley pithered with greater intensity, hoping that his mother, driven to distraction, would be persuaded on this occasion to relent and allow him to have the endpapers from *Monroe's Universal Reference Book* or *Modern Home Management*. He picked up the latter and flicked noisily through its pages.

'I've *got* to have some paper for this picture I've got to do for Russ,' he said, trying to make it sound urgent and important. 'If I'm *r-really* careful, Mom, can I cut the clean p-paper out of one of your books? I'll be that careful, I'll do it with a razor blade and a ruler. Nobody will ever notice. It'll look as good as –'

'No, I've told you a dozen times before, no!'

'B-but why? Why can't I? You never tell me *why*.'

'Because you can't, that's why and that's all there is to it. Anyway, it spoils them.'

'How can it spoil them? It's just plain paper; you don't need p-plain paper in a reading book. Anyroad, you never read them, they're just l-lying there wasted.'

'I'll give you wasted, and I'm not telling you again, no! Anyway, they're your dad's books. You wait till he gets back and ask him then, but I know what he'll say.'

Morley was tempted to wheedle, but he could see that his mother was on the brink of some dark emotion. It often happened when his father's return from the war was mentioned. If he provoked her further, he ran the risk of a thump or a kick on any part of him that she could reach – and there would be hours of awful silence afterwards. So he said, as one determined in spite of all obstacles to honour his obligations, 'I've r-really got to do this picture for Russ. I've got to get some paper from *somewhere*. That lumber jacket he gave me is b-brand new. I've got to give him something.'

'Well, you haven't got to do the picture now, this very minute,' his mother said irritably. 'Russ won't even be expecting anything. Just go down now and say thank you for the jacket. If he's there, that is. If he isn't there, go for a long walk up the Ickley Hills or something. Frank will be back any minute and I don't think I can stand the two of you under my feet.'

Morley was about to say that he had been for a long walk on the Ickley Hills yesterday but remembered just in time that his mother wasn't supposed to know. 'Ah, yeh, good idea, haven't b-been up there lately. Bit of fresh air'll do me good.'

He had said it too glibly and his mother was alerted. She gave him a hard look. 'You're not thinking of going to the pictures?'

'No, course not!' he said with virtuous indignation since it hadn't crossed his mind. Even so, he embarked on the tired old argument to punish her for her accusation. 'But I don't know *why*. Everybody else does, even that Joe Kinsella that s-serves on the altar. Yes, yes, okay, I know, I know.' His mother was advancing on him. 'It makes people work and you sh-shouldn't work on a Sunday. I know, I know.'

'Well, just so long as you do, that's all, my lad. And I don't care what other people do. You don't go and that's that.'

Morley made for the front door but couldn't resist shouting when he was on the step, 'Well, you shouldn't listen to the wireless of a Sunday then, it's just the same. All them people working for the BBC, just the same as the p-pictures – worse! And *they* work all day long. There must be hundreds of –'

'You cheeky sod, you wouldn't dare speak to Russ like that – or anybody else for that matter!'

He slammed the door but not before hearing her murmur, 'Anyroad, son, you'd have a job spitting it out.'

The bright Sunday road was deserted. The pig bin was on its side, its malodorous contents spilled into the road, and Reggie Kelp's half-starved dog, Tarzan, was happily picking through the mess. Someone had cut or untied it from the lamp post. It was always happening – usually to create a gap big enough for a goal.

For a brief period, long ago, there had been a small notice fixed to the lamp post, with instructions for the pig bin's use. Sadly, however, the rules were no longer always observed. The contents frequently included glass, chip papers, sweet papers, cigarette packets, dog ends, dog turds, and spent matches – and these often wet, since the lid was usually missing. In addition, the scruffs who gathered around it in the evenings spat in it, pissed in it, and Reggie Kelp, it was said, had more than once tossed off in it.

Whenever Morley's mother saw the pig bin on its side,

she always set it upright and retied it to the lamp post; she instructed Morley to do the same. But today, partly because he was wearing his new trousers and lumber jacket and partly to punish his mother for not letting him have the endpapers, he let the pig bin rest. And anyway, Frank the lodger was coming drunkenly into view at the bottom of the road.

Morley was bitterly ashamed that they had a lodger, even more so that it was Frank. But Canon Reilly had been very persuasive with his mother. Wasn't she a good Catholic? And wasn't her house close to the Aero Works where Frank had already got a job? And wasn't he from one of the most respected families in the whole of County Meath? If that was true, then Frank was the black sheep of it all right, his mother was always saying.

If he hurried, he could be inside the Pinders' house – where Russ was a frequent visitor – before Frank spotted him: the last thing he wanted was a loud, embarrassing encounter with Frank near the Pinders' front gate.

On the other hand, when Frank was drunk he was good for anything up to half a crown – if there were others around to witness his generosity. And now he was with two companions. Furthermore, he had a piano accordion with him and Morley was intrigued. If he got a move on, he could ensure a meeting point with Frank well beyond the Pinders'.

Frank staggered up the road between old man Kirkham and Bashful Harold, hogging the conversation and gesticulating wildly, the accordion wheezing discordantly. Frank was in his Sunday best: navy pin-striped jacket and brown pin-striped trousers; beneath his nose was a smudged Hitler moustache done in soot.

'Well, will you look at who's here now,' Frank called out with great heartiness as Morley drew near, a safe half-dozen houses past the Pinders'. 'There he is, fellas, the apple of his mammy's eye! Now then, Harold, you old son of a gun, did you know your man here is a genius? He knows entirely everything, he does. Now then, ask him something, ask him anything under the sun. Ask him the seven wonders of the world.'

'You ask him,' said Harold, looking at the ground.

'I will, I will now. Now then, son . . .' He swayed suddenly and lost his thread. He turned to old man Kirkham. 'And you should see his drawings! Why, your man draws like an angel. Now, Mr Kirkham, you take a snap of Harold here, with a camera, okay? And this one, this young fella, will do you a photo just the same, exa-ct-ly the same with a pencil. A pencil! Now have yous got a pencil, Harold? Nipper? To show him.'

'I know what a bloody pencil is, you barmy bugger,' growled old man Kirkham.

'And I'm telling you, you won't be able to tell the difference. If you can tell the difference, I'll give you, five bob . . . or this ar-ccordion.'

They were an oddly assorted trio. Balding Bashful Harold, middle aged, neatly dressed, still living with his mother at the top of the road. Old man Kirkham with one lens of his glasses opaque and the other so powerful that his iris filled up the entire area and changed shape as he moved his head. And Frank the lodger, weighed down with the accordion, struggling to keep his balance, one eye closed against the smoke from the cigarette in the corner of his mouth.

Frank was silent for a moment. Then he turned to Morley. 'Hey, nipper, will you come here and I'll show you something. It will have you in stitches. Now, Harold, will you hold this awhile while I show the nipper here.' He struggled to detach himself from the accordion, reeling into the road, reeling back, losing his footing and falling backwards on to the gravel strip which separated road from pavement, the accordion hissing and wailing.

Harold grinned foolishly, looked at his shoes and said softly, 'Naw, I in't even going to touch it, I don't know nothing about it. If you got any sense, you'd tek it back now, this minute – leave it on the pub step, say you found it, I dunno, but don't go getting me involved.' ·

'Ah, stop whining, will yous. There's no harm done; sure, it's just a loan. It'll be back safe and sound as soon as the pub opens. And I'll bet you, they won't know 'twas gone.'

31

Frank, back on his unsteady feet, finally managed to free himself from the straps. The accordion landed on the pavement with a heavy bump and a screech. Frank, unconcerned, picked it up and leaned it against a tree, right into a pile of moist dog turds. He spat on to his hand and smoothed a lock of his grey-black wiry hair across his forehead. 'Now, take a look at this, nipper, sure and they were pissing themselves back in the pub. I was the life and soul of the party. Isn't that right, fellas? Now, look at me, nipper. I might not be up to your grand standard but I've added a little twist of me own.'

Right arm raised, left forefinger under nose representing a moustache, presumably forgetting the one in soot already there, Frank goose-stepped erratically up and down the pavement shouting, 'Hail, Hitler, hail, Hitler, hail, Hitler. And now for me new bit. Look, will you. Hail, Hitler, ha, ha. Hail, Mary, ha, ha, ha. Hail Mary, full of grace, the Lord is with thee, ha, ha, ha. Hail, Hitler, full of shit, the divil is with thee, ha, ha, ha.'

Morley felt very self-conscious as spectator to this absurd public display, and offended by Frank's blasphemy. Anxious to put an end to it, he said, 'Your dinner will be all d-dried up if you don't get a move on. And what's our mom going to say about that accordion?'

Frank paid no attention. 'Now, what do you think of that, nipper? How was I now?'

'M-Marvellous,' said Morley, scornfully – and added mischievously, 'I've just seen the p-priest going into our house.'

'Ah, sure and you're joking. The priest wouldn't be visiting on a Sunday, for sure. He'd be far too busy.'

'I'm off then,' said Harold to his fingernails. 'Come on, Mr Kirkham, I'll see you back.'

'Will you tell me, nipper, and which priest would that be?'

'Canon Reilly,' replied Morley, choosing the fearsome one of Upfield's two priests. 'I suppose Father Smythe's doing c-confirmation class and b-benediction and – oh yeh, there was something I heard about a visiting priest. Maybe he's helping out, so C-Canon Reilly's free.'

'Well now, son, it was you he came to see then, was it? Or your mammy? Yes, sure it's your mammy, a fine Catholic lady he'd be seeing. Not an auld sinner like me!' he finished with a strained laugh.

Morley frowned. 'Well, I don't know, I came out the house just before he came; but Canon Reilly's already seen me, this m-morning after Mass. And he must have seen Mom at the eleven o'clock, so who else . . . ?'

Morley was enjoying himself: the story was unfolding almost of its own accord and there was little tendency to stammer.

Frank pushed back his hair and rubbed at his soot-drawn moustache with a moistened finger. 'Now, er, Morley, son' – he had never called him Morley before – 'you know I've always liked you, admired your photos – why, was I not saying just as much to Harold and Mr Kirkham? Now, will you be doing auld Frank an auld favour? Just look after this instrument for a while and I'll . . .' He searched feverishly through his pockets. 'It's not for me but your mammy's sake. I wouldn't be causing her any worries, you understand, and I'm sure you wouldn't either. She has a great cross to bear with your daddy at the war. A lovely lady, but high strung, you won't mind me saying, sensitive.' His pockets proving unfruitful, he scrabbled in the lining of his jacket until a nicotine-stained finger shot out through a hole in the fabric. 'Will you believe that, son? Gone! Jaysus, and I had nine bob in there, I did. And three would have been yours. Now if you'll hide this instrument safely with a friend, or, well, sure and you're a bright lad, you'll think of something. Then let me have it at seven o'clock by the lounge bar door. Or, no, let me think . . . if you put it *inside* the pub – and tell anybody that comes, that you found it – and it will be four bob you'll get. Four bob on Friday, er, Morley?' Frank picked up the accordion straps and moved as if to drape them round Morley's shoulders.

Morley wanted nothing to do with it. Any minute now, the landlord of the pub might come running up the road with a couple of toughs or a policeman. He backed away. 'I would, Frank, but I'm in a r-rush. I'll miss the tram if I don't get a move on. I've got to see Joe Kinsella up Upfield. Er, p-put it in the shed or behind the dustbin before you go in.' And away he dashed before Frank could think of any other inducements.

A great burst of bass as the accordion hit the gatepost signalled Frank's arrival home. Morley glanced cautiously back to see him stagger along the path, struggling to free himself from the straps. He suddenly thought of the dog shit.

He continued walking down the road. In the last quarter of an hour, he reflected, he had told two deliberate lies. A lie to put a stop to Frank's clowning and send him back to his dinner before it became uneatable – and to spare his mother further annoyance. Then another to spare Frank's feelings when he was unwilling to help him hide the accordion. But surely they were only white lies, such as his mother told on those occasions when she had summoned enough presence of mind to claim she was right out of ink or baking powder or dried milk when Big Gwen Pinder was on the scrounge? Anyway, white lies were nothing compared to his Mortal Sin. Suddenly, his brilliant scheme to pose as a French lad during his confession went out like a light. It would be deception: far, far more serious than a white lie. And in the sanctity of the confessional. And another thing: Canon Reilly would surely question his accent, ask him where he came from, where his parents were. Good God, he might even speak French! Priests were educated, had been to university, or wherever priests go. They spoke in Latin after all. Why had this not occurred to him before? His heart pounded as he imagined the canon helpfully interrupting just as he finished confessing, 'I do a rude zeeng, eur, seveurn or eight times per week,' with, 'Aah, *Français*?' Then launching into real French, which he wouldn't understand. No, the whole pathetic plan was riddled with flaws and he was still no further forward in overcoming this one obstacle which lay between himself and, it seemed, perfect happiness.

Usually, he reflected, there were half a dozen obstacles just below the surface waiting to be worried about at the slightest provocation. He listed them: his protruding teeth, his stammer, being about an inch below average height for his thirteen years, skinny, about half a stone underweight, pale-looking, and having, according to his mother, neighbours and teachers, a permanent worried expression. Now, all these things seemed manageable. His teeth were being coaxed into place – about twelve to fifteen months it would take, they said at the dental hospital, if he wore his brace constantly and kept all the appointments for its adjustment. He had more control over his stammer now, even when he wasn't French, so that on a good day it was mere hesitancy that afflicted him. He thought that his stammer might disappear altogether when he discarded his brace, though when his mother had enquired, the dentist at the dental hospital had said there was no connection. Even so, he knew that the fear of people staring at his brace sometimes made him self-conscious, which made him stammer. As for his deficiencies in height, weight, colour and expression, they weren't particularly serious, though together he knew that they added up to an impression of, well, a weed. He recalled the time nearly eighteen months ago when he turned up at Scouts proudly wearing his new scout hat that Ron, his uncle, had got for him. Instead of approving looks, all he got were sniggers. The same thing had happened when he'd first appeared in swimming trunks at Upfield Baths. On his first appearance in long trousers at church, too – the new ones that fitted properly. He was just that sort of boy. But not for much longer. As soon as he was absolved from his Mortal Sin, he would somehow sort all this out. So what on earth was it called?

He found himself at the bottom of Woods Park Road – three or four hundred yards past the Pinders' – with no recollection of having walked there.

# Chapter 4

A 71 tram from town slithered to a halt at the Woods Park Road stop and Eric Beswick alighted, an old army haversack on his back. Morley was in no mood for an encounter with Eric but Eric had already spotted him. Eric spat, crossed the carriageway and spat twice more before reaching the corner where Morley stood resplendent in his red plaid lumber jacket.

'Warrow, Morle. What you been up to, then?'

Morley tried to think of a smart reply and failed. 'Y-You know, j-just hanging around. Been up your uncle's then, Ec?' He couldn't quite bring himself to call him Perk or Perky as most of the other lads did.

'Yeh. Caught eight pounder. Nine pounder. Tench. Our uncle said they should a been photoed. He only caught a few titches.'

Eric often went fishing with his uncle who lived in Brierley Hill in the Black Country and he usually stayed overnight. He spat again.

Eric was always spitting. He did not hawk, cough or even merely clear his throat, he just spat. When people asked him about this curious habit, he said that he didn't like the idea of his mouth being full of spit. Morley found it difficult to fathom Eric out and decide whether he was bright or dim. Never at a loss for an answer, his strange, clipped, expressionless voice had a slightly hypnotic effect, keeping listeners uncertain but respectful. He was rarely teased, though he cut rather an odd figure: almost normal from the front – tallish, slim, with dark hair and pale olive skin – but in profile, from the top of his head to his heels, he was almost a straight line, as if he had been trimmed with a plane.

Eric seldom dwelt on preliminaries. 'Heard this one then, Morle?'

Morley looked dutifully attentive.

'There was this kid called Fuckerarder. Went in this shop to get this chocolate. There was this bostin' tart inside. So he gets her down on the floor. Behind this counter. His mom was outside by the tram stop. She shouts, "Fuckerarder, Fuckerarder. Quick, the tram's acoming." He shouts back, "I'm doing my best, Mom. But I in't even got her drawers down yet."'

Morley laughed politely and loudly, though he had heard Perky tell almost the same joke to the scruffs round the pig bin a couple of times before. The last time, though, the kid was called Shoveitupper, and it was a different sort of shop, and it was a bus instead of a tram, and the kid was with his dad.

Morley doubted whether Perky knew the word for his Mortal Sin, but he was on his own, they were already close to the subject and he wouldn't get any funny looks from Perky either as Perky only had the one expressionless look. He tried an indirect route.

'Nice g-girls up Brierley Hill, Ec?' he began conversationally.

'Yeh. This ATS tart. Lives by our uncle. Bostin'. Whoa-er! Seen these photos. Took by her boyfriend. Showed me. Whoa-er! Skirt up. Legs open. Could see all her hairs. Whoa-er! Took them in these bushes. Whoa-er!'

Enormously excited, Morley wanted to know more, but found himself asking, 'Where d-does he get his f-films from, then, Ec?'

'Shop up Brierley Hill. They got films. All sorts.'

'Honest?' Films were nearly as rare as bananas.

'Yeh.'

'B-But when it was developed, the chemist might've got the p-police.'

37

'Naw. Boyfriend's in the RAF. Got a special RAF camera. For tekking photos over Germany. And that. Got special developer inside. Automatic. RAF don't take films up the chemist's.'

Morley wanted to get this straight. 'So he d-didn't b-buy *his* films in Brierley Hill, this RAF bloke?'

'Naw. Din't have to. Gets them from the RAF.'

'But you *can* g-get films in Brierley Hill, ordinary ones?'

'Yeh. Easy. Told you.'

Morley would have dearly loved a film but decided not to pursue the matter. He tried to steer the conversation back to the original subject with the hope that, this time, things wouldn't get so confused. 'I, I, I b-bet old Reggie Kelp wouldn't m-mind seeing them photos, Ec, ay? Wonder what he'd do if he seen them photos? I reckon he w-would go and have a good w-wank or t-toss off and that,' he said boldly. 'Funny w-words, in't they, Ec? Wonder what they call it up B-Brierley Hill?' Without waiting for a reply, he rushed on, anxious to find out what he wanted to know. 'Y'know that posh kid, Trevor? Him that l-lives in that b-big house up Eachley? He goes in Hiller's shop and he g-goes, "Ai say, Hiller, those acid drops were frightfully good; do let me know when you have a further supply. The whole family's awfully keen on them." Y'know, I often wonder what *he*'d say after a w-wank. I mean he w-wouldn't say, "I din't half have a neat w-wank," like Kelp 'cause he talks posh like the wireless. He s-says things like, er, "I walked up the parth parst the grarss, then had a barth," you know.'

'Funny thing to say,' Eric said.

'Wh-What is, Ec?'

'Going up the parth. Parst the grarss and that. When you've had a wank.'

'N-No,' said Morley, exasperated. 'I was just t-trying to show how he talks and that. You know, p-posh, *different*. I, I mean Kelp, or Nolan would say to us, "I just had a smashing *w-wank*."' He was inwardly cringing, wondering what his father or Russ would think if they could hear him now. 'Now, if this kid T-Trevor done it, what would *he* say to his posh mates?'

Eric, his face impassive, closed his eyes a fraction and paused half a second in thought. '"Ai say, I just hard a smarshing warnk, charps." That's what he'd say. But why you asking me, Morle? You do all them funny voices. Hitler and posh kids and that.' He added, a trifle uncertainly, 'You having me on?'

It had been in vain. Morley wanted to go but he couldn't resist a final feeble enquiry. 'No, no, Ec. Just w-wondered if there was another word for it. That's all, just w-wondered. Not *how* he'd say it but y-you know, what the p-posh word is.'

'You think too much, you do. Our old lady says, "That kid's mind's always on something else. He'll get run over."'

Morley was happy to accept the observation: it provided a means of escape. 'Yeh, s-suppose you're right. G-Gosh, yes, j-just remembered. Our m-mom said to try and get her some f-fags, from the caff. Better go; she'll wonder wh-what's happened.'

'See, told you. Think too much. You do. Like our old lady says. Where you get that jacket, then?'

Throughout their fractured conversation, Morley, conscious of the jacket's magnificence, had flicked bits of dust off it and fiddled with the buttons, waiting for Eric to make a flattering remark. 'Yank, th-that Yank. Russ. Goes up Pinders'. Goes out with that Beryl. Genuine Yankee job. Made in USA. Says inside.' He was talking in short flat bursts like Perky. 'N-Neat, innit?'

Eric shrugged. 'All right. Too bright for me. Seen loads of them.'

Morley was surprised. He had only noticed a few: two or three in Redwell and perhaps some in town. 'Wh-Where, Ec?'

'Up Brierley Hill. All the kids up Brierley Hill. They got them.'

Morley walked a few yards along the Bristol Road in the direction of the cafés near the Motor Works to support his claim about getting cigarettes. Then he walked back to Woods Park Road and peered cautiously around. Perky was safely out of sight.

He was now nearer to Micky Plant's house than Russell and the Pinders'. He wondered if Micky had come back from his holiday.

# Chapter 5

Apart from the first ten, which were owner-occupied, Woods Park Road was composed of rented, early thirties houses built by the Corporation. They were in blocks of two, three, four and six, and set at varying distances from the road. The roofs were of slate or tiles; the windows were flush or bay; and the walls were of brick or pebble dash. All, however, had identical cast-concrete canopies over their brown or dark green front doors. They all shrieked: Municipal!

Morley wasn't too keen on living in a municipal house. Although it was a minor problem towards the bottom of his long list, he felt that it reduced his status with more affluent schoolmates and, more particularly, distanced him from the delectable middle-class land of *Children's Hour* and his books, where municipal houses didn't exist.

Turning out of the right of way into Marshfield Drive where Micky Plant lived, Morley entered a subtly different world. Here the houses were all semi-detached, all the same shape and equally distanced from the road, and all being paid for. But here the builder had thrown in individual front doors and coloured leaded lights. In addition, every other pair of houses had ornate, projecting, box-room windows with latticed panes, while those in between had small, half-timbered gables above the main bedroom windows to make things fair. 'Private houses,' people in his road called them, either respectfully or scornfully. There was no institutional colour scheme imposed here. Colours were freely chosen and included pastels, delicate greys and beiges with a sprinkling of aggressive royal blues, scarlets and emerald greens. In some cases, the central drainpipe was included in the scheme, each vertically divided half carefully painted to match its respective front door. This resulted in some breathtaking combinations: maroon and turquoise, pink and acid green, and peach and black.

There was a profusion of house names: The Firs, The Hollies, Hill View, Beacon View and, less accountably, Glenside, Capri and Sorrento.

Because of the very warm weather, a number of front doors sported sun awnings to protect the paintwork. Morley could not remember if the Plants' had one. He hoped they hadn't.

They had. A red and white striped one. He rang the bell, rehearsing what he was going to say if either of Micky's parents answered the door. After two more rings and still no reply, Morley wandered round the back to see if the family was in the garden.

As he opened the back gate, he heard rattling, banging and muffled shouts of, 'Oi, quick, somebody open this door. Oi, quick!' The row was coming from the coal house where the hefty kicks being rained on the door were threatening to break the latch. A woman neighbour with pursed lips and a disapproving frown ducked behind the board fence when she saw Morley.

He hesitated for a moment, then called, 'M-Micky, that you?'

'Hurry up, quick, open this door!' came a muted yell.

Morley lifted the latch. A coal-dusty Micky Plant shot out, threw off his jacket, kicked off his shoes, pulled down his braces and charged through the back door into the house, shouting, 'Can't stop, gorra have a crap.'

Morley wondered what it was that Micky had done this time, although his imprisonment was not surprising: it was well known that Micky's parents were harsh disciplinarians.

Micky's father was the Superintendent and his wife the Matron of Redhill Asylum; although as befitted their exalted status there, they always called it the Hospital.

'Very nice, Micky's mom and dad, I always think,' Morley's mother would often impress on Morley when Micky came up in conversation. 'Now, I've got nothing against them. Always very polite, he always touches his hat to me in the street, but I reckon they're both a bit touched. They can't *help* it, poor devils. A lot of the staff there are the same; comes of dealing with all those patients day in, day out for years on end. Enough to send anybody mental.'

Morley's mother worked in the kitchen of the Asylum and he knew that this was her way of coping with the Plants' superior attitude in choosing not to recognize her when their paths crossed at work.

Micky was taking his time. Morley gazed around for something to interest him. Propped up inside the kitchen window was a nearly completed shield-shaped Union Jack overpainted with a Churchillian hand making the V sign; evidently waiting to be displayed at the front of the house as soon as Peace was declared. It was painted on card and extremely well done, obviously Micky's work. Morley examined it with grudging respect. The hand was simply though convincingly rendered in a way Morley would have been hard put to match. He wondered, not for the first time, who was the more talented. Sometimes it was Micky, sometimes he who came top of the class for art – at least according to the termly reports, which were regarded as gospel.

Micky appeared, put on his jacket and shoes, then frowned at his wristwatch. 'I've only got about half an hour, then Dad'll be back and if he finds me out, he'll belt me. You'll have to lock me in again.'

Morley was at his best in an emergency when he had little time to think too much. 'I'll keep near the back gate and when I hear your d-dad coming, I'll lock you in and pretend that I've only just come round. I'll say I came over the b-back from the field in case he wonders why he didn't see me in the road.'

42

'Yeh,' said Micky, unhappily regarding the keep of the latch, which was now hanging loosely on two protruding screws. He pushed them back, but when he gave a testing tug the shanks of the screws popped into view again. 'God, if he sees that, I'll be in for it.' He pushed the screws back. 'You can't really tell that there's anything wrong but *he*'ll soon find out. He always does, our dad,' he said, bitterly. 'What'll I do, Morley?'

'M-Matchsticks,' said Morley, trying to keep the triumph out of his voice. Micky looked baffled. 'You shove matchsticks in the holes. M-Makes the holes, well, smaller.'

Micky looked unconvinced. 'You sure?'

'Yeh, course.' But he knew that his assertion alone would lack conviction. 'Remember that p-pencil sharpener fixed on Miss P-Pryce's desk? It kept coming loose when you turned the handle and she got fed up. Then she got old Shagger to come and fix it, and he used matchsticks and m-made us all watch to show how b-brilliant he was, and he was the only b-bloke in the world who knew –'

'Yeh, yeh, I believe you. Can't say I remember. Got any matchsticks then?' he said, as if having suggested the solution, Morley should jolly well be equipped to carry it out.

Morley hadn't, so Micky sent him indoors to search for some in the kitchen cabinet, instructing him to remove his shoes first – Morley knew that Mrs Plant was fanatically house-proud.

Matches found and Micky urging speed, Morley worked them into the holes, broke them flush and drove in the screws with Micky's scout knife. They held. Micky sighed with relief, clambered back into the coal house and squatted carefully to avoid undue contact between the coal and his clothes. Morley closed and latched the door.

'Good kid, Morley,' Micky said, his mouth close to the crack of the door.

Morley savoured the rare praise and hoped that his assistance might lead to a closer friendship and earn a bit more of Micky's loyalty, but somehow he doubted it.

'W-What happened, then, Micky? Why did they lock you up?' he now felt confident enough to ask.

43

'Oh, there was a big row over our grandma when we came back yesterday. They all came, Gran, Grandad and Uncle Peter – he drove us in his car. I sat with our grandma in the back. Anyway, near Bromsgrove, there was this terrible stink and I just said, without thinking, "Pwwaah!" like you do, and our grandad turned round, a bit red, and gave me a look and opened the window a bit. Then it came again, long and worse.'

'What was it, Micky?'

'Our grandma, she farted.'

'Your grandma?' Morley marvelled and pictured small, delicate, straight-backed Granny Plant with her snow-white hair and gold-rimmed glasses, sweet, demure: a story-book grandma.

'Yeh, listen. Anyway, this time, instead of saying "Phwwaah", I was polite. I said, "All right, our gran?" But she turned away and our grandad said, "I think you've forgotten yourself, Michael."

'And I said, "Sorry, Grandad, I don't know what you mean, forgotten what?" He says, "I think you know what I mean, Michael."

'I say, "I don't know what you're on about, Grandad." And he made Uncle Peter stop the car.

'He says, "Michael, you're forcing me to say things I'd rather not say in front of Grandma." But anyway, he still said it. He goes, "You were rude, Michael."'

'And were you?' asked Morley. 'This time, I mean, was it you who, er, farted and let on it was your granny?'

'Naw, course not,' said Micky indignantly. 'It was our grandma all right, it was like . . . like an old navvy who just eats sprouts. She's done it before.'

'Yeh, b-but everybody *does* it,' said Morley. 'Even film stars.'

'But she can't help it. I think she's got stomach trouble or something.'

'So their house at Evesham stinks all the time, then?'

'No, course not! It's, well, different at home, I suppose she can go outside or to the lavatory or something but sometimes like in the car . . .'

Morley was fascinated. 'She came to see you in the play at school in that *Bishop's Candlesticks*. I mean, how did she manage then or, say, church and that?'

'She always sits by the door, says she might faint, says she wants nobody fussing but she needs fresh air occasionally.'

'Sounds as if e-everybody else needs the fresh air,' said Morley boldly. 'But she must f-feel it coming on, then?'

'Dunno, yeh, suppose. But listen,' Micky said impatiently, 'I haven't finished. When our grandad said I was rude, I thought he was blaming me for dropping one so nobody would think it was our gran.

'So I said, "I wasn't rude, really, Grandad, God's honour. I just think it was Grandma being a bit poorly." Then our gran cried. We went home and had our tea. Everybody was quiet and then our grandma let off another. I went up to my bedroom after that and painted my shield. I wanted to keep out of the way. Then if she let off again, they wouldn't think it was me.'

'But they did *think* it was you, in the car, or at least, your grandad just *said* it was you. And they locked you up for that? Since yesterday?'

'No, no, no,' said Micky. 'Just listen. Dad'll be here in a minute. Are you listening out for him?'

'Yes, don't worry, I can hear all right from here.'

'Well, I don't know what Grandad said to our mom, but today, just before she went to work, she said, "Michael, I know there might have been a bit of a misunderstanding yesterday. Grandma was very upset. And we can't have that. She's not in the best of health. And they might not ask you to stay with them again. Write a nice letter saying you're sorry."

'And I said, "They should send *me* a letter. *I* didn't do anything. Our grandad accused me and all the time it was our grandma."

'Our mom said she didn't want to *hear* what happened, just to send a letter.

'And I got mad and said our gran farted twice in the car and at tea time.

45

'Then Mom got really mad and said, "*What* did you say?"'

'And I said, "*Farted, farted,* our gran *farted,* the dirty old cow *farted,* right?" And our dad heard me up the garden and he shoved me in here. Then our mom went to work and Dad went for a walk and said he'd let me out in about an hour if I'd come to my senses and apologize and promise to write the letter, then he'd work out a proper punishment. Can you hear him coming?' There was panic in Micky's voice.

'No, don't worry, there's p-plenty of time, I'll tell you,' said Morley. 'But it doesn't seem fair to me. It was all your grandad's fault. I s-s'pose it was mainly 'cause of you swearing to your mom that made them lock you up.'

'Yeh, it was. But I've been thinking, our grandad didn't really accuse me of farting.'

'But you said he did!'

'No, what I think was that he didn't like me saying "Phwwaah" and then saying "All right, our gran?" *That*'s what he meant when he said I was rude. Like Miss Pryce would say if someone answered her back. When you've got no manners. Our mom would say it's a personal remark. It's best to just pretend you haven't noticed.'

'Or s-smelled, more like,' said Morley. 'But wouldn't it make it worse to write to your gran and say' – putting on a middle-class accent – "My dear Grandmother, I'm awfully sorry I made remarks when you farted. Love, Michael."' There was no response from Micky. Perhaps Morley had gone too far. 'Are you all r-right in there, Micky?'

'Yeh . . . okay . . . just got a touch of cramp . . . be all right in a minute.'

'You'd better let me let you out, then.'

'No, no, no. It's okay now. Trouble is, there's no room to stand up and I daren't sit down in case I get my clothes dirty.' There was the sound of a minor avalanche and a heartfelt cry of, 'Fucking hell.'

'Micky? You okay, Micky?'

'Yep, don't matter now, I'm all over covered in coal. Might as well sit in it for all the difference it'll make. It's my best suit as well. Still, that's their fault. Haven't you got a new jacket, Morley?'

'Yeh, Yankee job,' said Morley matter-of-factly. 'Got it from Russ, that Yank I told you about. I'm going to do him a picture as a thank you. A country scene: he's mad ab-bout the English countryside. He's seen some of my pictures already and he likes the watercolours b-best, likes the way I do trees and old buildings.' Aware that Micky might think he was bragging, he said hastily, 'I like that shield you've done. It's r-really neat, looks like it's printed.'

'Ah yeh, the old victory shield; still needs a few finishing touches. Won't be long now, Morley, the end of the war. Our dad says it's only a matter of a week or two, or even a few days. Talking about art, when is it we hear about the Art School? *You* haven't heard yet?'

'No,' said Morley. 'They don't tell us till J-June, I think. You looking forward to going?'

'Yeh, anything that keeps me out the house longer suits me down to the ground. Y'know, we'll have to start out well before eight and we won't get back till about half-five. Anyway, I'll be glad to finish with Redhill School. They don't teach you anything and most of my best mates went to the grammar the other year. Well, except you and one or two others,' he quickly added.

'You should have gone to the grammar school,' said Morley, careful to return a compliment. This was obviously a time for exchanging confidences. Dare he a little later bring up the subject of you-know-what?

'Perhaps I wasn't good enough,' said Micky modestly, 'but then, I didn't really try. I was scared of trying hard, then failing. And then they were always on to me, nagging; getting Uncle Peter and Grandad and our teacher to have a word with me. Then saying Dad and Grandad went to grammar schools and if I failed, I'd be letting everybody down. I got fed up and mixed up and in the end I didn't even bother. But y'know, Morle, if we don't go to the Art School, we'll be left school for ever next year. Unless I go to that private school, Hamilton House, and I'm not all that struck.'

47

Morley shivered. The prospect of starting work next year was horrifying, but he hadn't really thought about it until now. A year! Where on earth had his boyhood gone? He wasn't ready for the future, yet here it was speeding towards him at a frightening pace and full of uncertainties. Timorously, he tried to face it. Back to Redhill Council School and Senior 3A with Micky probably gone, along with four or five other familiar faces who would have gone to technical schools; and then, *work*! Or Balsley School of Art for three years and afterwards – well, it was too far off to contemplate, but perhaps becoming some sort of artist. His earlier anxieties about Art School vanished – going there was now imperative.

His thoughts drifted back to the day of the examination, one of the last of his innocence. He felt a curious yearning for it, though it had not been free of humiliation.

Morley, Micky and three other Redhill Council School pupils had sat the one-day entrance examination for Balsley School of Art in March.

The morning was devoted to the academic half of the entrance examination – general knowledge, arithmetic and English. Morley was reasonably happy with his general knowledge but didn't quite finish his arithmetic paper. He was particularly pleased, though, with his quick-witted response to one of the English questions. It read, 'Describe your favourite picture and briefly state why you like it.' Halfway through a description of *Went the Day Well*, a picture he had seen at the Rex in Redhill, he paused, neatly crossed out what he had just written, curved his left arm protectively around his paper to guard his discovery from less intelligent eyes and wrote instead about *February Fill Dyke* by B. W. Leader, a painting he had seen in Birmingham Art Gallery.

Comparing notes on the English paper at dinner time, it emerged that Micky's response to the favourite picture question had been *Rio Rita* starring Bud Abbott and Lou Costello. Morley smugly described his own answer. But Micky shrugged and didn't appear to be impressed.

'B-But th-this is an art school, stands to reason, that's the sort of picture they're on about. P-Paintings not f-films –'

'Yeh, yeh, okay, okay, knowall, but everybody knows that pictures are just as likely to be moving pictures as paintings. Everybody knows that. Isn't that right, lads?'

Two of the others were only too happy to agree, as they had offered *Lassie Come Home* and *The Mask of Dimitrios*.

The drawing examination was conducted in the afternoon. The principal test was called Pictorial Composition. Morley chose 'The Waterside Picnic'. He drew an ancient bridge reflecting itself in a wide river. Reclining against a tree in the foreground, an American army sergeant with a drink in his hand gazed across a laden tablecloth towards a glamorous, big-busted young woman in a two-piece bathing costume posing against an upturned boat. Though far more decorously posed and attired than all the other women he had drawn recently, it still gave him a pleasant thrill to draw her, particularly in these silent, formal surroundings. It also made him feel bold, modern and a man of the world. Then it occurred to him that the school authorities might disapprove. He reduced the size of the woman's bust slightly.

Still pleased with his daring, though, he described the scantily clad woman to the other lads at the short break allowed for the lavatory, ready to counter Micky's expected crack of 'You dirty sod, Morle!' with a smart rejoinder.

But Micky chose to look dubious; he glanced at the others, who shook their heads doubtfully. He said that you couldn't be too careful in an exam. They all nodded seriously.

Morley felt uneasy. His eyes darted nervously from one to another. He swallowed hard. He noticed their amused looks and quickly closed his mouth over his rabbit teeth and brace. 'Ah, well, it'll be okay,' he mumbled without conviction. 'Ar-Artists do all s-sorts of pictures.'

But acting, it seemed, on some unseen cue, they all shrugged and the subject was abruptly changed to religion.

Douglas Bruton, an evacuee, and a candidate from Redhill, hadn't put down his religion on his application form. One of the supervisors had asked for the missing information, but Douglas, orphaned in the London Blitz, did not know. He had promised to have a serious think about it.

'Stick anything down,' suggested Micky. 'They won't bother to check, even if they could.'

'Yeah, I suppose you're right; so what'll I put? What are you?'

'Congregationalist,' said Micky. And, as if making a virtue of it, 'But don't ask me to spell it. Hang on a bit, though, old Morle's a Roman candle. Stick that down.'

They all laughed except Douglas. 'Roman candle? Don't get it. Ain't that a firework?'

'Yeh, old Morley's a firework all right! No, but he's a Catholic – Roman Catholic – Roman candle! Get it?'

'Right, I'll be that, then. Do you know how to spell it, Morle?'

Morley tried to inject some dignity into his answer. 'I g-generally put down R.C., everybody kn-knows that means Catholic.'

'Cathlic. Catlick, cat lick a dog's arse,' said Micky. It was something the scruffs might have said.

They all laughed again.

Back in the examination hall, feeling bruised by his mates' attitude towards his art and his religion, Morley dispirit-edly erased the young woman's breasts for the second time. Then he remembered something. This morning, blatantly displayed on the back wall of the hall, had been a painting (this afternoon, because of the drawing tests, all pictures had been removed to avoid the influence they might have on candidates) depicting three *naked* buxom women shame-lessly parading themselves in front of two men and some sheep. *The Judgement of Paris*, it had said underneath. He cursed himself for allowing himself to be so easily manipu-lated by Micky, then smiled. *Rio Rita* Micky's favourite pic-ture! Abbott and Costello! He shook with silent laughter as he rubbed out the woman's breasts for the third time and recklessly enlarged them to beyond even their original dimensions. He even lowered the top of her bathing cos-tume. He was an artist. Artists drew nudes. Artists would be marking his work: they would understand.

The second drawing paper, and the last test of the examination, examined the candidate's ability in commercial art. From the three choices, Morley played safe and chose a design for a showcard advertising cigarettes; only a month earlier, he had done a similar subject at school. The paper stated that candidates must create their own brand or company name and compose a slogan extolling the virtue(s) of the chosen product or service. Morley did an improved version of his design of a month ago: a close-up of a gloved hand, fingers clutching a cigarette, partly obscuring the lower part of a front view of a trilby-wearing man's head. Over the background and cutting through the hat, he lettered, 'Smoke GASPERS'. His earlier version of the poster had continued with 'your faithful friend'. But Mr Ross-Armitage, who took them for art, had said, 'Mm, nicely composed, visually splendid, old chap, though does sound a bit as if the fellah's smokin' his dog, what?'

So Morley now mentally tried: 'Smoke Gaspers, your boon companion.' It smacked a little less of dog, more your best mate. Then he remembered once hearing old man Kirkham, between bouts of violent coughing, with Frank thumping his back and suggesting that he cut down otherwise he'd soon be in his grave, saying that it was the only pleasure he'd got left. Ah! 'Smoke Gaspers for pleasure . . . for most pleasure . . . for the greatest pleasure.' Nearly. Then he had it. It wasn't true of course – there was something much better, and free – but it sounded right. Along the bottom of his design he lettered, 'for the ULTIMATE pleasure'.

Balsley School of Art, emptied of pupils, where the entrance examination was held, was an impressive ivy-clad building of brick and stone with AD 1896 above its pillared entrance. The supervisors, wearing academic gowns, were masters from the school; two senior pupils, resplendent in their gold-edged bottle-green blazers, assisted them. Each blazer bore the school crest: an outline of an artist's palette enclosing the interlaced letters BSA; peeping from behind the palette were three fanned-out brushes; beneath was the school motto: 'PLUS EST EN VOUS'.

51

Ivy-clad buildings, gowns – the first he had ever seen in real life – and blazers were powerful symbols for Morley. It all seemed not far removed from the public-school world of Greyfriars, Rugby, St Jim's, and St Cuthbert's. One day soon, he might become a part of it. He was both thrilled and scared. He thought of all the splendid fellows who inhabited those other ivy-clad piles: Harry Wharton, Tom Brown, Tom Merry, Nigel and Dick the boy detectives. Cricket- and rugby-loving chaps, supremely confident, thanking the head after six of the best, enduring the punishment with a stiff upper lip – never, of course, blubbing, preferring the beating to sneaking on the real culprit, even though he was a sworn enemy and an out and out rotter. He wondered whether his despised name might for once go down rather well.

But would he have to change the way he spoke? Call his mom, Mum? Pepper his speech with 'I say', 'Thanks awfully', 'Top hole', 'Jolly good show', 'Ripping', 'Wizard'? How would his mother, his relations, the neighbours and the people at church react? Should he work up to it very gradually? Or simply have two languages, discarding his refined school accent as soon as he reached home?

Then a glance at the other very ordinary candidates around him brought him swiftly down to earth. He felt relieved though vaguely disappointed.

A few minutes before the end of the last test, one of the pupil-assistants strolled over to Morley and tapped him on the shoulder. 'Mr Boldmere wants a word with you; that gentleman over there,' he whispered, pointing to a supervisor bent over some papers at a table at the front of the room. 'Not now,' he hissed, as Morley, anxious to display alacrity, leaped up and all but knocked his chair over. 'Afterwards, when you're told to dismiss.'

There were some curious glances; Morley caught a glimpse of Micky Plant's smirk and raised eyebrows. He busied himself with some unnecessary shading on his Smoke Gaspers design, feigning unconcern, but his hand was shaking. Could it be about his bathing-costumed young woman with her over-sized breasts?

Mr Boldmere allowed half a minute to elapse before looking up from his papers. 'Ah, there you are. Now then,' he said, riffling through some buff-coloured forms, 'here we are.' He extracted one which Morley recognized as his own application form. 'Tell me, do you know what *Christian* name means?'

Standing stiff as a poker, hands behind his back, vastly relieved since he now knew what this was about, Morley said, 'Yes, sir, it means the name th-they give you wh-when you're . . .' But the word had slipped from memory. 'Wh-When you're . . . b-born,' he finished awkwardly.

'Ah ha, well, near enough. Yes, an appropriate name chosen by your parents at baptism. A baptismal name, a given name, a Christian name. Very well, so we've established the meaning of Christian name. Now will you tell me the meaning of *surname*.'

Eager to compensate for his previous lame response, Morley swallowed, took a deep breath and deepened his voice. 'Sir, it means your fam-mily name, taken from your father and h-his father and h-his father, though in Iceland' – this from an item in *Monroe's Universal Reference Book* – 'you take your f-father's Christian name and, and add on son on the end, so if his n-name's er, er, John you're called J-Johnson. But, sir, I kn-know what –'

'Well, well, your scholarship is to be commended,' Mr Boldmere interrupted with a mildly startled smile. 'But perhaps it's your very knowledge of Icelandic practice that has led to some confusion. Do you have your identity card with you by any chance?'

Morley hadn't: people seldom bothered nowadays. 'N-No, sir, I, I, haven't, but, sir, I c-can explain. I . . .'

Mr Boldmere ignored him. 'Now, if you will just take a look here' – gliding his finger to the top of the form. 'It asks for the applicant's surname, which, for the sake of argument, we'll assume means the non-Icelandic, English variety. But here we have Charles, followed by, on the next line, where the candidate is required to furnish his Christian name or names, Morley John. Now, is this correct? Or did you, as I suspect, in your excitement at the prospect of coming to art school, transpose two of the names?'

'Sir, I w-was trying to s-say, sir, people are always getting it mixed up. But th-that is, is right, sir, Morley Charles.'

'Unusual name,' said Mr Boldmere, though his manner suggested, at least for the likes of you. 'Any, er, special significance?'

'It's just a sort, a sort of, well, family n-name.' He had never understood why his mother had given him her own maiden name. But in case Mr Boldmere enquired further he added swiftly, 'It's like Russ, sir, R-Russell, very popular in Am-America, and, th-there's er, ah, Clark, Clark G-Gable, sir. Th-They s-s-sound like s-surnames but really –'

'Ah, Clark Gable,' said Mr Boldmere reflectively, seeming anxious not to display too much familiarity with the Hollywood cinema. 'Er, just refresh my memory.'

'F-Film star, sir, he's a f-famous f-film star, sir, he starred in, er . . .' He could only recall the name of one Clark Gable film. 'Er, *Honky Tonk*, sir.'

'Did he, indeed? Well, so you and he have something in common, you having perhaps what might be described as a, er, film star's name?'

'Sir,' said Morley uncomfortably.

'Well, make sure it's not wasted. Perhaps one day, if you work hard at it, we'll see your name up there in lights.' And Mr Boldmere raised his arm in an elegant gesture, sweeping it around as if indicating lofty buildings ablaze with neon.

Undecided whether to go along with the joke and pretend to be amused, or summon up the courage to look disdainful, Morley did neither. 'Yes, sir,' he mumbled, feeling very foolish.

'Are you deaf, Morley?' came Micky's voice from the coal house. 'That's the second time I've yelled at you. Are you still listening out? I thought I heard something.'

'Y-Yeh, you're okay, Micky, I think it was s-somebody n-next door. Somebody b-bouncing a ball.' He felt himself catching something of Micky's anxiety, which made him increasingly uneasy at the prospect of meeting Micky's father and lying to him, telling him that he had just this minute arrived over the back fence. He also felt the need for solitude so that he could re-examine what had now become his chief problem: the overwhelming need to go to Balsley School of Art.

'M-Micky, it might be best if I, I go now, before your d-dad comes.' But in case Micky thought him disloyal, he added, 'You see he, he mightn't believe I've only just got here. S-Sounds too much like a coincidence. And he might just guess I let you out. M-Might make it worse for you.'

'Mm,' said Micky reflectively. 'Yeh, if he sees you here, well, he'll wait till you've gone, then he'll say on your honour and all that, and was I locked up all the time, and yeh, he'll guess all right. Better hop it quick over the back. See you tomorrow in school. Morle, you won't say anything, will you, to anybody else? You're a good kid, Morley.'

'Naw, course not,' Morley promised, knowing that he almost certainly would, although discreetly, cautioning each listener never to breathe a word. He knew that if their roles had been reversed, Micky would wait until he had a large audience with Morley present and exploit the tale to the full, deriving great pleasure from Morley's discomfiture. Morley sighed inwardly. Life wasn't fair.

# Chapter 6

Morley dawdled to the Pinders' wondering whether the Art School examination papers had been marked. If they had, then his future was already decided. He felt his stomach lurch. Even if they hadn't, there was still nothing he could do about it.

Or was there? 'If you shall ask me anything in My name, that I will do.' It was so simple and appealing when delivered by Canon Reilly, Father Smythe, Sister Twomey and, to a lesser extent because from her it sounded forced, his mother. Sister Twomey always greatly emphasized the 'anything' and Morley now did the same. 'If you should ask me *anything* . . .'

Curing the sick, blind, deaf and lame, raising people from the dead, or restoring a severed ear seemed much more in Jesus's line, though, than ensuring that a thirteen-year-old boy passed the examination to Balsley School of Art. But the promise was clear enough: *anything*.

He remembered that he had invoked the same promise for a Meccano set for Christmas when he was nine but had got only a very inferior chemistry set whose contents fell very short of all the elaborate apparatus promised in the illustration on the front of the box. 'Cambridge Chemistry Set No. 1', he recalled with disgust.

Perhaps he hadn't prayed deeply or long enough. 'You

must storm heaven,' Sister Twomey told the little girl in Saturday instruction class whose guinea pig was close to death. The girl did so, but her pet still died. So Sister then explained to the class that the guinea pig's death must have been *meant*, that it was a painful but necessary part of Almighty God's divine plan. So asking for something in prayer wasn't exactly foolproof.

Anyway, he suddenly realized, he was in no condition to pray and ask for anything at the moment since he wasn't in a State of Grace. To achieve this, he must first confess and be forgiven his Mortal Sin. If he had been in a State of Grace, he could ask God for the proper word for his sin. And although God wouldn't tell him directly, he could expect that somehow, in some mysterious way, he would be led to the answer. Though, of course, when you *were* in a State of Grace, you wouldn't have any Mortal Sins staining your soul to worry about. He would have to find his own means of discovering the mysterious word.

Rude words, he reflected when he was once again in Woods Park Road, sometimes began with the same letters as their respectable counterparts. Well, arse did with anus; bum and bottom; and wasn't teat the polite name for tit? Then there was prick with peenus or something; and spunk with . . . with . . . what was it? Certainly something that began with s. Thinking of esses, what was the proper word for shit – apart from dung or droppings? If it had to be referred to politely, it was doing your business or biz. Though even these descriptions would be considered vulgar at school, where 'Please may I leave the room?' was the only accept- able term for going to do anything in the lavatory.

Once, in bottom juniors, a fearful smell was generated; not the more usual transient variety, this one gathered strength and hung around. The excited class was throwing meaning looks towards a mesmerized Philip Paramore, while his outraged desk partner, Norma Partridge, sought refuge in the aisle.

Miss Trembelow, flushed and worried, was finally forced to exclaim, 'Er, I think somebody has left the room in, his, er, her, er, their trousers; will, er, whoever it is, please go outside at once?'

Could he describe what he did in a similar polite school-teacher kind of language? 'Father, I did something rude in my trousers.' No, it was too vague, the priest might get the wrong idea and explain that it wasn't a sin – unless you had done it deliberately to offend or harm another. And it would be still left to a very embarrassed Morley to explain that he meant something else.

Some dictionaries actually had rude words in them, he remembered. Mr Ross-Armitage's did. It was in two big volumes kept on a shelf at the front of his art room. Perky Beswick had ushered Morley and a couple of others into the deserted room one dinner time, taken down volume I, expertly found the place and, straightfaced, pointed to: 'fart, *Taboo, n.* 1. an emission of gas from the anus.' Morley was amazed. That same evening he had eagerly consulted the slim dictionary section of *Monroe's Universal Reference Book* but found it disappointingly less broad-minded. It was doubtful whether there were even ruder words in the art teacher's dictionary – Perky Beswick would have found them already and pointed them out. Still, nothing would be lost from having a look. And even if toss off, rack off or wank were too rude to be included, he could still go through all the t's, r's and w's and possibly discover the respectable word – if it did, indeed, begin with the same letter.

God, what a complicated sin! He recalled the first time it had happened – and the only time it had been free from any connection with sex. Just a sensation which he had supposed, at the time, was peculiar to himself alone. It had been at the end of the Christmas term.

Mr Grant, full of boozy good cheer from, no doubt, a festive lunch-time session at the pub, said with almost criminal recklessness, 'Now lads, I must just pop out for a minute or two. So while I'm gone, here's a Christmas treat for you: do anything you like! No, no, wait. Choose any apparatus you like, but no more than eight . . . No! No more than, let me shee . . .' He swayed and counted his fingers. 'No more than four, four lads to each activ-it-y at any . . . for five minutes. Then all change! You understand? Five minutesh, then all change. And there's to be no nonsense . . . till I get back!' With that, anxiously patting his pockets, presumably to check that he was equipped with cigarettes and lighter, Mr Grant left the gym.

Most boys had changed but some – terrible sin – had not even taken their boots off. The air was thick with soccer and tennis balls flung or kicked from one to another or deliberately hurled at wall bars, light fittings and unsuspecting boys. An improperly secured beam – another terrible sin – bearing three boys crashed to the ground. A pile of shrieking lads lay in a tangled heap after sliding down a dangerously angled form hooked up to the wall bars. Four boys dangled from a climbing rope, three trying to debag the one above. Two rope-clutching braves launched themselves from the top of the ladder and, with piercing Tarzan cries, cut a swathe through the chaos below before almost swinging to the ceiling. The din was appalling.

Morley ran round the gym for a few minutes bouncing a football, dodging the missiles which now included pumps, shoes, boots, shorts and even pants. Then he saw a free rope next to the wall bars and grabbed it. He set himself the target of climbing to the top four times without pause – a normal PT lesson only allowed for two ascents. He added urgency to his endeavour by pretending to be a secret agent escaping from the prison yard at Gestapo headquarters: if he failed to reach the top of the wall – equalling the four rope lengths – he would be shot. On his third ascent, a few inches short of the top, an unfamiliar but exquisite sensation overwhelmed him. It started somewhere around his pelvis and spread through his whole body – making even his toes tingle. His escape from the Gestapo forgotten, but still prudently clinging tight to the rope, he closed his eyes, oblivious to everything except this novel, thrilling experience.

As the last spasm passed, he became aware that the terrible noise had stopped. He opened his eyes and had a bird's eye view of the class standing to attention and staring up at him. The returned Mr Grant was standing almost beneath him, sluggishly trying to follow the class's gaze.

When he finally got Morley into view, he said, 'Do I see an angel of the heaven . . . heaven-ly host above me?' There were a few polite titters. 'Or ish it the fairy atop, atop the Chrismash tree?' The titters grew louder.

Morley, in a curious state of torpor, stared down at him.

'What's the matter, lad, are you shtuck or something?' The class laughed heartily so Mr Grant said it again and added, 'Why not come down and join us, lad, if you can manage to get yourself . . . unshtuck.'

Mr Grant wasn't far off the mark. Later, in the changing room, Morley discovered a mysterious sticky wet patch on his pants and a lesser one on his PT shorts. Two or three weeks later, lying in bed, a hot-water bottle between his legs, and idly thinking of Sheila Godden doing her uninhibited cartwheels behind the gym, he discovered he didn't need to climb a rope to induce this remarkable feeling. And after that . . .

A familiar pattern of white paint on the pavement – spilled when a neighbour had been painting the top of his gatepost – prompted Morley to look up. He had gone five houses past the Pinders'. He turned back.

# Chapter 7

In the living room, which Big Gwen Pinder called the lounge, all was pandemonium. The Pinder boys – Brian, fourteen, Maurice, sixteen, and seventeen-year-old Graham – were leaping over and around the furniture, effortlessly dodging the swipes that Beryl, their sister, was aiming at them with a rolled up magazine.

They were laughing and mocking her. 'Aw, gee, Russ, honey, Ah get so lonesome when you're away. Aw gosh, you're so cute, Russy baby. If you leave me, Ah'll just die, Ah'll just die.'

Percy, Big Gwen's husband, was perched on a chair which stood on the table, painting the pelmet.

Beryl appealed to her father. 'Oh, Da-a-ad, please *do* something, they're being so *awful*.'

But her father chose to ally himself with his sons. He laughed his deep, throaty laugh, then said, in a high-pitched voice, 'Hey, big boy, come down over here and give your cute lil' ol' baby a cute lil' ol' kiss.'

Graham and Beryl were confronting each other across an armchair. Beryl stepped one way, then the other, while her brother feinted provocatively but easily kept out of reach. Beryl suddenly lashed out. Graham ducked, opened the door behind him and slid through, slamming it as he went. 'Ah'll just die, honey, Ah'll just die,' came his voice from the hall.

61

Beryl wrenched open the door and ran after him. The front door banged and then Beryl's shrieks could be heard from the road. Maurice and Brian rushed out to join in the fun.

Morley sat in the alcove to the right of the fireplace with a mug of tea and a couple of home-made scones. Both tea and scones tasted just a bit unusual. The chances were that the baking tray used for the scones had recently done service for something else, and perhaps the dried milk in the tea had been tainted by whatever had previously been in the tin. Or the mug might have once held white spirit, or Grandad Pinder's Steradent and false teeth. And no doubt next Sunday's joint would also taste unusual if the paint-filled roasting tin that Percy was now dipping his brush into was restored to its proper function.

When any of the Pinders needed something, they chose the most immediate route to getting it. They scrounged it, charmed it out of a neighbour, converted it from something else or used the next best thing.

'Would you like another scone, junior?' Big Gwen asked from the kitchen doorway. 'Junior' had lately become Big Gwen's tag for Morley. He quite liked it.

'Er, no thanks,' said Morley. 'They're v-very nice but I couldn't manage another, and I haven't finished this one yet.' He was hungry enough but Big Gwen's scones might even be poisonous and he was in no fit state to die at present.

'Get it down you!' boomed Percy's voice from his perch near the pelmet. 'You could do with a bit of building up. Couldn't he, cock?' he said to his wife. 'A puff of wind and he'd take off.'

'Well, he's a bit on the lean side,' said Big Gwen a little more kindly. 'But you can't force him if he isn't hungry. Why don't you take a few home with you, junior, and give some to your mom? Russ loves them, always takes half a dozen with him when he goes. He shares them with his buddies back at the base, doesn't he, Percy?'

'Sure does, honey. I guess his buddies just love your home cooking.' Then, standing back on the table to admire his handiwork and reverting to his native Brummie, 'Now how about that, cock? What d'you think of that, our kid?'

The pelmet was in pale ochre – a colour similar to one of the colours camouflaging the Motor Works where Percy worked.

'Very nice,' said Morley, though he had noticed two or three small errant streaks on the wall where the pelmet joined it.

'Mm, very nice,' echoed Big Gwen, without looking. She inclined her head slightly. 'I think I can hear Russ getting up. I hope he feels better.' She turned to Morley. 'His foot still keeps on playing him up. He was in quite a lot of pain when he came this morning, so I gave him two aspirins and sent him upstairs to rest.' She added in a widely mouthed whisper, 'He said the pain's in the ends of his toes that aren't there. You can't credit it, can you?'

Russell had lost two of his toes from a shell splinter in the Ardennes Campaign last year and now worked at the US Post Office in Sutton Coldfield.

'It's a well-known fact,' said all-knowing Percy, looking around the room as if for something else to paint. He got down from his table and looked at each of them in turn. 'When we was in France in the last lot, there was blokes lost their whole legs and arms and, you wouldn't chuckle, they got chilblains on their fingers and toes. Chilblains! On their fingers and toes that was blown off! Years after!' He gesticulated with his brush and several tiny drops of paint descended on the carpet.

'Shh, he'll hear you,' said Big Gwen.

Russell, his hair tousled, came into the room, walking rather awkwardly. 'All okay now,' he replied, in answer to Big Gwen's enquiring look. 'I reckon I'm fit enough to beat this fellow,' he said, nodding at Percy, 'any time he likes: a hundred yards, a mile, five miles. You name it, Mr Pinder, I'm ready.'

'I was just saying to the wife – wasn't I, cock?' Percy began, 'that in the last war, I knew blokes that had their –'

Big Gwen gave him a shove. 'Russ doesn't want to hear about the last war, he's had enough of this one. How about

63

a nice cup of tea – or coffee, Russell, and a couple of my scones?'

'Well, coffee would be just fine, but use the stuff I brought. Don't waste your precious ration on me. And I can't really use a scone right now: I ate plenty before I came.'

He made himself comfortable in an armchair. 'And how are you, Morley? You okay?'

'Yes, fine thanks,' said Morley. 'Oh, and, er, thank y-you very much for the jacket, Russ, it's smashing.'

'Yeah, suits you fine – and fits,' said Russ, eyeing him approvingly.

'Oh, er, and Mom said to do another p-picture for you, a watercolour scene, as soon as I can get hold of some decent paper.'

'No, hold on, I saw the jacket as a kinda payment for that portrait you did, so the score's even. And the jacket didn't cost me, I got it from a buddy that owed me a small favour. But I was gonna get round to asking you to do a painting for me, anyhow, for a regular fee.'

Two weeks before, Morley had done a head and shoulders of Russ in uniform against a stars and stripes background. He had gone to great trouble to get the insignia and the curious upside-down stripes just right.

'Well, p-perhaps I'll just do you another one first,' said Morley, adding not quite truthfully, 'Mom said it's only fair, an expensive jacket like this, not to mention the coupons. And she said that one day soon when she g-goes to the p-pictures and sees an Am-merican picture, she'll think that's where our M' – he found it difficult to refer to himself as Morley – 'where his pictures are – halfway round the world.' This was a pleasant reflection of his own but somehow it seemed that his own ideas carried more weight if he ascribed them to his mother – or someone else.

'Yeah, that's quite a thought, Morley. And if you're real sure about another picture first, well, I'm certainly not going to fight you about it. I just love all your country scenes. But what I really want from you some time is a picture with some of those quaint old buildings; that seems to be what

64

the real England is all about. Is there maybe some place, real close by, where there's buildings with those crooked roofs? Somewhere I could visit easy; then tell them back home that I've stood right on that very spot and it's near where the young artist and my girl live.'

Morley nodded. He had already planned a subject for Russ's picture: the crumbling, disused barn which lay between the Motor Works and the Bluebell Woods. (The scruffs called it the Spunkbag Woods since, apart from blue-bells in the spring, it was also carpeted, all year round, with discarded Durexes.) It was a good subject if you ignored the dumped rusting prams and bedsteads, rotting mattresses and other refuse which littered the place, and adopted a viewpoint which cut out the edge of the unfinished hous-ing estate and the camouflaged roofs of the Motor Works. But it was hardly a place to take Russ.

Big Gwen came in with Russ's coffee, more tea for Morley and a plate of scones. 'I'll put what's left over in a bag for you to take back with you,' she said to Russ. Then, hearing Grandad Pinder murmuring upstairs, added, 'What's he on about now? Silly old twerp, I'd better go and see to him, he sometimes loses his way to the lav.' She noticed some flour on her hands and dusted them on the front of her pinafore. It was almost a caressing gesture and Morley found himself aroused, though he had the idea that the process might have begun earlier, perhaps when he had thought of the Spunkbag Woods. He casually lowered his mug of tea to his lap to mask his condition and tried to concentrate on something neutral.

The entry gate burst open. 'Here she is, our wench!' said Percy from the kitchen where he was painting a cabinet in dark olive – another colour similar to that used on the Motor Works. 'We thought you'd got lost. Old Russ just sent out a search party. Where've you been? For a run round the Ickleys?'

'Oh, I've just been walking round the block a few times,' sighed Beryl. 'I guess I just needed to be alone for a while. Hi, honey,' she said to Russ, bending down and kissing him on the mouth.

'So what have you done with your brothers, then, are they wandering around the block as well?' asked Percy coming into the lounge holding his brush aloft. A tiny droplet fell on Russ's shoulder but Morley noticed that Percy's dark olive was almost the same colour as Russ's olive drab tunic.

Beryl said distantly, 'Oh, they went off to see somebody's motorbike or something. I dunno. I couldn't care less.' Then to Russ, she said, 'And how's my little soldier baby been while I was gone?'

Morley wasn't sure what to do: he would be in the way if he stayed in the lounge and Percy would be likely to overwhelm him if he went into the kitchen.

But Russ didn't seem to mind Morley's company. He said, ignoring Beryl's frown, 'This young artist has just promised to do me a special picture. Some day soon we'll all go to some real quaint old place and watch him at work. Okay, that's the deal, Morley?'

Morley nodded eagerly, deciding that he would have to find a place he could show to Russ with pride. Somewhere approaching the Real England, that idyllic land which featured in most of his books and which he imagined to exist somewhere well beyond the urban sprawl where he lived. Perhaps Russ would get hold of a car.

'How about that, baby?' Russ said to Beryl. 'A picture I can send home and say to the family, this scene is close by where this English babe lives?'

The remainder of the afternoon passed very pleasantly. Russell, lying back in his chair with Beryl on the floor beside him, her arms and head in his lap, talked about his life before the war. Morley sat on a small stool made by Percy at what he considered a proper distance from the couple and listened.

Russ was a good storyteller and Morley was transported to the house in the little town near Milwaukee; Russell's high school and college; his fishing and shooting expeditions during vacations; and the woods where Russ's grandfather had an encounter with a bear. Morley asked questions, intelligent ones, he hoped, since most people seemed only to ask the

Yanks about obvious things such as film stars and cowboys and Indians. He also knew better than to ask about the war.

Russ took Morley's questions seriously and gave him thoughtful answers. Morley began to relax. He even fancied that he had grown in stature and that his upper teeth were a little less rabbit-like. His anxieties about Mortal Sin, starting a new term at school tomorrow and passing for the Art School receded a little.

At about twenty to six, the Pinder boys came back and disappeared into the front room. A few minutes later they came out, grabbed some scones from the kitchen and sprawled on the settee.

Big Gwen came in from upstairs carrying a bundle of sheets which looked, at first glance, as though they had been smudged with Percy's camouflage paint. 'I don't know who's been giving him chocolate. He doesn't really appreciate it, just gobbles it up like he does everything else. He doesn't understand it's rationed and precious.' She laughed as if to make light of it. Morley guessed it must have been Russ. 'You'd think chocolate would block up his system, wouldn't you, and save us a lot of trouble, but it seems to have the opposite effect.'

'*Mo-o-om!*' cried Beryl.

'I guess I'm guilty,' said Russ. 'I thought I'd give old Mr Pinder a treat. I didn't know it might, er, complicate things.'

'Oh, that's all right, Russell, how could you know? But you see, in his state, he can't –'

'*Mo-o-o-om!*' wailed Beryl. 'We don't wanna kno-o-ow! Quick, get that stuff outta here.'

'Keep your hair on, duck, what d'you think I'm doing? That's why I brought them down. I can't put them in the bath because his yesterday's stuff's in there bleaching. The sheets he gets through, I can't –'

'*Mo-o-o-om!*' yelled Beryl. The boys grinned. Big Gwen took the sheets outside.

'I think I'll get the worst off with the hosepipe, Perce. Will you fix it on the tap?' came her voice from the garden.

'No, cock, leave it,' shouted Percy. 'Come in here for a few minutes and take all that weight off your feet. I'll give you a hand later. The news is on in a minute.'

Morley was vastly relieved to hear her washing her hands in the kitchen.

'What's all this fuss about the news, then?' she said, coming in and taking off her pinafore.

'Just sit down and listen,' commanded Percy. 'There's a lot going on. For all we know, the war might be over and you wouldn't want to miss that, would you? What do you think, sergeant, can't be long now, can it?' But without giving Russell a chance to reply, he carried on. 'Hey, you lot, do you know what? Do you know what last Friday was? Three guesses.'

'Day after last Thursday,' said Graham.

'Pay day,' said Brian.

'Da-a-a-ad!' whined Beryl.

'No, all wrong!' Percy smirked. 'It was old Adolf's birthday! And, dear me, you wouldn't chuckle, I clean forgot to send him a card! I bet they'll say on the wireless in a minute, "The Führer was furious the other day, he said to Goebbels, 'Mine God, dat swinehund, dat Percy Pinder don't send me no birthday card.'"'

'Why, has he suddenly turned into an Italian?' asked Maurice.

Percy ignored him, then slapped Morley on the back and said cryptically, 'You never know what you'll hear on the news do you, our kid?' Then, turning to Graham, who was fiddling with the volume knob, 'What's happening to that wireless, Gray? You sure you got it on?'

Graham looked at the back. 'Yeh, course, Dad, it's just warming up: the valves are all lit. Any minute now.'

Maurice got up from the settee, went out to the front room, returned and beckoned to his father. Percy followed him out, closing the door behind them.

'What's going on?' said Beryl. 'First he tells us to shut up and listen, then he starts talking. Then, when the news is starting, he goes away! He's cracked, our dad,' she went on, swivelling her finger on her temple. 'Everybody says so.'

Morley knew his mother certainly did; she said that was where Morley got some of his daft ideas from.

Beryl screwed up her face. '*I* know what's –'

'Shushsh,' the others said in unison.

'I think you're *all* daft,' said Beryl, tossing her head, 'except my handsome soldier.' She pouted her lips and stroked Russell's cheek. But even Russell was signalling quiet, putting a finger on her lips.

There was a crackle from the wireless and the announcer said, 'Before the news bulletin, here is an SOS message. Will anyone who knows the whereabouts of Morley Charles please telephone Scotland Yard, telephone number, Whitehall 1212.' Percy came back into the room humming tunelessly and sat down. 'It is believed that Charles has lost his memory and is probably wandering aimlessly around. He was last seen in the Birmingham area.'

Morley Charles! Morley stiffened and felt a hot flush creeping up his neck. Had he heard right? Had he really been listening? Anyway, it couldn't be him. Someone else with the same name? Or perhaps the announcer had said a name that was just similar to Morley Charles. He risked a cautious look around him. Big Gwen was smiling, Beryl and Russ were in a clinch and Percy was humming at the ceiling. Brian and Graham were expressionless. So no one else had noticed the similarity in names. He must have been mistaken.

But there it was again. 'Morley Charles . . .' Morley felt paralysed, was barely breathing. Now he should be up and laughing, exclaiming on the coincidence. But the moment was gone. '. . . thirteen, with medium brown hair, blue eyes . . .' How could this be? It *was* him! How? Why? 'He is easily recognized because . . .' There was a pause and an odd, strangled sound. 'Because he has a wooden leg, a glass eye and is completely bald, and, and, when he talks, he has –' There was a splutter, a crackle, then a low continuous hum. Then all around, the explosion of suppressed laughter.

He remained rigid, not knowing what to do or say.

Maurice came back into the room. Percy slapped Morley on the back again and said, 'Orright?'

Big Gwen smiled. 'You should have seen your face, junior, it was a picture.'

'Did you guess?' asked Brian.

'You gave the game away, our Beryl,' said Graham sourly.

So it was a trick! The feeling was depressingly familiar: the butt, the clown, the victim, the stooge. That's what he was; that's how others saw him. Images of other humiliating experiences flashed by: his new scout hat, the swimming trunks at Upfield baths, Uncle Walter trying to teach him to wink, the milkman to yodel, Perky to whistle through his fingers, his first attempt to smoke. All seemed to be accompanied by peals of derisive laughter.

'It was only our Maurice,' said Big Gwen. 'They are a silly lot, aren't they? Percy's got one of those . . . What are they, Russ? Yes, mikes. He's got this mike joined up to the wireless set. He was in the front, in the dining room talking into it.'

It was too late for Morley to say that he knew all the time: he knew that his face had shown he had fallen for it. But he still had time to grin and enter the spirit of things and say in a sportsmanlike way that they really had him that time. He couldn't, though, even manage a strained smile and anyway felt disinclined to try. It was what the announcer Maurice said at the end of the SOS, when he referred to the way he talked. That was mean, below the belt. He wanted to cry but didn't dare.

Everyone's attention, however, was on Beryl and Graham.

'You spoiled it, our Beryl,' accused Graham. 'Didn't she, Bri?'

'I did not!' said Beryl, fiercely. 'You all shut me up. All I said was –'

'You said, "You're not doing that wireless trick again." Didn't she, Bri?'

'So what? The wireless trick!' she said scathingly. 'It's corny. Anyway, I didn't get time to finish with all of you on to me.'

'Yeh, but what you *did* say was plenty to let on what we was up to!'

'*Were* up to,' said Maurice.

'And any fool'd know what was going on!' Graham continued.

At this, Morley shrank even further inside himself. He was incapable now of retrieving any dignity from the situation.

Big Gwen must have noticed. She came over and put a sympathetic arm round his shoulders. 'It was only in fun, duck; only a joke, they didn't mean any harm.'

Her contact produced no arousal, just the security that his mother found it hard to give him. But he would rather not have needed comfort. He didn't want to be that kind of person. He longed to be confident, ready for anything, unconcerned about what others thought or said. Like Alan Ladd. And instead, here he was, showing himself up, more like Stan Laurel.

Protected by the noise of the argument in which nearly everyone was involved, he confided to Big Gwen, 'I j-just thought tha-that Maurice was m-making fun of m-my stammer. I didn't m-mind the w-wooden leg and that, it w-was very funny. B-But he s-said about the way I talk, or was g-going to say.'

Big Gwen shook her head and laughed soothingly. 'No, no, no, duck. Nothing to do with that; anyway, I thought you were pretty well cured now. No-o-o! No, what our Maurice was *going* to say was, "Morley Charles can only talk German 'cause he's lost his memory, er, for English." He was thinking about last Christmas, see. Remember? When Percy gave you all that sherry and you took off Hitler? We didn't half laugh. But he couldn't get it out, see, for laughing, about your Hitler, remembering about it. It wasn't anything to do with, er, your, er, stammer; like I said before, you hardly do it nowadays, do you?'

Morley still felt troubled: how did Big Gwen know what Maurice had been thinking? But then she added, 'They did it on me! With me, they said I'd done a bunk and the police were after me 'cause I hadn't paid the rent!' She laughed heartily. 'But it was easy to guess after a bit because it was Percy who was doing it and he can't put on his voice like our Maurice. Beryl wasn't there that night so we kept quiet and did it on her the day after. Our Maurice overdid it a bit, said she was a Jerry spy. But it had her going for a time all right. With Russ, they didn't make it funny enough and he believed it, poor devil. Our Maurice said that all the men in his regiment had to report back to US Army something or other – where was it? Belgium, back to the fighting. He was going to say it was only for men over eighty-five but the wire came out the wireless or something. Anyroad, Russ took it in good part.'

So he wasn't the only victim. This put everything in a new light. But a light no brighter than before. Now he felt ashamed of his over-sensitive reaction, the response of a weakling, a sissy – a girl. Lost in his misery, he had completely forgotten the huge success of his Hitler impersonation. He wanted to explain, somehow put things right, laugh loudly in a sportsmanlike manner, but Big Gwen's attention turned to Beryl.

'One more wisecrack out of you, Graham, and you're for it!' said Beryl, armed with a small Welsh-costumed doll she had grabbed from the mantelpiece.

'Yeh, I'm terrified,' jeered Graham from the settee.

'Don't you worry, I'll get you all right and no mistake!' Beryl narrowed her eyes and tried to look menacing.

'Not with that you won't!' said Big Gwen. 'That doll's precious. I've had that over twenty years.'

'Don't worry, our mom,' said Graham. 'She wouldn't dare.'

Beryl suddenly smiled but her intention still seemed clear. 'You asked for it, you barmpots,' she said, holding the doll above her head.

Russ closed his eyes. Percy, from the back kitchen doorway, boomed, 'Pax, pax, pax, children. You know what that means, Russ?'

Maurice said, 'You've forgotten your Yankee accent, sis.'

Brian was pretending to take refuge behind the settee although there was only a three-inch gap.

'You'll all get it in a minute,' said Beryl, now taking purposeful aim and advancing towards her tormentors. As she did so, her hip caught one of the projecting shelves of the plywood fireplace. She yelled in pain and dropped the doll.

The fireplace, a creation of Percy's which covered the municipal iron range, shuddered and a lone securing screw, complete with Rawlplug, came out of the wall. The five-foot-high structure fell forward, flinging on to the carpet and coffee table, with a series of great crashes, the best Coronation mugs and tankards, ashtrays, vases, dried flowers, a framed photograph of Russell, dolls in national costume, a Dutch clog and many other treasures.

There was a brief glimpse of the cobwebbed Triplex range behind, its grate filled with a dusty assortment of papers, cigarette ends and soot, before Graham and Russell leaped to catch the fireplace in mid-flight. They steadied it and leaned it at a safe angle against the chimney breast. Russell winced with pain as he went back to his chair.

Brian and Maurice had also jumped up to lend a hand but, in the process, dislodged the settee from the bricks which supported its rear – Percy had no doubt purloined the castors for something else. It crashed down backwards and sideways, its arm knocking over a standard lamp, which took with it the wireless set from a small occasional table.

'You stu-u-upid bugger!' yelled Percy at Beryl, all his customary geniality gone.

Grandad Pinder came through the hall door wearing what may have been one of Big Gwen's nightdresses, stained here and there with what looked like yellow ochre.

'Mo-o-o-om!' wailed Beryl between sobs. 'Get – him – out – of – here!'

Grandad wandered through the wreckage on the carpet, his bare, ochre-flecked feet miraculously avoiding fragments of glass and china, having a conversation with an imaginary companion, and disappeared into the garden.

Morley felt superfluous. He wondered if he should offer

to take something home to repair, but didn't want to draw attention to himself. He felt drained. It was time he went. He wanted to just slink out without saying anything in case he stammered, but that wouldn't be very polite. He stood up and murmured, 'Thanks for having m-m-me. I better go now.' He had an impression of nods and vague smiles as he swiftly made his exit through the back door.

He walked home, mentally kicking himself and gritting his teeth. God, he had nearly cried, and in front of Russ who probably *had* behaved like Alan Ladd after they'd played the same trick on him. Looking back, it was obvious that the Pinders had been up to something. He would have to explain later, say he had felt under the weather, had earache, but what a neat trick, he hadn't half laughed about it later – when his earache had gone. But then, perhaps, apart from Big Gwen, nobody had really noticed his unmanly reaction in all the chaos that followed. He wondered if Big Gwen would mention it to his mother. No. Gwen was okay, she wouldn't burden his mother in her state with anything like that.

Somewhat consoled, he reached his house. Reggies Nolan and Kelp were at their usual post by the now righted pig bin but looking away from him. Morley silently opened his garden gate and tiptoed along the path to the back door.

# Chapter 8

Morley's mother was in the back kitchen opening a tin of Spam. She had that sour, tight-lipped expression which meant that Something Was Up.

'Hello, Mom,' Morley said with forced brightness, trying to sound her out.

'I'll hello you, you little swine. You don't half show me up you do,' she said in a vicious whisper without looking at him.

'What have I d-done now, then?' Morley asked, raising his voice with a brave show of innocence but thinking guiltily of missed confessions, missed communions, stiffened areas on sheets and socks, rude drawings and a flux of other shameful possibilities yet to take proper shape.

'Quiet, *he's* in there,' hissed his mother, meaning Frank the lodger, jerking her head towards the living room and pulling the door fully shut.

'But, Mom, I haven't d-done anything,' protested Morley, hoping, at least nothing you are likely to know about. But she had obviously found out something. And it must have been since she had last seen him at dinner time.

'You know, my lad, only too well,' she said witheringly.

His guilt deepened but he said carefully, 'I've been down the P-Pinders all afternoon – I've only just got b-back. Go and ask them if you don't believe me.'

'And before that?' She looked him straight in the eye. It *was* something to do with church.

He took his time. He desperately wanted to know, yet he wanted to delay the moment of accusation. Co-operatively, he said, 'Well, after dinner, I saw Frank coming up the road with Mr Kirkham and that Harold. I stopped and had a talk with him.' Then, with the pathetic idea of directing his mother's interest elsewhere, he added, 'Gosh, he wasn't half d-drunk. He was doing this s-stupid Hitler act, y-you should have seen –'

'I don't want to *hear* about him,' snapped his mother. 'What did you do then – after that?' So it wasn't Frank mentioning Canon Reilly's mythical visit, then.

He felt on slightly safer ground now. He squinted at the ceiling as if finding difficulty in remembering the rest of the afternoon's events, so innocent and inconsequential as to be already half forgotten. 'Oh yeh,' he said, sounding quite surprised at the recollection, 'I know, I saw old Eric Beswick coming off the tram. He'd been up his uncle's.'

Ah, but that was it: somebody had heard their rude conversation from behind a hedge or through an open window. Their talk about the ATS tart; legs wide open, no knicks, seeing her hairs, his excited interest, his pursuit of the subject, Kelp tossing off. He knew he was blushing. What else had he said? More about tossing off. It didn't seem fair. Whatever it had sounded like to the unseen listener, he was only trying to find out what you called it – for confession. Perhaps the mysterious listener was a Catholic who knew his mother and felt obliged to tell her. 'Disgusting, Mrs Charles, what he was saying. No, I couldn't repeat it. It was too filthy. But the really upsetting thing is, a nice boy like him! Who'd have thought it?'

Though very unsure of himself, Morley pressed on. 'Up Brierley Hill his uncle lives. Oh yeh, they caught some tench.' And with another pitiful attempt at diversion, 'That's f-funny, I didn't think that there was a r-river up Brierley Hill, did you, Mom? By the way, Dad used to go fishing didn't he, with Walter? I r-remember . . .' At the same time he was thinking of what sort of innocent explanation he could possibly offer against the evidence of a respectable Catholic witness. 'Did D-Dad have his own rods then? Are they s-still here, Mom?' he finished feebly.

'Never you mind about all that,' said his mother with a deep sigh. '*I* know and *you* know what I'm on about. What did you do after that?'

Relieved that all the likely things had been eliminated, Morley was now genuinely mystified. He shrugged. 'Went to see Micky Plant; t-talked about the Art School.' No need to mention the coal house with its association of crime and punishment. 'And, oh, he'd been up his grandma's, came back yesterday.' He debated whether to mention Micky's grandma's problem. In a good mood, his mother would laugh like mad at something as ridiculous as the high and mighty Plants having a regularly farting grandma. Another day.

As if by telepathy, and wanting to get in on the act, from the other room Frank let off a long rumbling trump ending in a little squeak.

His mother seemed not to hear. 'Oh yes.' She nodded triumphantly. 'I *knew* we'd get there in the finish. I've just had Mr Plant up, I have; while you were out enjoying yourself. Oh yes! Micky's dad. I was that *embarrassed*; I'd still got my pinafore on and my hair was in a mess. I was in your bedroom trying to tidy up – why you can't fold your clothes up like a normal person, heaven only knows; and you never took your malt! Frank opened the door to him. Frank!' She bared her teeth and shuddered. 'Filthy, dirty swine; stunk of beer – and other things. I just didn't know where to put myself. I came down and there was Mr Plant on the step. Oh, very polite he was, oh yes, very polite all right. "Terribly sorry to bother you," he said. And Frank just hung around, the stupid, gormless bugger. To get rid of him, I said, "The window in the shed's got stuck, go and see if you can loosen it," and do you know what he said, Mr Plant? He said, "If it's all the same to you, Mrs Charles, it might be as well if Mr Charles heard this as well." Mr Charles! Frank! Your dad! Ughh!' She glanced at the living-room door, lowered her voice and almost spat the words. 'Dirty sod might have woke up. I'll have to disinfect that settee: I'm sure I could smell dog shit on him. And it was *you*, wasn't it, that let him out? It was *you* that started all this. *You*, with your mind filled up with rubbish as usual – just like that pig bin. No wonder you can't ever think straight. I'll never be able to look those Plants in the face no more.' Her accent and choice of words were slipping; she was beginning to sound like May and Grandma Morley.

Morley was horrified by events and shared his mother's distress, though there was indignation mixed with his guilt. He said very cautiously, 'Wh-What did you s-say to him?'

'Never you mind what I said,' his mother said, as if determined to show that she was not ready for conciliation, but she answered nevertheless. 'I said Mr Charles was still stationed overseas and Frank – Mr Conlan was just sort of staying for a bit. And I don't know what he thought about *that* for a start off. Stupid bugger!' Morley didn't know whether she meant Frank, Micky's dad or himself.

'B-But he n-needed to go to the l-lav,' protested Morley gently. 'I was just trying to be helpful. In fact, if I hadn't l-let him out, he'd have broke the lock right off to get out. In fact, I m-mended the lock 'cause he'd already broke it a bit.' Hearing his own words, he realized he had really done nothing to feel guilty about: there was nothing to be ashamed of in releasing his friend from the coal house to go to the lavatory. He risked raising his voice. 'Why does it always have to be *me*?'

But she carried on. 'He said you'd interfered with – what was it? "A justly prescribed punishment." Pfff. And he said their house was covered in coal dust; on the carpet, on the stairs, on the lav, in the basin. Everywhere! Still, I'm not bothered about all that: that's their affair. But I asked him to come in, well, I'm always one to try and be polite, and he looked around and saw Frank's dirty plate on the table from dinner time, well, it wasn't dinner time, the dirty sod never ate it till nearly three; and the tablecloth wasn't on – just a mat. And you know I always like us to have our dinner all

78

together properly even though he hasn't got any manners and it makes me heave to watch him eat. And there was this vile smell everywhere; and I'm always very particular, heaven only knows. But I bet he noticed all right. Oh yes, I bet he thought that's what it's like in municipal houses.'

She was feeling sorry for herself. She sniffed and took a hanky from her sleeve. 'I could have understood if he'd gone round the Kelps; they say the Kelps don't know what their bath's for and they keep the coal in it. And all them stinking bones in their front garden. But I'm not like that. I always try and do the best I can and make everything nice for everybody.'

Morley was afraid she was going to cry but her anger was not yet spent. 'And if it hadn't been for *you*, if *you* hadn't interfered, everything would have been all right.' She blew her nose.

Morley played a martyr's role. 'Okay, yeh, it was all my f-fault, shouldn't have took no notice, heard old Micky sh-shouting out and w-walked away, pretended I didn't hear – that's a sort of l-lie that is, lying by omission Father Smythe calls it.' That would get her. 'You needn't worry, I won't go there no more, no fear. W-Won't have anything to do with him, won't talk to him. And if we both pass for the Art School, it'll j-just be the same: I'll ignore him. And if I see him drowning or if it looks like he's going to get run over by a bus, I'll walk away.' Careful, he was overdoing it. 'And if he goes to the Art School and I don't, well, there's always Reggie Kelp and Reg Nolan and the other scruffs to knock about with.'

Reflecting later, he was quite pleased with his performance.

With lots of deep sighs, his mother had gradually calmed down. After tea she had gone to Big Gwen's to retell the tale no doubt, with frequent reminders that, although they couldn't help it, the Plants were mental.

Tea had been a very quiet, civilized, slightly uneasy affair with a spotless white cloth. His mother had put the margarine in a dish May had given her years ago. There were also serviettes, not seen since Christmas. His mother wore a challenging look which made it very clear that these tea-time refinements were perfectly normal and not to be commented on. Frank was unusually silent but threw occasional puzzled glances at Morley.

His mother had traced the sources of the vile smell – on Frank's coat and one of his shoes, and consequently on the lino, mat and settee – and with a furious face and much pine disinfectant, dealt with them.

Now with Frank down at the pub again, Morley had the house to himself. He sat at his mother's dressing table studying his face in the triple mirror. He wasn't strikingly handsome but, full face, his features were neat and even. He adjusted the side glasses and examined his left and right profiles. Again, quite presentable – no peculiarities. So why oh why was he so often an object of ridicule? It must be his manner, or the queer expressions which he was only half aware of but were frequently commented on. 'Always look worried, you do,' Perky Beswick would say. Then there was his mother's, 'For goodness sake, duck, put your face straight.' And shopkeepers and adults in general: 'Cheer up, son, it might never happen.' And then Big Gwen only two or three hours ago: 'You should have seen your face, junior.'

Eyes closed, he recalled the way he had felt when Maurice the fake announcer had said his name on the wireless. Then, when he thought he had exactly reproduced his reaction, he opened them. His mouth was gaping, his lips drawn back, exposing his errant teeth and his brace. So was it the sight of his frequently odd expression, the sight of his brace, or both? Well, at least he could try keeping his mouth shut when it was not strictly necessary to open it. Though, come to think of it, he had tried something like this already. He remembered an attempt at mouth-closing at school, when Mr Ross-Armitage had said, 'You okay, old chap? Spot of toothache, what? My old nanny used to swear by chewing on a clove. Seemed to do the trick. Or get your ma to give you a spot of brandy, what?'

The trouble was, braces were not all that common. They

attracted attention – perhaps more than merely sticking-out teeth. After all, Reggie Kelp's teeth were crooked, had gaps and were always dirty, but Morley had never heard anybody commenting on them.

Apart from the children at the Dental Hospital, Morley only knew of one other person with a brace, a girl in Senior 1A. He did not know her name. But once at playtime when the talk was about girlfriends, someone said, 'She'd make a neat tart for Morle, they'd make a neat pair.'

Glasses, of course, were much more common than braces. There were two wearers in Senior 2A alone. One of them was Margaret Quinn, who was, none the less, greatly admired by the lads. She used her glasses like lorgnettes, raising them, still folded, whenever she wanted to see the blackboard. 'Blind as a bat I am,' she would say with a laugh when some mishap caused by her short sight befell her. And people would smile in sympathy – but with respect.

There was a lesson to be learned there, Morley realized: it was about confidence. Perhaps he ought to go around smiling broadly, boldly exposing his teeth and brace to the world, countering the familiar curious looks and questions with a Margaret Quinn-like laugh and an airy, 'Just temporary till next year.' Or, in the right company, 'Just a bit of temporary ironmongery.' He might even add, 'Pretty common in America. That's why the Yanks have got such good teeth when they're older.' Everyone was impressed with the Americans' nice teeth: they were what people noticed – after the superior uniforms and glamorous accents. Yes, that's what he would do if he passed for the Art School, and with anyone else he might meet for the first time.

From the road outside came the periodic thump of a ball hitting the pig bin. Morley peeped through the window cautiously. The descending sun hung just above the tower of the Mental Asylum; and in the orange-tinted street, Reggies Kelp and Nolan, Eric Beswick and three of their cronies were playing football. Kelp was in goal, each of the others shooting at the pig-bin and lamp-post goal whenever he could secure the ball.

Morley envied these lads, clearly untroubled by nagging thoughts of physical imperfections, the prospect of school tomorrow and Mortal Sin.

Nearly opposite, Maureen from next door and a plain-looking friend were doing handstands against a garden fence. Maureen seemed to have a pretty good idea of what she was about. She had tucked her frock modestly into the elastic of her pants but every so often contrived to make the frock come adrift to display her white knicks and a narrow band of naked skin below her vest. Every time this happened, she shrieked in mock alarm and stole furtive glances at the footballers, who were, at the moment, too engrossed in their game to respond. The plain girl, in navy drawers, was making pitiful attempts to imitate her friend. Maureen seemed to like plain companions, probably because they increased the effect of her own modest charms. But Morley wasn't moved: a vision of a younger Maureen with a candle streaming from each nostril and impetigo scabs round her mouth and chin was still too strong.

Later, some of the lads might saunter down to the handstanders and there would be furtive talk and laughter. Morley did not belong to this world of easy friendships between girls and boys with its innuendoes and casual touchings. He had, though, long known the pangs of love from a distance, and even at nine had had a violent crush on a girl of about the same age who he saw weekly at Mass. But his love had died one cold, winter morning when the girl, after fulsomely blowing her nose, had closely examined the results in a dainty lace-edged handkerchief. There had been other secret passions as well, although they had no connection with the powerful images he conjured up to accompany his nightly activities. Then usually mature females such as Big Gwen, the nurse from the Dental Hospital and May, his aunt, seemed more appropriate.

He took another look at his left profile in the mirror and opened his mouth. Then, using two fingers, he pressed hard against his upper teeth. He had planned to do this in five-minute sessions half a dozen times a day to assist the work of his brace and thus shorten the time to his teeth's correction. But he often forgot or became bored and sometimes a bit scared that he might do some damage.

Something was vaguely disturbing him. Swiftly, he ran over all his most recent thoughts but it was merely the need for a piddle which sought his attention. He went downstairs, fingers still pressing against teeth.

He had some difficulty performing with one hand and his aim was poor, and he had not lifted the seat. He decided to make a proper job of it and blame it on Frank. In this way he could punish his mother, and Frank for upsetting her, at the same time. He piddled all over the seat, the cover, the floor and the wall behind the pan.

'No, Mom,' he could hear himself lying later, 'I didn't go to the lav except after tea. Must have been Frank; probably went just before he went down the pub.'

He relented. Releasing his fingers from his teeth, he looked around for something to clear up with. The shiny lavatory paper was no good. The floorcloth from the back kitchen? No, he didn't like the idea of his mother using a wee-soaked cloth, that was much too harsh a punishment for her; *he* didn't fancy the kitchen floor being wiped with piddle either – even though it was his own. What about Frank's towel? He laughed; serve the dirty old sod right.

Frank's was the only towel in the bathroom. He and his mother kept theirs in their respective bedrooms to prevent Frank using them.

The WC and its environs cleaned up more or less satisfactorily, Morley washed his hands and went into the living room. Open on Frank's chair was *Reynold's News.* His eye was caught by an article about Hitler's birthday. But after the first paragraph, he found his mind invaded by thoughts of school tomorrow. Monday was not a bad day and there was art after morning playtime. But like a veteran actor who has played the part many times yet still suffers from stage fright, Morley was filled with the familiar dread that this time school would somehow defeat him.

# Chapter 9

When his mother woke him on Monday morning, Morley knew neither who nor where he was. Then he became aware of formless unpleasantnesses, which somehow had to be dealt with.

As he got reluctantly out of bed, his thoughts began to sort themselves out. The most overwhelming one was going back to school. The next – though now far behind – was his Mortal Sin. In fact, if there had been someone (not God) with the power to give him the choice of: you don't have to go to school but you've still got your Mortal Sin; or, the problem of your Mortal Sin is solved but you still have to go to school; Morley would have chosen the former without hesitation and gratefully gone back to bed.

He didn't hate school or even really dislike it, apart from woodwork; what gave him the jitters was just the awful wrench from weekend to Monday, or worse, holiday to first day of term. In an hour or so, perhaps in the middle of assembly, he knew he would have more or less adjusted.

After his Weetabix and, under his mother's watchful eye, his malt and cod liver oil, she said, 'There's a letter from your dad.'

Morley had learned not to ask too many questions about his father's letters: they were likely to make his mother tight-lipped. So he simply asked, 'And, er, he's okay?'

'Yes, fine,' said his mother flatly. 'Says he's just started fourteen days' local leave in a nice billet with a nice old man. Oh, and he says he's got a hat and a badge for you and some other bits and pieces.'

'Wow,' said Morley, his spirits rising. 'Is it a field cap, you know, a Jerry one? One of those w-with the –'

'If that's what you asked him for I dare say that's what he's got you.'

He pushed his caution aside in his eagerness to know more. 'And the b-badge. Did he say if that was a Jerry one?'

With a deep sigh, his mother said, 'Look, I'll read you *exactly* what he says and then perhaps you'll be satisfied.' She took the airmail flimsy from her pinafore pocket, scanned down to the bottom and read, '"Tell the lad I've managed to get a Jerry forage cap for him and a Jerry badge with the eagle and swastika and a few other odds and ends. Tell him I will be writing to him soon." Satisfied?' she said, returning the letter to her pocket. 'Now don't ask me *any* more because that's all he says.'

When it was time for Morley to go to school, her mood towards him softened. She followed him to the front door. 'Your teeth look ever so much better, duck – I was only saying to Big Gwen the other day. And you're not nearly so hesitant when you talk either.' She never said stammer. 'But you do watch the *way* you talk in the class, don't you, duck? I mean, I'd like the teachers to think you come from a decent home. Just because we don't live in a private house . . . It's only that I heard you talking to that Reggie Kelp the other day and well . . . you know what I mean, duck?'

Morley did. She was still smarting from her meeting with Micky Plant's dad yesterday. But she had nothing to fear. Morley spoke as he considered appropriate to circumstances: rough with the scruffs, very careful with Miss Pryce and Mr Ross-Armitage.

He smiled and nodded reassuringly. 'Oh yeh, Mom, g-good as anybody – better than a lot.'

Morley's jitters had subsided a little with the news of his hat, badge and unknown bits and pieces. He paused at his front gate and spied out the land. Reggies Kelp and Nolan were just down the road kicking a tin can to school. It was difficult to tell whether this would speed or retard their progress as Kelp's only objective was to kick it as far ahead as he could, while Nolan favoured passing it from one to the other. He was impressing this on to Kelp with shouts of 'Give us it here, you prat! Pass it over, you cunt!' Morley had the urge to catch them up and tell them of his new possessions, then thought better of it. The outcome was all too predictable; it would go:

MORLEY: Got this Jerry hat and this Jerry badge – silver, Gestapo – and all this other Jerry stuff – loads of it.

NOLAN: S'ave a look, then.

MORLEY: In't got them with us.

NOLAN: Show us tonight, then.

MORLEY: Our dad in't brought them back yet.

NOLAN: Where's your dad then?

MORLEY: Still abroad, in the army still.

NOLAN (*jeering*): Anybody could say that! I could say I got this Jerry tank and he could say he's got this whole SS uniform. But you can't see them 'cause our dad's gorrem.

KELP (*who is almost incapable of telling the truth*): Tek no notice of Morle. He's a liar and I bet his dad is and all.

Maureen stood at her gate next door waiting for her friend, and meanwhile answering 'Yeh' or 'Naw' to a string of questions and directions her mother was flinging at her from the doorway. She ignored her mother when she saw Morley.

'Seen you in your posh jacket Satday. You din't see me. You was dreaming about something: you had that funny look on your face. Orright, are you?'

'Yeh,' Morley said, wondering if he was still looking peculiar or whether it was an ordinary enquiry. 'Got the j-jacket from that Beryl Pinder's b-boyfriend, that Yank, Russ. R-Real American: says so inside. And I got this stuff off our dad, Jerry stuff, Gestapo hat, b-badges, everything.'

Maureen said, 'Our uncle in the Paras got our Pete all that sort of stuff and all. But when our Pete went in the RAF, our mom said it was in her road and there weren't nowhere to stick it all; so she chucked it in the bin. Our Pete din't half get on a line when he come home on leave.'

'Chucked it all away!' exclaimed Morley, shocked. 'B-But you could have g-give it . . .'

Maureen's eyes were looking over Morley's shoulder; her plain friend had just appeared round the corner from Eachley Lane. They greeted each other with loud giggles and then set off for school talking and laughing about some escapade of the previous evening.

Kelp and Nolan had disappeared round the bend. Morley decided to hang on a bit longer and join somebody else on the way to school. Whether or not he told them of his Jerry acquisitions, he would feel more secure with company. Most school-bound children were in couples or groups. There was only Fatty Yardley, walking resolutely alone, absorbed in his *Wizard*. Then the Betts twins came round the corner, Bobby and Roy. They were identical except for a small V-shaped scar on one twin's forehead, but Morley had forgotten which. They were neatly turned out in identical brown jackets, grey trousers and Fair Isle pullovers. They were always particularly neat and clean but Morley's mother still regarded them as scruffs because they hung around the pig bin, their mother carried on with a man while her husband was away, and they had adenoids.

The twins were a little on the pale side and their mouths hung permanently open, affording a clear view of the gum they were always chewing.

Morley fell in beside them. 'Warrow, tw-winnies,' he said.

'Warrow, Borley,' they answered, looking at him with their amused eyes and chewing noisily.

'What you got this m-morning, then?' The twins were in 2C, Mr Preen's class.

They shrugged. 'Writig, s'pose.'

'What s-sort of writing?' asked Morley. 'English, history, geograph-phy?'

'Yeh, s'pose,' they said, then added brightly, 'we got footer the safters, if it dod't raid.'

'If it raids,' said the twin with the scar, 'we go id the gyb,' they finished together.

'Old ma Pryce g-generally gives us compositions, first day back,' said Morley. 'What w-we did – done in the holidays. Or something b-barmy like that,' he added, to convey an indifference to school to match the twins'.

'Sobetibes we have pictures id the gyb,' said the scarred twin, shifting his gum from one side of his mouth to the other.

'Yeh, but they id buch cop,' said his brother, similarly moving his gum.

'Nothig dod't happed id theb,' they said, as if tickled by the idea.

'Well it's much better than l-lessons,' Morley said, '''cause you can always nod off for a b-bit.' He only just managed to avoid saying, 'dod off'.

'He's always doddig off anyroad, 'cept id footer,' they said, each referring to the other.

Morley was familiar with pictures in the gym. It usually happened when Mr Preen was appointed to fill the gap of a teacher's absence. Then 2A and whichever class he was teaching would all jubilantly troop off to the gym and watch films.

Mr Preen owned both the cinematograph and the curious collection of silent films. Morley had seen them all – many twice. They included: *The Amazing Story of Starch*, *New Ways with Ferro-Concrete* and *Guilty Chimneys*.

'We got old Ross-Armitage after p-play,' Morley said, as he and the twins turned into the pupil-thronged main road. 'Bit old b-but he can't half draw. He showed us these p-pictures of these horses he did, d-done. W-Wow, you should have s-seen them.'

The twins smiled with their eyes, worked their chewing gum on to the tips of their tongues and squinted down to see how it was going, but said nothing.

Morley said, 'Our dad got us all this Jerry stuff, Gestapo hat, this eagle badge with a swastika, silver.' Since he had not yet got the items, he allowed his imagination to soar. 'A-And a load of all these other b-badges, Panzer, Luft-w-waffe, Kriegsmarine, SS, oh, and *l-loads* of other stuff.'

The news made no impact. 'We got peds,' they said, delving into inside pockets to produce handsome marble-effect fountain pens. One twin's was maroon, the other's royal blue. Both had gold clips and bands.

'Deat, id't they?' they said. 'Brad dew.'

'Wow,' said Morley, 'wh-where did you get them?'

They grinned at each other, then at Morley as if he was slow on the uptake.

'Our Boss got theb for us,' said the scarred one, 'ad he gib our bob wod ad all.'

'Add he gib our bob wod ad all,' said the other, slightly out of synch.

Boss was Moss, the man Morley had heard about from scandalized whispers between his mother and Big Gwen, a GI who visited the twins' mother when her soldier husband was away.

'There's Stadley. He's brought his caseball,' said the twins, spotting a classmate on the other side of the road. Stanley's hair was blond, almost white. He was bouncing a leather football.

'Stad,' the twins yelled, 'give us a gabe?'

They dashed off across the road. Without their diverting company, the sight of the school chilled Morley afresh.

The building was large and modern. It was two-storeyed and of pale brown brick – at least in those modest areas not occupied by glass. Mr Ross-Armitage gleefully referred to it as the Shredded Wheat factory.

Morley skirted the main building and entered a landscape of deep trenches, clay spoil heaps and brick stacks, littered with builders' boards and rusting reinforcement rods. Around the edge of the site were several large, creosoted wooden huts and the earth mounds of half a dozen air-raid shelters. In the middle were two brick and glass buildings linked by a covered way. These were all that had been built of the senior department of the school when in 1940 the government had ordered the cessation of all non-essential building. One of the buildings was a gym. The other comprised an assembly hall, staff rooms, offices, storerooms and a large reception area. The assembly hall was divided by a seven-foot-high wall into two temporary classrooms. Mr Preen and 2C occupied the half that opened on to the reception area. Morley's class had the half with the stage.

Morley walked to his classroom wondering what sort of mood he would find Micky Plant in after the almost certain beating from his father; what he would say and how he would say it.

# Chapter 10

Now that the morning was well under way, it seemed to Morley that the holiday had never been – although his task now was to re-create some of it. 'Holiday Experience,' Miss Pryce had announced brightly, as if inspired, writing it on the board. It was received with groans; and one of the girls reminded her that they had the same subject on the first day of every term. Miss Pryce replied that the title was unimportant, it depended on how imaginatively one used it; and she supposed that no one had the same experience *every* holiday.

Morley considered his possibilities. The trip to town where he had pretended to be French in the Midland Educational to improve his chances of getting some watercolours; he had failed but the experience had been interesting. Not to be written about, though – this was his secret. Three or four gloomy, lonely walks. A visit to May's on a rainy day, where he had spent most of the time reading *The Pictorial Book of Knowledge*. He thought of his unusually crowded weekend: Russell and his gift of the lumber jacket, the wounded soldiers outside the pub, Frank and the accordion, the wireless trick, the Pinders' fireplace, Micky Plant's imprisonment and its aftermath. Plenty there, but nothing that he cared to write about. A holiday preoccupied with thoughts of Mortal Sin and marked at the beginning and end by missed confessions.

A holiday best forgotten. He turned his attention to last year's holidays: Easter, summer, Christmas.

Last Christmas. Or wasn't it just before Christmas? At any rate, it had been very cold; his mother had insisted he wear his balaclava.

It was Sunday morning after Mass. Morley had just come out of Hiller's shop in Eachley Lane, and there were Reggies Nolan and Kelp and Neil Gunn, bound for the Ickley Hills. Having nothing better to do, he joined them. They walked over Redwell Hill and the golf links talking about football, the pictures, girls – which meant smut – and what they would do if they became rich. By the time they reached the pine woods on the side of Beacon Hill, the subject was school. Kelp said his favourite subject was art because you could muck about and didn't have to write anything. Morley was struggling to make some suitable contribution when a man appeared from the trees beside the path and fell into step alongside. He touched his hat and said in a cultured voice, 'Morning, young men. Please forgive my eavesdropping but I couldn't help overhearing your, um, observations, um, on art.'

The Reggies and Neil stared at him. Morley observed him a bit more discreetly. He was a pleasant-faced, crinkle-browed man with longish greying hair. He wore a brown trilby, a fawn, well-fitting overcoat and a lemon-coloured scarf.

Out of the side of his mouth, Nolan said, 'Come on, let's bugger off.'

'I'm an artist myself,' said the man, 'but my speciality is, um, sculpture.'

The Reggies and Neil were silent.

'Is that s-statues?' asked Morley, who knew perfectly well but thought someone ought to say something.

'That's absolutely *right*,' said the man, almost eagerly. 'You are, um, obviously well informed.'

'Let's get going,' muttered Kelp. 'I wanna gerra cake from the caff. Leave ol' Morle to it, I'm starved.'

They walked quickly ahead.

The man called after them, 'I wonder if one of you, um, young artists would give me, um, a hand with my work.'

The Reggies and Neil walked faster, leaving Morley uncomfortably placed between them and the man.

'It's worth, um, half a crown,' he added.

They stopped. Nolan said, 'Okay then, we'll give you a hand.' He pointed to Morley. 'Him, he can draw a treat. He drawed Black Bob out the *Dandy*. Better than the one in the *Dandy*. He's the best drawer in our school, in't he, lads?' The others nodded. 'He can draw you anything you want.'

'No, you don't, um, quite understand.' The man smiled. 'I need a, um, model. I mean I want one of you to pose for me. You see my usual, um, model is indisposed – ill. And time is short. I've been commissioned, you see, to make a piece of sculpture – a statue to, um, epitomize – express the, um, spirit of youth. It's for, um, ah –'

Nolan interrupted. 'You mean you want to copy one of us for half a crown?'

'Er, yes, exactly,' said the man, his eyes stealing towards tall, fresh-faced Neil Gunn.

'Yeh, he'll do it,' Nolan offered, noting the direction of the man's eyes. 'He'll like being copied, old Neilie.'

But Neil didn't agree. 'No, don't fancy being copied, don't like it.'

'Course you do, Neil, it's dead easy; *and* – half a *crown*? Nothing to it. Anybody can do it. He'll do it,' Nolan said confidently.

But Neil was adamant. 'Naw, it's just one of them things I never fancy. Anyroad' – suddenly rounding on Nolan – 'if it's all that easy, why don't *you* do it, then?'

Nolan was apologetic. 'Can't. I'd like to but I can't keep still, never could for long; runs in our family. I'd be hopeless, mek your statue all fuzzy. One of them'll do it.' He nodded towards Reggie Kelp and Morley.

The man hardly glanced at hunched up, shivering Morley, his chattering protruding teeth prominent through the small opening of his balaclava. He seemed hardly more impressed with slack-mouthed, uncoordinated Reggie Kelp either. But not having much choice, he asked, 'Well, how about it, young man?'

'Ten bob,' said Kelp firmly, acting the tough guy, squaring his narrow shoulders and puffing out his pigeon chest.

The man's face dropped, but Nolan gazed at Kelp approvingly. 'Yeh, Kelp's worth ten bob easy, and we'll keep him still for you. Where you doing it, round your house?'

'No, no, that won't be necessary, and it doesn't matter if he moves a little. All I want to do is to make a brief sketch or two, here, now. Take only eight or nine minutes at the most. The sculpture – the statue will be made much later in my, um, studio. But' – regretfully – 'this is hardly a, um, ten-shilling job, though. How about, let's say, four, um, bob?'

'Yeh, okay then,' agreed Kelp. 'What you want me to do?'

'Well, to begin with,' said the man briskly, 'let's just get off this path and find a more secluded spot.'

This done, he instructed Kelp to lean against a tree. 'No, just relax, be natural, don't do anything special.'

Morley and the others watched with interest. The man didn't have any special equipment. He rummaged through his wallet until he found a used envelope and opened it out. Then he looked at Kelp and made an astonishingly crude drawing. Morley was dismayed: Kelp could have done better himself. Unless, he thought, this was modern art beyond his understanding.

But Nolan and Gunn had no such reservations. They looked from the drawing to Kelp and back to the drawing and collapsed with helpless laughter.

'Now we need a drawing showing a little more, um, natural form,' said the man, searching for some more paper. 'Just slip your coat and jacket off, if you would. Only for a minute or two,' he added quickly, as Kelp looked about to protest.

The man then did another equally crude drawing. When it was finished, he said, 'Now, young man, um, this may sound rather strange to you but in, um, serious art circles, it's considered quite normal. Just drop your trousers and, um, pants for a moment.'

This was too much for Reggie Kelp. 'You can bugger that for a start off, mate,' he said, beginning to put his jacket on. 'I'm bleeding perished already.'

Nolan said, 'Mek it five bob and he'll do it.' And to the protesting Kelp: 'What you going on about? A lot of statues are *all* bare, I seen them in ol' Armitage's book. Great big bare blokes chucking plates and whatsits. Blimey, you'll still have half your clothes on. So stop whining and gerron with it.'

'Look,' offered the man, 'I'll make it six, um, bob if you will do exactly as I ask. All right?'

Kelp nodded reluctantly and after a few more clumsily obeyed instructions, was posed more or less as required. The spectacle was grotesque: Kelp's trousers were round his ankles, his hands high above his head so that his jersey and vest were hoisted just enough to expose his private parts.

The artist became quite animated now, drawing furiously but without looking at the result. Morley felt very uneasy but didn't know why. Nolan and Gunn were rolling around out of control, laughing so much that they were unable to give voice to the jeers the situation called for. Unconcerned by the commotion, the man now asked Kelp to hold on to the pose and turn round, for just a little longer. This time he didn't actually draw. He simply stood, hands thrust deep in trouser pockets, staring, shaking and breathing heavily. 'Just – need – to commit images to memory – now,' he said, eyes on Reggie's rear.

Infuriated by the indignity of his enforced posture and by Nolan's and Gunn's laughter, but probably afraid to drop the pose lest he should not be fully paid, all Kelp could do was shout, 'I'll get you, you rats, you dirty rotten rats! You wun't get no money, you see! You rats, I'll get you!'

But the artist had finished. 'That's it – fine,' he said sheepishly, handing over six shillings to the rapidly dressing Kelp. 'Super. So I'll, um, bid you good day, then.' And he hurried off through the trees.

'He's fucking barmy,' said Kelp. Then yelled into the trees,

95

'Oi, you, lah-de-dah, gorra screw loose or summat? Where was you when the brains was give out? Lah-de-dah tosser!'

And now Morley was a tosser. A real one. He felt almost nostalgic for that winter day in the woods when tosser was merely another rude word. He remembered his resolve to look in Mr Ross-Armitage's big dictionary at the end of the art lesson. But the urgency to get his Mortal Sin confessed had lost its edge. The sunlight streaming through the high hall windows, the restrained though lively chatter around him, David Meyer bent over his book beside him, the continuous low rumble from the class on the other side of the wall: the reassuring familiarity of it all made sudden death while in a state of Mortal Sin seem very remote. He would, before long, somehow sort his problem out; and he *might* take a look at the dictionary today or – and he could feel the relief sweeping through him – leave it until next week's art lesson. There was no hurry: next Saturday was not his usual Saturday for confession. And if he broke his routine, there might be awkward questions from his mother.

He glanced at David Meyer's exercise book; he had written a page and a half. David was tall and well built and looked about fifteen. He associated with older boys, or boys who looked as mature as himself. He seemed to like Morley, though, and encouraged and applauded his occasional impersonations. He would even happily pass the time of day with him in the playground – provided none of his tall, mature friends were around to claim his more serious attention.

He wondered if David or any of his mates did it. The thought disturbed him. He didn't want to think about it.

David looked up and winked when he became aware of Morley's eyes on his work. He looked at Morley's book, which bore only the date and the title. He liked to flatter. 'I suppose it's in your head, Morley, all complete. And all you've got to do is scribble it down.' He turned back to his own work.

Morley smiled, stretched and tried to think. His mind drifted to a holiday in Weston before the war. The only

96

holiday he could clearly remember spending with his father. He dismissed the idea of writing about it. Anyway, he had only been seven at the time. He offered up a brief prayer for his father's safety, then wondered if it would have any effect in his present state.

Miss Pryce called out, '2A, please, the noise has once again risen to an unacceptable level. Please, a *little* quieter.'

As if not to be outdone, Mr Preen's flat, nasal voice came from the other side of the dividing wall: 'Now if you *must* talk, make sure I can't hear a single word – unless you need to say something to me, that is,' although only twenty minutes ago he had demanded absolute silence. Then, to an unheard question, he said, 'Well, yes, you can say thank you – if it's for the dictionary or rubber you are borrowing, but not for anything else.'

The rumble from his class continued.

Morley decided that true experiences were out: he wanted to escape from his world of scruffs, municipal houses, lodgers and priests; he certainly didn't want it revealed to Miss Pryce – who might think his background was common. Until a year or so ago, he had often adapted William stories for holiday experiences but he could no longer identify with the eleven-and-three-quarter-year-old William. He grieved the passing years.

David Meyer's watch said eleven minutes to ten. Time was getting on. He decided to base his composition on one of his favourite books, *The Mystery of Swallings End*. Swallings End would become Barnt Green, he would be Dick, and Micky Plant, Nigel. Micky would be pleased to find that he had been cast in the role of the more intelligent of the boy sleuths if he read it, or if it was ever read out to the class. He would write it in a style that Miss Pryce would approve of and pay very careful attention to quotation marks – Miss Pryce had emphasized their importance last term. He began:

It was a bright, sunny morning at the beginning of the Easter Holidays as my chum Micky and I set off for a walk to Tardebigge. We had sanwiches and (popX)* mineral water which we carried in our gnapsacks slung over our shoulders. It was a favourite walk which we had gone on many times previously.

As we walked through the village of Barnt Green my chum noticed something (funnyX) rum and said in a low voice "I say (MorleyX) old man

He decided to leave himself anonymous – it might help to reduce the groans if Miss Pryce read the story to the class.

you see that big, white house over there facing the Manchester to London railway line, the house with the stirrup pump notice in the bay window?" "Yes" I replied. "Well" said my chum "When we last came along here, the notice was in the window of the <u>door</u> and not in the <u>bay</u> window as it is now. Then on the walk previous to that it was in the <u>door</u> again."

He chewed the end of his pen and idly listened to Mr Preen who now seemed to be almost encouraging his class to talk.

'Talking is natural, don't get me wrong. *I* talk, *bricklayers* talk, *factory workers* talk, *everybody* talks. But it doesn't stop them from *working*. Now I wouldn't mind *you* talking if it didn't stop you *working*.'

"Don't get excited Micky" I said "there is a simple explanation. The (manX) gentleman was decorating his (front roomX)(loungeX) sitting room and temporaraly put the sign in his <u>door</u> whilst he did so." But my chum was not convinced. "I think its been done more than the once" he said. I said "We will come back this way on our return from Tardebigge and not by the roundabout country route which we usually do and check."

* Miss Pryce forbade crossings out: errors had to be enclosed within brackets with a cross inserted. Also it was common practice not to use paragraphs to divide different speakers – this was to conserve scarce paper.

Mr Preen was actually *telling* his class to talk now. 'Yes, all right, talk as much as you like. Talk your heads off for all I care. Go on, it doesn't worry me! Not one bit, I still get paid. But don't you *dare* come back here next year and complain to me that you couldn't get any jobs . . . Geoffrey, what did I just say?'

'No, I did not, Geoffrey.'

'No, that was a good ten minutes ago, Geoffrey.'

'Look, laddie, I'm not arguing with you. Get out. Outside that door. Now! Out, Geoffrey!'

If there was any reaction, 2A couldn't hear it, just the usual rumble.

Miss Pryce, smiling gently to herself, stood up. 'It's so tiresome when I am marking your English compositions to be continually confronted with I said, he said, they said, Miss Smith said, Mrs Brown said, Mr Robinson said, when there are so many much more expressive alternatives. We *whisper*, we *exclaim*, we *shout*, we *ask*, we *demand*, they *cried*, she *enquired*, Miss Smith *implored*, Mrs Brown *pleaded*, Mr Robinson *ejaculated*. Please remember that, 2A, when you are using direct speech in your work.'

Morley bit his lip and substituted more expressive alternatives to his existing work before continuing.

Fifteen minutes and a page and a half later he paused and read what he had written. God, on the last page he had mentioned his guardian . . . twice! He was too closely following the original story. Miss Pryce might enquire if it was true that he had a guardian – though probably not question the far-fetched adventure itself. How could he get rid of it? Putting it in brackets didn't help: it would still be there. And she would be annoyed if he crossed it out. It might be simpler to tell her that he *did* have a guardian, he thought ruefully. Trying to compress a whole book into a few pages had not been a very bright idea – and there was tons more yet. He thought about the most exciting part of *The Mystery of Swallings End*, towards the end. The blacked-out train rushing through the dark, rain-lashed countryside of Real England bearing a diguised German spy, about to be trapped by two boys barely older than himself; their supreme self-confidence and public-school accents carrying the authority to order two soldiers they had just met to do their bidding. It was all so . . . thrilling, and somehow uncomplicated and cosy at the same time. Compared with his own messy existence.

'*Geoffrey?* Come back, at once. This very minute!' Mr Preen's voice sounded faint, as if coming from the vestibule.

2A went quiet and listened. Miss Pryce paused in her marking and inclined her head.

'Geoffre-e-ey, co-o-ome ba-a-ack!' It was only just audible now, as if Mr Preen had gone into the grounds. 'Co-o-ome ba-a-a-ck, Geoffre-e-ey!'

The rumble from next door grew a little in volume, and one or two individual voices could just be heard. A gym pump sailed over the partition but someone caught it and flung it back. Miss Pryce smiled smugly and carried on with her marking.

Morley glanced at David's watch. Twenty past ten! No time to bring the story to any sort of satisfactory conclusion – and in a few minutes Miss Pryce might tell them to finish and give them mental arithmetic. He put brackets round his entire composition and inserted a cross at the end. If questioned, he would say the whole essay was a mistake; that he was writing about a holiday experience that had happened to a friend. Then, in the middle of it, it had suddenly occurred to him that he should be writing about an experience of his own.

He drew a pen line under what he had done and began a highly condensed version of *The Outlaws and Cousin Percy*. He had done it before in top juniors. He would be William, Micky Plant, Ginger. He would leave out Henry and Douglas to save time.

# Chapter 11

For nearly an hour, Morley had enjoyed a precarious contentment, almost lost in his painting of the still life that Mr Ross-Armitage had set up. As usual, the teacher had presented the class with a new problem to solve. This time it was discovering how to paint metallic objects convincingly. To this end the group included a brass candlestick, a silver vase, a copper pan and a chrome ashtray. Reclining in the ashtray was a lighted cigarette, its wreathing smoke adding a little animation to the setting. The cigarette was replenished at intervals by the spare one the teacher was smoking in readiness. One way or another, a lighted cigarette featured in all Mr Ross-Armitage's art subjects.

But now it was almost dinner time and along with Micky Plant's and two others, Morley's half-finished painting was pinned in the place of honour on the blackboard. The rest of the still lifes were pegged on cords suspended from the ceiling. Chairs and tables had been restored to their usual positions. Two girls in aprons, who regarded clearing up as the high spot of the lesson, were enthusiastically washing brushes and the bun tins which served as palettes. Morley and a small freckled boy called Nipper Horrabin were admiring Mr Ross-Armitage's demonstration painting, also pinned to the blackboard. The rest of the class was straining its ears for the bell, sometimes difficult to hear from the art hut, which was a long way from the main building.

The shelves housing Mr Ross-Armitage's books were a couple of feet away from Morley. His eyes were drawn to the lowest shelf, containing the biggest books; there between *Masters of the Twentieth Century* and *The Pictorial Encyclopaedia of Modern Art* was the big two-volume dictionary which might hold the solution to the problem of his Mortal Sin.

Margaret Quinn called out, 'Sir, I'm sure I heard the bell go.' The rest of the class murmured agreement.

Mr Ross-Armitage took out his pocket watch, squinted at it, shrugged and said, 'Okay, off you go, then. I can't really deprive your fond mamas of the pleasure of your charmin' company any longer, I suppose – unless you're among the unfortunates who have to endure school lunches.'

Morley stood irresolute as his classmates rushed past him, a withdrawn-looking Micky Plant among them. Although he wanted to forget his Mortal Sin for the time being, there was a persistent little urge to have a look in the dictionary and get it over and done with.

Anyway, there was no reason, he thought, why he shouldn't linger a moment and have a look at the van Eyck picture again. One of several Mr Ross-Armitage had shown them during the lesson to demonstrate the treatment of metals, it was in *The Art of the Renaissance*. He turned to the coloured, tipped-in picture of *Arnolfini and his Wife* and studied the very realistic-looking gold candelabra above their heads. At that moment the bell rang, quite distinctly; the wind must have been in the right direction.

Mr Ross-Armitage grinned as he made his way to the door. 'Sly little buggers,' he said under his breath; and to Morley, 'Well, at least *you* don't seem to be in a tearin' hurry.' He glanced at the picture in the book. 'Mm, it *is* pretty, isn't it? Sort of fifteenth-century photograph really. Anyway, don't let your lunch get cold, or I'll have your ma after me.' At the door he turned and said, 'Do close the door after you, there's a good chap.' He winked. 'And no lookin' at the dirty pictures when I've gone.'

Morley blushed, wondering if it was obvious that he *was* the sort of boy who liked looking at dirty pictures; and wondering if there really were any. The closeness of the dictionary was disturbing. He put the art book back, deciding to go home; then impulsively bent down and pulled out volume II of the dictionary. It was heavy. He put it on the nearest table and went to the door to check that it was properly latched. Just a quick look. He turned to the back of the book. 'Wank' and its definition was his first objective. Or – if it existed – the proper, polite word which might be similar, or at least begin with the same letter.

'Wane, wangle,' he read. Then 'Wankie'! His held his breath, until he read: 'town in W. Rhodesia, chief industry coal mining'. Then, 'Wanne-Eickel', another town, this time in Germany; then 'want', and then nothing vaguely connected with what he was after. He considered looking through all the w's, but that would take ages.

He looked for 'rack off'. 'Rack' was listed but none of its more than a dozen meanings was connected with his Mortal Sin. It seemed to be one of those words like 'set', which Miss Pryce had said had over fifty meanings. He remembered that they had covered all three blackboards.

He found 'toss', another word with several applications. Morley scanned the half-column of tiny, closely spaced type. Heads, cricket balls, matadors, ships in storms, salads and cabers were among over a dozen things commonly tossed. And 'toss' could mean, he learned, lightly shaken, casually thrown, flung violently, pitched, mixed, agitated or energetically hurled. It *could* at a pinch apply to what he did, and without the 'off' it was a perfectly respectable word. But it seemed pretty elastic. Would it do? He tried it, but without much conviction. 'Pray Father, give me your blessing. I tossed several times.' How many? He calculated, fearful of the result. January, February, March, over half of April. Three and a half times thirty. A hundred and five! Not that he had done it every day. Though sometimes he had done it twice – and on a few occasions three times. So, still close to a hundred. He quailed at the prospect of confessing to a hundred Mortal Sins. But it had to be done. He closed his eyes. 'Pray Father, I tossed over a hundred times.' No, it wouldn't do. He could hear Canon Reilly's response – but it insisted on being a pantomime Canon Reilly.

'Ah now, and *what*, my son, was it that you tossed? A ball, a coin, a pancake? Or a caber, was it?'

He smiled grimly, then glanced back at the dictionary. He couldn't believe his eyes; there it was, listed separately: 'toss off' in full! He read, '1. empty by drinking in one draught (from a cup, etc.) 2. write quickly and effortlessly: *he tossed off a letter to his friend*'. But that was it. He was unable to hold back his disappointment; the dictionary was almost his last hope. He would have been happier if he had gone straight home. He looked gloomily back at the entry – and heard approaching footsteps. Mr Ross-Armitage had forgotten something perhaps. He quickly closed the book.

Being discovered with a closed dictionary in front of him might suggest a guilty conscience. He opened it at random and found himself in the M section. He ran his eye down a column of largely unknown words until he came to 'minnow'. He heard the door open but forced himself not to look up. Adopting the look of one lost deep in study, heart racing, he read, 'a small, slender European freshwater cyprinid fish'.

It was Miss Pryce. He felt even more awkward than if it had been Mr Ross-Armitage.

'Does your teacher know you are in here?' she asked.

He nodded, incapable of speech. It crossed his mind that maybe she had come here to ask him if he really had a guardian. Or to tell him off for wasting precious paper in his exercise book. But no, surely, she was probably looking for Ross-Armitage: people said that she fancied him. The knowledge embarrassed him. His eyes dropped to the dictionary, and he had the absurd notion that 'toss off' was revealing itself to her through all the obscuring pages like an X-ray.

'Oh, it's *you*. You are in my form, aren't you? Yes, of course you are.'

Morley could still only nod.

'And what are you so earnestly studying, er, when you might be enjoying the sunshine or going to lunch?'

'Minnow,' Morley was desperately trying to say, while trying to think of a good reason for an interest in a freshwater fish, which certainly was keeping him from enjoying the sunshine or having his dinner. 'M-Min, m-min,' he began. 'I w-was l-looking up m-min–'

'Of course, minstrel,' Miss Pryce supplied, looking at the page. It was in bold type at the top. 'And this is by way of an extra-curricular activity, I suppose.'

Morley didn't know what extra-curricular meant. He looked up.

'I mean something in addition to your usual lesson. Of course, are you not one of the Art School candidates?'

Morley nodded.

'No doubt Mr Ross-Armitage has set you a task to further develop your talent. And are the other Art School candidates also engaged in this minstrel project or were they given a choice?'

Morley had almost worked out what to say. He would explain that he had already done a painting of a minnow for . . . Scouts? No, she might find out that he was no longer a Scout. Church? No, an American friend, a soldier . . . who was interested in such things. And all he wanted was something for a bit of writing to go underneath. He made a supreme effort. 'N-No, Miss, Miss, I, I on-only, only, er –'

'Ah, so you are the only one; which explains your solitary presence here. Well, I am afraid you will not find very much in a dictionary, comprehensive as this one seems to be. But I may be in a position to help you. Medieval musical instruments have been a particular interest of mine since university days. In fact, I once wrote an article on that very subject for a *national* magazine. Can you see the connection . . . with your minstrel project?'

Morley tried again but the effort was exhausting. 'But M-Miss, I w-was just, er –'

'Now if I can possibly put my finger on it, I will let you see a copy. But, please, as soon as you have finished your project, do not fail to let me see it; I will be most interested, *most* interested.'

Morley found it easier simply to nod.

He walked home slowly, wondering how it was that he had suddenly become saddled with a minstrel project. And why Miss Pryce was so eager to see the result. He had some vague idea that it might be somehow connected with Miss Pryce's crush on Mr Ross-Armitage. But wasn't Miss Pryce too old for –

'You here again, Morle? This where your tart lives, then?' It was Perky Beswick.

They were at the bottom of Woods Park Road not far from the spot where they had met yesterday and discussed the ATS girl.

Morley forced a laugh. 'N-No, no, Ec, just on my way home, you kn-know.'

'Bet you been thinking again. I can tell. You got that look. That sod Shagger kept us in. For nothing. I'll get him. You see. Bastard. Get our uncle up. He'll give him one. Wun't do it no more.' He spat.

Tearing his thoughts away from his own troubles and feeling pleased that Perky had problems as well, Morley dared ask, 'Wh-What you been up to, then, Ec?'

'Nothing.' Then he almost smiled, as if reminiscing. 'Me and these other kids. Got these tools and that. Files, chisels and that. Mucking about with them.' He made two fists and put them by his flies one in front of the other, then thrusting his pelvis back and forth, went, 'Ugh, ugh, ugh. That's what we was doing.' He did it again, his curious inflexible back making him look like some strange insect. 'Ugh, ugh, ugh.'

Morley glanced around to be sure nobody was looking. The road was deserted. 'That all, Ec?'

'Well, it was bad enough. And I was doing it worse. Worse than all the others. They was too frit. To do it like I was.'

'Sh-Shagger didn't give you one, then, Ec?' asked Morley uncertainly.

'What him? Give me one? Naw. Wun't dare. Just give us these barmy lines.' He spat. 'Fifty. Only done about twenty. "I must not be rude in woodwork." Load a crap.'

'D-Does your class do proper woodwork, then, Ec?' Morley knew that they didn't, none of the classes did, but couldn't think of anything else to say.

'Naw, just draw these tools and that. Mallets, planes and that.'

'N-No writing and that, then?'

'Naw. Not now. Used to. Last year. In 2B. Went and seen some of them Eyetie prisoners. Up the loony bin. Yesterday. They mek these toys and that. Out a wood. Neat. Carve out these statues. And flowers and that. Gonna get one for our old lady's birthday. You seen them? Them Eyeties?'

Before Morley could reply, a small boy of about four or five called out to them, 'We've got chicken salad for lunch.' He had dark curly hair and large, intensely blue eyes. He was regarding them through the bars of the gate of one of the private houses.

Perky stared at him, as if to put him in his place by the power of his look.

But the boy, quite unmoved, repeated, 'We've got chicken salad for lunch.'

Eric said, 'Huh,' and spat. 'That's sissy stuff. We got tripe and onions. In't we, Morle?'

'Twipe and onions,' said the boy, eyes wide.

'Yeh,' said Perky. 'Neat.'

'After,' said the boy, 'we're having some of my other gwannie's twifle.'

Perky thought for half a second and said, 'We got prick pudding.'

'Pwick pudding,' echoed the boy innocently.

This almost amused Perky; he developed his theme further. 'Yeh. And tomorrow we got bollocks stew. And cunt tart. Ever had them?'

The boy shook his head.

'Don't know what you're missing. Neat. Great. Smashing. Yum. Yum.' He had another idea. 'Tell your mom to

107

cook some. For you. For your dinner. Say bollocks stew. Say it now.'

'Boll-ocks stew.'

'Yeh. Now cunt tart.'

'Cunt tart.'

'Now say both.'

'Boll-ocks stew, and – cunt – tart,' said the little boy.

'Go in. Tell your mom. Now,' said Perky, preparing to run. The boy trotted off.

But his mother had already heard. She came round the side of the house, her face furious. 'You disgusting, dirty-minded guttersnipes! I heard you. And I'll remember who you are. I'll be coming to your school this afternoon, you'll see!'

Morley and Perky didn't stop running even when the bend in the road hid them from the woman's view. Perky shot into his entry while Morley, breathing painfully, dashed the further few yards to the safety of his own house.

God, more problems. He had a sudden thought: could the little boy's mother be the same person who had over-heard him talking to Perky about the ATS tart yesterday? Then he remembered, with some relief, that the idea of a witness to his vulgar conversation had only existed in his imagination.

# Chapter 12

Morley went to school in the afternoon via a roundabout route, self-consciously wearing his new lumber jacket, his hair flattened with Vaseline, a piece of sticking plaster above his right eye and a deep frown. He had considered putting on an eye patch – a green card affair which Frank the lodger had worn for a week after getting a fragment of metal in his eye at the Aero Works – but had rejected it as too conspicuous. Dick and Nigel the boy sleuths favoured more subtle disguises.

He sat through the afternoon's history and geography lessons in apparent studious concentration but sick with apprehension at the prospect of the entry of the headmaster and the mother of the little boy. The changes in his appearance, he explained to David Meyer and one or two others, were the result of wrenching open a stuck cupboard door in his shed.

'Then it s-suddenly flew open and hit m-my f-forehead and only j-just missed my eye! Then this jar of turps sh-shot out all over m-my hair and coat. Din't half sting. I had to stick this Vaseline on it, and change my coat. W-Wow, still hurts,' he added, rubbing his head and deepening his frown.

But the woman did not come after all. Later he painfully removed the sticking plaster and rumpled his hair before his mother saw him at tea time.

\*

Now he lay in bed unable to sleep. He had resolved not to do it tonight. But he had. The relief was fleeting and solved nothing. He felt guilty and let down, and even more worried. He wondered if the woman would come into school tomorrow and, if she didn't, whether he should continue to wear his disguise for the rest of the week – just to be on the safe side. He cast around for something to cheer himself up, something to look forward to.

If the woman had not come by the end of tomorrow afternoon – after that there was a good chance that she wouldn't come at all, he decided – he would celebrate his relief by going to town directly after school. He would get some paper from the Midland Educational for Russ's picture – and they might even have some watercolours this time. His entire being lusted after some nice new paints to replace the small collection of near-exhausted pans and tubes he had to make do with at present. A box of paints like one of those arranged under a fan of magnificent brushes in the pre-war display cabinet at the foot of the stairs. These were not for sale, though; and Micky Plant said that the colours were fakes anyway, like the fake chocolates in sweetshop windows.

Morley liked the anonymity of town; and if he went by himself he could be French. Perhaps he would keep it up all evening until he got home: an adventure! He saw himself striding confidently down New Street in his lumber jacket, new paints in his pocket; popping into the Kardomah for a cup of tea and a bun – something he had never done before on his own. He might wear the sticking plaster; it would make him feel even more secure and strengthen the image of a heroic French refugee. Afterwards there might be time to go with equal ease to Pets' Corner in Lewis's, the bookshops or the Art Gallery. Any mistakes, any hesitancy in his manner or speech would be seen as the natural behaviour of a foreigner.

Once, he had plucked up courage and gone to the Art Gallery by himself. But in spite of the lure of the paintings it had been a painful experience. The place had made him feel uneasy and awkward, constantly afraid he might be

110

unwittingly doing something wrong or inappropriate; and fearful that an attendant might speak to him. But tomorrow it would be different. He was excited, and just for a few moments he felt that he held the key to all life's problems. But then, just like the water that always mysteriously seeped back through the bricks in Grandma Morley's newly swept yard, his problems crept back. The little boy's mother, the absurd encounter with Miss Pryce and the minstrel project, and his Mortal Sin. He tried closing his eyes really tight, curling up into a ball and willing sleep to come. But if he did go to sleep, the night would be over in a flash and his waking thoughts would be even more despondent than those he was enduring now, and in an hour or two he would be back in school – the source of his most immediate problems. At least at the moment, nine or ten hours separated him from that. If only he had something to read. Maybe, in spite of his unsuccessful search yesterday, there was some forgotten book downstairs that he had not read for a long time. Something easy and light that he could briefly lose himself in.

He was in no mood to explain to his mother or Frank, if either was still up, why he had come downstairs, so he would go down as if to the lavatory and listen outside the living-room door to see if the coast was clear.

There was a strip of light under the door. He listened: not a sound. He went in and there was Frank sprawled out asleep in the armchair, his stockinged feet in front of the dead fire, a tiny empty tube of dog end on the lower lip of his open mouth. There was a grey caterpillar of ash on the book on his lap. The book was *Five Go Adventuring Again* by Enid Blyton. Morley smiled joylessly. Frank derided his books; westerns were the thing, he said. If he had been up to it, Morley might have woken him and artlessly enquired if he had enjoyed it, and then revelled in Frank's squirming explanation. Another time. He needed a chair to reach his books on the top of the dresser but was afraid that the movement might wake Frank. Anyway, he didn't feel like hanging around: Frank's socks stank alarmingly. He glanced around for some other reading matter. On the arm of the settee were yesterday's *Reynold's News* and tonight's *Evening Despatch*; *Monroe's Universal Reference Book* lay on the table. He would have to make do with that. About to turn off the light, he paused, his attention caught by the small framed picture of the Sacred Heart in the hall. The picture was at least a yard to Morley's right but even so Our Lord's eyes gazed directly into his. Morley looked guiltily back.

His bedroom was chilly. He put *Monroe's Universal Reference Book* on the bed and closed the windows. His mother insisted on wide-open windows as a precaution against TB. She had read that in some northern town, TB had claimed more deaths in one particular year than the Blitz. About to draw the curtains together, he noticed an unfamiliar brightness outside. Light was streaming through the uncurtained windows at the backs of some of the houses in Marshfield Drive. Of course, today was the end of the dim-out. It had been on the wireless, in the paper and Miss Pryce had mentioned it in class: 'My little garden will be quite startled at the novelty tonight.' But he must have been so preoccupied that he had forgotten, as must his mother.

He closed the curtains nevertheless as it made him feel more secure, and switched on the light. He climbed into his now cold bed and twisted around with the book until he found a reasonably comfortable position. *Monroe's Universal Reference Book* was thick and heavy; it needed to be since it contained everything you needed to know, at least that was what his father used to say, with a smile. Morley was its chief consulter and it had served his changing needs for years. He turned to the beginning: a hundred-and-fifty-page section entitled 'The Story of Mankind from the Earliest Ages to the Present Day'. It occurred to him that there might be a picture here of a minstrel that he could copy and have ready for when Miss Pryce asked him how his project was coming along. It might be easier, he reasoned, actually to get some sort of project together than attempt to explain to her that it had all been a ridiculous misunderstanding. But there was no picture. He turned idly towards 'The Complete

112

Home Physician' section and the book fell open of its own accord to the entry on stammering. Not really surprising as he had consulted it scores of times, chiefly to try and find reassurance from the last rather inconclusive sentence, which said: 'The sufferer must be taught to have confidence in himself, and he must also ensure that his general health is kept to the highest level.' And that was it: you were still left wondering if and when your stammer would actually disappear. He knew the whole piece by heart: nervous individuals, nervous trouble in the family, the particular difficulties with labial p's and b's and all the rest of it. He could have added that being French solved the problem entirely, at least when it was safe to be so.

Morley looked at other nearby entries to see what other people had to put up with. There was spinal curvature and squint. Squint. The rent collector had a squint, and whenever he heard his mother and Big Gwen talking about him, which was often, his mother would always end up by saying, 'Poor little sod,' or 'Poor little bugger,' but only after they had had a jolly good laugh. 'The remedy,' said the article, 'is to make the defective eye function normally by suitable glasses and to cover up the better eye for periods and so force the defective eye to work.'

He turned back a page and saw 'SPERMATORRHŒA – see NOCTURNAL EMISSIONS'. That struck a chord. Feverishly, he looked up the second entry and read, 'The occasional nocturnal emission of semen may be considered quite normal and the resultant loss of vitality only a temporary condition. If emissions become frequent, however, a doctor should be consulted, and he will usually prescribe a sedative such as bromide. The problem, though, is best dealt with at source by encouraging a healthy state of mind with an emphasis on games, sports and absorbing hobbies.'

Loss of vitality and the need to see a doctor made him feel uneasy but, these considerations aside, nocturnal emissions sounded right. He knew what the words meant but, to be quite sure, he checked them in the dictionary section of the book. 'Giving out, sending forth, discharging.' *Discharging!*

113

And at night! It described it *exactly*. Well, apart from the fact that he sometimes did it during the day. It did go on a bit about *curing* the condition: strange – he had not, in spite of it being a Mortal Sin, seriously thought about stopping. Still, the main thing was to get it confessed. 'Pray Father, give me your blessing for I have sinned. It is six weeks' – no, five if he went this coming Saturday – 'since my last confession. I had nocturnal emissions about . . . a hundred times. Oh, no, not since my last confession, Father, I was doing it before that but at that time I didn't know it was a sin.'

Yes, he would definitely go to confession this coming Saturday. He looked forward to the enormous relief he would feel on coming out of the confessional. Relief such as he had never experienced before; relief perhaps so strong that he would not feel like doing what he did again. God had been merciful, had directed him to pick up *Monroe's Universal Reference Book*, had mysteriously arranged for it to be on the table. He awkwardly offered his thanks then said a hesitant Our Father, again unsure whether it was really proper to do so while he was not in a State of Grace. His last thought before falling asleep was the consoling one that even if he did do it again after next Saturday, he now knew what it was called, and later confessions would be much less of an ordeal than this coming one.

# Chapter 13

Senior 2A was doing general science. Morley and David Meyer shared a book called *Senior Science Two*. Part of their task was to copy an outline drawing of a human body divided into five unequal parts to represent the proportions of its chemical make-up. The area representing water, the chief constituent, occupied the head, arms and trunk of the figure. Next came protein, filling the upper legs; then fat, filling the calf areas; carbohydrates, the ankles and most of the feet; and lastly 'others' – a mere two per cent – the toes.

A previous scholar had added a further section, an area above the legs which he had entitled spunk. Between the figure's straddled legs he had drawn an enormous prick and balls.

Working with a blue pencil, Morley included these in his drawing to amuse David and impress him with his audacity.

Mature David was suitably impressed. He gaped in astonishment. 'Hey, Morley, you can't rub coloured pencil out. I'd have thought you'd have known that.'

Morley frowned as if not understanding. He took his exercise book, held it at arm's length and slowly brought it to within a couple of inches of his eyes as if he had difficulty in focusing. 'Well, looks all right to me,' he said seriously, 'and she said to d-draw it just like it is in the b-book.'

Of course, Morley had had plenty of practice in rendering

rude drawings innocent and it was an easy matter to lose the vulgar additions by shading the whole background in the same blue pencil. He proceeded to do this, and David punched him gently in the ribs, saying, 'You're a bit of a wag, Morley.'

Morley felt light-hearted. The anxieties of being identified by the little boy's mother in assembly and when filing out afterwards were almost forgotten. Now at twenty to twelve it seemed increasingly unlikely that she would come at all. And as for the minstrel project, in his present mood it just seemed laughable, absurd. *And* he knew the name of what he got up to and was still firmly resolved to go to confession on Saturday. Not that he was particularly preoccupied with that either: when it did flash into his mind and cause a fluttering in his stomach, he told himself that it would be all over in four days – four days and fifty minutes at the most. His drawing was looking quite smart – and decent: a white, silhouetted figure set in a blue-pencil-shaded panel. He reinforced the outline of the figure with his pen while David looked on admiringly.

Above the muffled rumble of Senior 2C, Mr Preen's voice came loudly over the wall: 'Well, I can't see any difficulty, Geoffrey. Water *is* liquid; that's why I wrote liquid water on the board.'

Morley divided up his outline figure to show the proportions of its chemical composition – leaving out spunk – drew the arrows and wrote the labels, water, protein and the rest, in a fancy script of his own design.

David said, 'Wow, that's neat. Will you do mine like that, Morley?'

Morley took David's exercise book and did an even better version of the script. He felt generous, expansive, quietly excited. Tonight, he was going to go to town and be French. French all the time – not just when trouble threatened. He smiled to himself, savouring his secret. He had hardly stammered at all since assembly. *Monroe's Universal Reference Book* was right: confidence was the thing. Even just thinking about being French made him feel confident. Life was looking promising.

116

Mr Preen next door was saying, '*Solid* ice? Ice is always solid, Geoffrey. No *need* to say *solid* ice.'

'Er, yes, I see what you mean. But with ice we don't say solid. We're using scientific language this lesson. The language of scientists. What *scientists* call these things.'

'No, they're not mad at all, Geoffrey.'

'*Geoffrey!*'

Morley gave David his book back and resumed his own work. He carefully wrote the title, 'Chemistry of the Body', in roman lettering.

There was only mild interest when the secretary, Mrs Crosbie, came into the room and had a brief word with Miss Pryce, but Morley felt himself going rigid.

Miss Pryce stood up, looked round, then beckoned Morley. 'Will you come out here, please, young man?'

Morley seemed to have lost the ability to stand. He made a desperate effort and clumsily got to his feet, barking his shin on the metal leg of the desk. His heart thumped painfully. The classroom looked oddly remote, almost blurred. The coming interview with the headmaster, and probably the little boy's mother, rushed through his head.

Yes, he had been there. No, it wasn't him. He was just going home from school. Then Eric Beswick had caught up with him. Eric Beswick had said all the rude words. No, he hadn't said any rude words at all.

No, he hadn't tried to stop Eric. No, he hadn't walked away, well, because . . .

Yes, he was ashamed. Yes, he was disgusted. No, Eric Beswick wasn't really a friend; he was older, in 3B, somebody he talked to because, well, he lived in the same road but . . .

Morley was at Miss Pryce's desk. In his wretchedness, his red lumber jacket and sticking plaster made him feel particularly foolish and conspicuous.

'Now,' she said, giving him an envelope, 'this is an extremely important message for Mr Grant in the gymnasium. Say, "I am sorry to intrude, Mr Grant, but I have an important note from Mr Church." Think carefully before you speak and then speak – slowly – and – distinctly.'

Morley stood outside the classroom, his chest still hammering, not quite knowing whether to feel relieved; trying to adjust to the change in circumstances. How did Mr Grant fit in to all this? He slowly made his way to the gym, full of uncertainties. Then all became horribly clear. This was such a serious matter that the headmaster had asked Mr Grant to deal with it. It was obvious: Mr Grant, although very fair, was one of the most expert caners in the school. The instructions for his punishment and the reasons for it were in the letter he was carrying.

Terror-stricken, Morley tried to remember what he had planned to say. Wasn't him. Had just happened to be there. Eric Beswick said all the rude words. Eric Beswick wasn't a friend, just somebody who lived in the same road . . .

*But Perky Beswick would be there as well!* Waiting to receive *his* punishment. How on earth could he say it was all Perky's fault in front of him? Even if he dared and his story was believed and he escaped punishment, Perky would make his life a misery afterwards and tell all his mates in the road. He could see the scruffs gathered round the pig bin, their jeers and taunts . . . He would just have to take his punishment. There was nothing else he could do. He squirmed as he thought of endless days of reliving the shame afterwards. And his mother's pursed lips and long, angry silences – she was sure to find out. Although his father was always being belted at school: he used to joke about it, almost boast. But this was somehow different.

'Over here, lad, if it's me you're after.'

Morley hadn't seen him, his view obscured by one of the brick stacks which stood all over the senior department site.

Mr Grant was outside the gym, conducting his lesson through an open window, a cigarette in his fingers.

Morley approached, resigned to his slaughter and, shaking, handed over the note.

Mr Grant took a long drag on the last bit of his cigarette, flicked it away and strode towards the entrance to the gym, opening the envelope and reading the contents as he went. Morley followed.

'What do they think they're playing at? That's the second bloody fixture they've cancelled. Sorry, lad,' he said, noticing Morley trailing him, '"scuse my French. No, there's no reply.' He waved him off.

'These are *both*, eur, sreepenny pieces, *madame*?' asked Morley, apparently puzzled, as he pointed to a new bronze and an old silver threepenny bit among the coppers he had spread in front of the cash register in Lyons.

'That's right, duck,' said the cashier. 'It comes to seven-pence, so we need one of them, that's a penny, and both them threp'ny bits. They *look* different but they come to exactly the same thing. And it's all money, in't it, duck?'

Morley frowned as if making an effort to understand, then smiled. 'Ah, *oui*, yes, *madame*, all is monay. *Merci*, thank you.'

As he turned with his tray, deciding where to sit, he had the satisfaction of hearing the cashier say, 'Always got such nice manners, in't they, Molly?'

'Who have?' said a voice from somewhere behind the counter.

'You know, foreigners.'

Confident again in his lumber jacket, and wearing a new piece of sticking plaster, Morley took his tea and cakes to a seat by the window.

He had been too late for the Art Gallery, and at the last minute the grand exoticism of the Kardomah in Corporation Street had unnerved him. Here in Joe Lyons he was on more homely, familiar ground. He had been here several times with Micky Plant and, many years ago, his mother. But this was his first unaccompanied visit and he was very pleased with the accomplishment.

He had managed to get some quarter imperial cartridge paper from the Midland Educational – although again, no watercolours. He had even dared to persist a little: 'You maybe have some undeur the counteur?' But the assistant had looked offended and said that they didn't do that sort of thing in *this* country. Then he had been to Lewis's and asked the way to Pets' Corner, even though he knew where

119

it was, just to exercise his being French. He had also quite unnecessarily asked a policeman and a young woman the way to Lyons in Colmore Row.

His thoughts returned to the events of the morning. The relief of not being punished had kept his spirits high ever since. And he had been so unusually talkative and stammer-free all afternoon that he had even fleetingly considered not being French for his evening's adventure in town. At the same time he cursed himself for his tendency to jump to conclusions. Just because Miss Pryce had used him as a messenger to go to the gym, he had immediately assumed that it was to do with the little boy. Why? 'Because you never stop to think, duck,' said his mother inside his head. He remembered that Nigel, the more intelligent of the boy sleuths, was always cautioning his slower chum, Dick, to remain cool, to observe and analyse before rushing in to action.

He made a game of it. He half-closed his eyes and went back to his classroom of the morning: the restrained chatter, Mr Preen's voice coming over the wall, David Meyer sitting next to him, Micky Plant, near the front, still withdrawn. But now he is a Nigel-like Morley, unruffled, quietly observant, analytical. Mrs Crosbie comes into the classroom. He casually looks up from his work. True, he is still half-expecting the little boy's mother to come in with Mr Church. But remember, this is Mrs Crosbie, who comes in nearly every day: it's hardly likely that *she*'s been sent to identify him. Well, how could she? You have nothing to worry about. All is well.

But what's that note she's got with her? God, a list of all the boys who live in Woods Park Road. Obvious, that's where the woman saw you. The headmaster has already checked all the other lads who live in the road; but as you live near the top, number 208, you're at the end of the list so that's why Mrs Crosbie has taken until nearly dinner time to get to you. Or the woman saw your brace and the note says, 'Send any boy in your class with a brace to me at once.' Or Perky has already been identified and snitched on you or told Reg Kelp or Reg Nolan and they've snitched . . .

Morley found that his head had dropped into his hands, his temple was throbbing and his hair was wet with sweat.

'Are – you – all – right – duck? Would – you – like – some – water?'

It was one of the Lyons' ladies; she put down a glass of water. Beyond her, he could see the cashier looking anxiously towards him.

'N-No, er y-yes, *oui, madame, s'il vous plaît, merci.*'

The relief was slower in coming this time. But when the two old ladies opposite, who had been gawping at him for the last several minutes, eventually left, some of his earlier humour returned. He resolved that from now on he would *force* himself to remain calm and collected when difficulties or danger threatened. He looked expectantly around the teashop, hoping that something might suddenly happen so he could put it to the test. But Lyons seemed an unlikely venue for an armed robbery, a riot or someone suddenly running amok. He cautiously went back to the morning's events – keeping his eyes open this time. Of course! Miss Pryce hadn't even chosen *him* as a messenger. She was beckoning to David Meyer. She always chose David to take messages. But Morley had caught her eye instead and she hadn't bothered to correct the mistake. He could now even recall her hesitancy and then the subtle shrug when he got out of his seat. What a bloody fool he had been: all that grief he could have been spared! But he would learn from his mistakes.

He finished his second substitute-cream bun and went out into a street thronged with homeward-bound office workers and bathed in the golden light of a sun half obscured by the Town Hall. He felt cautiously optimistic. School tomorrow seemed a not unpleasant prospect; from now on things would be better. He would even be cool and collected when confessing to his Mortal Sin. Or if he couldn't manage that, at least, as soon as it was all over.

# Chapter 14

Miss Pryce was absent the following morning so Mr Preen had to take 2A as well as his own class for arithmetic. He wrote problems on each of the two rooms' blackboards, then stationed himself in the doorway of the dividing wall and tried to keep order in both. But as the noise grew louder and the screwed up pieces of paper and other missiles flung back and forth over the wall became thicker, Mr Preen sent somebody into the gym, which was equipped with blackout curtains, to see if it was free.

Morley whooped delightedly with the rest when Mr Preen announced that they were going to see films for the rest of the lesson.

'Now going to the pictures, as you call it,' began Mr Preen when the classes were more or less settled on the floor, 'doesn't *have* to mean watching cowboys and Indians, gangsters, war, er, films or even strange ladies in bathing costumes singing and dancing on the wings of aeroplanes; interesting and entertaining as these films might be. No, there are other subjects just as interesting; fascinating subjects that film can bring to life for us. Well, of course, some of the things are already alive, er, already but, well, however . . .'

Morley, who had heard it all before, was paying scant heed to the content but studying Mr Preen's flat, nasal voice and wondering if he could improve his impersonation of it.

'Now let us consider our daily newspapers.'

There were murmurs of protest and groans: he was going to show them *From Forest to Front Door*. Again!

Mr Preen continued undeterred. 'They're so familiar, aren't they, that we are inclined to take them for granted. How many of us, I wonder, realize the long, complicated journeys and the complicated technical processes that they have to go through before they drop through our letter boxes, that is to say, from the time when they, er, weren't newspapers – when they were something else.'

The smell of feet in the gym grew stronger and the audience more restless.

'"Oh yes," *some* of you might say, "we understand all that, Mr Preen, we *know* that newspapers don't just happen, we *know* that they don't grow on trees." Well, I'm going to surprise you.'

'In a strange sort of way, they *do*!' Morley said, fingers pinched on nose.

'In a strange sort of way, they *do*!' echoed Mr Preen.

There were some splutters of laughter from those immediately around Morley, and David dug him in the ribs.

Morley felt a moment of triumph, then was alarmed at his temerity, and wondered if Mr Preen had heard. But Mr Preen was droning on.

At last, *From Forest to Front Door* was clattering on the cinematograph. It opened with shots of trees being felled with a check-shirted lumberjack shouting silently through cupped hands. 'Timb-e-e-er!' explained a caption set in a decorative border. The quality of the film was typical of all Mr Preen's curious collection: old-fashioned, grey and grainy. This one, however, was enlivened by a white vertical line which capered joyfully at the left-hand side of the picture.

Morley watched the antics of the line until almost lulled to sleep. For several moments, he was at the top of the climbing rope again, marvelling at a new, thrilling sensation flooding the whole of his being.

He came to with a guilty start and sought out in the gloom

123

the climbing rope which had caused that sensation, now neatly strapped to the wall with the others. He thought of his Mortal Sin. Then, more particularly, the means he would have to employ for getting to confession.

He gave the problem his full attention. He and his mother went to confession fortnightly on alternate Saturdays. As this coming Saturday was not his usual one for confession, he was very aware that a sudden announcement that he was going would make her suspicious and prompt awkward questions. His only plan at present was simply to go at half past eleven, and hope to avoid his mother, who usually went at half past ten – although he wasn't sure whether this could be relied upon. It was risky: their paths might cross, or somebody might see him and happen to mention the fact. He smiled at the irony: last week he had pretended to go to confession and had gone to the Ickley Hills; this week he would have to pretend that he was going to the Ickley Hills or somewhere, so he could secretly go to confession.

He glanced at the screen. The felled trees had now become paper pulp.

Why not simply come straight out with it and tell his mother that he was going this Saturday because, because . . . he had to go to the library in Upfield and might as well go to confession while he was there? But it would be so unusual, she would smell a rat. He had to go this week because the Saturday after . . .

From his post by the cinematograph, Mr Preen was explaining the process of the Linotype machine being operated on the screen by a shirt-sleeved, moustached man in a stiff collar.

Because the Saturday after, Mr Preen was going to take a group of pupils to town to see how newspapers were printed. But then she would accuse him of putting his trip to town first and his religion second. And question his sudden interest in newspapers. Art. That was more like it. With a more subtle approach.

'You know Mr Ross-Armitage, Mom, that old chap that takes us for art? Well, he's organized this trip to the Art Gallery

124

in town to explain about the pictures and that, just for those interested in art and those who might go to the Art School. Might be useful and that.'

'Mm, that's nice, duck.'

'Well, he was doing this list yesterday and I had to tell him I couldn't go.'

'Oh, why shouldn't you go, duck?'

'We-e-e-ll, it's on a Saturday, the one after next: you know, my Saturday for confession.'

'Well, duck, you know I'd *like* you to go but you can't really miss confession ... The Saturday *after* next, did you say? Well, what's to stop you going to confession this week, then?'

He went over it again. It seemed flawless. Even if his mother didn't make the hoped for suggestion, he could, very gently, make it himself.

On the screen, with the white line still dancing faithfully alongside, a newspaper boy in old-fashioned cap and breeches was walking jauntily along a gravelled drive like a speeded up mechanical toy. As he shoved a newspaper through the front door of a handsome villa he turned self-consciously towards the camera and mouthed, according to the caption which followed, 'All the latest news every day.'

The audience jeered good-naturedly.

The next film was *Holland's Watery Highways*. Although he had seen it before, Morley's interest quickened, as Ron, his uncle, had recently said that was where his dad's regiment was. But in the middle of Mr Preen's lengthy introduction, the bell went for playtime.

Morley continued to avoid the little boy's house. This afternoon, he took his now familiar roundabout route along Marshfield Drive. And there was Micky Plant coming out of his house.

'W-Warrow, Micky,' said Morley tentatively. It was the first time he had spoken to him since Sunday.

'Warrow,' said Micky shortly.

Morley tried to think of something well-distanced from

125

coal houses and belt-wielding fathers. 'F-Finished that victory shield then, Micky?'

'Naw.'

'Not done anything else then, pictures and that I m-mean?'

'Naw, nothing to speak of.' His eyes didn't seem to be looking at anything.

'Good about Miss P-Pryce b-being away this morning? Missing arithmetic and that?'

'She's away every month on Wednesday mornings. Don't suppose you'd notice. We had that student last time, then Mr Church a couple of times, Dai Davies and, oh, I don't know.'

'Oh yeh, course, I remember. Just didn't realize it was a regular thing.'

'She told us.'

'Must have forgot.'

'You would. She goes for a check-up somewhere, eyes or something.'

'Where to?'

'God, *I* don't know. D'you think I follow her around or something?'

Morley seached for another topic. He saw Saturday afternoon sparkling clear and bright: it would all be over by then. 'What you doing S-Sat–'

Micky turned to him, frowning. 'What are you doing coming this way to school, then? And what's that plaster?'

'B-Been coming this way, since Monday, well, Monday afternoon. And I hurt m-my head on our –'

'Why? It's a much longer way round for you.'

Morley shrugged, then saw an opportunity. 'Well, you know, thought I might bump into you.'

'Oh. Well, you didn't – till now. Why didn't you ring our bell, then?'

It had crossed his mind but Micky had looked so firmly uncommunicative all week that he had feared a rebuff. 'I was g-going to today. And I did yesterday as well, b-but you must have gone,' he lied.

'Oh . . . did you? Mm.' He looked a bit brighter. 'Heard the latest?'

They had reached the main road, which was streaming with school-bound pupils.

Morley eagerly gave Micky his full attention. 'N-No.'

'Shagger's away as well.'

Morley's spirits rose, then fell: he would probably be back by Friday. But he said, to keep Micky's attention, 'Has *he* gone for treatment an' all, then? God, if anybody needed b-bloody treatment, it's old Shagger. I mean, has he even ever done any r-real woodwork? God, remember –'

Micky was frowning at him. 'Who's telling this bloody story, anyway, Morley?'

Morley looked contrite, pleased with the 'Morley'.

'Yes, anyway, I dare say he *will* probably get some treatment all right.' This was a trick of Micky's to let things out a bit at a time.

'Oh?'

'But not the sort of treatment you're going on about.'

'No?'

'No.' He screwed up an eye and looked in the air. 'I'd say about, oo-ooh, four, five years. And hard labour.'

'Wh-Why? What's he done? Has he gone –'

'I'm telling you, aren't I? Listen.'

'Sorry.'

'I was late going home, *he*'s there today, changes his shift Wednesdays, so I hung around the shops a bit.'

Morley simply nodded: Micky was referring to his father.

'You listening?'

'Yeh.'

'Well, I saw these first-year kids who'd been in wood-work. Anyway they said, right at the end of the woodwork lesson, old Shagger goes barmy and lays into these other two kids in their class . . .'

It wasn't easy to hurry Micky in this mood. Morley tried a little goading. 'What's so new ab-bout that? He's always b-bashing kids, he had a go at me once, he –'

'Oh yeh, oh yeh! Did he break your wrist with a mallet? Did he stab you with a chisel? Did he put you in hospital? Did he break your nose? Did they fetch the coppers?'

Morley was elated: Shagger definitely wouldn't be there on Friday. 'God, I b-bet that's the first time old Shagger's ever used a chisel – or a mallet, in his life. Were the kids badly . . . ?'

But Micky wasn't listening. David Meyer and a tall friend from 3A were crossing the road in front of them. Micky hurried to catch up.

'Hey, Dave,' said Micky, 'this'll make you laugh. Shagger's started using the tools, at last.'

'Go on. What's he managed to make, then?'

'A mess! Started carving up some of the kids – literally.'

'You're kidding.'

'No, honest, he went berserk. Only used a mallet and chisel on them. Put two in hospital. They had to fetch the ambulance – and two coppers and a cop car.'

'Get out! Were they hurt very badly?'

'Bad enough. Could've been a lot worse if Grant hadn't come out the gym in the nick of time. Some kid fetched him. Neat thinking for a . . .'

Morley couldn't catch any more: they had turned in the school gates.

He didn't mind too much, his jubilation was too strong to harbour much resentment against Micky. He walked round the edge of the playground past unusually excited knots of pupils agog with the news, savouring his good fortune. Since September, the usual mid-week pleasant anticipation of the weekend had been spoiled by the anxiety of Friday morning's woodwork lesson. Last year, it had been on Monday afternoons and had added enormously to his dread of starting the week.

Morley had a clear memory of how eagerly he had gone into Mr Knox's wooden hut for the first time, filled with the hope that woodwork, like art, was something he might shine at. He had imagined the coffee tables, teapot stands and book ends that his mother would take more seriously than his art, and his father on his next leave would examine knowingly, with respect. But his hopes were short-lived.

'You don't talk, you don't run. You stand two to a bench, hands behind backs,' yelled Mr Knox. He was short, broad and ruddy-faced. His features were small and he had very little neck. He smelled strongly of beer and tobacco. Morley flinched when he caught his gaze.

Pencils, writing paper and limp, grey books entitled *Woodwork Practice I* were given out and the class was instructed to copy chapter one, including the illustrations. Mr Knox then gave them a challenging look, sat in his chair and buried his head in a newspaper. But even so, his presence was hardly less menacing.

The class worked silently, just occasionally exchanging glances, winks and shrugs. The room was dusty and smelled of linseed oil, damp and animal glue. From time to time, Morley took furtive stock of his surroundings. Large, unknown tools lay in racks or hung from pegs on the wall. At the back of the room was a large grindstone in a rusty housing and a glass-fronted cupboard filled with books and stacks of exercise-book paper. Near the blackboard was a coloured-pencil drawing labelled 'Halving Joint' and signed 'Shagger Knox'. Morley counted thirteen workbenches each with two vices. Of timber in the timber store – an alcove at the back – there was no sign.

For the rest of the morning and in the lessons that followed the pattern was the same: copying text and diagrams from the books, sometimes with an addition from the board. The class went through *Woodwork Practice I, II, III* and *IV*. When all four books had been worked through, they started all over again.

Mr Knox quickly established a reputation as a fearsome, unapproachable teacher, ever ready to respond with open hands, fists and the blackboard ruler to the slightest provocation.

Morley had been lucky, he had only been punished once. He and three other lads had been examining some G cramps hanging on the wall while they lined up for the playtime bell. Shagger had cuffed all of them. It was only a routine clout such as Shagger might dispense half a dozen times during a lesson. But Morley had relived it for days afterwards and had lived in nervous anticipation of another clout ever since. Or worse, being caned or hit with the blackboard ruler while the others watched. This had happened to about half the class. The odds were growing shorter, and Shagger even more quick-tempered. Soon it would be his turn to be called out to the front and made an example of. Only a couple of months ago, Shagger had beaten Alan Biddle across the shoulders, and then on the back of his legs so viciously that he had drawn blood. For sneezing!

It briefly occurred to him that, with Shagger gone, there would no longer be the feeling of glorious relief at the end of the lesson. But he felt that he could live with that.

He recalled the one or two lighter moments – although even these had been filled with awful tension. Once Shagger had invited the class to sit on their benches while he told them that there was no such thing as sawdust. This struck Morley as odd since he had just copied from *Woodwork Practice II*: 'Sawdust mixed with glue makes an effective stopping for small imperfections and nail holes in wood.'

'No,' he leered at the class, 'sawdust don't exist anywhere. If anybody can find me some sawdust, I'll give them five bob.'

Well, at least you won't find any here for a start off, thought Morley, half-afraid that Mr Knox could tell what he was thinking.

Then Micky Plant volunteered that he often got sawdust for his rabbits – from Kershaw's the woodyard in Redhill.

'No you didn't, lad. Oh no you didn't. There's no such thing as sawdust.' Micky looked as if he was about to protest and Morley was afraid that he might be caned for lying. But Shagger went on. 'Oh, no, lad, oh, no, what you went and got for your rabbits wasn't sawdust. What you got was *wood*dust. Stands to reason, lads,' he said to the others. 'It's the dust of your *wood*, not the dust of your *saw* what we're on about.' Morley was forced to marvel at his logic.

Later he had denied the existence of other familiar things. There were no such things as sandpaper, lead pencils or rulers. It was glasspaper you finished wood with and that definitely didn't have any sand in it. Lead pencils had no lead in them, it was graphite. And the only rulers he'd ever heard of were kings or queens: what you measured with was a rule – the 'er' didn't come into it.

Then there was the exceptional occasion after one play-time (David Meyer said later that he must have just heard that he'd had a win on the horses) when he again invited the class to sit on the benches, then asked, 'Any questions, lads? About anything?'

Morley had dozens. Was he a real teacher? Had he ever taught in another school? Was he barmy? How had he come by his queer name? And how did he dare write it on his things? Why did they have woodless woodwork lessons?

But now invited, no one seemed prepared to take the risk in case Mr Knox took offence at the question. Morley was equally afraid that he would take offence at their lack of response.

Mr Knox glared around the mute class. 'You think you know it all; no need to ask me nothing; all of you too clever, I suppose.'

He looked as if he was about to pounce on somebody. Morley's heart was beating wildly; if called upon, he would ask what sort of animals were used for making glue. But Mr Knox's eyes finally came to rest on Philip (Crapper) Paramore, who still sometimes suffered the nickname he had acquired after his little accident in bottom juniors.

Philip looked terrified. After a lot of throat clearing, he said, 'Please, sir, Mr Knox, sir, I think when our brother came to this school – a long time ago, before the war – I think, sir; they did a lot of writing, just like we do, sir – *more* I think, sir. But then, after – I think they made these sort of teapot stands, sir – and I think they took them home, sir.'

'Think!' repeated Mr Knox, incredulously. 'Think! The lad only thinks,' he sneered, jerking his thumb at Philip Paramore. 'He only *thinks* he's got a brother, that he only *thinks* come here, that he only *thinks* made a teapot stand, that he only *thinks* he took home. You should have been in the army, lad, like me. They would have soon sorted you out and stopped you only *thinking*. So now then, what's your question?'

Philip Paramore took a deep breath. 'Please, sir, Mr Knox, sir, will we be making – teapot stands – or something – one day, sir?'

The class held its breath, but Mr Knox said, 'You just in't ready yet, none on you. I'll know when you're ready. You're all too anxious, that's your trouble; you want to run before you can walk. You've got to learn all your theory first, get all that sorted out, then we'll see. Blimey, I'd look well giving you precious wood before you're ready. The quickest way to spile wood is to give it lads that in't ready.'

The unusual break was over. The boys got down from their benches and continued copying from *Woodwork Practice III*: 'French Polishing, Varnishing and Painting'.

The bell for afternoon school broke into Morley's thoughts. As he made his way to his classroom, he suddenly glimpsed God's Plan. He could almost see it in the form of a pattern. At the beginning of the Easter holidays he had truly *intended* to go to confession. He had even got as far as the church steps before realizing that he couldn't satisfactorily explain what he did. For this he had been *mildly* punished with a holiday filled with gloomy thoughts. But last Saturday when he had *no intention* of going to confession, the punishments had been much harsher. He counted them on his fingers. One: the Pinders' wireless trick; two: Micky's father's complaint to his mother and her anger afterwards; three: the little boy and the rude food and the hours of misery that had followed; four: the scare of being sent to the gym to be caned by Mr Grant. Oh, and the minstrel project.

But then, after *really* making up his mind to go this coming Saturday, God had not only relented but had rewarded him. The pleasant evening in town; Miss Pryce being away this morning. And now best of all: the end of Shagger. He almost danced the final few yards to the classroom. He stopped at the entrance. Things didn't quite fit. Nearly fainting in Lyons – he squirmed in embarrassment. Well, perhaps that was a little nudge to keep him on the right track. Then his father's promise of the Jerry souvenirs: that was on Monday morning, before . . . And what about the lads that Shagger had injured . . . And then Miss Pryce would have been away this morning anyway . . .

# Chapter 15

'He'd never a touched me,' boasted Reggie Kelp. 'If he'd a touched me I'd a knocked him flat, cut his ear'oles off, chopped his prick off, squashed his eyeballs in, jumped on his belly.'

'You and whose army?' jeered Reggie Nolan. 'You'd shit your pants if he just looked at you, you would.'

'Naw, I wouldn't. I in't never been frit of old Shagger.'

'Yeh, you was and I bet if he had a belted you one, you'd a blarted your eyes out and run home and told your mom.'

'Well he *did* belt me once, with the blackboard ruler, *really* hard, much harder than all the other kids and I never –'

Nolan whooped with glee. 'Thought he wouldn't dare touch you, Kelp, thought you'd flatten him, thought you'd chop his prick off and kill him and that!'

The Betts twins laughed, chewing gum glistening.

Morley knew what would happen next.

'Who d'you think you're looking at, *Morley*?' asked Kelp, kicking the pig bin viciously and adding to its many dents. '*Morley!* What a barmy name. I bet *you*'d be frit. A frit kid with a barmy name. *Morley!* I bet if old Shagger come at you, Morley, you'd ... you'd ... *maul* him!'

The Betts twins caught on. They grinned. 'Borley. Yeh, old Borley could *baul* hib to death! Like id that picture where that tiger cobe add bauled theb explorers to death.'

133

'I wouldn't mind mauling *her*,' said Nolan, looking towards Maureen, who had just come to her front gate. He hawked and spat in the pig bin. 'Yeh, I bet old Morley wouldn't be frit of old Shagger, more like old Shagger'd be more frit of old Morley.'

The others waited for him to explain.

'See, old Morley'd just open his mouth and old Shagger'd see that iron thing he's got stuck on his teeth and think it was old whatsit, old Frankenstein coming to get him.' He clutched at his throat. 'A-a-agh!'

They laughed, heartily because Nolan had said it.

Morley smiled tightly but felt the familiar painful stab of being the butt. And just when things were going well. Perhaps, though, it was another of God's nudges to remind him of his religious duties, and the teasing wouldn't last long. Please don't let things be spoiled, he appealed. I'm *definitely* going *this* Saturday.

'Hang on a bit, though, Morle,' said Nolan thoughtfully. 'You sure Shagger *din't* have a go at you?'

'No, no,' said Morley warily, 'only c-clouted me the once, o-oh ages ago.'

'It's okay, just that I seen you with one of them whatsits, them plasters on you the other day.'

'Qu-Quarry,' Morley said quickly. 'I was c-climbing up the quarry and this b-big rock came . . . come down and hit m-me on the head.' He was hoping his earlier less heroic explanation of the cupboard door hadn't somehow reached the scruffs.

'You dever had it od od Bodday bordig,' said the Betts twins, grinning, 'did you, Borley? We seed you.'

Kelp peered suspiciously into Morley's face. 'Funny it's all cleared up all of a sudden. Funny you can't see nothing there now. Funny sort of rock.'

'W-Well . . . it was only a . . .' Inspiration was deserting him.

But God answered his prayer. Nolan was in one of his periodic 'get Kelp' moods. He winked at Morley. 'Naw, Morley's all right, he heals up quick. If it'd a been you,

Kelpie, it'd took about a month. He heals up quick on his head 'cause he's brainier than what you are.'

Kelp said, 'Fuck off, Nolan.'

'No, serious, Kelpie, I'll prove it. What class are you in, twinnies?

'Bister Preed's.'

'Aah, but what's it *called*? What *number*?'

The twins looked at each other, then worked their little fingers into the backs of their mouths to release stuck gum. 'Two.' They paused. 'C,' they finished happily.

'See!' said Nolan. 'And what about you, Kelp?'

Kelp looked sullen and kicked the pig bin again.

'Yeh, don't like to say, see! But we know, don't we, lads? Yeh, Kelp's in old Davies's class. And what's old Davies? Teacher of all the dopey kids: 2D. And what about me? 2B. *Could* a been in the As but never bothered. But Morley's 2*A*. The only kid here in an A class.'

Morley reddened with pleasure and warmed to Reggie Nolan. He decided to leave while things were going his way and before Kelp could have another go at him. 'G-Got to go up the library, they're saving m-me this special b-book,' he explained. 'About cowb-boys and that,' he added, to suggest his taste in books was tough.

Out of sight in Eachley Lane, he remembered it was early closing – not that the scruffs would realize. He resumed his thoughts about God's Plan, which seemed much tidier, now that he knew Mr Knox's victims weren't badly injured. At playtime Mr Davies, who had been on duty, had dispelled most of the wilder rumours.

Eddie French in 1A had a sprained wrist, a gash on his head and badly abraded knees. His friend, Gilbert Hastings, had a bloody nose and several cuts and bruises. Most of the injuries, however, had been the result of the boys banging into workbenches and the workshop door, falling over the bricks and reinforcement rods that littered the site and into each other in their panic-stricken flight from a mallet- and chisel-wielding Mr Knox.

Nevertheless, Morley was forced to admit, they had still been

135

injured. Would God have inflicted even minor injuries on two innocent lads just to reward *him*? Unless, of course, the lads had to be punished for something *they* had done. That was it. Perhaps they'd been doing what he had been doing.

He went past the closed library as far as Hiller's shop, which was also closed. He walked back slowly, his mind now on his sticking plaster. If he didn't wear it at school tomorrow, his unblemished skin might raise questions among some of his classmates; Micky Plant would certainly make something of it – if he noticed. If he did wear it, he ran the risk of the scruffs seeing it at playtime. He decided not to wear it, but to rub where it had been to make it a bit sore, and hope for the best.

He turned into Woods Park Road aware that – should the scruffs notice – he was bookless. But they were playing football. Perky Beswick and Neil Gunn had joined them. It was a serious game: the pig bin had been moved about six feet from the lamp post and Kelp was in goal. No one paid Morley the least attention.

As Morley wiped his boots on the back kitchen mat he heard voices from the living room. Big Gwen. He liked it when Big Gwen came, it always lightened the atmosphere, although he hoped she had said nothing about the wireless trick. He went in. But it was Sister Twomey, sitting at the table opposite his mother. Between them was a pile of his drawings and paintings.

He cleared his throat. 'G-Good evening, S-Sister Twomey.' He felt a fluttering in his chest: had she come because he had missed two confessions?

'Ah well, here you are, so, er, young man. We were just admiring the fruits of this wonderful little gift you have,' said Sister, looking up from a sheet of Mickey Mouses, Donald Ducks and Plutos. 'The detail you have there is quite remarkable.'

Morley sat on the arm of the settee at a respectful distance from Sister. He relaxed a little, and reminded himself not to jump to conclusions: her visit was nothing out of the ordinary.

Sister's butterfly-like coif nodded with approval at a water-colour. Morley tried not to think of the bald head beneath the peculiar headgear. Joseph Kinsella from church had explained that nuns shaved their heads to show they weren't vain.

'Will you look at that now, that little twisting path going through the trees there; why, you could quite easily imagine yourself to be walking there yourself. Now is this a real place that you've painted, er, young man, or is it straight from that fertile little mind of yours?'

Noticing his mother's frown, Morley got up from the arm of the settee. 'A b-bit of b-both, Sister; it's b-based on the B-Bluebell Woods near the Frawley road.' *Only we call it the Spunkbag Woods, because that's where the Yanks do their tarts*, insisted a mischievous voice in his head.

'And was this little picture done entirely on your own, or did you get a little bit of help from your teacher?'

'Oh no,' said his mother, 'they're all done on his own – I think. Aren't they, duck?'

He nodded. How would she know, anyway? All his pictures ever got from her was a brief look and an expressionless, 'Mm, very nice, duck.' Though he knew that she wasn't above bragging about them to neighbours when it suited her.

Sister went steadily through the rest of the pile. Caricatures of Churchill, Hitler, Mussolini; half-timbered houses, a stone bridge, the Temple of Artemis at Ephesus copied from *Monroe's Universal Reference Book.*

'Would you believe, Mrs Charles, that I'm entirely without artistic talent myself? Why, I could not even draw a little straight line if it was to save my life, now.'

His mother hastened to claim that it was just the same for her.

Sister glanced at an officer of the Waffen SS, then at Morley's mother. 'Our Blessed Lord is very generous with his gifts and your son has been conspicuously blessed. But then each of us is at least blessed with some little gift. Though some of us fail to recognize the fact, or if we do are sometimes inclined not to use it properly.'

Morley felt guilt dimly stirring.

His mother said, 'Haven't you got some *other* pictures, duck? Where's that crib picture you did?' Her face was trying to convey something.

He understood: there weren't any religious pictures. And the only crib picture he could remember was a Christmas card he had made for May years ago.

He did his best to co-operate. 'I'm n-not sure. There's s-some at school and a few odds and ends in m-my reading books and that, but they're not, er . . .'

Before he could think of a way of stopping her, his mother had gone over to the dresser and taken down some of his books. She brought them to the table.

She flicked through pages of marginal drawings of German soldiers, women in fur coats and the interlaced initials of his name done over and over again. She tried another book: holly, fir trees, robins, tanks, aeroplanes, German military headgear. She picked up *Five Go Adventuring Again*. More fur coats, designs for a new type of rabbit hutch. Then she stopped at an ink drawing on a once nearly blank page beneath a chapter ending, frowned and turned the book sideways.

Morley knew it well. He had drawn it six or seven weeks ago – and confessed to it. It had originally depicted the standing up coupling of a naked man and a woman clad in a suspender belt, stockings and high heels. Fur coats would have been inappropriate disguises in this picture, so he had challenged himself to make it into something else. Bodies and limbs became gnarled tree trunks, boughs and roots. The woman's breasts became two of a string of melon-like fruits set among spiky leaves. He blacked out the couple's private parts, turning them into the mouth of a cave. Developing this theme further, he drew a jagged area of cliff face round the cave, two large boulders and a rock-strewn foreground. He didn't overdo it, though, stopping when he judged the original subject to be invisible to other eyes but still just intelligible to his own. He shaded it selectively using various hatchings and dots. The picture had a mysterious other-world atmosphere enhanced by the unintentionally ragged quality of the indian ink, which had spread slightly on the poor wartime paper.

Sister, watching his mother with polite interest, suddenly gasped then exclaimed, 'Why, will you believe that, Mrs Charles! May I?' She drew the book towards her. 'Now is that not quite remarkable? When you take just a brief little glance, there's nothing. Nothing but the empty grotto as the little Bernadette must have first seen it. But then, as you explore it further, you see the form of Our Blessed Lady taking shape. Her lips parted, about to address the little shepherdess. And look, you can even see a little glimpse of the girdle around her waist. But here, look, plain to see, the Holy Rosary weaving its way through everything, larger than life to emphasize its great devotional importance.'

She looked at Morley's mother. 'Now you do say the Rosary every night with, er, this young fellow, Mrs Charles. Yes, of course you do, confident that your little family will stay together if you pray together.'

Sister turned her attention back to the picture. 'I do believe that there is something else, over here, but very obscure. Ah yes, it's coming . . . yes, it's the face of Our Blessed Lord, very faint, yet seeming to look down with divine benevolence at the miracle he has wrought. Is that not truly remarkable?' She smiled broadly.

Morley looked at his mother, then at his picture. He wanted to laugh hysterically. Rush out and tell somebody. But who?

# Chapter 16

'Mr Knox was probably suffering from a condition that we sometimes call shell-shock,' said Mr Church from the platform.

There was a nervous titter from somewhere behind Morley. He composed his face to show it was nothing to do with him.

Mr Church raised his voice. 'Yes, some of you may well laugh but you are too young to understand. But I know what I am talking about. I was in the trenches in the last war and I understand only too well. I fought with men so badly shell-shocked that they were unable to fight. Some were actually shot. Yes, by our own side, for cowardice! Shell-shock can take many forms, though fear always comes into it. And was *I* afraid? you may wonder. Of course I was. Not shell-shocked, mind, but afraid. Brave men are always afraid: it's only stupid men who are not afraid. Yes, shell-shock can do strange things to a man. It often continues into civilian life. And then it might cause a man to do warlike things when it is no longer appropriate. It might cause him to imagine things that haven't happened. Take action against imagined enemies. But sometimes, in between, seem perfectly normal to everybody – even doctors. So remember that Mr Knox perhaps wasn't entirely responsible for what he did.'

There was another, much louder titter from behind Morley.

Mr Church frowned and scanned the audience.

Morley frowned to show that he was just as offended as Mr Church.

'Were you lads talking?' Mr Church thundered. 'Yes, you two, the twin lads.'

'Do, sir,' said the Betts twins.

'*I* think you were,' said Mr Church menacingly.

'Do, sir, it wered't us talkig, hodest, sir.'

Mr Church hesitated. 'Why were your mouths going up and down, then? Good grief, you're not chewing gum, are you? Out here,' he shouted, sweeping his finger from the twins to the edge of the stage. 'And you can get rid of that filth for a start off.' He addressed the rest of the school. 'If there's one thing I can't abide it's chewing gum. Where is it now?' he asked the twins.

They made a big show of swallowing. 'Gode, sir,' they said, positioning themselves at the edge of the stage.

He moved as if to clout them, paused and made them stand on either side of him. He gave them withering looks. 'Chewing gum – and in assembly. The cheek of it.' He turned to the hall. 'Chewing gum and cheek. *And* comics. And all from America. We could well do without those at Redhill School. Now it grieves me to say it, but the Americans have a lot to answer for . . .'

Morley thought about Russ. How he would always listen as if nothing was wrong when he stammered, and never attempt to finish sentences for him; as a result he rarely stammered now in front of Russ. And how when Percy Pinder had pointed out his brace, probably thinking that Russ had never seen one before, Russell had said, 'Why, half the kids in our neighbourhood had one of those some time or other. It's a good thing that you're looking after your teeth, Morley. Hey, one day when they're straight and you've got a bit more beef on you, you'll be knocking away the girls with a club!' And the ease with which he would say to someone he had not met before, 'Hi, I'm Russ, glad to know you.'

Morley tried it. He was relaxed, confident, right arm

141

extended. 'Hi, I'm Morle, glad to know you. Glad to know you folks. Yeah, that's right, Morle.'

Then he thought of the possible response. 'Come again. *Maul*, did you say? What sort of dirty bugger's name's that, then?' No, the next time, perhaps at the Art School, he would use his whole Christian name, but say it confidently. He glanced at his lumber jacket – Russ's gift. Only a few other boys in the school had anything close to it. He ought to start Russ's picture soon – the one he owed him for the jacket. He could start one tonight from memory: the old barn, but slightly changed and in a different setting, so it no longer represented the one in the Spunkbag Woods. On Sunday he could go with Micky to find somewhere really unspoilt, the sort of place he could show off to Russ, later, as part of the Real England. Or even Saturday afternoon – after confession. A nervous shudder shot through him; just two more days and a couple of hours.

He hadn't yet told his mother of the fictional visit to town with Mr Ross-Armitage. Last night after Sister had left, his mother had been agitated. It hadn't seemed the right time to talk about confession.

'. . . wounded, yes, wounded as much as losing an arm or a leg or being blind,' Mr Church was saying, 'so shell-shock might be described as an invisible wound, a wound you can't actually see, a hidden wound.'

Morley had never imagined his father shell-shocked. He had seemed too cheerful. No, of course it couldn't happen to him; not now, anyway, with the war nearly over.

'. . . officers are specially trained, and less likely to be affected. I was an officer, oh yes, worked my way through the ranks. I was a lieutenant a year before the end of the war. Nineteen seventeen, northern France. Yes, to keep sane it's a question of facing up to the worst that could happen, having faith in God, keeping your head . . .'

Morley looked at the Betts twins, apparently quite unmoved by their public disgrace. In their identical clothes they gave the impression of uniformed sentinels, though not very disciplined ones, mouths gaping, then smiling, turning their

142

heads in unison, and every so often chewing on non-existent gum.

Morley was consoled that others got into trouble as well as himself. Pleased, too, that it was the Betts twins: served them right after their contribution to his teasing last night. He imagined how he would feel if he was one of them, up on the stage. Looking down at all his classmates, the lads and girls in his road – the whole senior department – and Miss Pryce and the other teachers, all staring back at him. How could he avoid blushing? The smiles and winks and comments afterwards. Mr Grant in this afternoon's PT would say, 'Mm, you seem to enjoy hanging around in high places, lad.' And the changing room would echo with mocking laughter, Micky Plant's dominant. 'Making an exhibition of yourself like that!' he heard his mother say. 'Is that all the thanks I get for bringing you up properly? And after all I've done for you!'

He realized he wasn't up on the stage and smiled with relief. He wasn't too bad, he reminded himself: he was in an A class, good at art; he could, when he felt up to it, amuse people with his impersonations, which took a bit of nerve; and he could be French – who else would dare to do that? And when – if – he went to the Art School, people would see a very different, confident character. Of course, as soon as confession was over, he'd feel much more confident, anyway, *and* be in a proper state to pray that he would pass for the Art School. Tonight, then, he must explain away the change in his week for confession.

But that evening his mother was restless and edgy. Several times she seemed on the point of saying something and then apparently thought better of it. Affected by her mood, Morley found it difficult to concentrate on his drawing for Russ. Just at the end of the nine o'clock news it all tumbled out.

'Wasn't there a bit of trouble at school yesterday, duck? Didn't some teacher get aggravated about something? Wasn't somebody hurt?'

143

Morley nodded. 'Oh, yeh, I think there was a bit.' It was important to make light of it, although it depended on how much she knew.

'It wasn't anything to do with you, duck, was it? You weren't cheeky to anybody, were you?'

'No, no.' So that was it. She was worried he had been involved. Why? Usually she complained about his inability to stand up for himself. 'No, all it was, was this teacher goes a bit b-barmy and chases these kids. Wanted to frighten them a bit because *they*'d been cheeky and that. Mr Church said this Mr Knox got shell-shocked from when he was in the war. Cracked really, couldn't help what he done.'

'Did,' his mother corrected. 'But weren't they badly hurt?'

'No-o, not really. They'd fallen over a bit and the one kid had a nose bleed, s-so it looked bad.'

'Fancy a teacher behaving like that, I mean, it's terrible.'

'Well, he's just like them, those patients up at the Asylum. You know, you see them all the t-time and you don't get scared, do you?

'No, not those. But he's a teacher and Mrs Kelp said he was trying to kill them.'

'Mo-o-m,' said Morley, 'you say yourself you can't trust anything she says, and she's chased her own kids with a knife.' This was true. It happened when Reggie and his brother Ernie had stolen some money from under her pillow a year or two ago – it had been the talk of the road. 'No, this teacher goes a bit b-barmy and because he's a teacher, everybody naturally m-makes a big fuss, but that's all it was.'

She sighed deeply. 'No, I know you have to take things she says with a pinch of salt but . . . well, it was just that she said she thought she saw you with a sticking plaster over your eye and I just thought . . . just for a minute, that it might be connected with that teacher. Anyway, I told her that I'd have known if there had been anything wrong with you.'

Morley held his breath. He hadn't bargained for this. He tried to engross himself in his work.

'Ah well,' said his mother, going over to the sideboard. She straightened the runner and adjusted the ornaments.

144

She suddenly turned and faced him. 'There *wasn't* anything wrong with you, was there, duck? You *didn't* have a sticking plaster, did you?'

He could deny it outright – but that risked somebody else telling her. Safer to admit it. 'Well, er, yes, I did.' He shook his head and laughed while he struggled for an explanation. Door in shed again? Quarry? No, neither would do, he couldn't claim an injury which needed a plaster yet had completely healed in a couple of days. Anyway, talk of injuries worried her. 'No, look, Mom,' he said, thrusting his brow forward and hoping that the reddened area he had produced by vigorous rubbing in the senior lavatories that morning had faded, 'not a scratch, never was. It was . . .' He shook his head again and smiled ruefully as if at some embarrassing recollection. 'It was silly really, I s-suppose, but –'

'What do you mean, it was silly?' she said sharply. 'You weren't *pretending* you'd hurt yourself, were you? I sometimes wonder whether you're quite right, my lad,' she said, giving him a very searching look.

The reddened area *must* have disappeared: she had good eyesight.

'Oh, no, nothing like that, no.' Then it began to come to him. 'Well, our old art teacher, you know, M-Mr Ross-Armitage, brought his artists' oil paints in to show us. And he said that me and Mi – Meyer, David M-Meyer could have a go with them.' Better David Meyer, keep Micky Plant out of it. 'We did these pictures, only little ones, and we carried on in the dinner time for a bit – on our own, he t-trusts us.' That would please her. 'Anyway, I got this paint on my hand; I got most of it off. Then I came home, had my dinner, had a wash and I saw this purple paint, just over my eye, in the mirror. It must have got there off m-my hand or something. I tried to wash it off but it seemed to be in the skin, sort of stained. And d'you know what it l-looked like? Just like that purple stuff you stick on scabs and that, that st-stuff Reggie Kelp always used to have all round his chops.'

His mother's face cleared a little. 'Gentian violet, it's an antiseptic.'

'Ah yeh, that's it. Well, I didn't want to go to school looking like a scruff, did I? Anyway, it was getting late, so I just
s-stuck this plaster over it. When I got home, I got the paint
off with t-turps. Silly really.' And he grinned a little
self-consciously, as if ashamed at the absurdity of it all.

Morley breathed a sigh of relief as his mother went into
the kitchen. After a few minutes she came back and said,
'David Meyer, did you say? Isn't he that Jewish boy?'

Morley shrugged, 'I don't know about that, never thought
about it.'

'Yes, his father's got that men's outfitter's shop in Upfield.
Opposite Woolworth's. The older son serves in the shop; he
used to go out with a friend of Beryl Pinder's.'

'Y-Yeh, I know, but what's wrong w-with –'

'Oh, nothing. Nothing at all. *I*'ve got nothing against them.
I just wondered . . . that's all.'

She went back into the kitchen, still looking anxious.
Morley decided that any discussion about changed Saturdays for confession would have to wait.

# Chapter 17

Without woodwork, Friday had been pleasant and novel. Up until morning play, the boys in 2A had joined Mr Davies's class in the main school and were allowed to do anything they liked provided it was useful and they did it quietly. After break they had gone into the gym with 2C to see *The Amazing Story of Starch*, *Guilty Chimneys* and Mr Preen's new film, *Modern Marvels 3*, which sounded promising but turned out to be an account of the versatility of shale.

Now, at nine o'clock in the evening, with all the distractions of school behind him, thoughts of unconfessed Mortal Sin and the ordeal to come burned with painful intensity. His resolution to go to confession tomorrow had wavered only once, when his mother's strained face at tea time conveyed that this wasn't a good time to discuss anything, let alone changes in confession routine; and he had been briefly tempted to postpone it yet again. But after Frank had gone to the pub and the atmosphere had relaxed a little, the problem had been resolved with surprising ease.

'If it's confession that's stopping you, I don't see why on earth you can't go tomorrow. Might do you good to go two weeks running for a change,' his mother had said before he had even finished. It was as if she thought he lacked the wit for not thinking of it himself. She had gone down to Big Gwen's in a good mood.

147

It should have been bliss: Friday night, on his own, with five new sheets of quarter imperial cartridge paper. But he couldn't settle. His breathing was erratic, his stomach kept tightening and he kept finding his legs wrapped tightly round the legs of his chair. Every so often, he unwrapped them and planted them firmly on the floor. Mr Church had said it was important to be properly balanced and 'grounded' when you needed to concentrate on something important.

Morley was continuing with the drawing he had started last night, a scene based on his memory of the derelict barn near the Motor Works. But he was having problems with the end section of the building. Here were well-worn stone steps climbing in two right-angled flights to meet a battered door set near the apex of the roof. These were the features that gave the barn much of its picturesque charm. But Morley's perspective looked exaggerated and unconvincing. He had used his rubber so much that the paper was becoming grubby and thin; not much good for the watercolour he had intended to apply later. Nevertheless, he persisted – mainly to keep thoughts of external emissions at bay, for he had almost decided that the work was a failure.

The announcer on the wireless was describing how jubilant American troops advancing from the west had finally met equally jubilant Russian troops advancing from the east. The meeting had taken place on the River Elbe. All mixed up with thoughts of eye levels, vanishing points and constant verticals, came a mental image of thousands of soldiers, weighed down with weapons and equipment, thrashing about in the water, laughing, shouting, shaking hands. How did they manage it without drowning? he wondered distractedly. Why did they choose the river?

Then the announcer mentioned the railway bridge crossing the river at Torgau. Morley's wet thrashing soldiers turned into two thin, dry, rushing columns colliding in the middle of the bridge. Finally, his confused mind gave up struggling and he was back with external emissions. External emissions? That wasn't right. Shouldn't it be internal emissions – coming from inside? Although the emission was externally discharged.

He hurried to get a chair to reach *Monroe's Universal Reference Book. Nocturnal* emissions. Yes, of course, at night. He ought to write it down, though. He searched his pockets for his notebook before remembering that he had left it on his tallboy upstairs. He was about to tear a strip off the edge of the failed drawing to use instead, when his mother's voice said, 'What a wicked waste, spoiling that good paper. You could use the other side of that, and there's you always mithering for clean paper.' Yes, he could use the other side for sketching: it would be far superior to the thin lined paper of his Reporters' Notebook. On the way home from confession he could use it to make an on-the-spot sketch of the barn steps and later have another shot at the whole subject on a fresh sheet of paper.

'On the way home.' How wonderful that sounded. Again, he had a brief flash of the blessed relief he would be feeling walking from Upfield, through the allotments, through the edge of the Spunkbag Woods and sitting down to draw the barn with a clear, uncluttered mind. He carefully folded the paper – drawing innermost – so that it would fit into his jacket pocket. Along the top he wrote, in capitals, NOCTURNAL EMISSIONS, then rubbed it out and wrote the words backwards with two unnecessary spaces, just in case. He read the result a couple of times, forwards and backwards: SNOIS SIME LAN RUTCON. Satisfied but shaky, he put the paper into his lumber-jacket pocket and buttoned it up, ready for tomorrow. In about fourteen hours it would all be over.

When unencumbered with the need to remember, Morley's memory functioned perfectly. He knew by heart all the printed matter on Swan Vestas, Camp Coffee, Kellogg's Corn Flakes and HP Sauce – including the French translation – and the conditions of tenancy in his mother's rent book. At odd moments, long passages from *Tom Sawyer, Huckleberry Finn* and *The Mystery of Swallings End* floated effortlessly into consciousness. But ask him to get a half-pound of sugar and a quarter of marge, learn a few lines for a play or the answer to the simplest catechism question and his mind struggled like a trapped animal.

So it was with nocturnal emissions. He had studied the term written on the back of his failed barn drawing several times on the tram and twice as he walked the two hundred yards to the church gates. And although he had proved that he could easily repeat it without looking at the paper, he was afraid that inside the confessional it would either desert him or a different phrase would leap into his mind. Referring to the paper while in the confessional didn't seem right somehow, and also the priest might see him in spite of the curtain. He needed to brand it into his mind. *Noc*turnal, *noc*turnal, he recited as he walked along the curved drive to the Church of SS Peter and Paul, not *ex*ternal, not *in*ternal, *noc*turnal. *Noc*: think of knock. Think of it as a picture: his hand knocking the knocker of his front door – at night. To see if the trick worked, he forced his mind from the problem for a few moments and concentrated on the brick belltower of the church. He returned to his image: hand knocking front door, knock, nocturnal: still there. Nocturnal emissions.

As he approached the church steps, however, he couldn't resist one last look at the folded paper.

The church door opened and Sister Twomey emerged, clutching a big black umbrella.

Morley blushed. He tried to shove the paper in to his back pocket but the pocket was too small. He stood awkwardly, hand holding the paper behind his back.

'Why, hello, er, young man,' said Sister, joining him at the foot of the broad steps. 'We meet once again.'

'Y-Yes, Sister,' he said, trying not to think of his copulation/Lourdes picture and Sister's bald head.

'Ah, well, is it not strange now, months go by without our paths crossing and then twice it is in three or four days. I *have* seen you in Mass a few times, but' – she chuckled – 'you were always so quickly off. But then, perhaps you were rushing off to help your mammy with some little tasks around the house?'

'Y-Yes, Sister,' he managed to lie. He certainly did sometimes obey the priest's command, mostly politely ignored by the faithful, to 'Go, the Mass is ended' and sheepishly

150

slink out of the church with the people his mother called the weak-willed.

'And have you managed to produce any more little master-pieces since our last meeting, now?'

'N-Not really, Sister, just, er, a b-barn picture, only, er . . .' It was simply too complicated to explain. He clutched his paper even tighter.

A neatly dressed old man came out of the church and cautiously descended the steps on bowed legs. Sister said, 'You mind how you cross that main road, now, Mr Lenehan.'

'I will, now, Sister, I will, and God bless you.'

With Sister's attention on Mr Lenehan, Morley took the opportunity to transfer the paper to his lumber-jacket pocket.

'So.' Sister smiled. 'This, er, little barn picture, would it be sketched on that little bit of paper you have with you, there?'

'N-No, y-yes, Sister, b-but it's no good, it, it, went wrong, it –'

'Ah, I understand: the little artist doesn't want prying eyes to see his little mistakes, not even Sister's.' She chuckled. 'Ah, we all make little mistakes, now, but if you would prefer it if Sister did not see yours . . .'

Morley suppressed a sigh, unbuttoned his jacket pocket, unfolded the paper, picture side out, resignedly handed it over and tried to blot out everything.

'Well, young – ah, wait, I have it, *Crawley* – I have seen neater work that you've done but still and all, if Sister had done this now, she would think it a marvellous little achievement. But there is a little bit here that puzzles me.' She frowned and pointed.

'Th-That's where I had to keep rubbing out, wh-where I couldn't get the p-p-p-perspective right.' Morley was wondering morosely whether Sister would find a little baby Jesus in a little manger and three little wise men hidden in his tangle of corrections and re-corrections; and whether he should point out that she'd got his name wrong.

'And what, Crawley, will you do with this little sketch now that you have decided that it is a failure?'

Scared that she was going to ask if she could keep it, he

said in a rush, 'Well, I still need it. I br-brought it with me s-so I could go back to the b-barn later and get everyth-thing right and then do a new picture on a new p-piece of paper and use this as a sort of pr-prelim, prelim, rough . . .'

A handsome woman in a WAAF uniform approached, gave Sister a tight smile and disappeared into the church. With the force of a physical blow, Morley was suddenly reminded what he was here for. If he hadn't been delayed, his ordeal might have been half over by now.

But Sister seemed to have all the time in the world. 'Ah, so all your little problems are dealt with first, so it's only the final splendid version that you will be showing to your proud mammy. Is that how it is done, now?'

She began to refold the paper while Morley willed her not to notice his memory aid.

'Well, will you believe that? A little linguist as well,' Sister exclaimed, looking at SNOIS SIME LAN RUTCON. 'Now I wonder what language that would be. I know it is not Latin. And I don't think it can be French.' She shook her head. 'I'm afraid I will have to admit defeat. Ah, wait now, will you. *I* know, it's a little code. Ach, you lads with your heads filled with gangsters and war and spies. Is that not right, Crawley? And you wrote this up for a little friend to decipher? Or perhaps your little friend is challenging you?'

Morley nodded a lie, his agitation becoming almost unbearable. On top of this he had to make a superhuman effort to appear unconcerned.

There was some giggling from inside the church, which stopped abruptly when the gigglers emerged and saw Sister. 'Good mor-ning, Sis-ter Two-mey,' chorused three now straight-faced little girls as they decorously descended the steps.

'And have you worked out this little message yet, Crawley, from your little friend?'

Morley shook his head.

'N-No, n-not yet, Sister,' he lied again. He was prepared to lie further if Sister's next question was, 'And is your little friend a Catholic?' to which it would be easier to say yes. Though it would be still a lie if he said no, he reflected dismally.

But he was near breaking point; if he didn't get a move on, he might be too late for confession. And this time there was no feeling of relief at the prospect of postponing it for yet another week.

Morley's rather confused examination of conscience finished, he got up from the kneeler and sat down. He was sitting next to the woman in the WAAF uniform. He took a careful, sidelong glance. She was a warrant officer, he noted with approval. She smelled nice, had fair hair with a touch of grey and small crinkles around her eyes. She reminded him of a film star whose name he couldn't remember. She looked about the same age as Big Gwen.

In spite of his preoccupations, some automatic mechanism at the edge of his mind was already filing her image away for future reference. He wondered what she'd done.

Between her and the door to Canon Reilly's confessional was a woman with a nervous twitch. Just two more and then him. He shivered.

Two pews behind, four or five people were waiting to confess to the more popular, easy-going Father Smythe. Morley had almost changed his mind and joined them, but then decided that the canon's exclamation of outrage would still be preferable to the shame of Father Smythe's hurt silences.

The red light above the confessional went out and a serious-faced boy of about ten emerged. The woman with the twitch entered and the red light went on again. The WAAF, about to move along, turned to Morley and smiled. 'Would you excuse me, please?'

He blushed in awe and confusion. Her voice was cultured and as attractive as her appearance. He didn't know what she wanted, then realized that he was sitting on the strap of her bag. He mumbled something and leaped up. He knelt down again, trying to still his seething mind, hands clasped together so tightly that it hurt. Right, knocking the door. His hand on the knocker of his front door. Knock: nocturnal. But wait a minute, it could just as well remind him of an *ex*ternal door: external emissions. God, think of another door quick! Mr

153

Church's door in the main school. 'Headmaster' on a metal plate. An *in*ternal door, no. Forget doors. Knock . . . a shrine in Ireland; Wankie, a town in W. Rhodesia, chief industry coal mining; Wanne-Eickel, a town in Germany . . . Wank . . .

The twitching woman was coming out, after what seemed no more than a couple of minutes. In went the WAAF. Nice shiny stockings, shapely legs, part of Morley's mind recorded.

He slumped back in the pew, squeezed his eyes shut and tried not to think of anything.

There were sounds from the confessional but so low he couldn't decipher them. A continuous murmur . . . from the woman.

Then silence.

The murmur again.

Then Canon Reilly's voice, muffled but just discernible, '. . . both? At the same time?'

Morley held his breath. The woman's murmur continued, gently rising and falling, almost musical.

He was eavesdropping!

'What goes on in the confessional is a secret between just you, the priest and Almighty God,' Sister Twomey had said to the first communion class. 'So when you confess, keep your voice down but speak clearly. And if you are outside waiting to go in and you can hear what is being said inside, you must give a little cough, or give the pages of your missal a little rustle or make any other little noise to cover up the sound and distract yourself a little.'

Morley gave a series of little coughs but in between still caught Canon Reilly's muted, '. . . your own accord? You were not in any way forced . . . ?'

The musical murmur became so low he wasn't sure whether he was imagining it.

He waited for what seemed an eternity, crossing his legs into a tight double knot, until the woman came out. She looked composed but her eyes seemed intent on something distant.

There was a brief shaft of diffused light as Morley opened the door, then near darkness. He fumbled for the kneeler

154

and stumbled down on to it. He swallowed hard and tried to take a deep breath but his chest felt constricted. *This was it.* 'Pray F-Father, g-give me your b-blessing for I, I have sinned.' He gulped several times and made a halting Confiteor. 'It is f-five w-weeks since my l-last con-confession. I, I acc-ccuse myself of s-stealing s-some icing sugar, F-Father. Th-Three or f-four times. I, I'm n-not exactly sure.' So much for his determination not to stammer.

There was a long silence. Morley was about to repeat it, but the canon finally said, 'You seem to commit this sin with alarming regularity, my child. A sweet tooth, is it?'

Morley was startled: it had always passed without comment before. The only reason he confessed to it was to impress on the priest at the outset his scrupulous examination of conscience. Then he realized with a sudden shock that even if he *hadn't* stammered, confessing to the theft of the icing sugar had certainly given away his identity.

'Er, yes, F-Father, I s-suppose I have a b-bit.'

'And these were bags of icing sugar, or packets, is it, that you stole from the grocer's?'

'N-No, Father, n-no.' He swallowed hard. 'Only spoons, s-spoonfuls, Father. F-From our pantry. At home.'

From time to time Morley secretly made sweets: icing sugar, dried milk and cocoa mixed together with a little water, rolled into balls and allowed to dry. He got the chief ingredient, icing sugar, from the vast supply in the pantry. Two years earlier, May had given his mother twelve pounds of it. She didn't like to refuse it, but nor did she like to use it, because May's husband had acquired it and Ron, as everybody knew, was on the fiddle. His mother had iced just one cake with it before banishing the rest to the top shelf in the pantry.

It was really the uncertain moral status of the icing sugar which made taking it feel vaguely sinful: the small amounts of cocoa and dried milk, he decided, didn't count.

'And these spoonfuls,' said the canon, sounding grave, 'were they teaspoons, dessert spoons or tablespoons?'

'Er, not the very b-big ones. The m-m-medium ones, I think.' Morley was not well informed about spoon sizes.

155

This unexpected interrogation added frighteningly to his anxiety. What on earth was he in for when he confessed his Mortal Sin – Sins?

But 'Mmmmm' was the canon's only further comment.

'I d-day-d-dreamed in M-Mass. Three times. Ch-Cheeked my mother. T-Twice. Drew a r-rude picture in g-general s-science. Once. Missed –'

'Rude?' demanded the canon. 'A *rude* picture? Ah, but in science, you say? Biology, was it?'

'Er, yes, only th-they call it g-general s-science and I j-just –'

'If this is what you were being taught, then you cannot take moral responsibility for what you were asked to do.'

'B-But, Fath-ther –'

'Anything else, child? Anything more *serious*?' He sounded impatient.

'I told lies. Th-Though some of the l-lies were told to m-make people feel better, n-not t-to of-fend them. I, I don't kn-know how many times. Then I was with a b-boy who used s-swear words to a little boy and t-t-told him to repeat the words to his mother. *I* didn't s-swear but I didn't try and s-stop him – the big boy, I, I mean. Once.'

He was aware that he had deliberately said swear words rather than rude words to avoid the canon questioning him again. Would God think he was trying to mislead the priest by trying to lessen the offence? Was his confession already Imperfect? But there was no time to dwell on that; the real trial was yet to come. And now doubts about the authority of *Monroe's Universal Reference Book* began to assail him. Nocturnal emissions. They seemed to be things that *happened* to you – like a cold, not something that you *did*. All too often, books described a world different from the one he lived in, he thought gloomily.

'Anything else, child?'

Oh, God, eavesdropping. He would *have* to mention it. 'I, I, I overheard a b-bit of, er, somebody's confession, Father. I c-c-coughed and that b-but . . . er –'

'When?' snapped the canon. His silhouette behind the curtain loomed closer.

'J-Just b-before I came in, a few minutes ago, I, er . . .'

'Did you understand what was being said?'

'N-No, Father, I didn't hear m-much. Just two or three w-words.'

The silhouette became more diffused. Morley waited for a response but the following silence was so long that he thought that the canon had dropped off.

Frantically, he sought more sins to break the silence. What about the latest rude drawings he had done in his story books? No, he had confessed to those last time, and had not done any since. Prayers! 'And I m-missed my prayers s-s-several times. I can't rem-member how m-many . . .' He had an image of himself, inspired by countless films, waiting to make a parachute jump; it was almost his turn. He tried to hang back. 'And when I say th-them, Father, some-t-times m-my m-mind wanders off . . .'

He could still merely say, 'I do a rude thing,' but that was asking for trouble: the canon would pounce on it and ask him to explain. He recoiled at the terrible stammering shame of his explanation; if he *could* explain. 'Be a man,' said a voice not unlike Mr Church's. 'Don't panic, stay calm and stick to your original plan.' But he felt faint. Even kneeling, his legs were threatening to collapse. The confessional seemed airless, pressing in on him. It was his turn. The parachutist in front had jumped. Morley could see the dark ground, thousands of feet below. He was terrified of jumping into all that emptiness and just as terrified of not jumping. The dispatcher took away the hand restraining him from a premature jump and clapped him on the shoulder with the other . . .

NOW!

Was it I *had* or I *did*?

Be positive, *did*.

He scarcely recognized the breathless squeaky voice: 'F-Father, I, I d-did . . . n-noc, n-noc –'

'And it shall be . . . opened unto you,' finished the canon distantly.

'B-But, Father –'

'And equally, child, ask . . . and it shall be given to you.'

'But –'

'And seek . . . and you shall find.'

There was silence again. This time Morley was afraid to break it.

Then quietly and with unusual gentleness, Canon Reilly asked, 'Child, tell me, is *your* daddy away fighting in the war?'

'Er, yes, Father.'

'And your mammy: she is a good-living woman who waits patiently with faith – *and* faithfulness – for his return?'

'Y-Yes, F-Father, but –'

'It is good that there are such women.'

Relieved that the canon did not seem to know who he was after all – beyond the fact that he was merely the boy who regularly stole icing sugar – but desperate to confess now that he was so close, Morley raised his voice as much as he dared. 'But, F-Father, I did it a hundred times – m-more, th-this –'

'I know, child, I know, and you must continue to do so. Do it till it hurts, child. Storm heaven with your pleas if you want your daddy's safe return. Ask and it shall be given to you. Pray a thousand times and be sure that Our Blessed Lord will listen. And if it is in His divine will, your daddy will come back safe and uncorrupted by his sad experiences. This is a sad, wicked world, child, filled with temptation, but we must all be strong.'

'B-But, F-Father,' persisted Morley, 'you d-d-don't under, under, s-stand.' The effort was making him breathless. 'I, I d-did, I d-did . . .' He was pleading.

'Whisht, whisht, my child, calm yourself. Whatever is troubling you can confidently be left in the hands of Almighty God. Now you must make a really good Act of Contrition. For your penance say three Our Fathers, three Hail Marys, and a Glory Be. And, child, say a prayer for me.'

# Chapter 18

Morley sat on a front seat on top of the 144 Midland Red bus bound for Droitwich and May's. They had just passed the Plough, the last building in Redhill, and were now descending into a small oasis of unspoilt countryside in which the Famous Five might have roamed. On the right was an inviting, undulating landscape of small fields in a dozen different shades of green, sprinkled with clusters of farm buildings and isolated cottages, with Chadwich Manor and its lake set snugly in the deepest hollow. On the left were the densely wooded slopes at the beginning – or the end – of the Ickley range of hills. The environs of Birmingham were behind, hidden by the high skyline; the straggle that marked the beginning of Bromsgrove was yet to come.

Everything was intensely interesting. Morley turned his head from side to side and sometimes looked over his shoulder. Sheep grazing on a steeply sloping field all faced the same direction, except one, fatter than the rest, which was resolutely facing the other way. It reminded him of Fatty Yardley. He smiled. A boy, perhaps a little older than himself, a man's cap pushed to the back of his head, trousers tucked into wellingtons, was walking along a narrow field-path with a dog like Black Bob out of the *Dandy*. He was confident, you could tell by the way he walked; going about his own business in his own world, a world separate from

Morley's. A farm lad who in Enid Blyton's world would have called him *Master* Morley – at least if Morley had been one of the Famous Five.

The bus stopped outside a small square house with a window in each corner and a door in the middle. The chimney spiralled smoke above a triangular roof. A house such as you might draw when you were five. Red, white and blue bunting was strung under the bedroom windows and three Union Jacks fanned out above the door. There was a step-ladder near by, and an old man and a young woman in a turban stood back admiring their handiwork. The trimmings had obviously been left over from the Coronation: the middle flag bore a double portrait of the King and Queen and each of the white triangles of the bunting said 1937.

In 1937 he was five – and drawing houses like this. In the downstairs window was a card with 'WELCOME HOM' done in a not very skilled hand. A tree in the garden hid the rest. When the bus moved off, he craned his neck: 'WELCOME HOME BOB'. The next time he came this way, he would look out for Bob.

The bus rounded a long gentle curve between high hedges and the ribbon building began. Unusually, even this held his interest. That big house over there with the long sweeping drive, bay windows and brown half-timbering, well, he wouldn't mind swapping his municipal house for that.

Another house with a welcome sign: 'WELCOME HOME, RICHARD', done by a professional sign-writer by the look of it. Surely the forces weren't coming home already? The war wasn't over yet. Leave? No, more likely wounded. Richard with a leg missing, Bob with an eye gone – or blind. Then he wouldn't be able to see the sign; perhaps Bob was just scarred. He remembered the two soldiers in hospital blue outside the pub in Redwell, the one-eyed, terribly scarred one pushing his one-legged, one-armed mate in a wheelchair. He shuddered with horror, imagining a mutilated father. Or a silent father, face blank, all his energy gone like Harry Braithewaite, who sat outside the Asylum, victim of the last war and now of the Reggies' teasing. And Shagger Knox –

no longer responsible for his actions. He thought of himself, a boy with a brace and a stammer, with a legless, blind or crazy father to add to his problems. How would his mother cope? It was perhaps just as well that he was dead; killed on active service, a hero.

His mother had woken Morley at half past eight – much later than usual.

'Your dad's gone to heaven, duck,' she said, standing rigid, almost as if at attention, by his bedroom door. Tears sprang to his eyes but she was watching him closely and her look said, 'We'll have none of that.'

Downstairs, he didn't know how to behave: nobody close to him had died before. Until two or three years ago, it might have been all right to snivel a bit and be comforted by a then less tense mother, but at thirteen perhaps he should be comforting her. He had a fleeting impulse to put his arms round her and say something; though he didn't know what. He felt awkward; whatever he said would be wrong. The moment passed.

'How d-did it happen? Did he, er, die, er . . .'

'They never tell you. Just killed on active service, they always say. And I don't know anything else,' she said in a tone of finality.

Her lips were drawn tight, turned down more than usual. He knew better than to ask to see the telegram. He knew it was in her pinafore pocket, her hand clutching it; her last contact with her husband, his dad.

He noticed Frank's suitcase near the settee.

'I'd like you to go to May's for a bit until things are . . . settled.'

So that's what Frank's case was for. Big Gwen had borrowed theirs years ago and all his mother's attempts had failed to get it back. His relief was enormous – an escape from his mother's grief, no school, and May's. He could hear voices from the road, children still going to school, hurrying: it was nearly nine. Though curiously enough, Monday-morning school would have held no fears for him now. He

161

got up from the table and fumbled with the catches of the suitcase.

'You needn't look, it's all there,' snapped his mother before he could get the top open. 'Everything except toothpaste and your Lucozade – it was too big to go in and, anyway, it might have leaked. Have your malt every day; and if you feel you know what, don't forget your syrup of figs. Get yourself some more Lucozade or ask May to get you some. And don't just use their toothpaste: ask.'

Morley wanted to check if she had packed his art things but didn't like to ask: it wouldn't seem right being concerned about painting when your father had just died. How could he find out? He kept his art stuff in the dresser drawer. He went over to it, pulled it out, quickly scanned the jumbled contents. His new paper and the chocolate box containing his paints, brushes, inks, pens and pencils were gone. She *had* packed them. 'Oh ye of little faith,' he could hear Father Smythe saying.

'J-Just looking for my notebook,' he lied, rummaging round a bit longer for effect. 'I s'pose I'd better do a b-bit of school work: I only got fifteen out of twenty spellings last time. And my arithmetic . . .' Spelling and arithmetic seemed more appropriate in the circumstances. 'Ah, just remembered, it's in my p-pocket.'

He stood at the front door in his lumber jacket, wondering a little about its suitability, though his mother hadn't said anything. But then, he realized, she wouldn't. She would be far more likely to object to a black armband, or a black diamond sewn on to his sleeve. 'Just show,' she called these; and those who wore them 'shallow'.

She gave him a ten-shilling note and some change for the bus. He was delighted but careful not to show it.

'Be careful how you cross the road, duck,' she said. 'And be a good boy at May's and explain . . . what's happened. And if you're still there on Sunday, make sure you go to Mass – I don't think May goes any more.'

Her voice was lifeless. He was anxious to get away in case she broke down. She had never cried in front of him,

162

but he had sometimes heard quiet and anguished sobbing from her bedroom. He recoiled at the memory.

She hesitated before kissing him clumsily on the top of his head. He heard the door close before he had reached the gate.

The bus was approaching Bromsgrove. Villas, petrol stations, shops which would have looked more at home in a suburban high street, an electricity station, the Sir Walter Raleigh pub – not a country inn but a huge, recently built roadhouse – a breaker's yard, then a farm entrance. Morley had seen it before. Without its unlovely neighbours, it might have been the farm in *The Mystery of Swallings End*. He fixed his gaze there, head slowly turning as it got closer. He wanted a clear mental picture he could return to later and draw. He had only a couple of seconds: drive, rough track, barns, garden wall, gleam of pond, house with trees behind, lorry, a figure. His head swivelled right round and then the view was gone.

He felt pleasantly detached. A phrase Mr Davies had used at the time of *The Bishop's Candlesticks* sprang to mind: 'I am a camera'. That's just what he felt like. Apart from the mostly quiet, agreeable thoughts that accompanied whatever he was snapping, little else existed. The inside of the top deck of the bus with the changing landscape rushing by was the extent of life. His Mortal Sin, his Imperfect Confession, even the absurdity of the Lourdes picture, and all his other dismal preoccupations mysteriously left him alone. They weren't forgotten but . . . He waited for an appropriate image to surface. They were like unexploded bombs made safe: neutralized. He should always have been like this, he reflected, this feeling of living fully in Now. This is how you were supposed to be. Like Alan Ladd, Nigel the boy sleuth and David Meyer. And May and Mr Ross-Armitage and, it seemed, most people really, except his mother. The feeling wasn't entirely unfamiliar: hadn't he had it before? When? He shrugged and turned his attention to the beginning of Bromsgrove's long main street. A pub went by, the bus garage, two more pubs close together – the last the Queen's Head, where the bus stopped. He saw the driver get out and walk towards the lavatories beyond the wooden bus shelters.

He watched the progress of a woman hurrying up the street holding on to her pillbox hat against the occasional gusts of wind. She looked nice, a roll of chestnut hair below the hat, an indication of a shapely figure under the coat, nice legs. Surprisingly, there wasn't a flicker of arousal. She turned in his direction to check the traffic. Her face was little short of ugly: a tiny nose, thick glasses, lined forehead and almost no chin. The contrast between her face and the rest of her was startling. How strange of God, he thought, to have spoiled such a promising creation. She crossed the road and disappeared into a chemist's. Chemist's: Lucozade. He would remember to get some in Droitwich. He needed no persuasion to take Lucozade; it was like pop – only ten times the price.

Lucozade was the latest whim of his mother's, to give him more energy, she said. He had been having it regularly for the last month. Before that he had only had it two or three times when he was ill.

That was it, when he was ill. He felt well when he was ill. Or at least, he sometimes had this rare feeling of contentment and living in the present when he was ill. Not really ill with tonsillitis or racked with a bad cough or anything like that, but recovering from flu, say, or with just a slight cold. Lounging in the armchair, or lying on the settee with a rug over him, released from the usual need to steel himself to deal with people. But then, when people *did* call, he found he was able to function with ease.

Once Father Smythe came when he had flu, and Morley didn't dither or stammer at all. Until it occurred to him that the priest might think that there was nothing wrong with him, so he had to *pretend* to be his slightly awkward, hesitant self.

He was sure that he wouldn't stammer now, even if faced with . . . with . . .

The inspector coming on and finding him without a ticket! Now that was an idea to test his confidence. He took out his notebook, folded a page in half and tucked his ticket into the fold – just in case. He imagined the scene.

'I'm sorry, I can't find it' – searching calmly through his pockets. 'I must have dropped it coming upstairs.' (The conductor had issued his ticket downstairs when he was putting his suitcase under the stairs.)

'No, I assure you' – perhaps talking in a public-school accent like Nigel, the boy detective – 'I most definitely *did* buy a ticket. Check with the conductor if you like.'

'I am not in the habit of lying, or fare dodging, and I object . . .'

'Ah, ha, here we are' – finding it at last. 'Got caught in my notebook.'

Perhaps the inspector would touch his cap and say, 'Sorry, young sir, but we have to check. It's our job, you understand. I do beg your pardon.'

The bus started up and he became a camera again. The Post Office, the Red Lion, the *Bromsgrove Messenger* office, the Golden Cross Hotel, black and white buildings on the corner of St John's Street. A brief glimpse of the corrugated-iron market hall and St John's Church before they disappeared behind more shops. The street became narrow and then widened at the junction with Hanover Street where St John's Church came into view once more.

The bus was stuck for some minutes behind a brewer's dray waiting for a military convoy to pass before it could turn into the yard of Ye Olde Black Cross on the other side of the road. The convoy was very long, every vehicle precisely spaced. Vruumm . . . vruumm . . . vruumm. He found himself mouthing the sounds while his camera eye followed the course of each vehicle in turn, his head swishing back and forth like a tennis spectator in slow motion. Then his eye was caught by the arrangement of the slender spire of St John's rising above a mass of trees with a large, elegant house below, and the old terraced cottages lining Hanover Street curving towards it.

It was a nice composition. He made a viewfinder by arranging his fingers and thumbs into a rectangle as Mr Ross-Armitage had shown them. He held it at arm's length to get a close-up with a minimum of foreground and sky. Now a 'portrait' composition, turning the viewfinder to the vertical. And a long shot, bringing the viewfinder close to his eyes to allow more of the scene to come into the aperture.

The convoy passed, the dray turned into the pub yard, the bus moved off. Still gazing through his viewfinder he promoted himself to a movie camera, as he filmed the tail end of the dray disappearing into the yard. He panned smoothly (Mr Preen had told them about panning) to the other side of the street and filmed the entrance to Bromsgrove School. A public school like Greyfriars or Nigel and Dick's St Cuthbert's. To keep it clearly in view, he moved to the other side of the bus and turned round. And then he saw, through his viewfinder, that the bus had filled up; only the three seats alongside his own – the ones people usually made a bee-line for – were empty. Queer. Or rum, as Nigel would say.

Going out of Bromsgrove was a much tidier business than coming in from Redhill. The bus climbed a steep hill flanked by cottages, with a hospital on the summit, then dropped immediately into open countryside little changed since the last century.

Not for very long, though: coming along on the left, rapidly growing taller, were the wireless masts near Droitwich. Morley's arms were growing tired. He abandoned his viewfinder and ran his naked eye up and down each mast. He decided that he quite liked the masts, and gave them the same dispensation as railways and canals: an exciting addition to the countryside, not an intrusion like factories and suburban building.

On the other side of the road was the Swan Inn with a squat, steepled church just behind it and a row of willows bordering a nearby stream; then a large level area of ground divided into small, cultivated plots. The bus stopped opposite a curious building halfway between something from

166

*Grimm's Fairy Tales* and a cricket pavilion. The roof was a huge pyramid of thatch, far too big for its walls. A large sign read, 'Webb's Trial Grounds'. In front of the building were two beds of tulips – red and yellow.

The combination of flat countryside, willows and tulips put Morley in mind of Holland – and his father. He wondered how he had died. A ready-made image came into his mind, the action already in motion. All he had to do was direct the events a little.

He can see the flat landscape of Holland, red and yellow tulips stretching to a windmill-dotted horizon. Closer is a canal going through a badly shelled village of quaintly gabled houses. On this side of the canal are burnt out tanks – Centurions, he makes them – with charred bodies hanging out of the turrets, others lying on the ground. But his father can't be burnt to death, that's just too horrible to think about. He must still have an important role to play and then die a clean, instant death. So he and half a dozen other men are still alive, sheltering from enemy gunfire with only rifles and hand grenades left. On the other side of the canal are the Germans among their own disabled tanks – Tigers – but they still have an active machine gun. His father swims across the canal in the shadow of a shattered bridge, climbs to the other side, moves cautiously along the side of a building – it insists on looking like the thatched Webb's Seeds building – and tosses a couple of grenades into the middle of the German machine-gun post. There is a terrific explosion and splayed bodies fly out in all directions – just like the picture he has seen on the front of the *Champion*. He swims back, but at the bank he turns – he must not be shot in the back – and is shot in the chest. His mates grab him, pull him to safety. But he is already dead. His blood mingles with the red tulips. Peasants in picturesque costumes straight out of Mr Preen's film, *Holland's Watery Highways*, are coming along the canal in cheese-laden barges, unaccountably untroubled by the battle.

If he never learned anything different, that would be the way his father had died; that's how he would tell it.

The foreign-looking Chateau Impney swept by on the left; he was nearly there. Under the railway bridge, then Bullock's Café and other ancient timbered buildings all leaning at astonishing angles.

Russ would be over the moon, he reflected. 'And folks still *live* and *work* in these places? Well, I guess that beats everything!'

There was another place where everything was crooked. Where was that? Morley did not bother to rack his brains: it would come in a moment, everything worked well today. Something connected with Russ . . .

Of course, another American: Tom Sawyer. The graveyard where Tom and Huck witness the murder of Doctor Robinson. The board fence 'which leaned inward in places and outward the rest of the time, but stood upright nowhere'. And the graves: 'worm-eaten boards staggered over the graves, leaning for support and finding none'.

He felt a bit like Tom Sawyer now that he was an orphan – at least half an orphan – and going to stay with his aunt.

He got up and made his way to the stairs. A woman gave him an uncertain smile. He smiled back without a trace of bashfulness, the confident smile of the son of a war hero.

# Chapter 19

Morley's keen interest in whatever was happening around him hadn't abated. Even when occasionally his mind did wander, it didn't stray far. He was sitting on a pouffe in the lounge next to the half-glazed bookcase which housed one of the many attractions of coming to May's: the twelve volumes of *The Pictorial Book of Knowledge*. On his lap was volume eight, open at 'Painting'. Near by, Ron was standing in front of his baronial-looking fireplace rocking gently on his heels, hands in trouser pockets, jingling his loose change. May sat in an armchair and Ron's two friends on the sofa.

Morley was very conscious of his new status as the son of a war hero. He knew that everyone in the room knew, and that each was probably secretly regarding him with respect. Although he had hardly spoken all evening, he viewed his silence not as a failing as he might have done in normal circumstances but an indication of modesty and suffering borne bravely.

May was entertaining her guests with a story he'd heard before. He thought about Ron. Tall and handsome, Ron looked a bit like Ray Milland. Morley had heard his mother describe him as a spiv, a shady character, or a black marketeer, but to show she was fair-minded she would always add, 'Mind, you, he's always been very good to us,' or, 'He did have a lot to put up with,' or, 'He could have turned out a lot worse.'

Then, about eighteen months ago, in a rare expansive mood after a Family Ale, his mother supplied more details. 'He comes from ever such a rough background, you'd be surprised.'

Morley was. As well as looking like a film star, Ron talked posh in a mumbling though impressive sort of way.

'There were nine of them. And the mother . . . well, she just couldn't cope. But the father . . . Now don't go telling anybody, although this was a long time ago and he's dead now, but the father was vile. Ab-so-lute-ly *vile*. Vile temper, vile language, a really evil, vile swine; knocked them all about – even the little girls. He was wicked. As soon as the two eldest boys got jobs, he just stopped working, said he had a bad back, lay stinking in bed all morning till the pubs opened. Anyway, this is the part I was going to tell you about.' Her face twisted into a grimace and stayed that way as she continued. 'The father got too idle to go to the closet and he used to do his business in a bucket in the bedroom – no one else, just him – and it generally only got emptied when it was full up. He used to get one of the poor little kids to go and empty it out.' She released the breath she had been holding and shuddered. 'Ughh! Must have stunk the whole house out. You just can't imagine it, can you?'

'Mom, who told you about his d-dad and everything?'

'Oh, it was well known, they lived in a yard only a couple of streets away from us. Everybody knew what the Days got up to, they were the talk of the neighbourhood.'

'So how did Ron get sort of posh and, w-well, all the rest of it?'

His mother shrugged, her mind still probably dwelling on the nightmarish bucket. She lit a cigarette as if to drive away the imagined smell. 'We-ell, he puts it *on*. He had this job in Lewis's, on men's hats, that's when he first started putting it on, I think. Before that he sold things for wire-lesses and bits for cars. He even had a barrow in the Bull Ring once. Later on he sold cars in a big showroom in town, then he started selling them on his own account. He was up to everything, furniture, antiques, jewellery. But whatever

170

it was, you could bet your life he was on the fiddle. They say he even wangled his way out of the army.'

Morley was dismayed: at that time Ron was a valued relation, beating Micky Plant's dad hollow in wealth, smartness and style. 'How did he manage th-that, then?' he asked, hoping his mother might be wrong and that Ron was secretly working for military intelligence.

'I don't know the details but they were going to the Middle East or somewhere, and they had to have some injections and his went wrong. A bad reaction or they gave him too much or something. Oh, he really was ill, don't misunderstand me. But when he got better he made sure he never went back. Well, that's our Ron, it's his business. He's been very good to us, credit where it's due. And he'd do anything for our May.'

Morley turned his attention back to the book on his lap. The entry on Painting was subtitled, 'With Brush and Palette throughout the Ages' and continued, 'A short history of painting from the simple efforts of the cavemen through the glories of the Renaissance to the sometimes puzzling movements of the present day.' The idea of cavemen using brushes and palettes puzzled Morley. They couldn't have had them then, could they? It must be a mistake.

A burst of laughter made him look up. People described May as glamorous. She had naturally fair hair cut in a page-boy style, a classic, oval face, well-proportioned features with perhaps a slightly longish nose, and grey-blue eyes that impressed on you that you had the whole of her attention. She applied her make-up with skill and restraint and dressed with flair. The only thing that let May down – according to her few detractors – was her accent. She had never lost her strong Birmingham accent and was unaware of or chose not to bother about her quaint grammar.

'. . . I run all the way from Grey's in all that rain,' she was saying, 'and only just managed to catch it by the skin of me teeth. Then when I did get on, it was that crowded I had to stand up with all these bags and parcels. Wringing wet they was, well, I was and all. Anyroad, there I was –'

'I find that very hard to believe, Lizzie, impossible really,' one of Ron's friends broke in. Ron and his Droitwich friends always called her Elizabeth or Lizzie. Ron thought May was a common name. It hardly went with their surname, Day, either.

'What are you on about, Bob? Buses are always crowded nowadays and anyroad I told you it was nearly Christmas – I think it was the day before Christmas Eve and all the shops was just closing.'

'No, no, what I find difficult to believe is that there weren't dozens of gentlemen falling over themselves to offer you their seats.'

'Gentlemen!' May exclaimed with mock scorn. 'And what are them when they're at home? Anyroad, there wasn't all that many men sitting down as far as I could see.'

Ron, coins ajingle, laughed. Everybody knew that May was short-sighted.

'And the chap sitting by me was that old, I'd of give *him* a seat if I'd of been sitting down. Anyroad, there I was standing up with all me bags and that holding on to this pole.'

'Aye, aye, a Pole, eh!' This was Arthur, Ron's other friend.

May ignored him. 'I was hanging on to this *pole* and everybody seemed to be smiling, and I was smiling back like you do when it's Christmas time. Anyroad, all of a sudden, the bus stops dead and everybody shoots forward – you know how you do? No, course not, none of you lot would, seeing you've all got motors. So, everybody shoots forward, except me, I go *flying*.'

'Oh, you're suddenly in a plane now, Lizzie,' said Arthur. 'Was it a *Polish* plane?'

'If you butt in again, Arthur, I won't tell you no more.' May leaned over and slapped his wrist.

'Oh, there's more?' said Arthur, obviously hoping for another slap.

'Daft 'aporth,' said May, but she carried on. She seemed to provoke interruptions deliberately and she enjoyed dealing with them; it was part of her act. 'So I go flying, I land on the floor, bang me knee, me shoe come off, I laddered all

172

me stockings, me skirt come right up – right up to here.' She half-rose, indicated the top of her thigh and paused for reaction.

Both men whistled, Bob stamped his foot and Arthur cried, 'More, more.'

Morley glanced at Ron to see if he was offended but he was half-smiling. He had a sudden compulsive image of Ron's shitting-in-a-bucket father. He tried to erase it quickly as it interfered with the pleasant sensation that May's story was beginning to evoke.

'And one of me bags broke and everything come out and went all over the place. But . . . I was *still* hanging on to the pole.'

'Lucky old Pole,' said Arthur. 'Now I never had much time for Poles, but seeing that he'd got this blonde bombshell who couldn't keep her hands off him, well, I wouldn't mind swapping . . .'

'It hurt,' said May with a pained expression. 'Give us ever such a nasty bump, I can tell you.' She rubbed her temple, then ran her hand down her hip and thigh, which she inclined towards them. 'And I scraged meself all down here.'

'Hang on a minute, Lizzie,' said Bob. 'Seriously, what exactly happened? Did the pole break off or something? Did you complain? Get compensation?'

'No,' said May innocently, 'none of them things at all. See, it weren't a pole I was hanging on to at all . . . It was a *rake*!'

'A rake?' echoed Arthur. 'I suppose the Pole must have been a bit of a rake if he –'

'Naw, it was this old chap by us, see. He'd gone and bought this rake and I s'pose it wouldn't fit in the whatsit for the cases, the luggage place. So he had it stuck up between his knees, like, straight up in the air. That's why I thought it was the pole. That's why they was all smiling at me.'

'Shallow,' Morley's mother would say to Big Gwen. 'Now I know she's my sister but I *have* to say it, she's *shallow*. *Ever* so nice, *charming*, and *ever* so generous, I'd be the first to admit it. No, don't misunderstand me. But a lot of it is just *show*, duck, she just can't *bear* it if she's not the centre of

173

attention; and she's always so conscious about what she looks like. But there's really not much depth to her when you come to weigh her up. You should see the amount of stuff she buys: clothes, scent, undies, make-up . . . Talk about extravagant! But then *he* encourages her. Her hair, as well; always at the hairdresser's that wench is. Then there's pictures, dancing, and they're always going to some posh place for a meal – pfff, dinner *he* calls it. And the *drink* they get through!'

His mind filled with lingering thoughts of May on the bus floor, her long shapely legs on display, and not too bothered about her shallowness, Morley skimmed through 'Palestine' and the 'Panama Canal' in *The Pictorial Book of Knowledge* until he came to 'Paper: From Tree Trunks to Book Leaves'. He gave this more of his attention, comparing it with Mr Preen's film on the same subject. Then, a couple of pages later, he reached 'Paris: Queen of Cities, Mecca of Art and Fashion and Gay Capital of the Picturesque Land of France' and studied it with professional interest. It was a pre-war Paris. There were pictures of wide streets crammed with cars and curious buses – images of May again – with open platforms at the rear. Elegantly dressed people strolled along crowded pavements or sat drinking at tables on café terraces – blissfully unaware of the Occupation to come. He turned to the front of the book. 'First published 1938 Second impression 1939.' Only a year or two to go then. He rubbed his eyes: he was getting tired. How many of those strolling people were dead? he wondered.

Arthur said, 'Don't forget the ten o'clock news, folks; they might tell us a bit more about old Adolf kicking the bucket.'

May frowned. 'Rumours,' she said firmly. 'And anyroad, none of us want to hear anything about *him* for a start off.'

She turned to Morley, who was blearily trying to memorize Paris street and place names to enrich his spurious French background. 'Sorry, love, we've all been ignoring you a bit but when you've got your head stuck in one of them books, you seem to be in a world of your own and we don't hardly like to disturb you.'

Morley smiled. He didn't think he would stammer if he said anything but he decided not to risk it: Ron's friends were a bit intimidating.

'Well,' said May, 'I reckon it's time we all had another drink.' She topped up all the glasses including Morley's with the bourbon Arthur had brought. 'Now, love, we in't trying to get rid of you or anything: you can stay there just as long as you like. But if you've had enough of these boring old men, you can take your drink and all the books you want upstairs with you. Oh, and I've put a pile of *Lilliput*s and *Men Only*s out for you in case you want something a bit lighter. But honest, love, you don't half look tired. A good night's sleep'd do you the world of good. Anyroad, whatever you do, don't you go wearing your eyes out.'

Morley decided to take her advice. As he finished his drink, he had a terrifying vision of his mother wandering around her empty house, tearing up holy pictures, weeping loudly and shrieking the foulest obscenities at God. He shivered slightly; the image disappeared. He murmured his good nights.

May said, 'Sleep well, love.'

Ron said, 'Night, old chap.'

Arthur said, 'Mind what you get up to with those *Men Only*s!'

And Bob just grinned.

# Chapter 20

The Days had five bedrooms. The one Morley slept in was the third biggest. May had not got around to having it decorated yet and, although it was in good order, it lacked the flair of the other rooms she had had done up. Nevertheless, the beiges, muted browns and oatmeals of the previous owner, along with May's modern, cream-painted furniture and abstract-patterned rugs and curtains, produced an effect which to Morley was the height of luxury and good taste.

He lay in bed, still reading *The Pictorial Book of Knowledge* in spite of heavy eyes, loath to let go of the day. He had got to 'Post Office: The Incredible Adventures of a Letter'. On the right of the double spread was an inset panel entitled 'Round the World with the Postman and his Bag'.

A caption under a picture told what would probably happen to a letter arriving in Holland in the middle of winter: 'Then the postman in wooden shoes might push it on a hand sledge along the frozen waterways past the creaking windmills to its destination.'

The photograph showed a landscape not unlike the one he had dreamed up for his father's death. Flat countryside, bristling with windmills, slender spires thrusting up from the clustered roofs of villages, and an ice-covered canal in the foreground with the sledge-pushing postman. All it lacked was the tulips, but this was winter. His eyelids grew heavier. He looked at the remaining pictures with waning interest. Postmen in fur hats, peaked caps, turbans; delivering letters with bicycles, motor boats, punts, sailing boats, ox carts; and a white-clad Swedish postman emptying a post box fixed to the back of a tram.

He had had enough. Even the grown-up delights of *Men Only* were not enough to lure him out of bed to the pile on the dressing table. He closed his book and put it on the bedside cabinet. He turned off the ceiling light with the pendant switch above the bed and waited for the comfortable thoughts of earlier to return. But they eluded him. He felt unaccountably edgy. Thoughts of his Imperfect Confession drifted uncomfortably through his mind. He tried to lift his mood by reminding himself that he didn't have to go to school tomorrow, that the war was ending and that the death of his father excused him from having to do anything very much for the next few days. He tried to recapture the feeling of Nowness he had experienced on the bus but he seemed to have lost the knack. He felt that his mind would be invaded at any moment by as yet unknown fears that he would be unable to deal with. Even what he usually got up to at this time of night had lost its appeal.

The bedside lamp was still on, bathing the area around him with a mellow glow. He turned, about to switch it off, and saw the diffused shadow of his hand on the wall. He idly tilted back the shade, wriggled his fingers and watched the now sharply defined shadow following his movements. He thought about his father. Not the soldier hero but the father of years ago, sitting on the edge of his bed and entertaining him with his hand shadowgraphs. Birds, animals, human faces, including Oliver Hardy's and Churchill's. His dad was an expert. He remembered his father's bedtime stories. They were better than his mother's, although she read expressively and without faltering. His father sounded awkward and lifeless on the few occasions when he read. Instead he usually told stories based on what he had read for himself, seen on the pictures or heard on the wireless. Morley had heard his first William stories that way; and years later when he read the same stories, found all sorts of differences. His father was a good footballer and cricketer as well and could make you laugh.

Although he had always dutifully looked forward to his father's safe return, it had never been an eager or anxious business. He had been content that his father was alive out there somewhere, proud that he was a fighting soldier, sure that all in good time he would be back. Perhaps a little later rather than sooner because, just lately, he had harboured misgivings about their reunion. How would his father react to his brace? Would an awkward, weedy thirteen-year-old son who didn't seem to have achieved very much and wasn't much good at football and cricket fall below his expectations? He needed time to change. Well, at least, he didn't have those problems now. His father wasn't coming back. Ever.

At that, it really sank in. His face contorted, his eyes prickled and warm tears coursed down his cheeks. Soon he was sobbing and wallowing in the poignant memories that tumbled into his mind. His father helping him to build a den in the garden; sledging on the Ickley Hills with the sledge they had made together. And the last Guy Fawkes' night before the war with the huge bonfire that he and his dad had spent all day building; the recollection was vivid. He could smell the exciting acrid smell of the fireworks, see the intense magical colours of the Bengal matches that his father had told him to strike and hold himself, the smoke reflecting their red or green flames; hear the oohs and aahs from neighbouring gardens.

His father had been very popular. Even the then small scruffs would greet him cheerfully: ''Llo, Mr Charles.' And cheer when he invaded their football game, kicked the ball between the lamp-post-and-coat – later pig-bin – goal and gave the lad he'd pinched it from the credit for scoring. He could blow perfect smoke rings and had a trick of turning a half-smoked cigarette into the inside of his mouth with his tongue and closing his lips, the cigarette still smoking away inside. Then he would turn it out to its usual place, keeping an otherwise straight face. He sometimes did this when Percy Pinder was bragging about something and it would put Percy off his stroke.

But during his father's last leave, he remembered, once or twice his father's clowning had embarrassed him. He was a very different sort of father from William Brown's or any of the other fathers described in the books he read. Once he had overheard his mother say to him, 'You're just a great big kid, Albert.' And Big Gwen was always calling him a scream.

Morley was ashamed of his reservations. If he could have his dad back, he would settle for him exactly as he was and be forever grateful. His sobs increased. There would be no father around now to be pleased and proud if he passed for the Art School. If only he had been more careful when he climbed out of the canal – or whatever he had been doing when he got killed.

He tried to control his sobs – he didn't want May to hear – and console himself with thoughts of other fatherless boys. Tom Sawyer, Dick the boy sleuth, the many boys in school stories whose parents had died in car crashes or, for some reason, in India. Then there was Joe Kinsella and Armand Bechoux from church, Crapper Paramore from his own class, Douglas Bruton from 2B, and Stanley Bannister from Mr Preen's class – or was his father just missing? Ron, of course – and May and his mother, come to that. Reggie Kelp, who had never had a father to begin with; Reggie Nolan called him a bastard behind his back and Morley had only recently understood why.

A thought struck him. What about the stuff his father had got for him? The Jerry hat and all the other bits and pieces? Would somebody send them on?

'Selfish swine!' he could hear his mother saying. 'Self, self, self, that's you!' She was right.

But the thought just came – by itself. I didn't make it come, he silently protested.

Something else struck him, a terrible thought, far more terrible than the pattern of God's punishment and rewards

179

of last week. Had his Mortal Sin in some way helped to cause his father's death? He had not understood at the time.

Canon Reilly said, 'It is quite clear that beating somebody over the head with a stout stick or stealing their bicycle is sinful. We all know that, do we not? So it is the *secret* sins that we must be particularly on our guard against. Things that we might do, or just *think* about, on our own; in a field miles from anybody else; or hidden away in a deep cave high on a mountainside away from the world. These things can be just as sinful even though they do not *appear* to hurt anybody at the time.'

Morley thought of people quite remote from himself, crooks, perhaps, planning murder or robbery from their secret hide-outs.

'Nevertheless' – he looked at each member of the instruction class in turn – 'these secret sins can do just as much harm to other people. Like the invisible radio waves that are all about us' – sweeping his hand round the church – 'secret sinful actions send out invisible vibrations which spread like some loathsome, vile disease, infecting and attacking other people. Sins which seem harmless but which add to the store of evil in the world, which always leaks out and contaminates.'

Morley understood the words but to him they conveyed only germ warfare or poison gas, or Flash Gordon shooting invisible rays from his gun.

'How Satan chuckles and rubs his hands with glee on seeing a boy – or a girl . . .'

Now, over a couple of years later, he thought he understood. But he had *tried* to confess: it wasn't his fault that the canon had acted strangely in confession. Anyway, it was only recently that he had done what he did with a sense of sin; before that he hadn't realized it was wrong. Even now he wasn't *absolutely* sure that what he did was all *that* bad. Definitely not so bad as hitting somebody over the head with a stick or stealing their bicycle.

Father Smythe said that what really counted was what

180

went on in your heart. That if you committed a dreadful sin on a desert island and there was no priest available, you could confess directly to Almighty God, and be forgiven. And he had as good as done that on Saturday when he had gone to confession. He sighed with slightly uncertain relief and told God he was sorry.

May came in with a tray of cocoa and custard creams. She had changed out of her white blouse and dark slacks into an ivory-coloured turban and a long silky garment of the same colour. Morley had seen something similar in American pictures.

'I seen the light on under your door just now and I thought, I bet that little devil's still carrying on reading. Honest, I don't know where you find the room to stick it all; your poor old head must be busting.' She moved the book and put the tray down on the bedside cabinet where she was close enough to see Morley's tear-stained face. She sat on the bed and, as he half-rose, unselfconsciously put her arm around him and drew him close.

'I've been ever so thoughtless, love, leaving you on your own most of the evening. When Ron come home and I told him about what happened, we said it'd be better if his daft mates din't come round tonight – they nearly always come round of a Monday – but it was really too late to stop them. Anyroad, I hope you wasn't too upset with our daft talk, 'cause in a way I thought it'd be better if we carried on normal.'

'N-No, May,' Morley said, wiping his eyes. 'I like your stories. I'd heard the bus one before b-but you always make it sound new. And it's the way you tell it that makes it sound funny.'

'Well, to be truthful, that story's growed a bit over the years. No, but thinking about it, it wasn't *really* right carrying on like I did and encouraging them other daft 'aporths – but it's always the same when they come round. Mind, I med sure things din't go too far tonight and we din't drink all that much, and then you was so wrapped up in them books.

181

'Still, I'm glad them books of come in useful for some-body; we must of had them, ooh, five or six years now and do you know? I've never even opened one of them.'

'Did Ron get them, then, May?'

'Oh no, I was the one bought them all right.' She smiled. 'You'll think I'm daft but I liked the colour, that dark blue on the covers, and Ron had just got hold of that bookcase downstairs with the glass doors and we hadn't got nothing to stick in it, so I thought they'd look a treat in there and they'd go with the rest of the colours in the lounge. Anyroad, I felt sorry for the chap what was selling them, he looked that tired and sweaty. Let's see, it must of been August just before the war. He was one of them, you know, whatsits, commercial travellers, selling on the never-never. I paid cash. He couldn't hardly believe his luck, poor devil, must have med his day. Mind, Ron sometimes used them to check up on things when he was selling furniture and that. He was always at it, buying, selling, his head stuck in the *Exchange and Mart*, even when we was on holiday. That's just rem-inded me of something, but it's mostly about . . . your dad. Sorry, love . . . unless you *want* to hear.'

Morley nodded: his father was rarely discussed at home.

'Well, can you remember that time when we all went to Weston together before the war? You was about six or seven. Well, it was mainly jewellery then with Ron. He'd go all over the place to pick up something old or rare – if he could get it cheap. Well, this one particular night, he wasn't back, supposed to of gone to Bridgewater or somewhere. Anyroad, I could see your dad was dying for a drink. Not that he was a big drinker, but on his holidays or at weddings and that, he enjoyed a few pints. Your mom says why din't the two of us go off anyway, she wouldn't mind. She likes a drink but she's never been much of a one for pubs. We'd been at Weston for about five days by then and what generally hap-pened of a night was that one or two of us would stay be-hind to look after you while the others went in the town somewhere, or we'd all go down to this pub just round the corner – the Old House at Home it was called – and every so often, one of us would nip back to see if you was all right. You generally was,' she said, turning and smiling, 'with your crayoning and drawing and all that. And, anyroad, your mom would always get back for half-nine.

'Well, I knew Ron weren't too keen on this pub round the corner no more, at least he weren't that keen on the gaffer 'cause of something that happened at dinner time the day before. But we said we'd go there just to mek it easy for Ron to find us. When we did go up the town we generally went to all sorts of different places and we din't know their names.

'So me and your dad go down the pub round the corner. It weren't all that near the seaside so when we got there it was only about half full. I had a couple of gin and its and I was getting a bit tiddly. And your dad had got that look on his face when he was thinking about getting up to something. So I whispered, "Do your babby act, Alb." You know the one I mean?'

Morley did. It was one of his father's most appreciated party tricks.

'Anyroad, we're in one of these little alcoves with wood walls and that coloured glass – stained glass like our front door – on top, so the gaffer couldn't see us from behind the bar. Your dad starts his crying like a babby, quiet to start off with; and it was that real the way he done it. The couple opposite us seen what he was up to, but your dad just winked at them and carried on.

'The gaffer din't notice for a bit, but then one of the chaps he was nattering to says, "Alf, I'm sure I can hear a babby crying somewhere." The gaffer listens, then shoots out and looks all round. He sees your dad, all right, but your dad's just drinking quiet, all innocent. The couple opposite says they think the crying's coming out the bar – we're in the lounge, see – so he goes in there and your dad starts up again. Then the gaffer comes back and looks under all the tables and gets ever so aereated.

'"You better watch it, Alf," says one of the chaps by the bar, "you might lose your licence." But I think this chap knows it's your dad. In fact, a few of them are in on it by now. The gaffer goes back behind the counter and your dad keeps quiet for a bit. Then he starts up again, louder, and nearly everybody starts having a look, well, least pretends to be having a look. The gaffer goes and gets his wife out the back and they go everywhere looking behind curtains and out in the street even.

'When they come back, this other chap says, what's everybody going on about he can't hear nothing. He says to your dad, "Did *you* hear anything, mate?" And your dad says no he hadn't. And your dad says to me, "Did you, May?" And I says, "No and I've got perfect hearing." And then some others say they can't hear nothing neither.

'Then this first chap says, "Do you know what I reckon, Alf, I reckon you got a ghost. The ghost of some babby murdered hundreds of years ago." Another chap goes, "You better change the name of your pub, I reckon, Alf. You better call it the *Haunted* Old House at Home now." And everybody laughs. And somebody says, "Well, it'll bring you in a few more customers, Alf. They'll come from all over in charas; mek your fortune," but another chap says, "Frighten everybody off more like." Anyroad, the gaffer goes as white as a sheet and don't say nothing.

'Your dad thinks he's overdone it a bit. But I told him not to bother his head about it 'cause this gaffer can be a spiteful devil when he feels like it.'

'You mean that dinner time, when you said s-something happened?' Morley noticed some skin had formed on his cocoa. He loathed skin and hoped May wouldn't remind him to drink it.

'That's right, love, the day before. Me and Ron went in at dinner on our own – you and your mom and dad was on the beach. Well, what happened was, there was some lipstick on me glass, so Ron took it back and points it out to the gaffer. The gaffer gets another glass, bangs it down and pours me drink out the other glass into it. Never says a word. Ron says, no, he wants a new drink and all, one – what was it? – untainted by being in a dirty glass. You know the way he talks, love? Well he pours out another drink all right,

184

still never says anything, let alone sorry. He gives Ron a look like he could murder him. So I in't got no sympathy for him at all. So I says to your dad, "Don't bother, Alb, he deserves it. It's only tit for tat."'

Excitement stirred at the word tit. Morley stole a side-long glance at May, wondering what, if anything, lay beneath the silky material of the glamorous thing she was wearing. And the arm around him, if he chose, could be experienced as something thrillingly different from the sympathetic closeness of an aunt. But he tried to distract himself.

'So D-Dad s-stopped then, didn't do anything else to upset the gaffer?'

'Well, he stopped the crying all right, but once your dad gets started, well, there's no stopping him. That's to say, when your mom weren't around. I mean your mom used to like a good laugh all right, but she can't bear being showed up in public, the same with Ron and me. Oh, this'll mek you smile. Ron and me went to the pictures once, years ago, the Gaumont up town. Well, when the usherette showed us this row, I weren't thinking and I knelt down – genuflected like as if I was in church. It put Ron in a bad mood all through the picture. He just can't abide things like that. When we're out he expects me to be just so.' She straightened up a little and arranged her face into a prim lady-like expression. 'But you've got to have a bit of a laugh now and again, in't you, love?' She gave him a wide smile, showing her fine white teeth.

'Where was I? Oh yes, in the pub. Well, the gaffer gradu-ally calms down and soon he's drinking and nattering away with his regulars again. He's all right with most of them. Ron thinks it's only the holiday-makers he gets funny with. Anyroad, your dad gets some more drinks and he says all very friendly, "Nice drop of bitter you keep, landlord."

'The gaffer goes – I can't do his voice, but something like, "Well, we try and do our best, squire."

'"Mm, not bad at all," he goes and rolls it all round his mouth. "Mind you, it can't touch a nice drop of Ansells."

'"Ansells," goes the gaffer, "and what's Ansells when it's at home?"

'"Only the best beer in the country," goes your dad. "Brewed in Brummagem."

'"So what's your Ansells got that's so special, then?" goes the gaffer.

'Then your dad gets all serious but he's really just mekking it up as he goes along. He goes, "Well, for a start off, there's the special filtering."

'"Are you trying to tell me, me beer in't filtered?" goes the gaffer.

'"Oh, no, no," goes your dad, all gentle, "course it's filtered, your beer's *filtered* all right. Like I said, it's a very drinkable pint."

'"So what's wrong with it?" he says.

'"Nothing, but you see," says your dad, "Ansells is *triple* filtered. Yours is only done the once."

'"How do you mek that out, then?" he says. "I've been in this trade for over thirty years and I don't know what you're agoing on about."

'"Well all I can say is," goes your dad, "you just go up Aston Cross in Brum where they brew it and you'll see all the filters filtering the beer three times to give it its smooth taste, like. And then just you have a taste of it. I dare say they'd let you in all right, seeing that you're a landlord, and all."

'"What d'you tek me for?" goes the gaffer. "I in't going all the way up there just 'cause you come out with all this filtering tripe. I got better things to do."

'"That's all right, mate," goes your dad, very peaceful like, "that's all right with me. Just having a natter about the beer, that's all. No harm in that, is there?"

'The gaffer don't say nothing, just pulls a face, so your dad says, "Course, I could *show* you how they do it; demonstrate, like."

'You could tell the landlord don't quite know if he's having his leg pulled. He goes, "Get out of it, I weren't born yesterday, mate."

186

'But some of the others was saying they wanted to see how they done this filtering. Your dad had them, you see. He was like that, everybody listened when he got going.'

Morley thought of Mr Ross-Armitage: he also had the gift – and May. How he wished he had.

'"Only tek a minute," goes your dad. So he gets an empty glass off the counter, puts his foot on the table, teks his shoe and sock off. Everybody crowds round. Even the gaffer can't help looking. It was funny, I mean, some knowed he was having the gaffer on but they was all tekking it serious, playing their part, like.

'Anyroad, your dad holds his sock over this empty glass and pours his beer out his other glass through it. "Now," says your dad, "that's what's called your secondary filtering, what you don't get down here." All these chaps nod their heads like they understand what he's going on about. Then he says, "But now we come to the final very fine filtering what gives the Ansells its unique smoothness." He looks that serious that I had to bite me lips to stop meself laughing out loud. "So if my young companion will oblige," he says, just like a conjurer. And he looks at me, but I din't know what he was going on about. Then he looks at me legs and says, "May, if you wouldn't mind." And then it dawns on me.

'Now Ron – or your mom – would of curled up and died if they'd come in just then, but I was past caring about anything. I stuck me leg on the table, took me shoe off, undone me suspender and rolled me stocking down re-e-a-l-ly slow – like you see on the pictures – no, you shouldn't be seeing pictures like that at your age.' She gave Morley a mock reproving look and then a tight squeeze.

'Then all these chaps started whistling and clapping and shouting and I give the stocking to your dad and he rolls it down to mek it smaller and pours the beer through. But this time in me shoe! And d'you know what he done then? He goes and stands on the table and holds me shoe what's full of beer and shows it all around like a conjurer again and says – what was it? – oh yes: "Here we have perfection, ladies and gents, from your triple filtering." Then he only goes and starts drinking it out the shoe. And everybody cheers like mad and they all come out the bar to see what the row's about. Then he goes, "Mm, mm, smoo-oo-th, lov-erly."

'Well, these young fellers want a drink of it and all, honest. And he gives them the dregs to drink. And some ask him if we're coming in tomorrow 'cause they want their mates to see. And one chap says he wouldn't mind just having the one filtering, so long as it was done through me stocking, you could leave out the other filtering.'

Morley was transported to the pub. He could see the smoky lounge in mild, bitter and stout colours. He saw it a bit like a smaller, cosier version of the lounge bar of the Hen and Chickens, which he could glimpse from the outdoor where his mother sent him to get a Family Ale or a Nourishing Stout. But older, like the country pub in the film *Went the Day Well*. He wasn't quite sure how he would have felt, though, if he had really been there watching his father's antics. Was that the only way May remembered him? As a comedian? There was nothing there he could brag about to Micky Plant – or anybody else. Nevertheless, he felt relaxed and secure in the pub and didn't want to leave. He wanted May to continue, though he hoped that anything else she had to say about his father would be more . . . well, less ridiculous. He also hoped that May would mention her stockings again.

'And did Ron c-come back – to the pub?' he said, hoping that he hadn't.

'No, he never did. It turned out he went on to Taunton after, and he got this puncture on the way back. Good job he did: your dad and me'd really had a few over the eight by then. Anyroad, everybody's in a really good mood now and you got that feeling that they was waiting to see what your dad's going to get up to next.'

Morley held his breath, willing his father's next exploit to involve catching a robber or protecting May from some tough.

But if anything, it was the daftest of all. Morley squirmed throughout its telling. According to May, his father, on being told that they had run out of crisps, had pinched half a dozen carnations from the lounge's window sill, sprinkled them with salt, bitten off the heads and eaten them, with everybody, except the landlord, watching. And saying how much he had always liked the simple things in life, especially flowers. Then he had shoved the wet stalks behind a picture. The lounge had been in an uproar.

'Well,' said May, 'I was getting a bit anxious by this time in case somebody give the game away and the gaffer sees that half his flowers was gone. So I said to your dad we better go. But he still wanted to carry on. He pulled me stocking out his pocket, still wringing wet it was, and he says, "I know what, May, let's auction this, mek a few bob." But I really did have to stop him there.' She shook her head, sighed wistfully and wiped her eyes. 'That was our Alb.'

She suddenly peered at her watch. 'Love, just look at that time! I'll have your mom after me. Look, love, I know it's a waste but I'll leave the landing light on and if you need anything – some milk or cordial or something, well you know where everything is.'

# Chapter 21

Morley wandered the pleasant tree-lined streets close to May's house with no idea of where he was going or what he wanted to do. Earlier, eager to ride in Ron's Hillman, he had planned to go with May to Bromsgrove, where she had a part-time job. But Ron couldn't get the car to start, so Morley had merely seen May on to the bus, the attraction of Bromsgrove suddenly fading. As soon as the bus had drawn away, he had regretted his decision, remembering Woolworth's and the market hall and the curious graves of the engine drivers in the churchyard, who had been killed when the boiler of their engine had exploded.

A familiar problem, indecisiveness. The trouble was, once started on something, there was always the thought that you might have been happier or it might have been easier doing something else.

It was like that now. Perhaps he should get something to drink and maybe something to eat. He wasn't all that hungry or thirsty, though. Not so much as to drive him to overcome the anxiety of going into a café or teashop. Later, perhaps.

He wasn't quite sure where he was. He had simply walked at random since seeing May off, his head full of all the other things he could have done if he had gone to Bromsgrove. Still, at least he could go into the town centre and buy something to thank May for having him. Grown-ups did that.

He had felt grown-up yesterday, still in his confident mood, when he had stood on May's doorstep with his suitcase.

'Front garden's looking nice, May. I like those pink flowers and the daffs,' he had said, before telling her of his father's death. He was pleased with that. Nigel, the cooler of the boy sleuths, would probably have done the same.

A present, then. On reflection, it was difficult. If he bought scent or make-up, which he was sure he could manage if he was French, he would probably get the wrong thing. He was dimly aware of the mystique surrounding such things: just anything wouldn't do. And, of course, he would never know because, whatever he got, May would be pleased and grateful and insist that it was just right. Maybe he ought to leave it for the moment.

He was very fond of May. There was hardly anyone he liked better. She was never moody, she always listened to him attentively, she would look over his shoulder with genuine admiration when he was drawing or painting and ask questions. What he particularly liked was that she seemed perfectly happy to be seen with him in public and glad of his company. Unlike his mother: 'Put that face straight. Stop gawping. For goodness' sake, duck, can't you stop looking so vacant for a minute? Anybody would think they'd just let you out of the Asylum.' May made him feel . . . well, normal.

Yet now he felt uneasy about the way she had behaved last night. Drinking, flirting with Ron's shady friends – who had probably also wangled their way out of the army – and telling funny stories when her nephew's dad had just died, killed on active service. Never mind about the excuses she had made for not putting them off: she should have told them on the doorstep that it wasn't right for them to be there tonight.

What would they have done, though, if Ron's friends *had* stayed away? Played ludo or Monopoly? Talked in whispers about his dad, with Ron walking aimlessly up and down, trying not to yawn, jangling his coins as usual and communicating to Morley through May. 'Does the old chap want another drink? Does he want the radiogram on? Yes, go on, give the old chap a cigar. Won't do him any harm.'

And to be honest, he had quite enjoyed last night. And then of course May *had* spent the whole afternoon with him in Worcester, going into every likely shop in search of some proper watercolours when she had heard that was one of the things he most wanted.

It was not really May's fault; it was just that she seemed only to remember his father as a clown. That was what was really upsetting him. If what had happened in the pub had been a film, with Stan Laurel doing all the tricks, he would have laughed like anything. But he didn't want a Stan Laurel for a father. Who else had a father who cried like a baby, filtered his beer through his sock and ate flowers in a pub? He wanted to have had a father who had been more . . . dignified. Mr Ross-Armitage and Russ could make you laugh all right, but they didn't make fools of themselves. It was strange, he reflected sadly: he had only learned of his father's death yesterday morning and now he knew things about his life that even his mother didn't know. It might have been better if he had not known about them either.

The houses he was passing now were smaller and he seemed to be getting nearer to the main road; he could hear the occasional lorry or bus. Over the road was a shop. His spirits lifted a little: it was his sort of shop, not too grand, no more forbidding than Hiller's at home.

It was bigger than Hiller's and shabbier, the black paintwork on its double-windowed front blistered and peeling. The fascia read: 'Tobacconist Newsagent Sweets R. C. CRUMP Stationery Fancy Goods' in dull gilt lettering. The left-hand window was filled with elaborate displays of cigarettes of every brand imaginable. But everything was dusty and sprinkled with dead flies, and the red printing ink on the packets and showcards had been bleached by the sun, leaving only yellows and blues and a dingy range of greens and khakis in between. If that wasn't enough to dash the hopes of some naïve customer, 'DUMMY, FOR DISPLAY ONLY' was just visible on the back of one of the pyramids of joined together packets that had fallen over; and a hand-written notice on the door said, 'Turkish Only'.

Morley was reminded of the glass case of watercolours in the Midland Educational, which Micky Plant said were fakes. He turned to the other window.

The goods here were real enough and lay in sprawling confusion. Some of the flies were still alive. There were writing pads, airmail flimsies, bottles of ink, crayons, chalks, jigsaw puzzles, knitting patterns, and old comics for a penny. Towards the back of the window was a box of Love Hearts, its half-closed lid adorned with a small khaki turd. Near by, a black cat with a white throat sat on an untidy pile of tracing and colouring books.

It was a good job his mother couldn't see the turd, he thought. She would have forbidden him to go in and buy as much as a comic, warning him of typhoid, scabies, impetigo, infantile paralysis and TB. 'Those are the sort who wouldn't dream of washing their hands after going to the closet. There must be germs in there crawling about all over the place. I just can't bear to imagine,' she would say, twisting her face and shuddering.

But he was in a spending mood. Keeping the turd out of sight and reflexively rubbing his hands on his trousers as if to cleanse them of contamination, he considered the window's offerings. There was a model aircraft kit – a 'Timpo penknife model' it said on the label. But it was two and three, nearly a quarter of all he had. And say he found that there was something missing or broken when he was making it, would he have the courage to take it back and complain? A torch? The two in the window were of brown Bakelite covered with tiny blurred dots of bright primary colours. They looked cheap, one had a crack on the side and there were traces of rust on their switches.

Ron could get him a torch, anyway – though it wasn't the same as buying one for yourself – if he really wanted one. He wasn't all that sure that he did now.

He knew Ron could get lots of things. This morning at breakfast May had asked for some more nylons and Morley had watched a ritual he had seen Ron go through before. 'Tricky,' he said, stroking his chin, then drawing in his lips so that they disappeared, his other hand keeping the coins circulating in his pocket. 'It's a question of meeting the right chap at the right time. Could, I suppose . . . mmm. Then there's . . . mmm. I'll see what I can do.' As if there were tremendous obstacles but you could rely on Ron to overcome them.

He noticed another, smaller aeroplane kit in the window. It had no price on it. Somebody had scribbled all over the front and the box had been clumsily repaired with brown gumstrip. It looked like something from a jumble sale. He gave half-hearted thought to buying a comic. Then he saw them. In a small cavity between a puzzle and a battleship game, and almost covered by a *Rainbow Annual*. He turned away quickly so he could look again and repeat the thrill of discovery. Tubes of Winsor & Newton watercolours! The bands of colour on the labels were faded, but Mr Ross-Armitage would have reminded him that they were 'for usin' not admirin'.'

He visualized Mr Ross-Armitage's watercolour equipment: a scarred, paint-stained cigar box containing filthy-looking pans and screwed-up tubes, a chipped white saucer; and the beautiful sparkling work he produced from them. Quality materials, he insisted, when some of the girls turned their noses up. He was scornful of fancy accessories; described them as dabblers' bits of nonsense.

And, thought Morley, Ron could get *him* a cigar box – probably already had one lying around. At this moment he could think of no greater joy on earth than arranging new tubes of watercolour in a cigar box, adding the best of his brushes and a white saucer – the sort you stood egg-cups in – if he could get one from May. He shaded his eyes and took a closer look. There they were: three tubes with 'WINSOR & NEWTON LONDON ENGLAND' in raised letters on the exposed metal parts of the tubes. He bent down and fancied he could see more tubes in the shadow under the *Rainbow Annual*. Maybe there were others in the shop.

Casually, he looked inside. At the far end was a man reading a newspaper. He took a deep breath and boldly, with no thought of rehearsing, entered. He was French. His confidence faltered only a little when the man looked up, displaying a red blotchy face and a very disagreeable expression, as if resentful at the interruption of his reading. But as Morley approached him, a tiny old lady popped up from behind the counter on his left.

'What can I get you, my lovey?' she said. 'So long as it en't cigarettes or envelopes.' She had a pleasant touch of rural Worcestershire in her accent and looked so friendly and motherly and inspired so much confidence that being French was almost unnecessary. But Morley was already set in his role and it provided protection if the angry-looking man said anything.

'Ah *non*, *madame*, envelopes I 'ave. But do you 'ave any, eur, wateurcoleurs, please?' He smiled.

She may not have understood or had forgotten about the paints in the window for she said, 'No, my lovey, I don't think we've got anything quite like that.'

'Paints,' said the man, without looking up from his paper. 'He's agoing on about paints.'

'You don't mean paints by any chance?' asked the old lady.

'Ah, *oui*, *madame*, yes.' He widened his smile. 'In, 'ow you say, leetle teubes?' He illustrated the shape of a tube with his fingers. 'Paints of wateurcoleurs for making picteures.' He felt poised, free of the tension which usually urged him to get everything over and done with and out of a shop as quickly as possible.

'Well, let's see now, I think I do recall aseeing something of the sort somewhere about. Over there, I think.' She made her way round the perimeter of the shop, past the angry man to the fancy goods and stationery side of the business, and peered at the stacks of tins and boxes that lay on the shelves behind her.

Morley could simply have pointed out that they were in the window but he was enjoying his performance. He also harboured a faint hope that here inside there might be more, unfaded tubes of colour, perhaps still in their original boxes.

The old lady brought a cardboard box to the counter and sorted slowly through its jumbled contents. 'Now, let us see what we've got here, my lovey, shall we?' She picked up two tubes of Seccotine from among packets of dyes, liquid silk stockings and sticking plasters. 'Now is this the sort of thing you're after, my lovey? You did say you were after tubes?'

'*Oui, madame*, yes teubes, eur, but I regret zese are, eur . . .' He tried to remember the French for glue but couldn't. He settled for English. 'Zese contain gleue, *madame*.'

'Winder,' said the man, still reading.

'Now I come to think of it, I think I see them in the window,' said the old lady, replacing the glue and putting the box back on the shelf. As she leaned towards the window, she saw the turd on the box of sweets. She picked up a writing pad and, with surprising agility, gave the cat a resounding whack and yelled, 'You filthy, dirty, slovenly beast, Blackie!' The cat shrieked, leaped out of the window and disappeared through a door at the back of the shop. 'I'm agoing to rub your nose in that later, you'll see, *and* lock you in the cellar,' she shouted after him. She took the box of Love Hearts, complete with turd, and put them under the counter. Then she turned towards the window and scanned the contents, clicking her tongue and shaking her head. 'I can't rightly recall but they must be here somewhere.'

'Tell him to come in tomorrer,' said the man.

'Now, do you think you can come back tomorrow, my lovey? And I shall have them all ready for you.'

Morley was used to this sort of treatment. Without having to think, he said, 'Ah, *madame*, I, eur, regret I cannot, for soon I must depart for *Londres*, for London. And I will not return.'

Giving an exasperated sigh, the angry man threw down his paper, made his way to the window and, with much huffing and puffing and throwing aside of stationery and fancy goods, retrieved the paints, plonked them on the counter and returned to his paper.

Morley examined the paints with a beating heart. There were seven and not only were they Winsor & Newton's but they were *artists'* quality! Even Micky Plant had only got students' quality paints. Though artists' paints could cost him all his money. He had about eleven shillings. Ron and May would almost certainly give him something before he left. But eleven shillings for seven tubes of paint. What would his mother think? Not that he would tell her. They might even be more: Mr Ross-Armitage said that colours from rare sources could cost three times as much as the easier-to-get 'earth' colours. He read the labels. Lemon yellow, french ultramarine, chrome yellow deep, burnt umber, cobalt, alizarin crimson, and vermilion. No simple sky blues, brick reds, sea or grass greens as you got in children's paints. These colours sounded very serious – professional. No green, though. But greens were easily mixed. The labels on four of the tubes hadn't faded at all and looked as good as new. He carefully unscrewed the caps to check if they were still moist. They were.

'I don't rightly know where they come from, my lovey,' said the old lady, 'but I think that once upon a time they was in some sort of set. What I do know is that they must have been here for years and years.'

'Freeman's lad,' supplied the man, 'they was his.'

'Ah, it's all acoming back to me now,' said the old lady. 'They was young Leonard Freeman's. He was agoing to be an artist, was Leonard. Then the war come along and he had to join up. And then he got hisself killed. Got hisself killed on leave he did. Don't seem right does it, my lovey, to go and get killed on leave? But there you are. His poor mother give all his things away. She said they was no use alying around the house adoing nothing. So she brought in his paints and stuff and says if you can get a few coppers for them, you can put half of it in the Spitfire Fund.'

'British Sailors,' said the man, carefully folding the paper and putting it back on the pile. 'British Sailors' Society: he was in the navy.'

'Or, if we wanted,' said the old lady, 'the British Sailors. I

197

mean it wouldn't have seemed so bad if he had been akilled in the fighting, would it, my lovey? But he was killed on leave, with his friends in a pub in Birmingham.'

'Southampton,' said the man.

'Or it might have been Southampton, my lovey. I can't rightly recall.' She regarded him closely. 'You don't sound like you come from around here, my lovey.'

'Foreigner,' said the man, opening a paper from another pile.

'Maybe you come from foreign parts, my lovey?'

'*Oui, madame*, from France, Paris. Montmartre,' he added, remembering a photograph of the artists' quarter in *The Pictorial Book of Knowledge* last night. 'I, eur, escaped *avec* – wiz my fazeur before ze *Libération*. But alas, 'e was less fortunate zan I . . . ze *Boche*. Aah.' He felt heroic.

'That's nice,' said the old lady, sounding a little unsure of herself. Then more confidently, 'Are the paints all right, my lovey?'

'*Oui, madame, magnifique*, splendid.'

Leaning as close as her small stature and the broad counter allowed, she whispered conspiratorially, 'Let us say twopence ha'penny each, shall we? So that makes, let us see . . . one and fivepence ha'penny. Let us call it one and three, shall we, my lovey?'

'Huh,' the man exclaimed.

The old lady wrapped the paints in a piece of newspaper and twisted the ends like a wrapped sweet. 'Now I needs one of they and three of they.' She picked up a shilling and three pennies from the coins Morley had spread on the counter.

He was elated. Then he wondered if he was committing a sin of omission by not pointing out the paints' true worth. Taking advantage of the old lady's ignorance.

'Thou shall not steal,' said the seventh commandment. Which was not just avoiding breaking into an old man's isolated cabin and stealing his life's savings from under the bed while he slept, with a stout stick handy in case he should awake, the canon had explained from the pulpit in Mass. No, it also meant knowingly accepting too much change from a shopkeeper or a tram conductor, not paying debts, keeping money found in the street, cheating anyone of any-thing – including even the government – stealing employer's time by laziness and sneaking into picture houses without paying.

And 'Are we *bound* to restore ill-gotten goods?'

'Yes, Sis-ter Two-mey, we are *bound* to restore ill-gotten goods if we are able, else the sin will not be for-given,' his first communion class had chanted.

He had the opportunity to explain, if he chose . . . he had been given free will.

On the other hand, she had said one and three and he had given her one and three. Leonard's mother had said she *could* sell them for a few coppers . . . and they *were* sec-ond hand . . . and if *he* hadn't bought them they might lie there for years and dry up.

But he would think of Leonard when he used the paints . . . and put a bit more on the plate at church for a few weeks . . . and something in the British Sailors' Society when he saw a collector . . . or the Spitfire Fund, if it still existed.

His conscience satisfied, he made an elaborate show of his final thanks and farewell.

'*Merci, beaucoup, madame.* And you, *monsieur*, for your noble struggles in ze window. *Au revoir, madame et monsieur.*' He bowed.


Being the possessor of a set of new artists' watercolours kept Morley's spirits precariously high for the rest of the day. He hugged the idea to himself and thought of little else; though well aware that if he allowed himself to, the thoughts would be gloomy ones.

At tea time Ron presented him with a large cigar box. It was a magnificent affair with properly jointed corners and brass-plated hinges and clasp. Stamped deeply into the lid was the name 'Excalibur' set in a circlet of medals. An impressive green seal pasted across the opening crack read 'República de Honduras'.

'Smell it,' commanded Ron.

Morley did. It smelled rich and exotic. 'Mmmm, very nice.'

'Should do,' said Ron, 'they cost enough – when you can get them. The other smell's the cedar that the box is made from.'

'Mmmm,' murmured Morley again.

Later, he sat in the bay of the lounge window, a newspaper spread on the floor beside him. On it lay his new paints, the cigar box, his old chocolate art box and its contents, and three blue-edged, white saucers May had given him.

'No, we don't need them no more,' she had said. 'I don't really know why we hung on to them 'cause Ron got these modern ones, you know, where the egg-cup's stuck to the saucer in one, like.'

But Morley had problems. Although the cigar box was big enough to accommodate all his materials, he wasn't sure whether he really wanted to mix up his old coloured inks and students' and kiddies' paints with the artists' colours. There was something very satisfying about having the new things together, for however short a time, in all their unused glory: cigar box, new paints, saucers – which looked new – and the best two of his brushes, whose ferrules he had polished earlier with Silvo. All too soon they would acquire the scruffy look of his other stuff. Nevertheless, he continued assessing the quality and condition of his original materials, wondering if this or that might merit being included in the new box to make it look less empty – Ross-Armitage's was crammed full. But then, as the owner of proper artists' watercolours, would he ever again use the kiddies' paints? Maybe just the best of the students' colours.

Paints were for painting pictures with, not for fiddling around with or gloating over, he reminded himself. Anyway, he would be using them tomorrow. He was going to stay in all day and do a painting based on some suitable photograph in *The Pictorial Book of Knowledge* – maybe give it to Russ as payment for the jacket if it was good enough.

Originally, he had planned to go out and explore the surrounding countryside and draw from life but May had said that if he waited until Friday, when she was free, they could all go much further in the car to some villages they knew.

They sounded enticing, perhaps part of the yet undiscovered Real England. Feckenham, Hanbury, Inkberrow, Chaddesley Corbett, Ombersley.

'Ever so pretty, some of them are,' May had said. 'Sometimes of a nice evening Ron and me go to one of them for a drink, and go for a nice walk after. Mek lovely pictures at this time of the year. And tell you what, love, you could do us a nice picture – we'd pay you for it, wouldn't we, Ron? I'd love one of that old pub, the whatsit, the Bull at Inkberrow, with the church and all. We could drop you off and give you time to do your picture, then pick you up later and go somewhere else.' Which solved the problem of May's present – if he refused payment.

Morley got some water from the kitchen, unscrewed the cap of the lemon yellow, dipped in his moistened brush and carefully restored the faded band of colour on the label. Then he did the same with the vermilion and french ultramarine. These were the only labels which had suffered from their long exposure in the shop window. There was a detective play on the wireless. Morley had lost the thread of the plot, though for a long time afterwards, Inspector French of the play would spring to mind whenever he used the ultramarine. Holding the tube, waiting for the paint to dry, he had a sudden impulse to shove everything into the cigar box and mess it all up so that it resembled Mr Ross-Armitage's. He resisted it.

Feeling stiff, he stretched and yawned. It was very draining having your mind focused on paints all the time. He looked around. Ron was sprawled in his leather armchair, one hand holding his paper, the other circulating his coins in his trouser pocket. From the hall, he could hear May on the telephone.

Just as the play ended, she came into the room and said, 'Got a little surprise for you tomorrow, love.'

Morley's heart leaped. Perhaps they were going out tomorrow instead of Friday.

'I've just been talking to this woman we know. Don't live all that far away. Anyroad, her lad's had this accident and can't get out. And she thought it would be ever so nice if you was to go around and have a bit of a natter with him tomorrow morning; cheer him up a bit. And I thought it would be a nice change for you and all to be with somebody round about your own age – he's nearly fifteen. I'd of liked to go with you for a bit but' – she pulled a face – 'you know it's work for me tomorrow.'

Morley's heart sank. His modest plan for tomorrow suddenly seemed idyllic. Making new friends wasn't his strongest suit. 'W-Wow, great,' he said with forced brightness, trying to think of some way to get out of it.

'Yes, poor lad, he come off his horse in the holidays and broke his leg, din't he, Ron?'

Morley became even more dismayed. Not so much about the lad's condition but that he was the owner of a horse.

'Yes,' said May, 'he must be bored stiff on his own most of the time. He'll enjoy a bit of company. His name's You-jean.'

'Eugène,' corrected Ron, making it sound French.

'Well, I was near enough,' said May. 'Still, it's a funny name for a lad, in't it? I've never come across it before, have you, love?'

'There used to be one that served at Mass but he went in the navy.'

'Well, that's all right then,' she said, as if some awkward obstacle had been overcome. 'But their other name's another funny one if you ask me. It's Saint John-Cromwell really but you got to say Sinjon-Cromwell.'

'Sin*jn*-Cr*u*mwell,' corrected Ron.

'Well, whatever it is, they're ever such nice people. The father won't be there tomorrow 'cause he's generally down London most of the week. And his mom won't be there neither 'cause she does voluntary work on Wednesdays, Thursdays and Fridays; so you'll have the whole place to yourselves.'

That made things slightly better but . . . 'Does he go to school here, in D-Droitwich?' He had said it for something to say; he hoped it wouldn't be a grammar school.

'Oh no,' said May, 'it's miles and miles away. It's one of them boarding schools.'

'It's a jolly sight more than that, Elizabeth,' Ron chided. 'A *Borstal* could be described as a boarding school. Lord, it's one of the country's top public schools you're talking about.'

Morley's feelings were mixed. He thought of the awkwardness and coarseness that he felt in the company of Micky Plant's cousin Desmond. On the other hand, this was a not-to-be-missed opportunity to meet in the flesh a Dick or a Nigel, a Bob Cherry, or a Tom Brown. Or Eugène might be a real swell like Arthur Augustus D'Arcy – an aristocrat with a monocle. And perhaps he might have more in common with a public schoolboy than he did with the lads in the road – or even Micky's cousin Desmond, who only went to Hamilton House. And even if it all proved to be a big ordeal, it would still be something to have experienced, to swank about afterwards.

Morley went to bed feeling excited but anxious. He pretended to be asleep when he heard the bedroom door open. He wanted no more comic stories from May about his father.

# Chapter 22

Hitler was dead. The following morning's news bulletin was full of it, as was the front of Ron's *Daily Express*, though Morley noted rather sluggishly that the headline was in inverted commas. It raised a vague question, something Miss Pryce had said about their use other than to indicate direct speech. He thought of asking Ron but was becoming aware that the educated impression Ron gave was just that, an impression. It seemed that the rumours of the last two days were true then.

To Morley the image of Hitler was much stronger than that of his father. Perhaps not surprisingly: cartoons, drawings and photographs of Hitler confronted you everywhere. In newspapers, magazines, boys' papers and comics; on propaganda posters, novelty goods, board and target games and comic postcards. You saw and heard him on newsreels, impersonated in films and by every would-be comedian. Caricatures of him adorned walls and school text books. There were hundreds of jokes about him and several songs. He was probably talked about more than any other person alive or dead. He was regarded as a monster, a genius and a clown. Father Smythe said he was Satan made man, the epitome of evil. Morley had occasionally experienced a curious fleeting regard for him.

He wondered if Hitler had died on the same day as his father – the news reports said that he had died by his own hand two or three days ago. He found it strange to think of Hitler being dead as well.

Ron had taken May to work in his now repaired Hillman. How Morley wished he could have gone with them; or somewhere else, almost anywhere rather than this unknown public schoolboy's house. The cautious excitement he had felt last night had completely gone.

He dragged his feet, afraid that if he got there too early, Eugène's mother might not yet have left the house to go to her voluntary work. He couldn't remember either the address or directions for finding it for more than a few seconds together and had to keep consulting the notes Ron had written in his notebook. If only he could capture the easy mood of Monday on the bus. He tried looking forward to the relief he would feel when the visit was over but it failed to console him. After all, what was there when it *was* over? Perhaps three or four more days at May's, then home for school, confession and the now much more uncertain moods of his mother: a depressing procession of burdens. Even the thought of his paints refused to cheer him. It occurred to him to miss his appointment and go back to May's. He could tell her later that he had felt ill. She would understand but might feel let down.

'Be a man,' he told himself. Mr Church was always telling the boys to be men. 'Tek no notice,' Grandma Morley would say. And his father might have regarded the visit as an opportunity for a bit of fun. He pulled himself together with difficulty and found himself opposite R. C. Crump's shop. The news boards said, 'Hitler is Dead', 'Suicide of Führer', 'Hitler Dead – Official', 'Hitler Dies by Own Hand', all in inverted commas. As far as the Crumps were concerned, he remembered, he was supposed to be in London. Still, it wasn't likely that they would recognize him from across the road, particularly as he wasn't wearing his red lumber jacket – he had thought it too flashy for Eugène's. Nevertheless, he turned round guiltily and after a few minutes and with more luck than judgement found Augustus Avenue.

Number 14, or Salisbury House as it said on a wrought-iron sign, was much larger, older and more magnificent than

May's house. It had three different-sized, widely spaced gables, porticoed double entrance doors and at least some stained glass in all the windows. The two gateways were joined by a crescent of gravelled drive.

The gravel crunched loudly under his feet. He tried to reduce the sound when he saw a man with his back to him cutting a hedge at the side of the house. It was obviously one of the days when Eugène's father wasn't in London. Heart beating wildly, he reached the safety of the front porch unobserved and with relief: he hadn't rehearsed what he would say if confronted with an adult.

He pressed the bell push but could hear nothing inside. He pressed harder, still with no result. Perhaps it was broken. He waited, and then noticed an ornate lion's head knocker. He banged it loudly. Then he almost panicked as it occurred to him that the bell could only be heard somewhere deep in the interior of the house, and that soon an angry, limping boy would wrench open the door and yell, 'What the devil do you think you're doing? I'm not deaf! How do you think I'm supposed to run with a broken leg?' And the relationship would be spoiled from the very beginning. He resisted the urge to run away. He might have been seen already, and anyway there were footsteps approaching from inside.

A woman opened the door. His nervousness grew. Eugène's mother hadn't gone yet, after all. She was much older than he had expected, with grey hair and dry sallow skin. There was a thick powdering of dandruff on the shoulders of her long black frock. He tried to say good morning but the words stuck in his throat. He smiled tautly.

She stared at Morley as if waiting for him to explain his presence, then said, 'Ah, you must be the young –' She was unable to finish because her upper denture dropped down and she had to close her mouth and make some adjustment.

What passed as confidence for Morley was returning: Eugène's mother was hardly more awe-inspiring than the little old woman in Crump's shop. He couldn't help feeling let down, though: she was nothing like the stately, graceful, confident or jolly figures he had variously pictured last night when May had mentioned her.

'A very n-nice h-house you have got – r-really lovely,' said Morley, finding his voice and trying to sound grown-up.

She didn't reply but gestured him inside, closed the door and said with a peculiar grimace, 'If you'll follow me, I'll take you to –' But again her teeth defeated her and this time she had to use her hand to sort things out.

He followed her across a vast hall and up a wide staircase. The inside was as splendid as the outside. Everything was richly dark, the leaded lights glowing jewel-like and projecting their colours on to tiles, carpet and varnished wood. They went along a landing and up more stairs. She stopped at a door with a cardboard sign hooked to the knob, which said 'Do not Disturb'. In spite of this, she knocked, opened the door and said, without faltering this time, 'Your visitor, Master Eugène.'

And the penny dropped. A maid! Although the fiction he read, watched or listened to was awash with them, this was the first time he had seen one in real life. And the man outside must be the gardener. He was now in the realm of Nigel and Dick, and William Brown. Something else to drop casually to Micky Plant at a well-chosen moment.

But he had to cut his reflections short, as Eugène was awkwardly advancing towards him. 'Thanks, Pearson,' he said over Morley's shoulder.

He wasn't much taller than Morley but plumpish with dark, rather long hair and fleshy lips. The collar of his open-necked shirt was turned over a huge shapeless jersey. One leg of his cavalry twill trousers was cut short to reveal a plaster-encased leg ending in a grubby portion of foot. The other foot wore a threadbare, plaid slipper. If his appearance fell short of Morley's idea of a public schoolboy, his accent and confident manner did not.

He extended his hand. 'How d'you do. It's Rawley, isn't it?'

'M-Morley,' Morley corrected shyly. 'Er, how do you do.'

Eugène indicated a basket chair. He sat down himself on a lower, upholstered chair and with a small grunt swung his plastered leg on to a footstool. 'So you found us all right then? Sorry, superfluous question. I, er, bad show about your father.'

Morley mumbled his thanks and tried to erase a picture of his father sprinkling flowers with salt and eating them in a seaside pub. He gazed around him.

The huge room looked out on to the back garden. There was no stained glass here to impress the passer by, but what was impressive was the contents – no boy could ask for anything more. Which solved the problem of conversation, since Morley could think of nothing he owned, nothing he had done and nowhere he had been that would be likely to impress, surprise or even mildly interest his grand new acquaintance. At least to begin with, he could ask intelligent questions about Eugène's possessions.

'You look as though you like the den, old man,' said Eugène, following Morley's gaze. 'Do feel at liberty to browse around.'

Morley was only too happy to see everything at close quarters. One wall was filled with shelves crammed with books, games, construction sets and boxes promising unknown further delights; there was an Ensign camera, a portable wireless, a Bingoscope cinematograph and an Ernest Sewell cabinet of conjuring tricks. On top of one of two cupboards similar to ones he remembered from his infant school was a fort and a box which said 'Trix Railway' – relics of childhood, no doubt. A large table in the middle of the room held a half-completed Meccano model crane. Near the door stood a Hobbies' Gem treadle fretsaw, a workbench with a vice and two racks of tools above it, a punchball on a stand and, yes, it must be, a school tuck box! Something else he had only read about. A collection of model aircraft, some in solid balsa, some designed to fly, hung from threads drawing-pinned to the ceiling. They weren't particularly well made and some of the transfers were awry. Afraid that he might have to comment on them, he quickly moved over to the fireplace, above which hung a couple of crossed swords and a gun.

'Air rifle, ·22,' explained Eugène, 'BSA; and there's an air pistol, a Webley Senior somewhere, if you're interested.'

Morley wasn't, though BSA reminded him of Balsley School of Art: the same letters on the school crest. There was a plywood cubicle in the corner with a thick black curtain instead of a door. It made him think of a confessional. Then came the pleasing thought that he had identified it. 'A darkroom?'

Eugène smiled. 'Yes, a phase of early adolescence. No, actually I'm still keen but I've run out of developer and you simply can't get it anywhere. I've got heaps of bromide paper and hypo but developer . . . Must have a word with your uncle, see what he can do.'

Morley made a mental note to ask Ron if he could get him a film for his camera; he hadn't thought to ask him before.

'I'll show you some prints later, if I can put my hands on them. I'm quite pleased with one or two of them; trick effects is my speciality; ghosts coming out of walls and, er, other amusing ideas.'

Morley examined the Meccano crane on the table. It was huge and built from hundreds of pieces – some of them of a pattern he was unfamiliar with. He glanced at the box, a mouth-watering number 10 set. There was a steam engine near by. 'That's r-really neat,' he said.

'My father and I used to have grand times with that. Particularly with the steam-driven models. As you can see, I've just been trying to reacquaint myself with its half-forgotten delights; but you know, it's lost something of its former savour. There comes a time when one has to put away childish things, eh?' He gave Morley an amused, questioning look.

Childish or not, Morley would have been only too happy to spend hours with this particular Meccano – and for a few years yet – to compensate for a childhood restricted to making simple trolleys, hay rakes and incomplete cars and boats, which was about all that was possible with his own bits and pieces.

Of the conjuring set, Eugène said, 'Well conjuring's all right, I suppose, if one's awfully good at it – up to professional standards and all that. But just tinkering around with it is, well, rather puerile, don't you think?'

Morley continued to examine item after wonderful item,

while Eugène explained its history and function and how he rated it.

Morley had said little so far and didn't quite know where to pitch his accent. In addition to a strong tendency to lisp in the company of a lisper, become adenoidal with the Betts twins and talk as if dictating a telegram with Perky Beswick, his accent was pretty mobile within the lower half of the social scale, depending who he was with. He roughened it up considerably with the Reggies, refined it with David Meyer, Father Smythe and Micky Plant's cousin Desmond. He now had a strong impulse to match Eugène's, but that was going too far, and he realized he lacked the confidence that went along with it. Also, he imagined an occasion when he might be with Eugène and May together; the thought of the embarrassing consequences made him squirm. He settled for the middle-of-the-road accent with careful attention to grammar he used with his mother during their better moments together as well as with May and Ron, whose respective accents represented opposite ends of the class spectrum.

A large, dark reproduction of a painting under a grimy glass hung between two of the windows. 'Fisher Girl by Franz Hals,' Morley read. He said, 'Have you ever d-done any p-painting – pictures, I mean?'

'Well, only the stuff we're expected to do at school. But even there it's considered rather a Cinderella sort of thing. Got a chum who's a dab hand at it though, copies old masters in oils; dashed if anyone can tell the difference. But no, I can't really say that it's ever aroused my interest – possibly one of the very few things I've never really dabbled with. I do rather like decent paintings though. My father's got the beginnings of quite a respectable collection; some quite valuable stuff, I'm told. I can barely remember them myself. They were stored somewhere for safe keeping at the beginning of the war.'

The comment on Morley's talent in painting he had hoped for was not forthcoming; Eugène either didn't know or wasn't interested enough to bring it up.

Then, Shagger Knox-like, Eugène explained that the knife Morley had picked up from the table and referred to as a penknife wasn't a penknife but a yachting knife; that the swords he had asked about were foils; and the punchball was a striking ball. But Morley got binoculars right.

'Barr and Stroud, Admiralty pattern,' Eugène said reverently. 'Now *those* are a bit nearer my current interests. I'll tell you a little story in connection with those.' He gave Morley another smiling, speculative look. 'Ah, but later. I'm forgetting my duties as host. Be a good man, Raw – Morley – and yell to Pearson for some coffee – or tea, if you'd prefer.'

Morley would have preferred to do without either if he could be excused from yelling down to Pearson. But he could hardly refuse. 'Will she h-hear from up here?' he asked lamely.

'Good Lord, no, but if you go to the floor below and lean over the banisters she will. There's a bell over there but it's *kaput*. Just shout Pearson and when she appears ask for a coffee and whatever *you* want – tea or a Rose's if you like.'

With some misgivings but also the satisfaction that he had briefly become part of the magic world of his books, he did as instructed. Though when the maid did appear after two yells, he tempered his request with a little servility: 'Er, excuse me p-please, would you b-bring up two coffees, p-please? Thank you very much.'

On the way back, two thoughts struck him. One: if some of Pearson's dandruff fell into his coffee, would he be able to face drinking it? He didn't know whether dandruff floated . . . and if it didn't . . . he wouldn't know if there was any there or not.

And two: Eugène hadn't introduced himself but he had called him Morley; did he think it was his surname? Public schoolboys didn't go in for Christian names much – apart from Nigel and Dick . . . but they were bosom chums and cousins. So if he risked calling him Eugène, Eugène might think he was being familiar, but if he called him . . . He took out his notebook to be quite sure. Saint John-Cromwell. But you had to pronounce it . . . Lord, how *did* you pronounce it? And did you use both names, or just the Cromwell bit? But if he called him Cromwell or Cramwell or however else you said it, Eugène might think it a cheek – if Eugène was, after all, calling him Morley with the knowledge that it *was* his Christian name. He gave up and cursed his sensitivity and the way he always managed to complicate things, then went hot with embarrassment as he remembered telling the maid what a lovely house she'd got.

Back in the room, Eugène said, 'While you're on your feet, old man, just do this old cripple a small favour and you'll earn his undying gratitude. Go over to that bench and find a screwdriver, a big one.'

Morley was then instructed to roll back a large rug in front of the fireplace and unscrew four screws securing a small section of floorboard.

'You won't see anything but if you shove your arm in towards the window you'll find a book. Sling it over here if you would, and then put the board and rug back. Don't bother putting the screws back just yet.'

The book had a yellow cover and a title in French, but French beyond Morley's limited vocabulary. He gave the book to Eugène.

Pearson came in looking like a maid this time in a white cap and apron. Eugène stuffed the book behind him. The maid put down coffee and biscuits and quietly left.

'Have as much sugar as you like, old man. That's one commodity we seem to have plenty of. Go on, I know it looks like flour,' he urged, as Morley hesitated, 'but it's the genuine article, I promise you, it's just that it's powdered.'

Then Morley recognized it as icing sugar.

'Mother gets it from some no doubt dubious source.'

Morley took two heaped spoonfuls, thoughts of dandruff forgotten. Eugène had four.

From under his capacious jersey, Eugène fished out a twenty packet of Craven A and offered one to Morley. 'Sorry they're cork-tipped but they're the only ones Mother will smoke. Supposed not to affect the throat or the vocal chords and she warbles a bit, you know, charity concerts and that sort of thing.'

'Does your m-mother *give* you c-cigarettes, then, er . . . ?' He wondered whether to risk a Eugène or a St John – what was it? It wasn't well-mannered to go on not calling him anything. Perhaps later when he felt more confident.

'Hardly, old man. I trust she's blissfully unaware that she shares them with me. Though I'm scarcely depriving the old girl. She gets them by the cartload from somewhere.'

Morley thought he knew from where. Icing sugar, cigarettes and goodness knows what else. It explained the unlikely relationship between Ron and May and Eugène's parents. He could hear Eugène's mother saying to a friend of her own station, 'Oh, a frightfully quaint couple, awfully sweet, very amusing and perfectly all right in their own way.' It was a line, near enough, he had heard on *Saturday Night Theatre* on the wireless. He added silently, 'And can get you anything, darling, simply anything.'

Eugène handed the yellow book to Morley. 'Talking about pinching, cast your eyes through that.'

In spite of another quizzical look, Morley was entirely unprepared for what lay inside. A glance at the first picture plunged him into a state of seething excitement. He turned the pages slowly. The book had no text or captions but was simply a ragbag of reproductions, some in colour, of drawings, paintings and engravings. All kinds of styles were represented. Some of the pictures were crude, some beautifully and lovingly rendered. But they all had one thing in common: imaginative and complicated sex.

Morley was aware of Eugène's scrutiny. His legs were already crossed so one indication of his abruptly changed condition was masked. He brought the hand holding the cigarette close to his face, hoping to hide any give-away expression.

He found the book utterly compelling. Given the choice between it and the number 10 Meccano set, the Meccano wouldn't have got a look in. But he was shocked, and felt uncomfortable under Eugène's gaze; this wasn't something to be shared with somebody else. He took one last look at a scarcely believable picture of five intimately connected figures and reluctantly, though feigning lack of interest, put the book down. There might be a chance to see it later, perhaps when Eugène went to the lavatory. He looked up as nonchalantly as possible.

Eugène had a twisted, expectant smile. 'Pr-r-e-e-tty hot stuff, eh? As our Yankee cousins would say. Published in France, as if that isn't obvious. Nothing very coy about anything in there, is there, old man?'

Morley decided not to be drawn. He was fed up with playing a subservient role he didn't know how to reverse and was becoming irritated with Eugène's habit of throwing back his over-long hair every few minutes. The way he was now leering and licking his lips was even worse. 'Didn't you say something about p-pinching this book or something?' he asked primly, sidestepping the question.

For a second, Eugène looked disappointed. Then he said, 'Yes, I did, but like the smokes, I felt that I had no alternative.'

'From a-a shop?' Morley thought of Canon Reilly.

'Heavens, no. Hardly the sort of thing you'd find displayed in your average bookshop. No, it's Uncle Richard's. He probably doesn't know it's gone, though he's hardly likely to kick up a stink if he does. He's halfway to being gaga. It was in his study, slyly hidden behind a book on something so unutterably dreary – part of some twenty-volume work on the flora and fauna of deepest Patagonia or something – that the poor old cove probably blissfully imagined that no one would be interested enough ever to take it down.'

'S-So how d-did you m-manage to find it?'

'Aah, well, *I* was up to his little game. I noticed that this particular volume wasn't quite so dusty as the rest; and Uncle Richard never reads – apart from the racing papers. There's a lesson there for you, old man, somewhere . . .'

Morley grudgingly acknowledged Eugène's powers of deduction and was reminded of Nigel, the more astute of the boy tecs, though Eugène's appearance fell short of the tall, slim and jolly-looking boy in the illustrations.

He suddenly felt exhausted. He realized that in a more energetic mood he would have seized the opportunity to find out from Eugène whether the phrase he had tried to use in confession last Saturday was the right one. But he lacked the will and the cunning to nudge the conversation in the right direction. And somehow Mortal Sin didn't seem all that urgent now. Even thoughts of the French book failed to raise very much excitement.

It was his dad. Increasingly, scenes from May's stories of his father's exploits came back to torment him, all too readily confirming his own earlier, though only occasional, uncertainties about his father's behaviour. And now, for the first time, he had doubts about the manner of his father's death. Say he hadn't died a hero. Say he'd fallen drunk into a canal or under one of his own tanks, or been shot by his own side by mistake . . . or accidentally shot himself while clowning around. If he ever discovered that his father hadn't died a hero he wondered how he would learn to live with it.

'. . . justified the theft by telling myself that it was an essential but hitherto neglected part of my education,' Eugène was saying. 'I mean, if you waited for people to explain the more important things in life, you might die ignorant and unfulfilled, eh? The only instruction we ever get in that line is from Dr Lavish – our school chaplain – telling us the things we mustn't do but in such veiled language that half the men are more confused after his preaching than before he started.'

'Is *your* f-father in the forces?' Morley asked abruptly, following his own thoughts, hoping that Eugène's father wasn't and regretting his rude interruption.

But Eugène seemed not to mind. 'Yes, desk-bound, though. Whitehall, in some sort of advisory capacity. All very hush hush. Saw plenty of action in the last war though. A colonel, France, Flanders. Jolly near bought it a few times, apparently. Oh, this will interest you. One night . . .'

Morley descended deeper into gloom as Eugène's story progressed and almost ceased listening. Why can't you shut up, you fucking talking machine, he said silently, wearily racking his brains for an excuse to leave.

But Eugène was unstoppable. When he had finished with his father, it was cricket, motorbikes, shooting, riding, his holidays in Scotland last year and on the Continent before the war. Morley's half-hearted attempts to make appropriate comments during Eugène's rare, brief pauses, to demonstrate that he was at least capable of speech, only spurred him on. How he wished he could exchange Eugène for one of the scruffs – even Reggie Kelp.

Eugène offered him a cigarette and, as he bent over to light Eugène's, he considered pretending to have a fit. There was a boy in Mr Preen's class who had fits; sometimes you could hear the squeaking of desks being moved and Mr Preen's nasal 'Move back there, while I turn him on his side; no leave him be, give him air.' No, a weedy lad with a brace and stammer – the son of a clown who had accidentally shot himself – who had fits. It was an image he couldn't entertain, not even as a means of escape. But nothing else suggested itself.

Eugène seemed to be talking about Hitler. 'I mean, a man in *his* position, most unlikely. No, I'd stake my life on it, he's safe in Spain or Portugal at this very moment.'

This was a subject which normally would have interested Morley but all he could manage to say was, 'Well, er, yes, I w-wondered about –'

'He would have prepared himself, naturally, plastic surgery – ears particularly, they're always pretty tell-tale. His dental records would have been destroyed; all too easy to confirm the real identity of the corpse with those still around. They would already have some minion standing by who looked like him – with one of his balls already surgically removed, of course. Then, when the time was right, had him shot, made it look like suicide to fool the Allies that dear old Adolf had done himself in.'

Morley sat mute and miserable while Eugène developed his theme further, predicting a Nazi resurgence. What little confidence he had had earlier was entirely gone. His first encounter with a public schoolboy: a dismal failure.

# Chapter 23

In Morley's first art lesson in bottom juniors, Miss Trembelow had shown the class how to do sunset pictures. She pinned a piece of sugar paper on one of the blackboards and, starting from the top, filled three-quarters of it with horizontal bands of spectrum colours descending from cool to warm, finishing with a black silhouette of pointed roofs, trees and church spire, perforated here and there with crossed rectangles representing lighted windows.

Miss Trembelow said, 'Even those children who may not have been very good at art in the infants will now be able to make a nice sunset picture if they do exactly what I have done here.' She then instructed the children, one row at a time, to select the correct pastels from the big biscuit tin on her desk.

Morley had grasped the principle. He believed that he could do as well as the teacher. He had one of his rare feelings of confidence.

Mild confusion followed as pupils went back and forth choosing pastels and quietly arguing about which grimy colours were which. Intent on including power lines, pylons, a castle, a bridge and factory chimneys in his picture as well as the rooftops, trees and spire, Morley collected his pastels, pinned his paper to the middle one of the three blackboards and began his task. A band of blue at the top, followed by purple then red, just as Miss Trembelow had done. But in his version he dared to soften the edge of each colour so that it blended gently with its neighbour. He had also decided that, to impress everybody further, he would be the first to finish. Miss Trembelow wouldn't know yet that he was perhaps the best artist in the class: she would be impressed as well. And yes, he would put in a stained-glass window underneath the church spire.

'Are you the teacher now, then, Morley?' asked Nipper Horrabin from among the smiling group sorting through the pastels in the big tin on the teacher's desk.

Morley grinned shyly at the compliment as he rapidly smoothed red pastel with his finger. He glanced at Miss Trembelow's picture; her bands of colour were more-or-less straight; he would make his next strips more crooked, more natural. He put in the final, yellow band where the sky ended, then noticed there was a pink pastel in Miss Trembelow's tin. He added pink to the bottom of his sky. Next, with a cream pastel he had also discovered, he drew the half-disc of a disappearing sun complete with long-reaching rays. He stood back a step to admire his work, then wondered a little uncertainly about his departures from the teacher's example.

He looked up to see what the others were doing. He was surprised to find that that no one else was working along-side him at the blackboards: all the others had made do with their desks. One or two children were looking at him curiously. Miss Trembelow was bent over, helping someone at the back of the room. Someone sniggered. Miss Trembelow looked up and caught Morley's anxious eye.

She frowned. 'What on *earth* are you *doing*, boy? Who gave you permission to work at my blackboard?'

Morley felt himself trembling and a hot flush invading his face. He had thought that standing up at the blackboard was the junior department's way of doing sunset pictures, just as Miss Trembelow had done hers.

'Well?' demanded Miss Trembelow, as Morley struggled for an answer. 'Has the cat got your tongue?'

Junior 1A tittered.

'No, children.' She held up an admonishing finger. 'I am astonished, quite astonished that a pupil in Junior 1A should for some strange reason only known to himself, without as much as a by-your-leave, take it upon himself to work on the teacher's blackboard. I am simply . . . astonished. In fact I don't think that I have ever seen anything more astonishing in the whole of my life!' She came to the front of the room, put her hands on her hips and, fixing her eyes on Morley, addressed the class. 'Ah, but perhaps this boy thinks that he *is* the teacher.'

Fumbling, Morley tried to unpin his paper from the board with the vague idea of escaping back to his desk.

'Oh, no. Oh, no, no, no. No, if this boy wants to be the teacher, then the teacher he shall certainly be. He will remain out here working at the blackboard until his sunset picture is finished. But will he be a *good* teacher, children? Will he be able to teach us anything useful?'

'No-o, Miss Trem-be-low,' sang Junior 1A confidently.

'No, Miss Trembelow, indeed! And why will he not be a good teacher?'

Nobody seemed to know.

'Well, I will tell you why he will not be a good teacher, 1A, because . . .' She suddenly leaned close to the still shaking Morley and pointed to the bottom of his sky. 'What colour do you call this, boy?'

'P-Pink, I, I think, M-Miss Trembelow,' Morley mumbled unhappily.

'Pink, you think, Miss Trembelow, indeed!'

'And do *you* see any *pink* in *my* picture, 1A?' she asked, turning to the class and looking very puzzled.

'No-o, Miss Trem-be-low,' chanted 1A as if aghast.

'And what is *this*?' demanded Miss Trembelow, indicating Morley's half-sun and rays.

'The s-sun . . . I, I think,' whispered Morley.

'The *sun*, the boy thinks. Can *you* see a *sun* in *my* picture, 1A?'

'No-o, Miss Trem-be-low.'

'And are there *suns* in *your* pictures, 1A?'

219

'No-o, Miss Trem-be-low.'

'And *why* aren't there suns in *our* pictures?'

Junior 1A didn't know this either.

'It's because the suns in *our* sunset pictures have disappeared over the horizon, haven't they? Our suns have already *set*, haven't they?'

'Ye-es, Miss Trem-be-low,' they suddenly seemed to remember.

'You see,' said Miss Trembelow, smiling smugly, 'this boy cannot follow simple instructions, cannot do as he is told. He works on the blackboard, not at his desk like anyone else, and cannot learn how to do proper sunset pictures. And those who cannot learn, *cannot* become good teachers and teach others.'

A week or so later, still bruised by his experience, he had confided in May on one of her flying visits. They were alone: his mother was at the shops. She had listened without interruption, merely smiling; no derisive laughter as he had half-feared.

'Well, I shouldn't worry your head about it, love; I bet you know tons more about pictures than that daft old teacher any day of the week. She just sounds ignorant, to me, she does. I bet she was jealous 'cause your picture was better than what hers was. Anyroad, just 'cause your picture had a sun in it and she told you off and one or two kids laughed a bit, that's nothing. You should of seen what happened to me once.'

Morley would, he knew, feel much better if something worse had happened to glamorous May.

'I was at the pictures, see. With this chap – not Ron. It was before Ron. I must of been about eighteen. We went to this picture house what I'd never been to before – up Aston Cross, I think it was. Or was it Alum Rock? Anyroad, I had to go to the ladies, see. So I went in this door but it din't have anything writ on it. There was all these steps going up. I thought, funny. Well, I took no notice, went up these steps. They went on and on and then I come out in this great big space. How can I explain it? This place with all these lights shining on me. Ever so bright they was. I had to screw me eyes right up, I could hardly see where I was going. And there was all these people laughing. And some was shouting, "Get her off, get her off." Do you know what I'd been and gone and done?'

Morley shook his head, delighted but mystified.

'Well, I'd only gone and walked across the stage right in front of the screen, must of gone through the wrong door. The chap I was with, what was his name? Raymond, that was it. Anyroad, he said after that the picture was shining on me like as if *I* was the screen, shining on my coat and that and this film star's hands was moving all over my bust and that.'

Morley laughed aloud. He did feel much better already, and Miss Trembelow really did seem daft and old and ignorant and remote from the bright, jolly world of May.

'And remember, there was *hundreds* of people all looking at me – not just a class of kids like you had. For weeks afterwards, whatsit, Raymond, used to go around saying, "You didn't know May was a film star, did you? Oh yes, she's been on the pictures all right. She starred in this picture we seen up Alum Rock."'

In spite of May's consoling words, the incident of the sunset picture had still occasionally returned to haunt Morley during the intervening years. Although not recently. He wondered why he was reliving it with such enormous intensity now.

He sighed and tried to keep his mind on his watercolour painting. It was a Dutch landscape based on a photograph in *The Pictorial Book of Knowledge*. But his work looked flat and lifeless. The photograph wasn't much of an inspiration. 'Where windmills turn to hold the sea at bay,' said the caption beneath an austere black and white landscape devoid of foreground interest. The fields, roads, dykes, canal and horizon were all straight lines. And the rows of trees were all the same shape and size and evenly spaced, like toy trees, as were the windmills with their sails all set at exactly the same angle. Nothing to get your teeth into, as Mr Ross-Armitage would have said. He should have stuck with the coloured picture of the Norfolk Broads for Russ as he had originally planned, but a sudden impulse to paint a fitting setting to his father's death had prompted him to turn back the pages and find 'The Netherlands: Wonderland of Tulips, Wooden Shoes and Windmills'.

His legs felt cramped. He stretched and looked up, half-expecting to see Miss Trembelow and the classroom in bottom juniors. Ron was lounging in his armchair. The six o'clock news was on the wireless. There was an appetizing smell of chips coming from the kitchen: May was getting tea ready – or dinner, as Ron called it. The evening routine was already beginning to seem familiar.

Yes, all those years ago he had been upset about the sunset picture and May had put things right. And now he needed May to put things right again – *that* was what had put the sunset incident into his mind. But on this occasion May *was* the problem. If he did tell her that he was upset about her stories about his dad, she would simply make up something appropriate to please him. What he really wanted was for May to tell him something admirable about his father without being prompted. But how could he bring that about? Maybe with subtle hints. He was reminded of his similar quest to find out the name of his Mortal Sin but found the association of what he got up to with the life of his father distasteful.

He looked at the big expanse of sky in his painting, trying hard to forget that other, sunset sky. It could do with a bit of livening up. He wetted those parts not occupied by clouds, mixed a wash of ultramarine with touches of yellow and crimson to subdue it and applied it to the wet areas, allowing it to drift more or less at random. Then, checking that Ron wasn't watching, he sucked his brush nearly dry and blotted up the blobs of surplus paint where they had gathered at the dry edge of the horizon.

Suppose he did decide to broach the subject of his dad and May didn't understand, thinking it wonderful to have a father who played the fool and kept you in stitches all the time. Maybe there simply *weren't* any stories for her to tell that put his father in a serious, respectable or brave light.

He decided that the Dutch landscape was a failure. It depressed him. Two failures one after the other: the barn and now this. Even the tree he had introduced to add interest in the foreground looked unconvincing, overworked and muddy.

May came into the lounge. She was wearing a smart apron, not a pinafore like his mother's. 'Tea'll be ready in about ten minutes,' she said. She came over to the coffee table where Morley was working and peered very close to his painting. 'Oh, you've finished it, love; it's lovely. And it's that real I could just imagine meself having a walk down that road by them trees there. I never know how you do it, love.'

See, thought Morley, I'm right: you'd say anything to please. Look at that tree, anybody can see it's crap; anybody can *see* it looks made up. It's made up 'cause I didn't think to work from a real tree in the garden. And look at those clouds: old Armitage would say they look as if they'd been carved out of plaster of Paris. But he said, 'Mm, well, I've done better,' then wondered if it sounded as if he was bragging.

'Come and have a look at this, Ron,' said May.

Ron ambled over, coins jingling. 'Mm, quite artistic, old chap. Got a touch of Vernon Ward about it.'

What would you know about it, Ron? thought Morley, deliberately visualizing Ron's dad crouched over his bucket of shit, and, Who's fucking Vernon Ward when he's at home?

'Who's Vernon Ward when he's at home, then, Ron?' asked May.

'Landscape-with-birds johnnie,' said Ron. 'That print in the dining room's a Vernon Ward.'

'Well, you learn something new every day, don't you, love?' May said to Morley. 'I'm sure *I* din't know it was a whatsit Ward.'

'He's signed it clearly enough in the corner.'

'Yes, but *I* don't go round looking for chaps' names in the corners of pictures.'

Ron used his spare hand to stroke his chin and Morley could hear the sound of scraping bristles. 'Oh yes, one of the most popular living painters around, very much sought after. Saint John-Cromwell's got an original. Didn't you see it this morning, old chap?'

'N-No, Eugène said he thought all the pictures were put away for safety or s-something because of air raids.'

223

'Oh yes, if you're talking about his really old and valuable stuff, but he's hung on to a few lesser works to decorate the place.'

Morley revised his present jaundiced opinion of Ron – just a little.

'Oh, that reminds me, Lizzie, Virginia rang just before you came home,' Ron said.

'You din't tell me. That's You-jean's mom,' she said to Morley. 'Did she want me, then?'

'Oh, she enquired about your health, but no, she wanted to know whether I could get her a couple of dozen bottles of champagne, or at least some really decent sparkling wine for a friend of theirs.'

'And can you?'

'We-e-ell,' said Ron, 'almost certainly not real champagne but . . .'

Morley watched as he went through his performance: lips disappearing, brow furrowed, eyes squinting at the ceiling, hand vigorously scrubbing his chin. It was very tricky, depended on a lot of things, but Ron thought he might be able to pull it off.

'Oh, and I forgot, old chap,' he addressed Morley directly a second time – once was a rare event when May was there. 'She said Eugène had perked up considerably after your visit, said he'd been livelier than she'd seen him for ages.'

Morley was sitting up in bed with May beside him. He hadn't feigned sleep tonight and May had brought him cocoa and biscuits again.

They were talking about his visit to Eugène's and Morley had confessed that he had not opened his mouth more than half a dozen times and then usually to say yes or no, and that for most of the time he hadn't been able to think of anything to say.

'There's nothing wrong with being a good listener, love,' said May. 'And you must of cheered him up all right, else his mom wouldn't of said so, and Ron would never of just med it up: it'd never of struck him.'

224

That, at least, was true: Ron was very sparing with compliments. Morley was far from displeased but felt he hadn't *merited* what good he was supposed to have done; it didn't seem due to any ability. It was like finding five bob rather than earning it from the sale of one of his pictures. 'B-But I still can't think how *I* could have made him feel any better.'

'You worry too much, love. You *did* and that's all that matters. I mean, he really can be a moody little devil sometimes and his mom's always going on about how he never tells her anything. And he shuts himself in that room of his for hours on end in holiday times. Still, he's nearly fifteen and I s'pose that's an awkward age. He probably just *liked* you, love. Enjoyed your company.' She turned and smiled. 'You in't so bad, you know. And tomorrow it might all be different with you doing all the talking for a change.'

Tomorrow. Morley shuddered. He shouldn't have so rashly promised another visit. But the unexpected message from Eugène's mother to inform her son of a forgotten hospital appointment about his leg and his swift departure in a hired car had been such a relief that he had been only too eager to promise anything.

He didn't want to talk or think about Eugène, not now. He sought a means of changing the subject without appearing to be too abrupt. 'I can't imag-gine *you* being, er, awkward when you was – w-were fifteen, May.'

'Well, it probably don't affect girls so much, but I s'pose I had my moments.' She handed him his cocoa. 'Oi, get this down you before it gets cold.'

Morley gulped it quickly, imagining skin developing on it even as he drank, and considered how he might best manage the conversation. Definitely no direct questions about his father in any way that might alert May to his anxieties. Just get her to talk casually about herself and the family, and sooner or later his dad might crop up naturally – this time, hopefully, in an acceptable role.

'That was nice,' he said as May took his empty cup. 'Er, when you were at school, May, what lessons were you best at?'

'Ooh, let's think. Well not *much*, that's for sure. Weren't

225

too bad at sums and mental arithmetic – I worked in all these shops before I got married and I don't reckon I ever got diddled, or diddled anybody else for that matter. History, geography . . . mm, no. And English, well, writing stories was all right, but verbs and all them whatsits; and teach and learn, and borrow and lend used to get me mixed up a bit. Should of tried harder. Ron used to be always on about the way I talked, but then I only worked at shops in Nechells where everybody knew me, so it would never of done to start putting it on. I used to tell Ron, it's no good trying to be something what you're not. You've got to be yourself, haven't you, love?'

Morley nodded without conviction – not being very clear who his own self was anyway, and then always planning to be more like Alan Ladd or Nigel the boy sleuth.

'Now your mom was very good at English all right, nearly always come top. And she speaks nice – I don't mean put on, just nice. But then she worked in that big posh house in Edgbaston with that rich old woman, whatsername, so p'raps she had to watch the way she talked.'

As on Monday night when May had come in, the ceiling light was off and the only illumination came from the bedside lamp. Within its pool of mellow light and snug between the crisp, lavender-scented sheets, he should have felt secure and relaxed, eager to listen to more of May's reminiscences. But tonight he felt strained and full of foreboding.

'Was Mom still at school when you was – w-were there, May?' He had already worked out the answer, but since Monday night May had seemed less than perfect and he had the urge to test her.

'Oh yes, well, for a couple of years. Let's see, she's seven and a quarter years older than me, so when I started . . . she must of been twelve. Yes, 'cause for a couple of years she used to tek me to school with her – well, nearly a couple 'cause she left in the Easter.'

Morley was impressed but disappointed: he had harboured the feeble hope that perhaps her accounts of his father's exploits were due to a poor memory.

'When was it M-Mom m-met Dad then?' He hadn't meant to ask. It had just come out. He held his breath.

'When? Mm, must of been 1929 – no 1930, 'cause I left school in 1929 and I'd been working at the grocer's round about six months when your mom told us about him and I first seen him. I'll never forget, he come into our shop this night and – gosh, you'd of laughed.'

Morley braced himself.

'He'd got his arm in this sling, he was limping and all his face was twisted up and one of his eyes was closed. Anyroad, he goes up to old Arnott – that was our gaffer – and says in this daft voice, all high and squeaky like as if he was being strangled, "Sir, have you got a Miss May Morley working in this establishment?" I was bending down sorting out the shelves but I stood up to watch.

'Old Arnott goes all dithery. "Who, who are you, then?" he goes.

'"I? I am a long lost relation from overseas," goes your dad, "and Miss Morley is required at home urgent – urgently."

'"Well," says old Arnott, "well, I don't know, I mean, this is very unusual. She hasn't finished work yet. I mean, why is she wanted?"

'"Sufficient to say," says your dad, "that it is of a highly confidential nature, an emergency, as you as a man of business will understand."

'Well, I din't know him from Adam then, but when old Arnott weren't looking this chap winked at me; and, anyroad, I still had half an hour or more to go and I think, well, anything to get me out of work early.'

Morley felt cold and tense, his forehead moist. He found himself distractedly wondering how May managed to speak grammatically when her stories needed it or when she was quoting somebody else. Perhaps she *was* capable of speaking better. He didn't want to hear any more, although there was a perverse need to know the worst.

'Anyroad,' continued May, 'when we'd got outside he told me who he was. Said he had come to tea and they was waiting for me to come home but Walter said how old Arnott

227

used to keep me behind, working all hours. It was Walter who'd put him up to it to get me home early. Oh, it wasn't half a scream when . . .'

It was no good, he would just have to accept that his father was the way he was. Learn to live with it. Gloomily, he tried to salvage what he could. Perhaps his dad mainly clowned around when he was with May. That it was May who usually put him up to it. And wasn't May always making a fool of herself? Blundering around in picture houses; holding on to a rake instead of the pole on the bus, then falling over and showing her drawers to everybody; genuflecting in the pictures. Well that might be okay for an aunt.

A thought struck him. Say May had been his mother and she came to the Art School – if he passed – for a meeting or an exhibition or something. How ashamed he would be every time she opened her mouth! Yes, nobody was perfect. And his dad only fooled around on purpose, did things . . . from choice, to make people laugh, or to solve an awkward problem. Not out of clumsiness or short sight like May. And didn't *he*, after all, sometimes impersonate Hitler and Dai Davies and Mr Preen to make people laugh? *And* pretend to be French . . . and yes, go on, say it, toss off nearly every night! Say *he* had a son who found out all this about *his* father. He squeezed his eyes tight and waited for the roaring in his ears to blot out the awful thought. And would having had a father like Micky Plant's make him feel any better? Or David Meyer's? Mr Meyer, old, wizened, with his thick accent and thick glasses, behind the counter of his men's outfitter's in Upfield. But it would have been nice just to have had something, just a little thing, well, to be proud of.

'You selfish little swine' – he could hear his mother's scathing voice clearly – 'it's only you you're thinking about. Self, self, self, that's you. Who do you think you are, anyway, criticizing others; what's so special about you? You! You wouldn't dare say boo to a goose, you wouldn't; you curl up when anybody looks at you, you do; you can't do a simple job around the house, or be trusted to do a simple errand, you can't. It's only because *you*'re not worth bragging about yourself that you want something about your father to brag about. No thought about loving him; no thought about saying prayers for his soul in purgatory. Your mind's just full of rubbish.'

Yeh, yeh, I know: just like that pig bin, he answered silently. He held back the threatening tears, sighed deeply, changed it into a yawn then, aware that that sounded ill-mannered, tried turning it into a cough.

'Got a frog in your throat, love?' asked May, putting an arm round him. 'Shall I get you another drink, then?'

He wanted May to go away so he could be alone with his thoughts, but forced a tight smile. 'I think I've got a hair in my mouth,' he improvised, running his tongue round his mouth. 'From my paintbrush. From when I was painting.' He swallowed theatrically. 'It's gone now.'

'Mm, you be careful, love. Anyroad, where was I? Oh yes, we all knew a *bit* about your dad beforehand 'cause Walter and your dad worked at the same place and played for the same football team – that was Locke's, the works team.'

'Walter was about the same age as Dad, then?' He knew but wanted to keep things neutral.

'Yes, Walter's the oldest, then your mom, then me, then John who died. Yes, poor old Walter might of been a famous footballer if it hadn't been for his motorbike accident. Though they said he wasn't as good as your dad.'

Morley's interest quickened. He knew his father had been good at football and cricket, had more than once even resented it, knowing that he would never be able to compete but . . . 'H-He was *really* good then, May?'

'Yes, course: good at all sports, he was, but ever so good at football. Took football ever so serious at one time. There was them that said he could of been a professional – might of played for Villa even.'

Morley felt like weeping with relief – and remorse – but he held himself in check. Why did he never learn? Why did he always jump to conclusions? Why hadn't he taken his father's skill at games into account? Yet he had *known* that he had once played for the Motor Works team. He thought of the fort his dad had made him, and the trolley, and the

229

little table on the landing for his mother. He remembered his serious discussions with Percy Pinder, the books he regularly got from the library. Though he really hadn't known about the Villa. But May was probably exaggerating. 'D-Did they *r-really* say he was good enough to play for Villa?'

'Oh yes, they did, all right. We din't half used to brag about it.' May's manner was serious and full of respect. 'I'd of thought you'd of knowed all about it. I don't know the ins and outs of everything but he had trials and that. You'll have to ask Ron; Ron was a big Villa supporter once upon a time, well, I reckon he still is but he keeps quiet about it now, pretends he's keen on whatsit – rugger – but he'll tell you all right.'

Morley was satisfied. Nearly playing for Villa made everything else seem all right. It was something to treasure and certainly something he could tell Micky Plant about at a suitable moment.

He restored May to perfection again. Ron was all right. His mother wasn't too bad. He himself could be worse. He forgave Miss Trembelow and smiled at the sunset picture episode. And he would easily manage Eugène tomorrow. His mind now freed from most of its recent burdens, his Mortal Sin poised itself ready to fill the space, but he managed to push it aside: he could deal with that as well – later. He felt almost happy.

May's arm was still around him, her face close. He could smell her scent and feel the pressure of her breast under the thin fabric of the glamorous thing she was wearing. He suddenly felt terribly excited. He wondered if May could tell. He tried to forget that she was his mother's sister.

May gave him a squeeze. 'I bet your dad's probably up there now, having a little smile to hisself, looking down at us, hearing every word we're saying and knowing every little thing what we're thinking about.'

Morley doubted whether May was a believer but his conscience was stirred. God had been good; was this the way to repay Him – with impure thoughts? Somewhat reluctantly he allowed May to become his aunt again.

# Chapter 24

'On the shelf above the bench somewhere,' called Eugène, 'in the bigger of the two boxes marked bromide paper. But for heaven's sake don't open the small one while the curtain's open.'

Morley took down the boxes in Eugène's darkroom. Although there was a considerable difference in size between them, he spent seconds anxiously comparing them before deciding which was the bigger – just to be sure. On each, in red type, was the injunction 'OPEN UNDER SAFE LIGHT ONLY!' He understood: Mr Preen had demonstrated developing and printing under the stage in 2A's classroom. He opened the big box cautiously, not knowing what to expect. A surge of excitement shot through him. It was the yellow book again. Why hadn't Eugène told him what he was supposed to be looking for? He flicked through it quietly and quickly while he still had it to himself, then guiltily closed it at Eugène's shout of, 'Found it, old man?'

'Yes, j-just putting things back,' said Morley, mentally trying to coax his condition back to normal.

'Couldn't manage the old floorboards by myself,' Eugène said with a grin when Morley was seated and the book was between them on the coffee table. 'And what with being suddenly whisked off to the old hospital yesterday, I completely forgot to enlist your valuable aid in shoving it back in its accustomed place. Still, the darkroom's fairly secure: Pearson's got strict instructions never so much as to cross its threshold. Anyway, it was only a temporary measure; you can stick it back under the floorboards shortly. Shoving it in the printing-paper box was a stroke of genius, eh? Even Pearson's likely to be scared off by the warning label – she'd probably think it was full of gas or electricity. But one can't be too careful: she's got this compulsion to snoop and I wouldn't put it past the mater either. Now here's a little poser for you, old man, changing the subject only slightly: how would *you* go about checking that your personal stuff in cupboards and drawers wasn't being pried upon?'

Morley got as far as opening his mouth.

'I've been trying the time-honoured device of fixing hairs across the opening cracks – but with a few of my own refinements. Know how I do it?'

Morley thought he probably did; Nigel and Dick the boy sleuths had done it half a dozen times. 'W-Well, if I was –'

'Dust, for one thing!' exclaimed Eugène triumphantly. 'Good old-fashioned dust. Most glues are shiny even when they're dry – pretty tell-tale to someone alerted to the possibility of a trap. Sprinkle the glue with dust while it's wet – wherever you are there's always likely to be dust around.'

Yeh, there's plenty around here all right, thought Morley. A pretty dusty family generally, what with your old Uncle Richard's study as well.

'And be sure to keep your handiwork well distanced from the lock or handle. And never at eye-level if it's a door. If necessary, press the glue flat with, say, a knife blade. There's something you might find handy one day.' Eugène pointed to the packet of Craven A he had put on top of the yellow book. 'Help yourself, old man.'

So Eugène must have read the Nigel and Dick stories: he had been almost quoting, Morley thought, as he lit his and Eugène's cigarettes. 'Have you got oth-ther things, then, that you want kept private, er . . . ?'

'Perhaps the odd item or two,' Eugène said with the odd twisted smile of yesterday, 'but nothing frightfully important.

It's the principle of the thing. A fellow needs his privacy and the assurance that his things aren't being secretly examined.'

In spite of himself, and feeling much more receptive than yesterday, Morley's eyes kept stealing towards the yellow book, his excitement rising. He was sure Eugène was aware of his interest and was provoking him. Why else the pantomime of getting him to retrieve it from the darkroom? But he knew that his pleasure in looking at it would be spoiled in Eugène's company. It would be like going to a party full of pre-war luxuries with a toothache. He certainly wasn't going to *ask* if he could have another look – and anyway he had resolved to be good, although his resolve was much weaker than last night. Wait for Eugène to suggest it and then he would see.

'And *has* anyone b-been, er, looking – p-prying into your things, then, er . . . ?'

Eugène leaned back in his armchair, laced his hands behind his head and yawned. 'Without a doubt, old man.' He yawned again and Morley noticed with satisfaction two discoloured teeth. 'But inconclusive as to the identity of the snooper. Still, I've still got one or two more tricks up my sleeve to solve that little mystery.'

'Oh?' said Morley patiently.

'Well, to begin with . . .'

Morley repressed a sigh. He gauged that he had been here for over an hour, with Eugène talking non-stop throughout. He resigned himself to another long spell of unrelieved boredom which he would have to disguise as intelligent interest, and tried desperately hard to think of something to impress Eugène with when he had finished. The five-shilling consolation prize he had won in a children's colouring competition in *Reynold's News*? His friendship with a GI? His dad nearly playing for Villa? Or perhaps he could claim that his dad actually had. He pictured Eugène's blank face, his superior smile, his yawns and banished the idea.

It would be a good idea to find out if Eugène did have the Nigel and Dick books. If he casually sauntered over to the shelves to have a quick look, would it appear bad-mannered?

If nothing else, it would certainly relieve the tedium.

'T-Touch of cramp,' he said almost to himself, rubbing his calf. He stood up and edged sideways to the shelves containing Eugène's treasures, exaggeratedly flexing his knee.

Eugène was talking about fingerprints. 'You see, old man, french chalk's fine, provided the surface is dark, or transparent – like glass, for example. But there's a problem if the dabs are on a pale surface. Now I've experimented with soot, sieved through fine muslin . . .'

Nigel, the more inventive of the boy tecs, had explained this to Dick using exactly the same words! Morley smiled knowingly. 'Mm, v-very original,' he said generously.

He swept his gaze along the rows of books and boxes. Surely Eugène wouldn't display them openly, not after claiming that the ideas from them were his own. Then, just above his head, he caught sight of the familiar red and yellow lettering: *Nigel Accused* by Edmund Willis Frazer. He glanced at Eugène talking into space, then surreptitiously resumed his search. A bit further along was *Dick Stands Alone* and *A Spy at St Cuthbert's*. 'J-Jolly good idea,' he flung over his shoulder to show he was still listening. *The Mystery of Swallings End*, *Trouble at Dieppe* and *Mistaken Identity*. Eugène had probably got them all. He limped back to his seat very satisfied with himself. Eugène wasn't so bright after all, if it hadn't occurred to him that Morley might also have read the books.

Eugène suddenly leaned forward and looked at him levelly. 'You, er, didn't seem to be very interested in this book yesterday, old man?' He pointed to the yellow book on the table.

Morley was startled. 'Well, er, I . . .'

'You know, I took it to school a couple of terms ago and some of the fellows went practically berserk. One chap actually offered me a fiver for it. Had to keep a tight reign on it.' He stubbed out his cigarette. 'Still . . . How old are you, old man? Twelve?'

'Th-Thirteen . . . b-but only just.' To show his age hadn't been too badly misjudged.

'Mm,' said Eugène. 'Now here's an interesting thought, old man. If this book – shiny cover, notice – was ever offered

234

in evidence in court, well, the only prints on it would be yours. And – although this mightn't stand up – *I* have evidence that you opened it . . . this morning.'

Morley hoped his embarrassment wasn't showing. He was tempted to deny it. His voice, when he found it, sounded cracked and squeaky. 'Well I didn't kn-know it was the same book. I d-didn't understand the French on the cover. I j-just, well . . .'

'That's all right, old man. I'm not standing in moral judgement; just demonstrating the efficacy of my methods. But aren't you going to enquire how I know?'

Morley nodded obediently.

'Now just examine the top . . . there.'

Morley gingerly picked up the book. Four hairs were sticking out of the top edge. He opened the book and riffled through it. It looked as though the hairs had originally spanned two sections of pages: the other ends of each were still messily secured with glue to the flanking pages.

Eugène was smiling smugly. 'But no dust called for in this case.' He threw his hair back. 'And another thing: notice anything different in the arrangement of the room?'

Morley didn't feel co-operative. He shook his head.

'That picture I saw you admiring yesterday: I moved it.'

Morley looked around. The Frans Hals was facing the entrance to the darkroom.

'Just the ticket. Dark, you see: makes an unobtrusive looking glass – a real glass would be noticed. So from this chair, I had a *fairly* clear view of what you were up to – then the broken hairs confirmed it.'

Eugène lay back as if waiting for a reaction. Morley experienced the all too familiar feeling of being manipulated.

'Of course,' said Eugène softly, 'some fellows *prefer* studying this sort of thing in solitude, and if that's . . .'

Without thinking, Morley scrutinized a drawing of a maiden in a dungeon sandwiched between two naked young men, to prove that *he* jolly well didn't.

He turned a few pages. A kneeling man in a monocle was closely surveying the thrust-out posterior of a woman pulling down her flimsy pants. On the facing page the same woman, now naked save for stockings and high heels, was attending to the man with her mouth. Morley was even more thrilled and shocked than yesterday.

'What do you think, old man?' asked Eugène, licking his lips, his eyes gleaming.

Morley's mind was racing. He would have to confess what he was doing. But did it really matter on top of everything else? Was it something he could perhaps brag about to Micky Plant? How many pictures could he commit to memory to draw in private later? Why couldn't Eugène bugger off for ten minutes? But one thought overwhelmed the others: to put Eugène in his place.

He turned another page. A rather crudely drawn worm's-eye view of a woman, peeling off her stocking. He thought of May in the cosy Weston pub, of his father playing up the landlord – now with approval. He felt mischievous. He leisurely turned more pages, feeling like Mr Ross-Armitage doing one of his 'post mortems'. 'Oh, n-not too bad,' he said evenly, 'not too bad at all.' He hesitated, then added, as if reluctant to comment yet determined to be truthful, 'Except that . . . well, it's just that some of the p-pictures are a bit ins-sensitive and heavy-h-handed and some of them look as if the artists don't kn-know m-much about women's an-an-anatomy.'

Eugène's jaw dropped, then he quickly pulled himself together. 'Of course, you paint, don't you?' he now acknowledged. 'But how is it that *you* know so much about women's anatomy?'

Stung by the 'you', Morley said recklessly, 'Well, special books and pictures m-mainly and the –'

'You mean books like this one?'

'Well, yes, am-mong others. You see, artists are interested in the human figure, er, in action. Because if y-you can learn to draw bare – naked women . . . and men really well, you can draw p-practically anything.'

Eugène leaned forward and nodded seriously.

Morley heard May saying, 'Your dad had them, you see. Everybody listened when he got going.'

Eugène said, 'And where did you see books like mine, Moreton?'

'Morley,' corrected Morley, 'my Ch-Christian name, that is,' wondering if that made things any clearer. 'I've got this friend Ross-Armitage, m-much older than me, a very famous artist. He's got loads of books, all sorts, French – like this – but others as well, oh, from everywhere. I like the American and, er, Dutch ones best. And he p-paints from models in his s-studio – at his house. Bare – naked girls and women.'

'While *you* are there?' Eugène was wide eyed.

'Oh yes, funny, I've never really thought ab-bout it before but I suppose artists are a p-pretty broad-minded lot really, y-you know, think of it as just natural.' While he talked, he flicked over the pages with apparent indifference, greedily absorbing everything he saw.

Eugène offered him another cigarette. 'Didn't I hear you were at art school?' There was almost respect in his voice.

'September,' said Morley, lighting up and giving himself the benefit of having passed, 'I start then.'

'And will you be drawing naked models there?'

'Well, n-not in the first year,' Morley improvised, 'and then n-not all the time, there are other art subjects and ordinary subjects as well.'

'I'd forgotten, I was going to tell you yesterday about my adventures with the binoculars,' Eugène said a bit feebly. 'Over there at about seven o'clock, two or three times a week, a very passable piece of skirt disrobes right in front of her window.' He pointed towards a distant house through the trees at the bottom of the garden. 'Takes off everything – absolutely starkers, she is – though I can only actually see her upper part. She looks as if she's admiring herself in front of her glass – which is out of my vision. Then off she goes – to her bath, I imagine. Twenty minutes or so later, back she comes, still starkers, brushes her hair and then puts on her underclothes and her evening finery. One of the very few compensations of being laid up. Looks as if she's in the next room through the old Barr and Stroud's. Not so much na-*val* binoculars as na-*vel* binoculars, eh?'

Morley looked up from a coloured picture of a scantily dressed couple flying towards each other on swings, their private parts destined to mesh in mid-air, smiled politely and said, 'Mm, must be fun.'

Eugène leaned further forward and asked, 'Have you got a girl, Morley?'

He was on the point of saying no, because he didn't think that he looked the sort of boy to have one. But evidently Eugène thought him capable, he had Eugène's interest and his stammer was in retreat. He thought of his father in the pub again; he felt in a similar mood to when he was being French. 'There *was* a girl recently b-but the family moved away.' He was thinking of the girl he had worshipped across the aisle in church, whose appeal had vanished the moment she had examined the contents of her handkerchief with such fascinated interest. 'So I only had her for a f-few months. The others are more sort of casual friends really.'

'But I mean, did you, do you go out with any of them, just the two of you, on your own?' Eugène was agog.

Morley put down the book: he needed to concentrate on what to say next. He thought of Sheila Godden and Margaret Quinn from his class – if only it were true! 'Oh yes, we go for walks in the hills by us, up town – Birmingham that is.' He knew town meant London to Eugène's sort. 'The flicks, a caff – c-café sometimes. You know, the usual things.'

'Well, to be frank, I don't know if I do, really. You don't know what it's like being at school, and there's no one around here I know. I've got heaps of cousins but only one remotely near my age – and she's pretty puerile. Have you, do you, er, when you're in the country, do you ever *do* anything?'

Morley decided to look puzzled.

'You know, kissing and, er, hugging and that sort of thing.'

'Oh that, I thought that was the wh-whole idea. I th-thought for a minute, you meant something else.'

Eugène threw back his hair, shuffled to the edge of his chair and said very seriously, 'There's a proper way of kissing girls, isn't there? I mean you can't really sort it out from that book, can you? It's much too, er . . . But I've seen it in

238

films. Don't you put your left arm round the waist and your right arm round the shoulders, er . . . like this?' He held out his own arms as he had described. 'Or is it the other way around?' He reversed his arms' positions. 'I mean, a fellow needs to know these things.'

Morley certainly didn't know that there was a proper way – though he made a mental note to check in the next appropriate film. 'There's no special way,' he said quickly. 'It s-sort of c-comes natural – naturally. S-Some do it one way, some do it another. Some put both arms round your sh-shoulders and want you to p-put your arms round their waists. Some want it the other way round. But then wh-when you're lying down it's different because –'

'Lying down?' Eugène licked his lips. 'When you're lying down, do you, have you ever touched a girl's . . . a girl's . . . twinkle?'

Morley felt like laughing aloud at the infant language. 'Well, not with *them*,' he said carefully, 'at least with them only through their knicks. But two of them let me have a l-look. They were only t-twelve or thirteen, though.' He wondered if he dared make further claims.

Eugène was encouraging. 'So if not with them, with other, with older girls?'

'Only the one . . . and only once,' he began modestly, as if unwilling to reveal too much. Now that he had Eugène's undivided attention he wanted to make the most of it, impress him with his art and a supposed exciting life with grown-up friends. He chose one of the fantasies which had recently accompanied his nightly activities. The woman was an amalgam of the nurse at the dental hospital and the ATS tart Perky Beswick had told him about. 'It really goes back to the drawing and painting. This Yank, a master sergeant he was, wanted this picture done of him to send to his folks back home. So I did this painting in watercolours with the Yankee flag behind. He paid me twenty-five bob. I b-bought a jacket and some paints with it.

'Well, he showed it around, and other people wanted their pictures done as well. Now some artists just copy from photos but I always p-paint from real life, 'cause if a picture is to have any real value, it m-must have the artist's p-personal touch and not be a m-m-mere superficial likeness.' He was quoting Ross-Armitage. 'Otherwise, you might just as well make do with a photo, and forget the painting.'

Eugène was impatiently tapping his new and shorter plaster cast. Morley took the hint.

'Anyway, this ATS girl wanted a picture to send to her boyfriend overseas – probably heard about it from this Yank. So I went round the house – she was on l-leave – and drew this picture of just her face and finished it off at home. When I took it back, she gave me ten bob and a packet of f-fags. And she said would I do her another one, different this time. "Come round Friday," she said. But it had to be finished in the one go 'cause her leave would be up by then and she had to go back on the Saturday morning. Anyway, when I got there she was only w-wearing this white silky thing and this turban.' He was remembering May in his bedroom. 'And she wanted me to draw her whole figure. She'd been drinking, she had this big bottle of Yankee bourbon. She gave me some and she said, "I hope you won't be too bashful but I want to take this off" – the wh-white silky thing – "'cause that's the way my boyfriend likes to see me." Then she laughed and said this was another boyfriend.'

Eugène's mouth was open, his tongue active. 'And was she naked underneath?'

'You bet, well, except stockings and high heels,' Morley said, visualizing Jane in the *Daily Mirror*. 'Well, she couldn't keep all that still so it took a long time. Oh' – with sudden inspiration – 'she k-kept getting cramp and had to stretch out a b-bit and walk round.'

'Tell me what you could see when she walked around.'

'Oh well, everything, all her hairs and that. Oh, and she kept coming over and l-looking at the drawing.'

'And while she was looking, was she very close?'

'P-P-Practically pushing. Mind you, she'd had a few by then – probably didn't really know what she was doing. Anyway, I finished the drawing off, and she said she liked it and went to get some money from her handbag, and I –'

'Did she have to bend over to get the money, and did you see her from behind, and were her legs apart, and could you see her other little hole?' Eugène was lying back, hand under the hem of his jersey.

'Er, sort of, but she'd only got eight and three in change. She said she would send another five bob in the post – unless I wanted something else instead, and she gave me this funny look, and sort of winked.'

He wanted to leave it there, not only because he was disinclined to describe aloud his own imagined physical actions but also because he was uncertain about what precisely you did and the appropriate terms to use. Anyway, the fantasy rarely went much further – it hardly needed to for his own requirements.

He finished rather lamely, 'So I s-said I'd like something else, er, and then it happened.'

'What did?' demanded Eugène.

'She p-put my hand on to her, er . . . twinkle.'

'And did you put your fingers in?'

'Mm.'

'Right inside?'

'Yes, er . . .'

'All the way?'

'Mm.'

Eugène closed his eyes, his fingers still busy. He wriggled around in spite of his plaster-encased leg and let out a classless, 'Who-o-er,' then asked breathlessly, 'Did, did she come?'

He was surprised that Eugène said come, just like the Reggies, and even more surprised at the idea of women coming as well. 'Mm, qu-quite qu-quickly.'

'And did she shoot all over your hand?' Shoot, another word the Reggies used.

'Mm.'

'And what about you?'

'She j-just did the same . . . to me.'

'With her hand?'

241

Dare he claim even more? Perky had often described other ways and well, there were plenty of alternatives in the yellow book. 'Yes w-with her hand . . . At first.'

'And then what? Not with her *mouth*?'

'Mmm,' he said neutrally but he cringed as he said it.

His account, meagre as it had become, seemed to be having a profound effect on Eugène. He was working his hand violently and hissing through gritted teeth, 'And did you . . . shoot . . . all . . . over her . . . everywhere . . . and were her . . . legs still wide apart . . . very wide apart . . . and was her twinkle . . . still . . . open . . . and . . . and . . . ? Shush, quiet, quiet . . . who-o-er, who-o-er, who-*e-e-e*.' He collapsed backwards, then rubbed his leg above the plaster, grimacing.

Then, with no reference to what had just happened, Eugène dabbed under his jersey with a grubby handkerchief, gestured to Morley to take a cigarette, took one himself and continued his monologue on the re-emergence of Hitler and a Fourth Reich that he had begun the previous day.

It was a relief when, half an hour later, Eugène got his second wind and the subject returned to what it had been earlier.

'You're a lucky old so and so, old man,' Eugène said, 'living in the wide, real world, free to come and go as you please, not subject to the monastic constraints I have to endure for most of the year. I mean, when you're at school, you are forced to resort to practices, that, er, people like you might find perhaps a little difficult to understand. Oh, I'm not talking about pansies, heaven forbid. But you know, if you're perfectly normal like me, and the real thing's not, er, available, is there anything wrong in, say, two of you with, er, similar inclinations, er, combining forces? I mean, it's really far more *natural* with two people. Far more natural than doing, er, things, on your own.'

Morley's relief turned to unease. He tried to hide it, tapping his cigarette to free it from ash, politely attentive but contemplating flight.

'Don't misunderstand me, Morley, I have nothing to do with people who *prefer* their own sort. No, no, give me a girl every time, oh yes. But at school, people like me have limited resources. And, I mean, well, one needs the release. I mean, if one doesn't do *something*, one can become ill, one's system can get poisoned, can't it? So you can either fly solo or make it more natural, more interesting with a chum, and imagine, er, that he's a girl – just for the time being, to practise, get things right – until the real thing's available, eh, you follow?'

Eugène was waiting for an answer. Morley asked, 'What's a solo flyer?' though he had a fair idea.

'Sorry, it might be slang confined to school. Well, someone who does it unassisted, er, tosses off . . .'

Something prompted Morley to look baffled.

'. . . well, masturbates in solitude, because he's an oik, and can't find anyone else. But you, Morley, have had experience with girls – and women. And you must know simply heaps more than I do and . . .'

He let Eugène carry on. He had the word. *He had the word!* He mustn't forget it. Master: think of schoolmaster – Ross-Armitage. And bait: think of . . . Perky Beswick fishing – bait, bait. He had to write it down, *now*.

He asked for the lavatory. 'That l-lime juice, and all that tea b-before I came out,' he explained.

Eugène gave him directions and a suspicious look.

In the lavatory, Morley wrote 'masterbaits' in his notebook. While he piddled he mouthed, 'Father, I masturbate . . . I masturbate . . . ed.' Masturbated. Yes, masturbated. What an ugly word. 'For an ugly deed,' said Canon Reilly from far off. But the word was uncannily familiar. He had heard it before somewhere. He knew it was right. He absolutely *knew*.

He washed his hands. He felt brighter now, and Eugène had become easier to handle. But he still wanted to escape as soon as he decently could. Back in Eugène's room, he noted for the first time that the room smelled musty . . . and of something else . . . unpleasant.

The telephone rang from somewhere downstairs.

'Damn,' said Eugène. 'A pound to a penny it's the mater

243

fussing about something. Look, be a good fellow and open the door, would you?'

The ringing stopped and Pearson's shouting voice could be heard, though the words were barely decipherable. Eugène cocked his ear and frowned then held a finger up as if Morley was about to interrupt.

Morley tiptoed back to his seat. He glanced at Eugène; his collar was dirty and his skin looked greasy and the hand he was holding up was the one that had been busy under his jersey. Seen round the pig bin, he might easily be taken for one of the scruffs. And his mother would have been disgusted at the condition of Eugène's lavatory. Even the yellow book, with its association with Eugène, now seemed to have lost a little of its savour.

How wonderful it would be, he thought, to be in an antiseptic-smelling chemist's buying a bottle of Lucozade. As soon as he was free, that's what he would do. Pity it couldn't be used as an excuse for a quick departure. 'Ah sorry, old man, just remembered, got to go and buy a bottle of Lucozade, urgently. If I don't take it regularly, I get this terrible . . .' He smiled at the absurdity of it. Ah, but maybe something on similar lines. Obedient to Eugène's still warning finger, Morley quietly searched through all his pockets, knitted his brows and went through them again. As Eugène showed no interest, he took off his jacket and started fiddling with the lining.

Pearson's voice stopped but there were no ascending footsteps.

Making it seem very important, Eugène said, 'Well, no urgency it seems. Possibly not for me after all. Might have been a wrong number, or simply a message for Pearson from the grocer or some such. Although . . .' At last noticing Morley's anxious searching, he asked without much curiosity, 'Lost something, old man?'

'Mmm, I'm sure I b-brought them with me.'

'What?' asked Eugène rather irritably, half-stifling a yawn. He turned to the table beside him and flicked through the pages of the yellow book.

Morley had only a sketchy idea of what he had suppos-edly lost, and none about what it was supposed to deal with – though certainly not fits. 'Oh, these t-tablets, I have to take them every so often, er . . .'

Eugène was studying a picture in the yellow book. He squinted, then turned it as if better to work out what the tangled figures were doing to one another. 'Is it so terribly important that you take them now? Can't you wait until you get back to your aunt's? What are they for, anyway?'

Big Gwen came to his rescue. He couldn't remember what she called them but her descriptions were vivid. 'I g-get these headaches – not ordinary ones,' he said, to show he was no sissy. 'This b-blinding pain comes at the back of my head and coloured lights start f-flashing on and off. Th-They can last for hours. B-But the thing is, I can feel them coming on, so if I take a couple of my tablets straight away, I'm usually okay.'

He was tempted to explain the origin of the complaint with something heroic, but it might get back to May, and eventually to his mother. If the tale of blinding headaches got to May, he could admit that he got headaches, all right, but suggest that Eugène was exaggerating. He would buy some aspirins to produce in evidence when he got the Lucozade, just in case.

But Eugène said, 'Well, that's easily solved: simply go back to your aunt's, take your whatever they are, then come back here for lunch. It'll probably be ham, potatoes and salad. Pearson can easily set another place. Mother may have al-ready suggested it to her, in fact.' He suddenly smiled. '*And*, we can have it up here in the den,' he added, as if it was an invitation impossible to resist.

Morley felt trapped.

Then the thought of eating a *meal* prepared by the dandruff-shedding Pearson – and in the company of greasy Eugène and his even greasier right hand – made his stomach heave. But it strengthened his resolve to escape, even if it endan-gered the friendship. Having a public schoolboy as a friend was certainly a valuable acquisition, but not at any cost.

245

He stood up. 'Thank you v-very, very much, that would have been very nice but I wouldn't have been able to stay for long anyway b-because, because' – in desperation – 'I've g-got these pictures to do, for the Art School, and if I don't get the tablets soon, I won't be able to work.'

'Aah, the old pictures again, eh?' said Eugène with unexpected good grace. 'Not nudes, this time, I trust?'

Morley laughed in relief. 'No, l-landscapes, farms, trees and fields and that.' Then fearful that Eugène might say, 'Well, bring your stuff round here, old man. Might be amusing to watch you work,' he added, 'They've got to be done from real life, d-done on the spot; so I've g-got some walking to do f-first. Out in the country.' He blushed, thinking of himself probably sitting in the bay window in May's lounge copying another landscape from *The Pictorial Book of Knowledge*.

But Eugène obviously hadn't noticed. He had resumed his study of the yellow book. 'Mm, your aunt said something to Mother about you having to go out and paint or something.'

'Yes . . . er,' said Morley, grateful to May, and just failing to muster the courage to add 'old man'. 'I've got to get th-this collection together before the end of the month and I'm b-behind already.'

With a rash promise of yet another visit, Morley shook Eugène's hand, before remembering again what he had been doing with it.

He washed his hands thoroughly in the bathroom before letting himself out.

The air outside was sweet and refreshing. He breathed deeply.

# Chapter 25

Morley gave himself eight out of ten for the way he had coped with Eugène. Then he scrupulously reduced it to six and a half as he remembered that the only times Eugène had shown any interest in him was when he was lying.

Canon Reilly said that there were different classes of lies. 'If an old lady – an old, dear friend of your mammy's who you call Auntie Pauline – is wearing a vile, terrible, horrible hat, and she asks you, "Now do you like the fine hat I'm wearing?" would you reply, "Ah no, Auntie Pauline, I do not: it's a dreadful old thing you have up on your head there"?'

'No, Canon.'

'And why would you not?'

'Because she would get upset, Canon.'

'She'd get aggravated, Canon.'

'Be sad, Canon.'

'She might cry, Canon.'

'Ah, yes. And would not your mammy be also upset? And clout your head when Auntie Pauline was gone home?'

'Yes, Canon.'

'So tell me now, what would you say?'

'Say, "Yes," Canon.'

'Say, "It's very nice," Canon.'

'"Lovely hat," Canon.'

'"Smashing hat," Canon.'

'"Best hat I've ever seen in my whole life, Auntie Pauline,"
Canon.'

'Ah now, there's no call to overdo it, Joseph Kinsella. But
have you not, all of you, just told a lie?'

'Yes, Canon.'

'Well, let's see now, have you not given yourself a bit of a
problem?'

'Yes, Canon.'

'So now, what you must be really clear about is your *intention* in telling that particular lie. That if you told the lie out
of genuine kindness of heart to spare your auntie's feelings
and those of your mammy, then you can be assured that
Our Blessed Lord will understand, and perhaps smile a little
at your innocent deceit. BUT . . .' And the canon thundered
on with dire warnings of what would happen to you if your
lies were told with *bad* intentions.

Morley calculated that he had told more than one class of
lie at Eugène's. The ones told to make his escape from
Eugène's unnatural preoccupations and Pearson's dandruff
were all right: they *were* to spare another's feelings. But what
class of lie had been his claims to have girlfriends and experience with an ATS tart? They were definitely far more serious lies than his father's light-hearted stories about filtering
the beer in the pub to make people laugh – even Our Blessed
Lord might have smiled at that. No, *he* had lied to make
himself seem more important and interesting than he really
was because it was the only way to get Eugène's attention.
Which was vanity, or was it pride? Another sin. *And* these
lies had been about indecent things. Lies with *bad* intentions.

He would have to be truly sorry for them. Though at least
with lies, you only had to say, 'I told lies, Father,' and then
how many times; you didn't have to go into details.

He was walking towards the main road and the Church
of the Sacred Heart to find out the times of confession on
Saturday – just in case he decided to go, supposing he was
still here on Saturday. Anyway, he thought with relief, he
*definitely* knew what to call his Mortal Sin now. A further
reassuring thought was the discovery that the sin was so

widespread. According to Eugène, most of the boys at his school were at it, and doing far more sinful versions of it into the bargain. He was hardly one among a tiny minority, as he had previously feared. But at the same time he found it disturbing.

Among his own acquaintances, the only boys he knew who did it for sure, because he had seen them and they openly talked about it, were Reggies Nolan and Kelp, Reggie Kelp's brother Ernie, little Bernard Inch and Perky Beswick. But you expected it from them: they got up to everything else you weren't supposed to do as well. They used bad language, played up at school, pinched things from shops, played the wag, got into the pictures without paying. And they were scruffs – apart from Perky Beswick – ragged-arsed, down at heel, dirty scruffs. There *were* lots of other lads who talked, laughed and joked about it. But then people talked about all sorts of things they didn't do themselves.

A year or so ago, long before he had started doing it himself, a then first-year boy from Mr Preen's class asked him one play-time, 'Ay, mate, heard the one about the kid having a bath?'

'N-No,' said Morley, pleased to be singled out and asked.

'Well, he was racking off in his bath, see.'

'Yeh,' said Morley, who vaguely knew what the term meant but didn't then know why on earth anybody did it.

'Well, he come, see, shot all over the place.'

'Yeh?'

'Well, you know the way spunk floats on water?'

'Ha, yeh.'

The boy wagged an admonishing finger and said, 'You dirty little bugger, so that's what you get up to when you're having a bath, is it? And at your age an' all.' And he went off to tell his mates, who all stared and sniggered when the blushing Morley was pointed out.

Come to think of it, *did* spunk float on water? He had never noticed. He would check.

So did that boy and his sniggering mates do it? Or did they just go round getting a kick out of sneering at people who did? Though it didn't matter if they did do it, for as far as he could remember they were mostly scruffs as well. He did it himself, he allowed, but he didn't like to think of public schoolboys doing it. And so openly. And with each other! The idea of Nigel and Dick at St Cuthbert's, Bob Cherry at Greyfriars and Arthur Augustus D'Arcy of St Jim's doing it filled him with revulsion. And as for Billy Bunter and Fatty Wynn . . . ugh.

Of course, Eugène's school might be an exception from the general rule – like Eugène himself. It might be – what was it? A lesser, no, a minor public school.

Minor public schools seemed much worse than no public school at all. He had come across the phrase two or three times and it usually sounded damning. He had also heard it in the film *The Triumph of the Regiment*, coming from the colonel explaining the caddish behaviour of a junior officer. 'Well, what can you expect from a fellah who comes from a minor public school and then some provincial red-brick affair that calls itself a university?'

Yes, in the better, the major public schools, he consoled himself, things would be sure to be much closer to the schools in his stories. Though if he accepted this, his friendship with a *minor* public schoolboy wasn't much to brag about after all. But Ron had said that Eugène's school was one of the best in the country. Although what did Ron know about . . . ?

He found himself frowning so deeply it hurt. It was an effort rearranging an unyielding real world to make it fit into his ideal one.

The Sacred Heart Church was on the other side of the main road. He crossed over and copied into his notebook the times of confession on the notice board: 10 a.m. to 12 noon. It would only be a week since his last, if Imperfect Confession, so he didn't *have* to go this coming Saturday, he reminded himself, his proximity to a strange church making his heart thump wildly. He wondered whether to go in and say a prayer to try to catch a glimpse of the priest and see if he looked friendly. But no, he would leave it for now, and anyway, he was hungry.

There was no need to be French, he decided, when he went into a small, friendly-looking shop in the High Street to buy a Cornish pasty. But although the short, thick-set, confident youth who served him didn't cause him to stammer unduly, he made him feel lanky and awkward as most small, confident people did. He walked up to Victoria Square, eating as he went, ducking his head under shop awnings until he became aware of his true height again. The pasty was nice but . . . different. When he had eaten down to the last third, he discovered there was swede in it. He loathed swede. He retched and spat half-chewed fragments into the gutter. There was never swede in the ones he bought from the cake shop in Redhill. He glanced around to see if anyone was watching and threw what was left away, trying not to think of the concentration camp victims who would have been glad of it.

Some of the shops in Victoria Square were decorated with Union Jacks and trimmings. Soon there would be flags everywhere, as there had been at the Coronation. He wondered whether to buy one, then realized it might not be right to put up a flag outside his house with his father so recently dead. He turned his mind to his new paints and the pleasing prospect of going back to May's and using them again. First the Lucozade – and some aspirins. There was a chemist's near the picture house.

The elderly woman in front of him fidgeted and tutted at the slow progress of the long queue. She wore a fur coat that smelled of mothballs and a black, shiny straw hat decorated with faded artificial roses, which wobbled when she moved. He laughed to himself and mentally impersonated Canon Reilly. 'Now, is that not a dreadful, terrible old thing that you have perched on your head there, Auntie Pauline?'

The chemist was a sprightly, balding man with a chubby pink face and gold half-glasses like Canon Reilly's. He did everything with brisk, exaggerated movements: bending down, stretching up, climbing his little ladder, opening drawers and glass-fronted cabinets, scooping and weighing, and bouncing in and out of a door at the rear of the

251

shop. He was very eager to please, with a cheery though respectful word for everyone. Nevertheless, in spite of being in a conspicuous place in the centre of the town, Morley had decided to be French – just to be on the safe side. Waiting in queues increased his nervousness and the likelihood of serious stammering.

The chemist's method of finding a required item was curious. Morley watched in fascination as he stabbed his forefinger towards half a dozen things in turn before targeting the correct one with a little triumphant cry of, 'Ah!'

When at last it was her turn, the fur-coated woman read out her needs one at a time from a piece of paper. Morley wondered why she didn't simply give it to the chemist to save time. But if the same thought occurred to the chemist, he didn't suggest it but just obeyed each command as it came.

'Sanatogen . . . Steradent . . . Corn caps – the Carnation ones – not your German ones . . . Chloradine . . . Clarke's Blood Mixture.' In between, things so apparently unmentionable that she had to lean over the counter and whisper them. The chemist leaped to it with increased alacrity. Bend, stretch, up and down the ladder, under the counter, into the back room, finger jab, jab, jabbing before pouncing on the objective; his triumphant 'Ah!' this time mixed with relief. The old lady inspected each item carefully before putting it into her huge handbag. Then she double-checked her change and moved slowly up the counter, securing clasps and zips and putting on her gloves.

The chemist gave Morley a slightly frosty smile and said, 'Yes, young man?'

'Give me, if you please, a bottle of, eur, Leucozade, *monsieur*.'

The man's smile broadened, his customer apparently seeming more interesting than he had at first supposed. He bent down to a shelf and stabbed at Wincarnis, Ribena, Roses, Kia-Ora and other bottles until his finger found the Lucozade. 'Ah!' He put it on the counter and surveyed the sprawl of coins Morley had put there. He stabbed the air above each in turn before homing in on a half-crown. 'Ah!

That is what we need, this big silver chappie, but you will need some change.'

Pleased with his effortless performance in front of a large audience, Morley couldn't resist becoming a little *more* French. *'Je*, I do not, eur, *compre* – undeurstand,' he said, raising his eyebrows, extending his hands and smiling a regretful smile. It was a mistake.

'Change,' the chemist repeated. Then, *'Monnaie,'* in what to Morley sounded like very fluent French.

Morley went rigid with terror. He found himself nodding as he thought with desperate speed: He's going to say something else, he's that sort of man. What about being Dutch, Danish, Polish? No, he had already said *monsieur*. What other language used *monsieur*? None that he knew of. He was a French boy who had lost his memory. Or a Russian who thought for a moment that he *was* in France – he'd been in France until yesterday when naturally he had called men *monsieur* and used the odd French phrase, but no, he didn't actually speak French. He was in a school play, a gendarme in *The Bishop's Candlesticks*, and was practising the accent – but then he would have to return to being English and . . .

There were lots of people in the queue behind him; perhaps the chemist would be too busy to say anything else, just *au revoir*; he could cope with that.

The chemist didn't. He gave Morley his change, then, as he wrapped the bottle in newspaper, said very conversationally, *'Vous êtes ici en vacances?'*

Morley felt paralysed, he had stopped breathing, the thumping in his chest was his only movement.

The fur-coated woman seemed to have had second thoughts about one of her purchases. She thrust a bottle under the nose of the chemist, almost pushing Morley aside. 'Are you *sure* that this does the same thing?' she demanded.

The chemist gave Morley an apologetic smile and said, *'Excusez moi, s'il vous plaît,'* before turning to the woman. 'It's exactly the same preparation, madam, the same Clarke's Blood Mixture. As I said earlier, we haven't the tablets in at the minute but I do assure you that this does exactly the same thing. I *will* check, though, just to make doubly sure.' He turned to a cabinet behind him.

Morley hurried until he was safely on the other side of the Salters Cinema. Not that he expected to be chased, but he felt more comfortable hidden and distanced from the scene of his near-disaster. Even though nothing had happened, he reacted almost as if it had. He imagined the chemist's stream of French; the stammer becoming so disabling that he wouldn't be able to explain – supposing that he could think of an explanation; the stares and comments of the customers as, cringing, he made his escape. And the fear, whenever he was in Droitwich for ever afterwards, of bumping into somebody who had seen the incident and would point and laugh and whisper to their friends.

He had calmed down enough by the time he had reached the Raven Hotel to consider the future of being French. He had been aware of the dangers that the role could lead him into. But this time he had been really reckless: the chemist was no R. C. Crump. He was educated, probably had letters after his name like the one in Redhill – MPS, was it? Whatever that meant. He sighed. He had enjoyed being French. Still, he didn't have to give it up entirely, he could still use it in certain shops, with tram conductors and other people in authority, if he carefully weighed up things first. And avoided people who looked as if they had been to grammar school. There were ordinary people too, he suddenly remembered, people like Harry Braithewaite, the patient who sat on the seat by the cast-iron lavatory near the Asylum.

Morley wasn't entirely convinced with Harry Braithewaite's French but there must be lots of people around Harry's age who had picked up a bit of French in the last war. Perhaps he should be Dutch after all, or come from some country with a language that not many people knew. It would mean finding out new words, though, and it wouldn't be so easy as –

'You barmy twat,' yelled a boiler-suited young man on a bike, swerving violently to avoid Morley who had just stepped into the main road without looking.

'You hadn't oughta to be let out without your reins on, you hadn't,' the cyclist continued over his shoulder. 'Dopey twerp, beetle-headed dromedary.'

Morley was left shaking, though more from fear of the incident being witnessed than being nearly knocked flat. He looked round anxiously but there was nobody except an old man on a bench on the other side of the road engrossed in his newspaper.

William, Ginger or Tom Sawyer would have yelled back something smarter and put the man in his place, he thought enviously. Even Reggie Kelp would have been ready with something, if only, 'Same to you with brass knobs on, mate,' or, 'Watchit, son, watchit.' And all of them would have felt better afterwards.

Morley felt much worse. He crossed the road very carefully, wondering if it was going to turn into one of those days when it was one thing after another. And why did such embarrassing things always happen to him? He couldn't imagine them happening to Nigel and Dick – though they were fictional. He needed to be more alert. What had Mr Church been going on about recently? Be awake, daydreaming means you are half-asleep; you can't function properly when you are daydreaming. He would be a camera again, aware of everything around him.

He gazed intently at the houses he passed, but they refused to interest him. What about counting all the houses with green doors? No, make it more interesting by *guessing* the number of green doors between here and May's. Thirteen, he decided.

The sun, which had been in and out all morning, now lay behind a bank of dark cloud. It was getting chilly. Morley quickened his steps. He had only seen three green doors so far, but this was not Marshfield Drive, still less Woods Park Road: here everything was much more refined with stained and natural wood colours predominating. He would be lucky to see another three before May's. He decided to guess the number of steps it would take instead. Four hundred. No, it would never turn out to be a round number like that. Say 387. He counted each time his right foot touched the ground. This wasn't quite being alert to your surroundings but it was a move in the right direction and kept your mind from wandering towards unpleasant things.

By the time he reached 119, he realized that he had vastly over-calculated: at this rate he would reach May's at around two hundred. But if he changed his target figure now it would be cheating. He decided to count *every* step, right foot and left.

At 209, with this revised method of counting, he had almost reached May's road. He turned the corner. There, standing outside the house, was Ron's green Hillman. Damn! He slackened his pace, counting forgotten. Although he liked Ron, he always felt shy and uncomfortable with him when May wasn't there. He suspected that Ron felt the same way about him. So much for his cosy three or four hours alone with his new paints, making cups of tea whenever he felt like it, having one of Ron's cigarettes, maybe even looking for the key to the brick-built air-raid shelter where Ron kept his luxury goods – just for a quick look around. He retreated into the road he had just come from to review the changed situation. He cast himself in the role of Nigel, the voice in his head speaking with Nigel's imagined accent. An accent breezier than Eugène's.

Does it have to follow that Ron is at home because his car is outside?

Yes, Ron never walks anywhere, not even to post a letter in the box at the end of the road.

He could have run out of petrol and been forced to walk or go on the bus.

Ron never runs out of petrol, he has coupons galore, two or three five-gallon drums of it in the garage and probably several more in the air-raid shelter.

It has broken down again.

In that case, it still means that Ron is at home, waiting for somebody from the garage or one of his mates to arrive with whatever is needed.

But why isn't the car on the drive? It is always on the drive when it isn't in the garage.

Ah, because Ron has just popped in *briefly* for something.

256

Papers, or perhaps clothing or petrol coupons . . . for a client. It would hardly be worth the effort to drive in and then back out again for such a short visit and such small items. In a few minutes he will probably be gone.

Very pleased with his deductions, Morley turned round. He would walk two hundred right-foot-only paces back the way he had come and stroll back. If the car was still there, he would repeat the performance twice more only. If it was still there after that, it would suggest that Ron was going to stay put, so he would resign himself to Ron's company. Though there was always the hope that on seeing Morley Ron might find an excuse to go out anyway.

After his first jaunt, the Hillman was still there. He started on his second, deciding to make it 250 paces this time. The sun looked as if it had gone in for good and the first few drops of rain were falling. A middle-aged, masculine-looking woman tending some potted plants in the shelter of her porch gave Morley an enquiring look. He wasn't surprised, as this was the fourth time he had passed her house; soon he would be passing it again. She probably thought he was up to no good. Clutching a bottle wrapped in newspaper didn't help: it could be mistaken for a blunt instrument. She might confront him on his way back; she looked the sort who wouldn't hesitate. She might be perfectly polite and merely say, 'May I help you, young man?' But even then, what could he say? Being French was now out of the question. Anyway she looked at least as if she had been to grammar school. And she might know May or Ron. He could simply tell her the truth, he thought with amusement.

Ron was nice enough. It was just that talking to him was difficult. His conversation when alone with Morley was usually confined to talking about the things he owned. Often the things he was wearing or had about him.

Once it had been his wristwatch. 'You see, tells you the time in New York, Sydney and Moscow as well. Or anywhere else you want depending on how you set it up – with this knob here, you see. And with this you can use it as a stop watch.' He opened the back. 'Jewels, twenty-three of them, diamonds. Try

257

it on. Yes, suits you. Cost a mint. Only two ever made; the other was for some Arab johnnie, a sheikh or something.'

Then there was his fountain pen: 'D'you know what that's made from? Well, it's not vulcanite and certainly not Bakelite, no. That's ivory, hand-turned, pre-war of course, twenty-two carat gold band, clip and filigree. Filigree? That's the gold pattern set into the ivory: skilled job. And look' – unscrewing the barrel – 'unusual filling system, eh? Patent valve. Not too many of these about, I can tell you. Fourteen carat gold nib. Go on, try it, write something. Borrow it if you like when you want to write something special on one of your etchings.' Ron always called Morley's black ink drawings etchings. Everything Ron possessed was unique, rare, hand-crafted, hand-tooled, hand-turned, specially made, irreplaceable, antique, pre-war, impossible to come by, the best there was or unbelievably expensive.

Morley always racked his brains on these occasions to say something sparkling, as many of Ron's things failed to interest him, while Ron, presumably sensitive to Morley's stammer, always did his best to spare him the effort, anyway, by talking continuously. The result was that all Morley was able to contribute was forced exclamations of, 'Wow!' 'Coo!' 'Honestly?' 'Gosh, I never knew that!' 'Good heavens,' whilst trying to banish insidious images of Ron's father's unorthodox shitting habits and wondering if Ron knew that he knew.

Morley decided to avoid passing the plant-tending woman's house again by making a detour which would, he hoped, lead him back to May's from the other direction. He turned into the next road on his left – the road he had taken earlier on the way to Eugène's – and saw May some way off coming towards him.

At least it looked like May. There was something different about her. Her coat for one thing, long and flapping, much too big for her. And anyway May was at work, he had seen her go.

When she saw Morley, the woman ran towards him. It *was* May. She was wearing Ron's military mac, and a headscarf, a rare thing with May. And glasses!

Something was wrong. Something had happened to Ron. He had high blood pressure, according to May – which reminded Morley that he had forgotten to get some aspirins at the chemist's. He began to run himself. Ron's car outside the house had meant something after all, something far more serious than he had supposed. And not illness either, or May would have been with him. No, Ron had been arrested, the police had caught up with him at last, as his mother was always predicting.

'Oh, love,' wailed May, throwing her arms around him. 'Oh, love.' She pressed her face close, her glasses digging painfully into his cheek, and sobbed.

Morley was scared and confused. This was more difficult to deal with than his mother's tearless response to his father's death. His eyes prickled in sympathy, he put his arms round her shaking body and awkwardly patted her back. In the process, the expensive, paper-wrapped Lucozade fell to the pavement with a muffled crack.

She pulled her face away a little and tried to speak. Her eyes were puffy, her cheeks streaked with mascara. Beneath the headscarf her fringe was damp; her glasses were smeared and spotted with raindrops. It was raining in earnest now.

She took a shuddering deep breath and managed, 'He in't dead, love,' before being overcome with sobs again.

'Wh-Who, Hitler?' said Morley, not daring to give voice to the impossible hope which stole into his mind, in case May dashed it. 'He d-d-didn't d-die after all, then?'

May almost pushed him off, then grabbed his shoulders and held him at arm's length. She sniffed, made a huge effort and, mouth twitching, said, 'No, you silly, soft, bugger.'

Morley had never heard May swear before.

'Your *dad* . . . your *dad* . . . he in't dead,' she stuttered, and resumed her weeping.

259

# Chapter 26

Morley closed his eyes and let May's words fill his entire being. Nothing else existed outside this glorious, marvellous, *miraculous* news.

May released herself, searched for a handkerchief. 'I must look a sight, love.' And becoming aware of the rain: 'Let's get in, love, out the wet.'

Morley kicked the broken bottle of Lucozade near the foot of a tree on the grass verge. They made their way back arm in arm, May overcome with sobs again and only able to answer Morley's anxious questions with nods and head-shakings.

'He's ok-k-kay, then?'

'N-Not b-badly wounded or anything?'

'Nothing, er, missing?'

'Eyes okay?'

'And his mind, n-not sh-sh-shell-sh-shocked or anything?'

Assured on all these points, Morley was content to leave it at that while he savoured the sensation of having a father again. Then he relived the moment when May had said, 'Your *dad*, your *dad*, he in't dead, love,' and the eerie tingling feeling that had crept up his spine.

And when, after a while, he became aware of them again, thoughts of Eugène, public schools, being French, chemists and men on bikes seemed absurdly trivial.

The woman tending her plants looked up curiously as the strange couple went past. Morley gave her a broad, confident grin.

Both bars of the electric fire were on in the lounge against the sudden chill. On the coffee table were two bottles of champagne, a bottle of whisky, a syphon of soda water, lemonade, biscuits and several blocks of chocolate. Ron stood in the bay window looking out, still keeping the coins moving in his pocket. He didn't turn round when May and Morley burst in, and Morley suspected he was trying not to cry.

'Brilliant news, old chap, isn't it?' he said, staring at the rain-soaked garden. 'Brilliant.' He shook his head and blew his nose.

May recovered quickly. She took off her mac and headscarf, wrenched off Morley's jacket, grabbed a couple of towels and, vigorously rubbing her hair and bidding Morley do the same, said, 'We'll just get comfy first, shall we, and then we'll tell you all about it. Ron'll start off.'

Ron was ponderous and anxious to promote his own part in events. With much back-tracking and repetition and between several swigs of whisky, he explained how lucky it was that he had been at home when Morley's mother telephoned – a chance in a thousand. That on his way to Birmingham, after having completed some business in Worcester, he had broken his journey to make some phone calls from home and pick up some stuff – something he only did very occasionally in the middle of the day. Then, about to get in his car to set off for Birmingham, he had heard the phone and rushed into the house. If the phone call had come only fifteen seconds later, he would have been gone. Hours might have elapsed before Morley's mother could have got in touch again.

May told him to shut up about all that and get on with it; the lad wanted to hear about his dad, not Ron's pithering about.

Morley, however, was content to allow the tale to unfold in its own good time. It was like going to the pictures and seeing the end first. So he knew it ended happily but wanted to enjoy every second of what led up to it. And, anyway, nothing else at the moment would have interested him.

When Ron got to it, information about his father was sparse. With minor chest and shoulder injuries, he had been a patient in a field hospital when part of the building collapsed. There were deaths and injuries but Morley's father had escaped without a further scratch. In the ensuing confusion, there had been an administrative blunder. The telegram his mother received should have merely informed her that her husband had been slightly wounded.

'Sounds like a mix-up, and they sent some other poor devil a telegram saying *her* husband was only wounded, then after, they had to go and tell her that he was dead after all,' said May sympathetically.

They were quiet until Ron said it didn't have to follow as they didn't know how the mistake had been made. Morley was only too relieved to accept this: that his father's life had been paid for, so to speak, by somebody else's death would have spoiled things a bit. He corrected the scene at the canal so that this time, as his father pulls himself out of the water and turns, the German bullet strikes him ten inches higher, in the shoulder.

May refilled all the glasses and sat on the floor leaning against Ron's chair. She said, 'Then your mom rung *me* up, at work – Ron'd give her the number – and said how this officer come round the Asylum – her next door told him where it was. And they let her off work for the day and she went home in this car with him, with a special driver and everything. Then he told her what Ron's just told you. You should have heard her, love, your mom on the phone, laughing one minute and crying like mad the next, and I could hear that friend of hers, that Big Gwen, crying and all.'

There had been more crying at his father's return to life, reflected Morley, than at his death.

'Anyroad, after all that, I couldn't of done no more work than fly in the moon. So I come home. Ron come round and fetched me, bless him. But, course, you wasn't here when we got here, and we knew you wasn't still at Eugène's 'cause Ron'd rung him up.'

Ron took a huge gulp of his whisky. 'Yes, I forgot to say. I naturally rang Eugène's immediately I heard the news, but that maid of theirs said you weren't there. Though I did wonder. Were you? About a quarter to twelve?'

'Yeh,' said Morley, 'we heard the ph-phone, but the maid didn't come up, and Eugène thought it might be a wrong number or something. It was just after that I left.'

'She probably genuinely forgot you were there, old son.'

Morley felt the familiar stab of mortification but it immediately evaporated.

'Anyway, it didn't really matter because, on reflection, I thought it better if Lizzie told you.'

'I should think so and all,' said May. 'The way you'd of told it'd be more like telling him his dad'd died all over again.'

Ron smiled and circulated his money.

'Anyroad, where was we? Oh yes, we din't half have a game finding you. We looked *everywhere*!' And May explained that they had scoured the town, where she had kept jumping out of the car to see if he had gone into a shop or café.

'She even did you the honour of putting on her glasses,' said Ron.

Then they had explored the roads leading to the countryside to see if he had gone sketching. In between, they had returned three times to see if he had come back. On the last homeward journey the car had broken down at the top of the road and they had had to push it home.

So *that*'s why it had been left outside: the drive was too steep.

'Radiator this time,' said Ron. 'Just loike a colander.' He bit his lip in embarrassment at his lapse into his native accent. Morley smiled to himself.

'So we didn't have no car now, did we?' said May. 'But I couldn't stand sticking in the house. I kept going in the road, then looking out the upstairs windows, smoking one cigarette after another, putting them down and forgetting them. It's a wonder I din't set the house on fire. So I thought, car or no car, I'm going out to look for him, perhaps he's gone back to You-jean's. But I din't want to phone them up again, see, I wanted to see you meself. I just couldn't wait to see your little face when I told you.'

Morley didn't care much for the 'little face' but May was easy to forgive, particularly as, at that moment, she drew her knees up till they almost touched her chin and hugged her long, shapely legs, displaying her stocking tops and a glimpse of what lay above. Sitting by the hearth on the pouffe, Morley was excitedly aware that he would be able to see even more if he moved his head to the side a little. He hesitated. This wasn't the time and anyway he had decided to be good. He edged safely out of the way, not before he had, without really thinking, committed what he had seen to memory.

No one could leave the subject alone. As the afternoon wore on, the story was told again and added to with things originally thought too trivial to mention, or forgotten. May remembered that his mother and Big Gwen had run out of change in the middle of their phone call. They had had to go to a shop to change a note but had then used the shopkeeper's private telephone.

Morley could see it vividly. The telephone box in Eachley Lane. The shop would be Hiller's. And Big Gwen confidently handling everything, charming Hiller into letting them use his phone, looking very smart as she always did in public – at least until you got near enough to see the tiny spots of paint here and there on her coat and shoes.

Then Ron speculated about his father's wounds. He talked about entry and exit holes; bullets, shells and splinters; artillery and infantry weapons; and dwelt at length on what a 9mm Schmeisser could do.

Morley began to feel alarmed. He saw May elbow Ron sharply in the knee.

'But there again,' Ron said, 'it's quite possible that there was no penetrating wound *at all*. He might have just been caught in the blast of mortar or artillery fire and thrown against a wall or a tree or something. Probably won't even have a scar to show for it.'

But Morley wanted a scar. Preferably one from a small-calibre bullet, without too much surrounding damage. Or

264

better still, a neat three- or four-inch furrow along the shoulder from a glancing shot. Now that would be *really* something to tell Micky Plant about.

Morley knelt down for the first time in weeks to say his prayers. In God's presence, he felt shy and unworthy. He didn't feel he had earned his father's return, and was over-whelmed by God's generosity. He explained that he wasn't sure that he was in a State of Grace and therefore did not know whether his prayers would carry much weight but he would try his best given the circumstances, and would con-fess, making a Perfect Confession, as soon as he could.

He said a decade of the Rosary, thinking of the first of the five glorious mysteries, the Resurrection. It took him a long time as his mind kept drifting towards the plans for the fol-lowing day; Ron and May would take him on a brief tour of the local countryside in the morning, then Ron would drive him home while May went to work to make up for this after-noon's absence.

He wasn't happy with his unmindful praying. He was about to start all over again, thought better of it, then settled for the longer Act of Contrition and the Confiteor to make up.

He snuggled down in bed and found himself able to re-sist dwelling on images of Big Gwen, the ATS tart, Sheila Godden, the nurse from the dental hospital, the student teacher, the WAAF warrant officer and May as they oblig-ingly flitted by, minus most of their clothes or in some way negligently displaying their underwear. Instead, he thought of a well-wrapped-up May in an over-sized trench coat, her smudged, tear-stained face, bedraggled blond fringe beneath her headscarf – still managing to look glamorous like a star in a picture about refugees fleeing from the Germans – against the scudding, dark clouds and the rain; her hands grabbing his shoulders and his tingling spine when she said, 'Your *dad* . . . your *dad* . . . he in't dead.'

He went through the scene again. It was better than the best part of the most brilliant film he had ever seen. Perfect

265

. . . except for May's glasses and the ridiculous dropping of the Lucozade. He tried to erase them when he watched it for the last time.

He dreamed of his father in an army greatcoat that came down to the ground and a vast black beret, now having to wear glasses as a mysterious result of his injuries. They were like May's with blue transparent frames. He was dragging a reluctant Morley to confession in Eugène's darkroom.

'Pray Father, give me your blessing, and have you got, if you please, a bottle of Leucozade?'

'That will put lead in his pencil,' Canon Reilly bellowed to the people waiting outside.

'And, F-Father, I, I was F-French on m-m-many occas–'

'You were WHAT?'

There was a burst of maniacal laughter from outside. Little Bernard Inch, Reggies Nolan and Kelp, the Betts twins and Perky Beswick were having a 'shooting' match.

'See that, twinnies,' said the Reggies, 'we hit the wall. Neat, ay?'

'But we cobe first; did't we, Perk?' protested the Betts twins.

'It in't a race. It's how far you shoot. Start again!' commanded Perky.

Nigel and Dick were also at it.

'Jolly good shot, old man,' said Dick, as Nigel's hit the ceiling.

'Nothing really,' said Nigel modestly, 'but what a topping pain.'

'Jolly decent pain,' exclaimed his chum. 'Absolutely ripping.'

'Quiet, me lads, I want to know what this barmy twat has been up to,' pleaded Canon Reilly. 'So it was French you were, was it? And did you do it alone or with someone else?'

'M-M-My own, Father.'

'And did you do it once or billions of times?'

'He never stops,' shouted Reggie Nolan.

'Can't,' shouted Kelp.

'Does it everywhere,' said Perky. 'Air-raid shelter. Bed. Bath. Confession. Pig bin.'

266

'Do you not realize, you dopey twerp, you beetle-headed dromedary, that every time you are French it offends Our Blessed Lady and causes her pain, severe pain, grievous pain . . .'

'Neat pain,' yelled little Bernard Inch.

'You are never right my child, never right in all this world. If you persist in being French, you will also wind up in a lunatic asylum. Why, Upfield Asylum and Redhill and the one at Catsfield are full of people being French, so they are. With their hands bound, chained up at night, their mouths sealed with sticking plaster to . . .'

The priest suddenly became the chubby-faced chemist. 'Now, why don't you forget this French nonsense, young man? Interest yourself in sports and absorbing pastimes. Why not try rubbing your threepenny bit, like a normal chappie, like everyone else does.'

'Yes, try tinkering with the old anatomy, you oik, you cad, you confounded bounder,' chorused Nigel, Dick and, now, Eugène. 'Awfully decent, thrilling, wizard, topping pain.'

# Chapter 27

Ron talked about cars throughout the entire journey. Cars in general, cars he had owned, the car he was going to get next and the car he had now. He explained how lucky he had been to get a new radiator at such short notice. 'Just *like* a colander,' he said emphatically of the old one, as if to demonstrate that he jolly well knew how to pronounce 'like' properly. He explained how a car engine worked, then described the electrical system. Just before Bromsgrove, he invited Morley to operate the lights, indicators and windscreen wipers. Later, on a deserted stretch of road in the heart of the Enid Blyton country, he told Morley to take the wheel.

Morley wasn't keen until it occurred to him that this was another valuable experience to brag about. 'Yeh, drove our uncle's car. Oh, about a couple of miles, I reckon. Mm, about forty, or a bit over,' he would say to Micky Plant. He leaned over and steered gingerly while Ron kept a restraining hand on the bottom of the wheel. Morley noticed that the speedometer needle was teetering just below the twenty mark, but then it was probably playing up, like the old radiator. Ron took over after about a quarter of a mile, when the beginning of Redhill appeared over the high horizon.

Morley didn't learn much about cars, his mind too occupied with trying to enjoy the passing landscape, anticipating his mother's mood, thinking up bright responses to drop at appropriate moments during Ron's monologue, and trying to banish occasional but vivid mental pictures of buckets full of Ron's dad's shit being carried down old steep stairs by a dirty infant Ron to the closet in Ron's boyhood yard. So as usual, his only contribution was a sporadic, 'Wow!' 'Aah!' 'Ha!' 'Goodness!' or 'Really?'

As they approached the lower end of Redhill, Ron said, 'I won't come in with you, old chap. I'm in a bit of a hurry and I can't afford to let this chap down again. I'll try and pop in and see Mum on the way back, if I can.' Which almost certainly meant that he wouldn't.

Ron *was* nice, Morley reflected, but now he wanted breathing space to recover from the strain of thirty minutes of Ron's company and prepare himself to meet his mother. Would she kiss him? Should he make the first move and kiss her? Would his mother expect him to carry on as if nothing had happened like when his father had died? Or was it possible to talk freely about him now?

'If you're in a hurry, Ron, you needn't take me all the way. D-Drop us just before the t-tram terminus. I, er, w-wanted to get Mom something from the cake shop, anyway,' he lied – to spare Ron's feelings. 'And, er, th-thanks for everything.'

He stood on the pavement buttoning his lumber jacket and fiddling unnecessarily with the locks on his suitcase until Ron's car had safely disappeared towards town.

It was quiet, the children were still in school. All that could be heard was the muffled thumps and rumbles from the Motor and Aero Works. Morley gazed around him: the hump-backed bridge, the cottages climbing Cock Hill, the white house with the fake black timbering, the green-domed tower of the Asylum through the trees, the cake shop over the road. Everything was as it had been on Monday when he had caught the bus to May's – except for a bonfire in the making at the foot of the quarry and a modest strip of bunting across the front of the cake shop. But the familiar scene *felt* different – pleasantly different, transformed. 'Inhabited by a benevolent spirit,' as Miss Pryce had once said, about something or other.

He crossed the road, eyes alert for cyclists. Harry Braithe-waite from the Asylum had forsaken his bench by the urinal and was passing the time of day with a tram driver and another man by the terminus clock. Morley's eyes were drawn to the other man. He was smallish with a friendly, sun-tanned face, dressed in a brown uniform, on the knee of his trousers a curious, round yellow patch.

Gosh, an Eyetie! One of the prisoners Perky had told him about. He looked at the man in awe. An Italian soldier in an Italian uniform, with Italian thoughts in Italian going through his head. An *enemy* soldier – well, sort of. Here in Redhill! He felt a thrill of excitement even greater than when he had first seen Russ. Perhaps tomorrow he would come down with Micky Plant and have a look at them – even try and talk to them.

He walked homewards along the narrow footpath beside the quarry, which ran its erratic course along the first two hundred yards of Eachley Lane. Just before the war it had been fenced off from the lane with sturdy wooden fencing in the hope of stopping people from climbing its, in some places, dangerous, almost vertical, faces. But now all that remained were a few supporting posts and the odd lower rail half-submerged under falls of rock. Over the first three or four winters of its existence, every single paling had been stolen for fuel and, more particularly, for sledge-making. The palings had been six foot long, four inches wide with arched tops. Two of these, cut to length, and you had the ready-shaped sides of a sledge.

Morley remembered the Reggies' sledge, a massive affair with the palings left at their original six-foot length and topped with the Kelps' coal-house door. He thought of his own small sledge, built with wood bought from Kershaw's the woodyard. Strange, he had been thinking of sledging only a few nights ago, though then his thoughts had been those of a fatherless boy, remembering never-to-be-repeated winter days on Beacon Hill with a daredevil Dad. Now it *could* happen again. An immense feeling of joy surged through him.

He asked himself a question. Say his father hadn't died and come alive again, but had just gone on living, the result would be just the same – an alive father; *but*: would he have felt as happy as he did now?

Well, for one thing, if his father hadn't died, he would be in school now. And he wouldn't have been to May's, got new paints; met Eugène and found out you-know-what; discovered what seemed to be the beginning of the Real England around Hanbury, Feckenham and Inkberrow.

But apart from all that . . . He drew a graph in his head: a slightly crooked horizontal line representing the minor ups and downs of everyday life. At the news of his father's death, the line plunges down at a steep angle; on his father's return to life, the line shoots up forming a V but continues to rise till it is much higher than the original plateau, before resuming its slightly crooked, horizontal course.

He wasn't entirely happy with the diagram. It wasn't as simple as that. But one thing was obvious: his father's resurrection didn't just cancel out his death but came with enormous interest.

He put down his case, flexed his fingers and picked it up with his other hand. He listed his assets. A *father*; a mother, surely much happier now than she had been for years; the Art School – yes, he must have passed; the end of the war – it had begun to really excite him now; real artists' paints . . .

He turned in to Woods Park Road. The pig bin was upright, and with its lid on. Was it always the *same* bin, he wondered, or did the collector put the full one on the lorry and replace it with another? He had never noticed. He would check next time he saw it being collected. Or put a chalk mark on this one. Or ask. There was no rubbish round it either, not so much as a potato peeling. Perhaps . . .

'Oi, Morley!' hissed a voice behind old man Kirkham's ragged hedge. Morley started. Reggie Kelp rose from his hiding place and pushed his head through a gap just above the top of the fence. 'You just come up Eachley?'

'W-Warrow, Reg, er, yeh, why?'

'Seen the school board man?'

'N-Naw.'

'Y'sure?'

'Er, yeh.'

'Huh, our Ernie said he seen him coming up Eachley, but our Ernie's always been a big liar. Anyroad, don't hang round talking to us, just in case he's really coming.' And he bobbed down again. 'Oh, neat about your dad.'

Where was he? Paints – artists' paints; a pound and a new protractor and slide rule from Ron ('Might find them useful with the old artistic activities, old chap,' he had said naïvely); ten shillings from May; the cigar box. And in his case the two drawings he had begun this morning and which he would later paint: the Bull at Inkberrow for May, and crooked-roofed cottages with the church at Feckenham for Russ. What else? Ah, May was coming on Sunday. Could life be better?

He was at his front gate. From the back of his mind, a disturbing shadow crept forward. Confession. He had promised. At the earliest opportunity. And that meant tomorrow. He suddenly remembered that tomorrow was the day of his supposed visit to the Art Gallery with Mr Ross-Armitage, so he had a ready-made excuse for going out. But wouldn't that be selfish? Wasn't it his *duty* to stay at home with his mother on his first full day back? Wouldn't she expect it? Anyway things might be . . . busy tomorrow. It wouldn't be an ordinary Saturday. And there was May's picture to finish before she came on Sunday. He really only had to go once a fortnight. And he had, at least, *gone* last week.

He would see.